God of River Mud

God of River Mud

A NOVEL

Vic Sizemore

WEST VIRGINIA UNIVERSITY PRESS
MORGANTOWN

Scripture taken from the New King James Version. Copyright © 1982 by Thomas Nelson.
Used by permission. All rights reserved.

ISBN 978-1-959000-02-0 (paperback) / 978-1-959000-03-7 (ebook)

Library of Congress Cataloging-in-Publication Data
Names: Sizemore, Vic (Victor Maynard), 1966– author.
Title: God of river mud : a novel / Vic Sizemore.
Description: Morgantown : West Virginia University Press, 2024.
Identifiers: LCCN 2023019862 | ISBN 9781959000020 (paperback) | ISBN
    9781959000037 (ebook)
Subjects: LCSH: Identity (Psychology)—Fiction. | Faith—Fiction. | Families—West
    Virginia—Fiction. | Appalachian Region—Fiction | LCGFT: Domestic fiction. |
    Queer fiction. | Novels.
Classification: LCC PS3619.I98 G63 2024 | DDC 813/.6—dc23/eng/20230501
LC record available at https://lccn.loc.gov/2023019862

Cover and book design by Than Saffel / WVU Press
Cover image by Varga Jozsef Zoltan / Shutterstock

For Vaughn Sizemore

Contents

Book One

Mill Creek Presbyterian Church
12 Church Street, Ripley, WV
*MORNING WORSHIP

Sunday, May 15, 1954
Prelude: "Intermezzo"
Call to Worship
Invocation

Hymn No. 6, "Praise, My Soul, the King of Heaven" (First three stanzas only)

Declaration of Faith

Gloria Patri

Meditation

Apostles' Creed

Prayer of Confession and Choral Response

Prayers of Supplication and Intercession

The Lord's Prayer

Sacrament of Baptism

Presentation of Tithes and Offerings

Doxology

Prayer of Dedication

Anthem: "O Savior of the World"

Scripture Lesson: Romans 1:8-17

Hymn No. 139, "Lamp of Our Feet" (Hymn of the Month)

Sermon: "We Are All in Debt"

Hymn No. 395, "0 Zion, Haste"
Benediction and Choral Response
Postlude: "Festlied" Meyer

*Ushers will seat those who are late.

OUR HOSTESS this morning is Mrs. Sharon Gorvin.

USHERS serving us today are Jim Gorvin, Mason McIntire, Jack Dorman, and Robert Johnson.

DEACONS serving us this morning are Allen Combs, John McPeeks, Jesse Stuart, and Luke Kennedy.

THE JUNIOR YOUTH GROUP will meet at the home of Mrs. Jim Harvey and the Pioneer Youth will meet with Mrs. Mason McIntire tonight at 6:00.

DR. STONE will speak on "The Social in the Social Gospel" tonight at 7:45.

WEDNESDAY
2:00—Executive Board, Women of the Church
4:00—Brownie Scouts
7:30—Choir Practice

The beautiful arrangements of flowers have been placed in the sanctuary this morning by Mrs. J. M. Spears in memory of her mother, Mrs. Randy Proctor.

SATURDAY

It is with great joy that Jim and Sharon Gorvin invite you to the wedding of their daughter, Sherry, to Mr. John Marten, here at the church, at 3:00 p.m. Afterward, all are invited to a celebration in Jim's new barn. Come hear Big Randy Crowder and his Mill Creek Boys. Hear his "pickin' and singin' boy" Little Randy's high lonesome voice and listen to his tricks and yodeling and singing folk-style ballads. Listen to young banjo sensation Zechariah Minor do his fancy finger work. Festivities begin at 6:00.

Having Put His Hand to the Plow

(Zechariah Wycliffe Minor, 1954)

WHEN ZECHARIAH and the Mill Creek Boys played the memorial barn dance for his pal, Ricky, Zechariah felt like he'd been baptized in the Spirit twice, three times if he counted what happened in his dad's Studebaker with Izzy Manzano after the dance—thinking secular music would bring down the Spirit was pushing it already; attaching it to the lust of the flesh was outright blasphemy. He knew he was skating on thin ice with God.

Izzy didn't dance with everyone else. She stood over to the side and watched him play his banjo, her hair so black it sometimes shimmered in the light with flashes of blue like a grackle's wing. That night she wore a white skirt with a blue and pink poodle embroidered on it and glasses colored to match the scarves around her neck that also matched the poodle on her skirt. There in the big barn, she floated among the earthy colors of loggers, mill workers, and farmers, like a bright flower tossed onto a creek full of brown fallen leaves.

Then, as the individual bandmembers came together and melded into one multipart instrument, the Spirit hit Zechariah and he lost himself entirely in the music. On "Pike County Breakdown," and then on "Sunny Mountain Chimes," he pushed at the front of the tempo like a coal train barreling into fog, with Ricky's dad Big Randy on mandolin racing alongside him. It was like God Himself was pouring the music into the top of Zechariah's open skull, rivers of it from on high, and it was up to him to keep it flowing through him, out the spout of his banjo onto the thankful crowd.

When this happened to him, as soon as Zechariah became aware of it, the moment had already passed, but the glow of it lasted for hours, or a couple of days, and when he was there, boy howdy, how he played. Big Randy had told him more than once he was good enough to play Bean Blossom, and Big Randy would know.

Izzy leaned close to speak into his ear after the dance and her warm mouth smelled of Wrigley's mint gum. "You were exquisite tonight," she said. "Your fingers moved so fast, they were a blur."

Still flying high, he impulsively said, "Want to go for a drive?" His mom had forbidden him to court Izzy since she was Catholic, not until she accepted the Lord as her savior.

Izzy grinned at him. Her big brown eyes looking like Natalie Woods's. She said, "You'll have to go ask my papa."

Her dad was outside the barn where the fellas sat on hay bales, smoking pipes and passing around moonshine jars. Zechariah could hear his laughter and loud northern accent and would normally have been terrified, but still riding the triumph of his glorious performance, he did it. He asked. Her father called him banjo boy, and said, "You're Reverend Minor's boy. A preacher's son."

"Yes sir," Zechariah said.

"They're the worst ones," Jeff Parker said, and all the men laughed and nodded as he sipped from the jar of shine.

"Then you remember what the Good Book says about how you treat a lady," Izzy's dad said.

"Yes sir," Zechariah said.

Her dad slapped him on the shoulder and said, "You have a real gift there, son."

Zechariah turned, and through the crowd gathering their things to leave, Izzy's big eyes glowed with admiration, and it was all aimed right at him.

She came to see him play on Saturday nights at the regular barn dances. He'd heard her play Bach at the school talent show, and Rachmaninoff in her parlor one afternoon. He felt like a hack around her. She was a technician, had taken real lessons before moving to Millwood, knew theory. Zechariah just had a knack for playing stringed instruments. He could barely read music.

He confessed his feelings of insecurity to her that night, as they were parked on a logging road out by Little Mill Creek.

"Anybody can read music on a page," she told him. "You have that *je ne sais quoi.*"

"I don't know French either."

She laughed and scooted herself across the seat to be next to him and took his hand. That led to necking, and necking led to petting, and Zechariah was so bold as to touch her hip, and then her breast, and instead of stopping him, she kissed him harder and spread her legs in her poodle skirt so that Zechariah thought for sure that, mixed with her perfume, he detected a familiar aroma: the flowery smell of unmentionables his mom and his sister Hannah both had under the bathroom sink in a box, what women used to make their privates smell like flowers. It was too much for him and he couldn't stop it; he spilled his seed into his underpants.

His face burning, he said, "It's time I get you home. I don't want to face your dad if we're late." He walked her to her front door, horrified that he might have a wet spot on the front of his dungarees but unable to sneak a glance and find out. He checked once he was back in the car, and to his great relief, in spite of the cold wetness he felt on his manhood, his dungarees were dry. He drove home and answered his mom's questions about how the barn dance went, told her it was swell, which she already knew because Big Randy had called to brag about Zechariah's performance, said he believed it was an expression of love for Ricky from his best pal Zechariah, said he would be forever grateful and never forget it.

Once that was over, Zechariah hurried to his room, locked the door, and abused himself into a tube sock while he fantasized about Izzy sneaking into his room, standing before him, and stripping off her clothes. He only got as far as her bra hitting the floor and her standing before him in nothing but white panties with her black pubic hair showing under the fabric before he spilled his seed for the second time that night. He threw the sock under his bed, changed his underpants, and threw the soiled ones under the bed too. If only he could marry her, the joys of heaven and earth would open up to him in their marriage bed. He could release his seed inside her. They had to be married or it would be sin. She was Catholic, so they would be unequally yoked, and that would be sin as well. He wept in love and longing for Izzy.

Ricky had been killed in Korea, at a place called Pork Chop Hill. He'd been older than Zechariah by almost four years, but they played hillbilly music together in the Mill Creek Boys, and when Zechariah played music with the older fellas, any age span accordioned in until nobody was old or young, but they were all just musicians together doing what they loved. Ricky had been a swell guitarist, moved it into B natural, B flat, while his brother Little Randy liked those easy chords. Ricky could sing too, could call out the high lonesome better than Bill Monroe—it put a lump in Zechariah's throat, hearing him sing like that.

The night of Ricky's memorial barn dance had, instead of being a mournful affair, turned out to be the best, the most momentous, night in Zechariah's life so far. He'd played like a recording star and then had glimpsed the promised land with Izzy in his dad's car. It all converged to feel like he was on the cusp of something big, something life changing.

As he lay on his bed contemplating these things, his dad's unmistakable three-tap knock came at his door, then the knob rattled on the locked door. He rubbed his face, pulled his dungarees back on, and unlocked the door.

His dad gave him a funny look and he knew it was because his door was locked.

"I was getting ready to put on my pajamas."

"I heard it went well tonight," his dad said. He stepped into the room in his suit pants and undershirt.

"Yes sir," Zechariah said. "It was swell."

"That was a good way to memorialize your pal," his dad said. "I know he was a fine guitarist."

"He was the best."

His dad turned on the expression he used when he was admonishing the congregation and aimed it at him. "Was Ricky saved?"

"I think so," he told his dad. "A lot of the music we play is gospel." That was true. Something else he knew about Ricky, which he didn't say to his dad, though he didn't know if Ricky was saved or not, was that when they played music together, he loved Ricky, loved him like they were blood brothers—or closer even than that—and he knew Ricky, whether he drank a little hooch or not, had a pure, good soul.

"Playing gospel music doesn't make you saved any more than wearing feathers in your cap makes you a chicken." Zechariah's dad stood straight-backed and peered down as if he were behind his pulpit. "Millions of billions of years in the burning torments of hell, where the worm dieth not." He shook his head. He said, "Son, D. L. Moody said, 'People seem to forget that there is no door out of hell.' What do you think Ricky would say to you right now?"

Zechariah waited silently.

"I'll tell you what he would say. He would say, 'Zechariah, we were pals, and you knew I was going to hell. Why didn't you share Christ with me?'"

"I'm sorry," Zechariah said.

"It's time for you to get serious about the things of the Lord," his dad said. "There's a pastor's conference at Pinewood Bible Institute in the fall. No discussion. You will be accompanying me." With that, he turned and left the room.

Zechariah lay back on his bed and cried for the second time that night.

After that night, when Zechariah left the house with his banjo, he felt he had to sneak around his dad as if he were slipping out, not to play hillbilly music, but to smoke and drink with unsaved people. When he left to spend time with Izzy, he felt as guilty as if he were visiting a whore in a house of ill repute.

Izzy's house was big and new. Her dad was a lawyer who worked for all the logging companies and not just one. Izzy's mom was short and fat, had houseplants all over the house, and had hired Stephanie Rule's mom to cook their meals and clean house for her. As far as Zechariah could see, all she did was read romance novels and tend all her plants, but she was friendly and nice. Izzy's dad was friendly and nice too. Izzy had three younger brothers who pestered the two of them when he was over there until Izzy cried out to her mom to make them stop and her mom would chase them off.

Not long after the glorious memorial barn dance, he sat in the parlor of Izzy's big house and watched her play what she had learned so far of Rachmaninoff's Second Piano Concerto. He'd never heard it before and didn't know who Rachmaninoff was or much of anything about classical music. He knew who Mozart was, and Bach because of "Jesu, Joy of Man's Desiring." Izzy's mom and dad had an expensive hi-fi in a polished walnut console and a bookshelf full of records.

He wasn't expecting much from the classical music, but Izzy was wearing tan capri slacks, and when she sat down, her soft thighs spread on the sides like those horse-riding pants. Seeing her there like that made his heart race like he'd been down at the ballfield chasing pop flies.

That's when her dad clattered through the front door, and when he reached the parlor, he stopped and turned to the two of them. His suit was rumpled, he had an old brown briefcase, and his eyebrows were so thick that they met in the middle.

"So, you are the banjo boy?" His accent was from up north, his vowels short. Sounded rude without meaning to.

"Yes sir." Zechariah stood up straight and prepared for the handshake in which her dad would squeeze his hand hard to test Zechariah's manhood.

He didn't squeeze the way Zechariah thought he would, and as they shook, Izzy said. "It's not just banjo, Papa. He can play anything with strings. He's a *virtuoso*."

"Anything with strings?" her dad said. "Anything at all?"

Zechariah's face felt hot. "Anything I've come across so far, yes sir. Banjo's my favorite though. Right now, anyway."

Izzy's dad smiled and nodded. To Izzy, he said, "Is banjo boy joining us for supper?"

"Papa, *stop it*."

Her dad walked through the parlor to the kitchen, singing to the tune of "Oh Danny Boy," the words "Oh banjo boy."

"Shut your mouth, papa," Izzy yelled after him. "Why do you always try to embarrass me?" Then she sat down, flipped her sheet music back, and started Rachmaninoff's Second Piano Concerto again from the beginning. Zechariah sat beside her to be her page turner, and as she played, he was swept up in the music. It carried him into a state of floating euphoria so that when she stopped, he didn't remember turning pages at all, only that he was in love with the whole world, and with Izzy Manzano, who sat with her beautiful thighs spread on the piano bench at the center of it all.

"Are you okay?" She rested her palm on his forearm. He came to himself and realized that his arms were covered in goose bumps and his eyes were full of tears. He blinked and they broke free and ran down his face.

"This is it," he said. "This is life."

She threw her head back and laughed. "I knew you'd like Rachmaninoff."

"The music," he said, "yes, that. But you too. The music *and* you." The only thing for him to do from there was to tell her he loved her, which he did. She said she loved him too and kissed him to prove it. He had a vision of the two of them married, both professional musicians traveling the world—who knew, they might live in New York City. He saw them in bed each night, making passionate love, he saw them sitting together at recitals and graduations and weddings and concerts, their own children so strong and talented like them. Zechariah would touch those soft thighs without shame, and it would not be a sin.

Once she got saved.

"Here," she said, standing from the piano. "Papa has a record of Arthur Rubenstein playing it. I didn't want you to hear him before I played it for you because then you would know how bad I am."

"No," he said. "You were amazing."

"Wait till you hear Rubenstein play it."

She walked across the parlor to the record shelf and started sliding records out and back in until she pulled out a red one. "Come sit," she said. They listened to all three movements, and Zechariah did love it.

When it ended, he was exhilarated, felt like standing to applaud, but he said, "I liked your version better."

She leaned into him. "That's because you love me."

Her little brothers banged through the front door and ran down the hallway to the kitchen. Her mom's voice back there sounded frustrated and perturbed.

"Will you stay for supper?" Izzy asked.

"I can't," he said. "My mom gets upset when we skip a meal without telling her before she starts making it."

Izzy nodded. "Maybe tomorrow?"

"I'll ask," he said. What he didn't say was that he wasn't allowed to court her, that this glorious time in her house was an act of willful disobedience to his mother's direct and specific prohibition—when Izzy got saved, they could revisit it, but before that, no contact that would lead either of them to, in his mom's words, "develop feelings." He walked home and lied that he had stopped to play a little Indian ball with the fellas at the grass lot.

Two weeks later, after a regular barn dance, in the back seat of his dad's Studebaker parked in a wide spot out on the logging road, she whispered to him, "I'm ready." It was awkward and fumbling and he released his seed almost as soon as he was inside her and she hugged him hard and laughed and said it was all right and told him she loved him, and he declared his undying love for her and asked her if she would marry him, and she cried and laughed at the same time and said, "Yes, yes. A hundred times over: yes."

The weekend before Zechariah's dad forced him to attend a pastor's conference at PBI, he preached a sermon called "Are You an

Idolator?" Zechariah had lived the most glorious summer, played hillbilly music constantly, saw Izzy almost every day—they made love when they could get alone, which wasn't enough for Zechariah, so he took to dreaming of her as he abused himself in his bed. His mom and dad hadn't paid much attention to his coming and going because it was the summer his dad pulled their church out of the Southern Baptist Convention over their going soft on modernism and secularism.

This night, his dad preached about how idols aren't just things made of wood and stone that the heathens worship, but anything that a person loves more than they love God. "And that," he preached, "is the thing God requires of you, the thing you must put behind you." He continued, "Whatever just popped into your head, *that's* your idol. That's what you have to lay on the altar of sacrifice."

The invitational hymn that night was "Is Your All on the Altar," and Norma played it over and over on the organ, while Zechariah's dad instructed people to take a pencil and a scrap of paper from the deacons who were passing them around. "Write what popped into your head when I told you anything you love more than God is your idol. I won't know if you're lying, but God will. Write it down."

Zechariah wrote *Izzy* on his slip, added *and hillbilly music,* and quickly folded it in half. The hymn played as his dad talked and people wrote down their idols. Women cried as they wrote.

Zechariah's mother wasn't crying. She sat straight and still. He peeked over to see what she'd written. In her neat blocked-in cursive, she'd written *My Family.* On the other side of his mom were his little brother and little sister. Taking care of the family was all she had, as far as he could see, besides decorating the bulletin board in the church foyer for each new season and teaching Children's Church on Sunday mornings.

After the service, Zechariah's dad moved the congregation to the grass lot across the dirt road, above the banks of the Ohio River. There was a bonfire that Ben Hodges and Bobby Pearson had slipped out earlier and got blazing. At the fire, Ricky's dad played his guitar and led them all in hymns, and in between, people took turns standing and testifying, telling what idol they were giving up. The shifting glare and shadow on their faces made it feel like they were there to tell ghost stories, and the reflection of the firelight stretched out across the dark river. Congregants took turns telling everyone what their idol was, renouncing it in Jesus's name, and throwing their paper in the fire.

Zechariah watched as his mom testified that her love of her family had consumed her and supplanted her love of God, and how it had caused her to have her priorities upside down. The fire was taller than she was. She leaned out and threw her paper. It fluttered to the ground. Didn't make it to the fire. Zechariah's dad started singing "I Surrender All," and the congregation joined in. Ben Hodges stepped in, snatched up her slip of paper, and turned to hand it back to her, but she had already disappeared into the group of women, all dark figures just beyond the flickering orange firelight. Seeing she was gone, Ben Hodges wadded it tighter and threw it like a dart into the fire.

Zechariah's dad brought the singing to a stop and said, "Anyone else? Anyone else ready to cast off your idols and commit your all to the Lord?"

Zechariah stared at the ground to wait this one out. Why would God demand he give up the two things he loved best in the world? How was that okay? He could tell just by the tone in his dad's voice that others were welcome to come forward too, but this call was being issued straight to him, Zechariah. The long, awkward moment passed, and his dad drew the meeting to a close with a benediction. Zechariah spun on his heels, hoofed it to his bedroom, and locked the door.

———

The first day of the pastor's conference, Zechariah's dad woke him early so they could run by Ron's Barber Shop and get their crew cuts shaped up. Ron opened early just to meet them. After their trims, they pulled onto the blacktop road and left Millwood, wound their way to Charleston, drove through Charleston, right by the capitol dome there beside the Kanawha River, rode alongside the river for a while, and then plunged into the steep winding roads of the Appalachian Mountains, roads that must have once been deer or Indian trails widened with dynamite and blacktopped. On one side a steep drop of craggy rocks and trees fell away hundreds of feet into the New River Gorge. On the other side a jagged rock wall rose from the roadside—the black rock of the mountain's innards, wet and dripping. At the top of the rock wall, the forest above hung over like a bad haircut. In places, small trees sprouted at precarious angles out over the road, their roots clinging like gnarled fingers to the jagged rocks.

His dad's gray felt hat rested between them on the seat of the Studebaker. The seat springs were hard and high, and now, sitting where Izzy usually did when he was driving, Zechariah felt not like a young man, but like a child. He tensed his legs when they went around curves to keep from sliding in his wool slacks into his dad's hat. The hooked choke handle buzzed when his dad let up on the round clutch pedal—he'd never noticed that when he drove the car.

His dad had said little on the trip so far. He was a preacher and considered his words, but he also could say a mouthful with his silence. After Zechariah got the point and knew full well what was coming, his dad began.

"Son," he said. "Brother Roloff said that if you had the cure for cancer, you'd tell people about it, right?"

"Yes sir," Zechariah said. No trip with his dad went without a stretch of admonition and exhortation.

His dad stared at the road, shifted, muscled the steering wheel. He had a few straight little pieces of cut hair crisscrossed inside his ear. The road curved out to a short straight stretch. The silver bar down the middle of the front window lined up with the white line on the far edge of the road. From the passenger seat, the car hood looked like it jutted halfway into the oncoming lane.

"If," his dad said, "you have a way to keep folks out of hell, and you're not sharing it, how's that different?" He put his hand on the gearshift but didn't raise his foot to the clutch to shift.

"It's not, I guess." The car climbed, winding up a mountainside. Pressure bubbles filled his ears.

"It's worse. An eternity worse." His dad's voice now sounded like it was coming from the other side of a closed door. Zechariah tried to yawn hard and pop his ear bubbles. It didn't work.

"That Manzano gal you're sweet on, has she gotten saved?"

"I don't know." He knew all right: she and her whole family were Papists, Mariolaters.

A coal truck loomed around the curve from the other direction. The choke handle buzzed. Both the car and the coal truck looked too wide to pass, and Zechariah held his breath, squeezed in his pee, and waited to be crushed. Or pushed over the edge of the cliff to fall and watch the rocks below rush up to smash him. The coal truck passed, and he breathed relief.

"It's high time you got serious about eternal things." His dad peeled out his fingers from the wheel, readjusted his grip.

The air bubble in Zechariah's left ear popped; then the right one popped too. The car engine and road noise came roaring in. His own voice sounded pure and clear in his own ears as he said, "I'd like to play hillbilly music." He'd recently bought finger picks and taught himself Earl Scruggs's three-finger rollover style, and his banjo had such a sweet tone in the high register. His fingers curled, wanting to grip his banjo at that moment.

"That's a swell hobby," his dad said.

"I could be a recording star," he said. "Big Randy says—"

"Big Randy." His dad cut in. He sighed heavily and said, "First, Big Randy is an unsaved man with ungodly priorities. Second, and more importantly, just because you can hit the ball over at the grass lot doesn't mean you can go trying out for the Cleveland Indians."

Zechariah managed not to cry, but tears did fill his eyes.

"I'm sorry," his dad said, "but it's high time you got straight truth and tough love."

According to the sheet in Zechariah's PBI Pastor's Conference folder, his first session was "Practical Aspects of Personal Soul Winning," and was "mandatory for all PBI students." The room was full of rowed wooden chairs facing a small pulpit with a cross on the front. Fellas, and a few gals, sat ready for the lesson. Zechariah found a chair between two fellas and settled in.

An old fella walked in and straight up to the small pulpit. He was a large man, over six feet tall with wide shoulders that hunched over. His crew cut was white, and his glasses had thick black rims. He stood at the front and without warning started praying in a deep, booming voice. When he finished praying, he stepped to the side of the pulpit, took off his glasses and twirled them in his fingers, and launched straight into the lecture. "Twelve practical rules for soul winners," he said. "Number one: go in pairs. Reason one, it is the pattern set by our Lord when he sent the disciples out in twos. His wisdom in this is evident."

Zechariah sat through two more sessions on Friday. On Friday

GOD OF RIVER MUD / 19

night, he sat through the church service in despair because the Mill Creek Boys had them kicking up dust in the Gorvins's new barn and Raymond Walters was playing banjo in his place—they were going on without him just like they had gone on without Ricky when he went off to Korea. Zechariah crumpled his program into a wadded ball and sat squeezing it until his hand cramped up.

Saturday night was Dr. Perkins's keynote sermon. Zechariah sat beside his dad in a wooden slat-backed chair on the left side of the lecture room, three rows from the front, beside an old upright piano against the wall.

At the front of the room, a fella sat at an overhead projector with his suit coat off and his sleeves rolled up. He took off a silver wristwatch and balanced it on his leg. The projector tilted back on a wooden chair so the display on the wall beside the pulpit was a glowing yellow trapezoid with the wide side on top.

The fella slid a transparency onto the projector. A warped black circle slid up on the wall. Fellas milled around but most had sat down. A minute later, Dr. Perkins's son pulled down the circle and put up the number 900. Dr. Perkins stepped behind the pulpit, pushed his glasses up with a finger, and arranged his notes. The overhead fella pulled the 900 down and put up 1,800. Dr. Perkins nodded to a gal Zechariah had seen earlier with a nametag that said *Evangeline*. She stepped to the piano and played the intro to "At the Cross." Zechariah stared at the back of her—she was a large gal and her mass spread out on the piano bench. His dad elbowed his arm, leaned into his ear, and said, "That Evangeline sure can tickle the ivories, can't she?"

She played through several hymns. The congregation sang. The fella at the overhead stared down at his watch, though there was a clock on the wall above the piano. Every minute he took down the number and put up another, each minute the number grew by 900.

They sang "Alas and Did My Savior Bleed," "Nothing but the Blood of Jesus," and "Bringing in the Sheaves." The pastors belted out the hymns as if they were in a volume contest. They also seemed to be in a contest to see which of them could remember the third verse of each hymn without having to reach under the chair for a hymnal.

Dr. Perkins said, "I trust you gentlemen have found this time in God's word to be profitable for doctrine, for reproof, for correction, for instruction in righteousness; that the fella of God may be perfect, thoroughly furnished unto all good works." He took off his glasses. "I cannot imagine," he said, "a more important theme than the one we've dealt with these past two days."

He picked up his sermon notes and pulled his Bible from under the pulpit. He said, "No less a preacher than D. L. Moody said that he believed he had done more for Christ through personal soul winning than through all his preaching. We all need to be reminded," Dr. Perkins said, "of what is on the line here."

Could it be true that Ricky was burning in hell for all eternity, no getting him out, lost forever? Zechariah silently prayed and asked the Lord to have sent a believer, put a soul winner in Ricky's path in Korea to give a clear presentation of the gospel to him. Please Lord, let someone have done that, he prayed. Please have saved Ricky.

Dr. Perkins preached, "According to Billy Sunday, we need to quit fiddling around with religion and get to work leading this old world to Christ."

What about Izzy? She needed the Lord, plain and simple. He could win her. They could be soul mates and bedmates; their marriage bed could be pure and undefiled—the thought made his manhood start to swell and fill up his slacks, so he made himself concentrate on the sermon.

At the one-hour mark, the number 540,000 was up on the wall. Dr. Perkins stepped to the projector. He said, "There are 2.5 billion people in the world today. A population explosion such as the world has never seen. The mortality rate is 1.9 percent. That means 1 out of 50 people alive right now will die this year." He pulled off his glasses and used them to point at the number on the wall. "There are 31,536,000 seconds in a year." He turned and looked out over the congregated pastors and students. "That means, each second, fifteen souls leave this world and go out into eternity, where they must stand before God and answer for what they have done with His Son."

Dr. Perkins seemed to grow larger as he stood, still pointing with his glasses at the number that swelled upward into the bright trapezoid on the block wall. He bellowed out now, "How then, shall they call on Him in whom they have not believed? How shall they believe in Him of whom they have not heard? How shall they hear? They won't. Do you hear me, men? They won't without you and me."

The number grew to 540,900.

"These numbers represent the souls that have gone out into eternity while we met here for this final session. The overwhelming majority of them without the saving knowledge of Jesus Christ." Evangeline started playing "Have Thine Own Way," and Dr. Perkins went into the invitation. "Gentlemen, are we still afire with the desire to win souls, or have we grown complacent with worldly comforts?"

"Lord," Zechariah prayed silently. "Please let me play hillbilly music for You. Let me marry Izzy. I'll win her to You. I'll get her saved."

"Have Thine Own Way" ended and Evangeline went straight into the intro for "I Surrender All." The preachers sang. Zechariah prayed, "I do surrender all, Lord. Use me and Izzy and our music in mighty ways." Izzy could be his helpmeet. He didn't have to give up the one thing he loved most in the world to please God—surely God didn't want that from him. All he had to do was get Izzy saved.

"Men," Perkins said, "and ladies too. If you said just now, 'They must hear, Lord send me,' stand up."

His dad stood immediately. After only a second, he stood as well. It was settled then: he would play hillbilly music and give God the glory. He would marry Izzy and win her to the Lord.

"No," the Lord said into his mind. "You cannot serve two masters. It is them or it is me."

"But, Lord," he prayed silently.

"No," the Lord said clearly. "How can you do less than give me your best, and live for me completely, after all I've done for you?"

He could run from it no longer. God wanted him to give up not just Izzy, but his banjo, and the hillbilly music he so loved. He stepped out into the aisle, left his dad singing the invitational hymn. Instead of going down front to kneel and pray, he walked to the back of the room. He let himself out and closed the door gently behind him. He hurried down the hallway to the men's room. The sound of the pastors singing muffled in the hallway. When the men's room door closed behind him, the singing was only barely audible. One sink sprouted from the wall with a looped pipe under it, and one urinal beside it went all the way to the floor. The toilet had a wooden stall built around it, with a swinging door and latch hook.

Inside the stall, he sat on the toilet and thought of Izzy. Could he give her up? She was so sweet and talented and beautiful. He fantasized about their being married and began dreaming of her standing in front of him taking off her clothes. His manhood responded as it always did to these thoughts of her, and he couldn't help it, he started abusing himself right there in the stall.

As he was rising to release his seed, the Lord barged into his dream of Izzy with another vision: it was the edge of the New River Gorge and a meaty mass of human flesh sprang from the earth and rolled like a swollen creek down a mountain crevice—anguished faces, flapping arms and legs, twisting, churning torsos. Then, off a cliff as high as Hawk's Nest, they hurtled for a brief instant into the sunlight, and then tumbled over themselves, screaming, and crying, into the dark and craggy gorge below. Endless bodies continuously tumbling over the edge like a great rushing waterfall of faces and arms. Their souls sprayed like spume out into misty air and disappeared into eternity. Which ones flew off to hell, into eternal torment and flame? Most of them. Almost all of them.

His manhood had gone soft. "I'll play music for you," he repeated as he wept. "I'll be a good husband to her. I'll get her saved." He wept aloud, "Let this be my calling, Lord. Not that. Lord, please let me play music and marry Izzy."

For His response, the Holy Spirit put Luke 9:62 into Zechariah's head, what Jesus had to say to those who want to follow him but would hold on to something from their old life: *no man, having put his hand to the plow and looking back is fit for the kingdom of God.* This broke him. His own soul hung in the balance. God would not play second fiddle to anything or anyone. There was no other way.

"Here I am, Lord," his choking voice echoed in the toilet. "Send me, send me." He had to drop himself into that tumbling mass of humanity and plant his feet firm and cast wide his arms. He had to catch all he could. Nothing compared to so great a salvation—anything else he could possibly do was wood hay and stubble in comparison. Dung to be burned. He saw it now. He saw it clearly. He must serve the Lord with his all.

"Forgive me, Lord," he prayed. "I will be a soul winner. Take my life and let it be . . ."

The door opened and a fella's leather soles clacked across the tile floor. He stood outside the stall and peed into the urinal as hard as a cow on frozen ground. He passed gas into his trousers as he peed. Zechariah breathed slowly and quietly like he was hiding from a killer. The air inside the toilet bowl was freezing cold on his manhood, and the smell of the pink deodorizer puck the fella out there was peeing on felt oily in his nostrils. The fella snorted, cleared his throat, and spit into the urinal. He zipped his trousers and left without washing his hands.

Zechariah stood. He tucked in his shirt all around, zipped his trousers and buckled his belt. He adjusted the shirt and trousers, so fabric didn't clump or bind against his waist. He unlatched the stall door, took a deep breath, and stepped out to go stand with his dad and the other pastors.

Welcome to Clay Free Will Baptist Church
Sunday, September 19, 1954
Morning Worship

PRELUDE   Mrs. Joana Belcher

Pledge to the American Flag
    Hymn #344, "Mine Eyes Have
    Seen the Glory"

Pledge to the Christian Flag
    Hymn # 231, "Stand Up Stand Up
    for Jesus"

WORSHIP IN PRAISE
    Hymn of Praise # 41, "On Christ
    the Solid Rock I Stand"

WELCOME TO GUESTS
    Tessie Davis

WORSHIP IN MEDITATION
    Scripture Reading   Tessie Davis
    Morning Prayer   Archie Gwinn

WORSHIP IN GIVING
    Offertory Hymn #487, "Jesus Is a
    Friend of Sinners"
                        Sandy Phelps

WORSHIP IN PROCLAMATION
AND DEDICATION

MESSAGE "God Said It, I Believe It,
            That Settles It"
                        Pastor Jerry

INVITATION   "Jesus Is Tenderly
#136   Calling"

BENEDICTION

"Turn Your Eyes   Sandy Phelps
    Upon Jesus"

The peace lily was placed in the
sanctuary today by Colley Goins in
memory of his dearly departed wife
Shirley.

Church Training
    6:15 (Please be prompt)

Church Calendar
Sunday
    9:15   Sunday School
    11:00   Morning Worship
    6:15   Church Training
    7:30   Evening Worship

Monday
    6:30   Handbell Practice
    7:30   Choir Practice

Wednesday
    6:30   Youth Choir Practice
    7:00   Deacon's meeting
            Pastoral search commit-
            tee meeting
    7:30   Prayer MeetingSunday
            School Study Course
    8:30   Chancel Choir Practice

Extended Session: Peggy Bunch
                         Nancy Dalton

Counting   Tom Friend
Committee: Henry Driggers
                         Archie Gwinn

Deacon Visitation: Henry Driggers

The Flesh Lusteth against the Spirit

(Jordan River Goins, 1954–1964)

JORDAN BAGGED his first deer in 1954, the year he started first grade. He was six years old and had only been in school for two months. He shot it with the new .410 shotgun his dad had bought him, using a pumpkin ball load. He'd already bagged squirrels with the .22 his dad had given him for his fifth birthday, but never a deer—he'd seen his dad bag deer though. As far as he knew, hunting was just what boys did.

His dad had taught him how to load the .410 in the living room with red plastic shells of six shot. It was heavier than his .22, so that when he lifted it, he pulled his shoulders up like he was standing in the cold river. When he broke the gun down like his dad showed him, it lobbed the shells out over his shoulder. With it broken down, he put his eye to the back of the barrel; the inside tube was a bunch of circles leading to a glowing center, not like a light at the end of a tunnel but like the glowing hallow moon in a hazy night sky. The outside of the black barrel was swirled with shimmering blue and dull orange and brown, like oil on a mud puddle.

His dad sat on the footstool beside him and adjusted his grip as he pulled the gun butt into his shoulder. "Here's how you aim it." His dad's head was low beside his face, the Brylcreem smelled like a barbershop. "Put that bead on a squirrel," his dad said. "Take a breath, and slowly squeeze the trigger. Don't ever pull a trigger. You'll jerk the barrel and hook your shot off target."

"I know," Jordan said. "You told me already."

"I'm going to keep telling you too. Shooting a buck is not like shooting squirrels. You get excited. A man will do that if he's not careful. If you let that feeling get ahold of you, you're going to pull the trigger and miss your best shot." His dad let go of the gun and sat back in his chair. "I'm not just telling you. I'm telling myself. It'll still happen to me if I don't watch out."

The buck Jordan killed was a spike and his dad took him through field dressing it, step by step, having Jordan do as much as he could, but doing the delicate parts, like cutting around the anus and tying it off so no more shit got on the meat. Jordan had gut shot the buck, so the intestines were ripped open, and the shit was out already; stunk so bad that Jordan had to back away to keep from vomiting up his Cream of Wheat.

He had seen deer hanging in his dad's meat shed. This was the first one he had seen field dressed and it disturbed him. That deer ate and pooped and didn't want to die, just like Jordan. He'd learned in Sunday School that his mom was in heaven, and he'd be there too someday since he'd prayed with Miss Arneda and accepted Jesus into his heart. Because he had a soul that lived on after his body died.

"Do deer have souls?" he asked his dad.

"No, sweetie."

"So, they don't go to heaven or hell when they die?"

"Nope. Only people go to heaven or hell. Deer and squirrels and turkeys and such, when they're gone, they're gone."

Jordan stared at the carcass.

"Don't worry," his dad said. "He died fast. He didn't suffer much. Got to be real careful when they're gut shot," his dad said. "Don't worry. It happens to everybody now and then. Bad angle. Deer takes a step. You don't want shit on those tasty loins though."

Once the buck's innards lay in a glistening pile for coyotes and buzzards, his dad said, "Indians who used to hunt these woods would take a bite from the deer's heart. They believed they got a little of the deer's spirit that way. It would make them strong and fast like the deer."

"If a deer has a spirit, why don't it go to heaven?"

"That's just what Indians believed. They didn't know about God and Jesus."

"Are we going to eat its heart?" Jordan stared at the clump of innards and swallowed hard, trying not to vomit in front of his dad.

"No," his dad said. "Number one, I don't eat organ meat—lotta fellas think I'm crazy, but I just don't. Sorry. Number two, eating raw meat will make you sick. French people eat raw horse meat. Can you believe that?"

Jordan let out a breath, relieved he wouldn't have to choke down a bite of raw deer heart.

"Here's what we do when you kill your first deer." His dad reached up his bloody hands and with his thumbs smeared blood down each of Jordan's cheeks. "You are a deer hunter now."

"When can I get a rifle?"

"When you're twelve."

Six years was Jordan's entire life so far, a time span too immense for him to even imagine, but his dad was not a man who changed his mind and begging only made him mad.

"Come on," his dad said, spreading out his canvas tarp to roll the carcass onto. "Now comes the fun part: dragging this fella out of here."

After dragging the carcass across the blacktop road, they dragged on through the Jacksons' yard, the Gillenwaters' yard, the Troys' yard, and then around to the side of their own house where Jordan's dad's meat shed was. Inside, the shed smelled strong of Clorox, like it always did. His dad hoisted the carcass up inside the walk-in refrigerator he'd built himself with insulation, wavy metal walls, and a broken air conditioner he'd picked up down in Charleston and fixed himself. The two weeks that deer hung in there felt to Jordan like a year. He put on his coat and went into the freezing cold meat shed, stared at his first kill in the dim light of the hanging bulb.

When the two weeks of aging were over, Jordan and his dad put on their winter coats and headed out to the meat shed early on a Saturday morning. His dad got right to work and explained to Jordan what he was doing and why. He opened the flanks to the inner loins, he cut along the hip bone, and then sawed through the spine with a hand saw, separating the butt and back legs from the rest of the carcass. He broke down the hind quarters, found the ball joints in the pelvis, and separated the legs from the butt.

He set Jordan up on a wooden box at the other end of his butcher block table with a boning knife. "I'm going to be seaming out the cuts now, and I'll send you pieces like this." He held up a big chunk of bone and meat. "Your job is to use that knife and cut all the good meat out of these. This silver skin . . ." He pulled at the meat, exposing a seam of white inside the dark red meat. "If you can see through it, then don't worry about it, you can leave it and we'll grind it with the meat. Cut the rest away." He pointed at two metal tubs on the floor. "Grinding meat goes in that one. Scraps go in the other."

Jordan focused on getting all of the good meat off the bones. He worked in rapt concentration as his dad seamed out meat, removed the femur bones, pulled sirloins, explaining as he went, even though Jordan had watched it all several times before. When his dad started turning the ribcage this way and that, slicing the meat from between the ribs and throwing it into the grinding tub with Jordan's scraps, they both stopped talking and worked their knives in silence, and Jordan believed, even though the cold in the meat shed had gotten into his bones and made him start shivering, he was content.

When they were finished, spread out on the butcher block before them were globs of dark red meat. His dad pointed at each one and named it: "Sirloin, round tip roast, tri tips, top round, bottom round, eye of round, inner loins, venison flat irons, venison chops, stew meat." He pointed down at the tub Jordan had filled with scraps. "Grinding chunks." He grabbed the back of Jordan's neck. "That carcass was 130 pounds. This here is close to seventy pounds of meat. You know what you've done here, Jordan? You've just provided all the meat we'll need for winter, and more. We'll give the ground meat to the preacher."

That evening, his dad fried the tri tips with salt and butter and baked two potatoes. They listened to *Dragnet* on the radio as they ate, and it was a clear night, so they didn't lose the broadcast at all, and Jordan thought to himself that he was the luckiest boy in the world.

"When I grow up, I want to be a butcher man like you," Jordan said. "And I want to be a truck worker man like you."

His dad shook his head. "Mostly I just change tires on school busses," he said. "If you're strong enough to do that, and you still want to, I guess there's no good reason you couldn't."

"I will want to," Jordan said.

"Wait and see," his dad said. "People change as they grow up, sweetie. You're a lot smarter than your old man is. You got your mommy's brains. You'll be able to do anything you want to do. You don't want to be an old grease monkey like me."

"I do," Jordan said. "I'm going to be a hunter and a truck worker."

His dad hugged him. "Come on, sweetie," he said, "let's get this meat wrapped and into the Coldspot freezers."

Jordan didn't believe his dad when he said he was not a smart man. His dad knew everything. When men brought their deer for him to process, they always wanted to stay around and pick his brain about hunting and fishing and working on cars. Jordan's dad was Colley Goins, and it wasn't just hunters who shut up when he spoke. People in Clay County stepped aside for him to walk by, and as his boy, Jordan, enjoyed the doting attention of church women. They had gone to making over Jordan after his mom died. They looked too long at him with sad eyes, and he knew it was because he didn't have a mom anymore, and it made him feel sad too, but it also made him feel deeply happy at the same time because of the attention he was getting.

Jordan's mom hadn't wanted him to fall in love with hunting and fishing. She told him he was her little girl and needed to do girl things. She'd wanted Jordan to play with dolls and learn to make cookies, even ordered him a frilly pink apron from Sears Roebuck that he refused to even try on, not even when she begged. Jordan had been four when his mom's skin turned dark and leathery, and her eyes turned yellow. She was too tired to cook or do housework anymore, so Jordan's dad started buying TV dinners. A lot of the time she was too sick to do anything else either.

Jordan could feel his dad's mute frustration and took it as a sign that she wasn't as sick as she said, and he treated her like she wasn't sick, but lazy. Then she started acting crazy, because of her liver, and then she was just in her bedroom day after day while Jordan went in and out of the house—it was just part of life that his mom was back in the bedroom sick. Then one day her spirit went up to heaven to be with God and left her body in the bed, dead as a shot deer out hanging in the meat shed.

While his mom had ordered the apron, his dad had gotten him a pair of brown leather boots for hunting. Jordan couldn't try those boots on fast enough and wore them with his chin up high—his dad wore his own boots all the time. Except to church. He was an outdoor man. When he wasn't away at work or fixing up the house, he was down at the river fishing, up in the woods scouting or hunting, or in his meat shed where men paid him to process their kills. Fish, turkey, deer, one time a black bear. Jordan was there for all of it, the eager helper. In his mind, his dad had never done any of it without him.

When his mom got too sick, Jordan stayed with Miss Harriet Gillenwater during the day while his dad was down the river fixing trucks. Harriet had a boy named Harry who Jordan played with. Miss Harriet taught the two of them to read and count and was making them memorize their times tables. The Gillenwaters' house was right on the river, and she let them go down and fish—Jordan was determined to catch himself a muskie one day—or take his .22 and hunt squirrels. One day the summer before he and Harry started school, they were at the riverbank behind Harry's house shooting at birds and Harry's dad walked down with his fishing pole and tackle box. He laughed and said to Jordan, "You sure are your daddy's girl."

"I'm not his girl." Jordan scowled hard at him and put his hands on his hips. "I'm his *boy.*"

Still laughing, Harry's dad said, "You're his *tomboy*, that's for sure." He stepped onto the path down to the sandbar. "Hell," he said, "you're a better shot than any of the boys hunting those woods right now."

With that, Jordan decided *tomboy* was a special category of boy, and started telling people that's what he was, a tomboy, and people he told agreed heartily and seemed to admire him for it. It was going to be okay. He was going to be okay.

When Jordan started school at Clay Elementary, the teacher made him go to the girls side for bathroom breaks and tried to get him to play hopscotch and jump rope with the girls at recess. He went to the girl's bathroom but refused to play with them. Instead, he played baseball, and marbles, and cowboys-and-Indians with the boys, insisting on being an Indian because they were the best hunters. The boys didn't like Jordan. Perry Taylor, Timmy Jackson, and Ralph Davis were the worst; teased him and called him names all the time. Harry didn't join in with them, but he was part of their group and didn't tell them to stop, and he made it clear he didn't want to play with Jordan anymore either.

The girls teased Jordan too. Not one teacher stepped in to make it stop. The boys didn't want him on their team, but he refused to go away, and he played rougher and harder, refusing ever to give up at any game. The girls didn't want him around and it hurt his feelings even though he had no interest in jacks, pick up sticks, hopscotch, or jump rope.

Being a tomboy was exhausting. People kept wanting to treat Jordan like a girl and he had to keep reminding them he was not a girl; he was a tomboy. He had no use for girl things. He didn't wear dresses and skirts, he wore dungarees. People wouldn't just let him be. They kept trying to get him to act like a girl. He felt betrayed by all the people around him except his dad, who let him do as he pleased at home. Dress like a boy. Hunt and fish. Read about hunting and fishing in his dad's *Field & Stream* and *Outdoor Life* magazines.

When Jordan was twelve, he developed a heavy crush on Barbara Smith and slipped her a Valentine's Day card he'd made. She thanked him but gave him a funny look like he was crazy. He nursed the crush, dreamed of marrying her, of hunting and filling up a freezer with meat to feed her and their children.

Jordan was still twelve when his own body betrayed him. It started growing titties. He lay in bed at night and wept. He had a recurring dream when he was between waking and sleep: he was out hunting and a stranger would pop up and shoot at a deer on the other side of him, and the bullet would rip across his chest, taking off the budding titties, and he would feel such a wave of relief, but then he would come fully awake and there they would be, the cursed growth on his chest. He would daydream, fully awake and aware, of taking his sharpened boning knife and slicing them off, then wrapping up his chest in bandages until it healed back good as new without boobs.

While he was still reeling from having titties growing on his chest, his body hit him with another betrayal: he started bleeding down there. He'd always known he didn't have a dick like a buck but had more like what his dad called the doe's lady parts. Jordan hadn't worried about the difference until his own lady parts started bleeding. He didn't know anything about pads or tampons or anything like that. He yelled and screamed and ran across the blacktop road and into the woods, bleeding down his leg. He hiked to the creek that gullied down the mountain and lay in the water that streamed no wider than his own body. He gazed up through the creek break in the leaves and wondered that he was such a freak, a boy in his spirit and a girl in his body.

Jordan's dad bought a new television set and put it beside the radio, two big wooden cabinets that filled up one wall of the small living room. He let Jordan stay up late on Saturday nights so the two of them could watch *Gunsmoke* together. One of those Saturday nights, Jordan came out like he usually did for the show. He could see his dad was uncomfortable all through the show so that neither of them could pay attention to it.

When it was over, his dad walked to the television set and turned it off, sat back down, cleared his throat, and said, "We have to have a little powwow, sweetie."

"About what?"

"Things are going to have to change around here."

"Like what?"

"Like, for one thing, you're starting to grow into a young woman—"

"No, I'm not," Jordan shouted.

"Sweetie."

"I'm not."

"Don't flip your lid," his dad said. "Listen. I've asked Miss Peggy and Miss Arneda to take you under their wings and teach you how to do the things you need to know how to do. Teach you how to act right."

"How do I not act right?" Jordan yelled.

"Settle down. They've agreed to teach you how to act like a girl."

"I don't want to act like a girl." Now Jordan was crying.

"You have to," his dad said, leaning forward and raising his voice. "I was wrong to bring you up the way I did. I was selfish. But you have to set those things aside now and learn how to grow up proper."

Why was his dad changing toward him? What wasn't proper about the way he was learning to be a hunter? "No," he cried. "No. It's not fair."

"It's not about fair and unfair. It's about what is."

Jordan didn't understand what that meant.

They both sat silently for what felt like a long time, and Jordan picked at a knobby spot in the cushion fabric. Eventually, his dad said, "And when you walk around the house now, you have to wear different clothes." He shifted nervously. "Different underthings. Women's underthings. I'm a man and you're growing into a young woman. That's how it is, and it's got to be done proper and right."

That night Jordan wept into his pillow. The next day, after church, he hiked back to the creek and lay on his back in the water. Pastor Young's sermon that morning had been about how the soul and the body were at war with each another, and people should follow the spirit, not the body. Jordan's spirit was a boy. His body was a traitor just like the preacher had said, but it was impossible to defeat it.

Or to hide it. It was growing tits. What kind of cruel joke had God played on him?

He lay in the creek and half dozed, and dreamed that he was bleeding again, and the blood came faster, and faster, and then gushed like a pig's slit throat, and flowed down the mountainside, and through the culvert under the blacktop road, and on into the Elk River, and his spirit would be gone from his bled-out body. It'd be no different than a deer carcass when its spirit, whatever its spirit was, left its body. The coyotes could eat it; he didn't care.

Jordan turned fifteen two days after her dad married Doris Wagner. Doris's first husband, Berlin, had been a line-haul truck driver before he'd fallen asleep on the Pennsylvania Turnpike and plunged his Peterbilt over an embankment. Doris was a thin little thing, prissy and prim. She might have looked a little bit like Audrey Hepburn from a certain angle, like maybe she could pass for the movie star's ugly twin—Audrey had soaked up all the pretty-juice in the uterus and she got the backwash. People still told Doris they were spitting images. She believed them too. Had three Audrey Hepburn dresses that she rotated through, one green, one red, and one sky blue, all with white polka dots on them.

Doris did not like cooking or housework, she refused to put venison on her plate, and she screwed up her face at the meat shed like it was a pile of manure. "You don't have any problem eating a hamburger down at the Tastee-Freez," Jordan told her. She got angry and defensive, and Jordan's dad said, like he was tired, "Jordan, just let it drop." Doris and Jordan's dad didn't even seem to like one another much. She needed a man to take care of her now that her husband was dead, and Jordan figured her dad was marrying the woman to keep the house. And to rub off on Jordan, make her start acting girly.

Jordan had let Miss Peggy and Miss Arneda pick out pleated wool skirts and blouses for her, bobby socks, black-and-white saddle shoes. She wore the skirts awkwardly and habitually tucked her blouses in at the waist. She chafed in the bra and walked through the school hallways angry and ashamed. She overheard classmates talking about how she walked like a boy, and she heard Mrs. Simmons say to Mrs. Miller one day after she had walked past, "Poor thing. She's never going to find a man to marry her." She bit her tongue and walked on instead of reeling around and shouting at them, "Who says I want to find a man?"

Changing for Phys Ed was daily torment. Jordan was called all sorts of slurs: man-girl, butch, dyke, he-she, hermaphrodite. They jokingly speculated about how big her wiener was, and occasionally asked her to pull it out and show them. Beyond saying things like, "Very funny, Janet," and "I can't help it," she kept her head down and took the abuse like a dog that knew its owner would get bored of beating it soon enough if it hunkered down and waited. She could have kicked all their asses, but what would that prove? That they were right about her.

As things grew tenser at home with Doris—who had taken over the house, acted like it was hers, and demanded Jordan follow a whole new set of rules—Jordan developed a deep friendship with Susan Nichols. Susan had a twin sister, Sandra, who had died of whooping cough when they were ten. Her mom was their class's homeroom mother, had a list of all their birthdays, and brought cupcakes to school for the class to celebrate each one of them. Jordan's birthday was August 10, so her cupcake day would come at the end of the school year, and she would share it with five other classmates who also had summer birthdays.

All of their teachers seated them alphabetically, and in five of seven classes her desk and Susan's were side by side. They conversed all day long, carrying on their conversations on notebook paper when they had to be quiet for class. The two of them liked playing jokes, and one time they met early at school and stretched cellophane wrap across the toilets in both bathrooms. It was a real gas. They didn't get in trouble and their classmates talked about it for days.

Jordan was fifteen when the tension between her and Doris broke into a shouting match that ended with Doris calling her a bull dyke and her acting the part by giving Doris a fist right to the mouth, busting her lip so the blood ran in around her teeth while she sputtered and cried. Jordan's dad took Doris's side and that's how Jordan ended up living over at Susan's house. Susan's dad was a Watkins Man and traveled all over the place selling things. He was hardly ever home, but when he came back for a few days, he brought Susan 45s for her three-speed record player. Jordan took Susan's dead sister Sandra's bed, and they spent their evenings watching television and sitting on the floor, leaning back against the bed, listening to Susan's favorite records. Jordan longed to be at the river fishing or in the woods hunting, but she also loved being with Susan. A song called "Love Letters" by a colored woman named Ketty Lester was Jordan's favorite. She also liked the Shirelles, Patsy Cline, and Connie Francis. Elvis Presley got on her nerves.

Jordan lived with them for six months, and then on through the summer; then she was sixteen and they were going into the eleventh grade. It was the first year since she'd killed her first deer that she didn't bag a buck; she didn't even go hunting once and didn't care. She and Susan were together day and night; "joined at the hip," as Susan's mom told people. Oddly, when they changed side by side for Phys Ed, the other girls ignored them intensely, except for furtive side glances. They didn't tease Jordan anymore, but it was obvious there was something about her they found disturbing, the more so because Susan seemed to be okay with it. To find it attractive even.

One night, they were in bed talking about television shows, and Jordan said of the Dick Van Dyke Show, "Don't you think it's weird that Rob and Laura don't sleep in the same bed?"

"They can't on television," Susan said. Then, laughing, she said, "If they don't sleep in the same bed, how do you think they got Ritchie?"

"Maybe they reproduced like trees," Jordan said, and the two of them laughed together.

"Maybe Rob jumped into Laura's bed with her," Susan said.

Without even thinking, Jordan crossed the two steps between their beds and slid herself under Susan's covers. "Like this?" she said.

"I guess so," Susan said.

They lay there like that in awkward silence for a long time, then Jordan got up and slid back into her own bed. They fell asleep without saying anything that night, but after that Jordan crawled into Susan's bed at night for a couple of hours. At first Susan joked nervously, "Oh, Rob," and Jordan responded, "Oh, Laura, I love you so much," and one of the two of them would say, "Let's have a baby."

Then when they were alone together, they used the pet names Rob and Laura. In the evenings as they lay in bed, they cuddled. The night of the Christmas dance, which they attended together without dates, Jordan crawled into Susan's bed and cuddled her from behind, both of them facing the wall, as had become their way. She softly rubbed Susan's leg, and when Susan lay still and let her, she moved her hand slowly around to her stomach, her breasts, and then finally she pulled up Susan's nightgown and slid her hand into her underpants and rubbed her until she writhed and squirmed and caught her breath in her throat.

After that night, they both would use their hands on each other one or two times a week. They called it *that*, and eventually Jordan also used her mouth on Susan, and they called it *the other thing*. Susan never did the other thing for Jordan, only did that, but Jordan didn't mind. She liked making Susan feel good.

She didn't allow herself to do anything like dream about a life together with Susan, she had a constant, low-grade sense of doom from the start—it would come to no good. She was in love though, just as in love as any boy could be with a girl. So, she wrote Susan a love letter to tell her how much she loved her, how much she loved when they did that to each other, how good it felt, and how she loved doing the other thing to Susan because Susan was so good and so beautiful, she deserved to feel good.

Maybe Jordan didn't pass the letter along like the normal notes they passed during school all day because she wanted it to feel special, or maybe she was sabotaging herself because she didn't believe she deserved to be in love and happy like a normal person. She propped the letter on Susan's pillow one morning before school, thinking she would find it, read it, and respond with a letter of her own during seventh period study hall. She worried that Susan wouldn't pick it up, but she left the room before her anyway, hoping it would be a fun surprise. She watched Susan all day, waiting for a glance or a smile that gave away that she'd read it.

Susan didn't find the letter on her pillow. Her mom did while they were at school. When they came in that afternoon, she was sitting on Susan's bed, her face splotchy from crying.

"Jordan," she said flatly, "you need to leave this minute."

Susan said, "What's the matter, Mom?"

Her mom didn't answer her. She repeated, "Jordan, you need to leave this minute."

"Mom . . ."

"My clothes are in the dresser—"

"Get out," Susan's mom shouted as she stood like she was going to fly at Jordan with her fists. Jordan's letter, all four pages of it, was open in her left fist.

Back at her dad and Doris's house, Jordan feared this trouble was the biggest she'd ever been in. She lay in the bedroom that was once hers and had since become the room where Doris sewed dresses from a stack of Butterick patterns. Jordan gathered the patterns from the bed and stacked them beside the sewing machine, trying not to mess anything up but knowing Doris would say she did.

Susan was not in school the next day. She was not in school the day after that. Jordan rode her bike up the blacktop road back and forth past Susan's house and never saw her or her mom. She didn't come back to school the whole week, and on Sunday they were not in church. On Monday, Jordan's dad told her Susan had been sent to live with relatives in Missouri.

"What happened over there?" he asked.

"I don't know."

"Sweetie, we don't believe that's true," he said.

Doris said, "Nobody believes you don't know. What did you do over there?"

"I didn't do anything," she said. "She was my best friend." She shut herself in Doris's sewing room, lay on the bed, and cried. Susan, her love and constant companion for so long, had just disappeared from her life, like she'd died. But she wasn't dead. Jordan briefly considered going after her, finding her, declaring her love, asking her to run away together. That was all a stupid fantasy. How would she get to Missouri? And then what? Susan's mom sure wasn't going to let her be with an abomination like Jordan.

Jordan was an in-between person—didn't belong anywhere in the world and yet there she was, smack dab in the world all the same. Mrs. Simmons was right: she would never find love because the people she fell for were off limits, her desires sinful and perverted. Her existence was despised by God like Sodom and Gomorrah, what Pastor Jerry preached was so disgusting to God—*cherem* in the Hebrew, he told them, *anathema* in the Greek—that the only way God's holiness could be satisfied was by Jordan's total destruction. Her choice: throw herself on God's mercy and beg to be transformed or be destroyed.

The following Sunday, she walked the aisle during the invitation and knelt at the altar—partly because she was terrified she would be found out for what she and Susan had done and partly because she was so exhausted from being a weirdo—and let the words of the invitational hymn be her prayer. "Search me, oh God," the congregation sang, "and know my heart today. Try me, oh Savior, know my thoughts I pray."

"Please, Lord," Jordan prayed, agreeing with the words. "Please."

"See if there be," the congregation sang, "some wicked way in me. Cleanse me from every sin and set me free." She sobbed and begged God to change her, to make her a normal person. "Cleanse me from this sinful thing I am. Set me free, oh God. Set me free."

On their way home, her dad said, "Sweetie, I'm glad to see you did business with the Lord today."

"Me too," she said. "I feel like a brand-new person." And she did. Or at least she thought she could feel it starting. It would take time was all.

She saw Doris's jaw clench. Doris didn't say anything at all.

Bible Baptist Church
(Independent, Fundamental)
Ironton, Ohio
March 31, 1968

Jim Dooley   Pastor

Musical Prelude	"Come Thou Fount" Dorcas Dooly

Announcements

Hymn #447 "Are You Washed in the Blood?"

Opening Prayer	Pastor Dooly

Silent Prayer and Confession

Children's Message	"God's Three Rs" Pastor Dooly
	Children Dismissed to Classrooms
Special Music	"His Eye Is on the Sparrow" Ladies Trio
Offertory	"In the Garden" Dorcas Dooly
Special Music	"Fairest Lord Jesus" Dorcas and Carol Dooly
Message	"The Teachable Heart" Pastor Dooly
Invitational Hymn	"Have Thine Own Way Lord"
Benediction	"Blessed Assurance" Dorcas Dooly

Do You?

Some parents say, "We will not influence our children in making choices and decisions in matters of religion."

Why Not?
The radio will!
The television set will!

April Fools Afterglow: Tonight the teens will go on a "destination unknown" afterglow. Fellas and gals, you won't want to miss the April Fools hijinks that Ralph has planned for you. Meet in front of the church directly after evening worship to "load up" and see where you "end up."

Deacons Meet: Today at 6:00 the deacons will meet for their organizational meeting. We would urge all active deacons to be present.

Appreciation: During a time like this we realize how much our church family means to us. Your expressions of sympathy will always be remembered.
—The family of O.A. (Hank) Custalow

Sally Ramsey would like to thank the Lady's Fellowship for the delicious meals they supplied to her family while she was out of sorts after the birth of little Michelle. She doesn't know how she would go on without her sisters in Christ.

Mark your calendar! Next Sunday, April 7, we have the privilege of hosting the Pinewood Bible Institute jubilate. They will be ministering to us in music in both services, and Zechariah Minor, evangelist and Pinewood Bible Institute professor, will bring us a message from the Word of God. Mr. Minor gives a spirit filled presentation of the gospel and many are being saved under his preaching. You won't want to miss this day. Bring your unsaved loved ones.

If the Son Hath Set You Free

(Berna Cannaday, 1968)

BERNA MADE her way to church that Sunday morning in 1968, and things already felt different, if not momentous. She tight-roped the edge of the road between mud ruts and long wet grass, trying to keep her feet as dry as possible. Morning sunlight was slanting in through tree leaves, making the dewy grass sparkle, and the Ohio River was low to her left, on the other side of fenced-in corn fields, deep and wide. A special singing group was coming from Pinewood Bible Institute and the morning service was going to be all music and no preaching. Not that she minded the preaching, but the music at the church was her favorite part by far. She'd only recently started going to church, for something to do after her mom grounded her from all but school for being easy and letting boys fuck her.

It had all started the previous year, her junior year of high school, when her best friend Linda started going together with Jimmy Creed and abandoned Berna. Before that, people called her and Linda the twins, and she and Linda's mom playfully pretended Berna was her daughter as well—Berna called her mom just like Linda did, and she obviously liked it. Berna and Linda said I love you to each other too—when they said goodbye, when they ended a phone call, their signoff would be, "Love you," "Love you more." They slept together in Linda's bed for sleepovers—no sleepovers at Berna's, not ever. They held hands walking from Linda's house to school in the mornings. They even gave each other little smooches on the cheek when they were hugging.

Berna knew through all of it that Linda's feelings weren't the same as her own, and she knew without being told that her own feelings were too sick and perverse to speak into the world. In her fantasies, she and Linda left Ironton, started over together where nobody knew them. More than once, her longing to tell Linda she didn't just love her, but she *loved her* loved her, had almost gotten the best of her.

Then Linda dropped her like a hot potato for Jimmy Creed, a tall, skinny boy with a tuft of dark peach fuzz on his chin and zit clusters on his forehead. Linda didn't even know him all that well. Berna sat with the two of them in the cafeteria and tried to be a good sport and act like it was fine, like she was happy for Linda. Now Berna had all this free time too. Seemed like there was nothing to do for it but start dating as well. Except, instead of going together with one boy, she went out on dates with a lot of them, and if they tried, she let them fuck her. She liked the attention, the being wanted so hard.

She'd seen Gerald's pigs fuck. She'd seen dogs do it too—once she saw a boy dog get his dick stuck inside a girl dog, and the two of them ran down the road ass-to-ass yelping like they were about to die. When dogs fucked, what she noticed was how the boy dog's body jerked in and out with the rhythm of a machine, while its neck stretched and its face went blank as a shark's, the brain shut down while the body did what it was programmed to do by instinct.

When those boys climbed on top of her, rutting and panting, they were like dogs—how their brains shut down until they blew their load. During all their grunting and huffing, Berna discovered she could float up out of her body a few inches and watch it happen, like the body they were putting their dicks into wasn't even hers. She didn't ever feel the slightest inkling of love for any of them—hell, she already knew there wasn't a boy in that town worth marrying. She loved Linda, so marriage lay beyond the stratosphere of Berna's fantasies.

One day after school, Linda approached her as she walked across the parking lot cradling her books.

"We need to talk," Linda said.

"Talk then." Berna stopped walking, turned, and faced her.

Linda stood and said nothing for a long instant, and an awkwardness that had never been part of their friendship swept in and swamped it. "What has happened to you, Berna?"

"What do you mean?"

Linda slapped her hands to her hips, cocked her head, lowered her eyebrows to indicate Berna knew full well what she meant. "Why have you all the sudden started doing what you're doing? With boys?"

"What am I doing?"

"Stop it, Berna. We're best friends."

"Are we?"

"We always will be." Linda started picking at her cuticles, a nervous habit that made them peel back and bleed. Jimmy Creed was sitting in his mom's green Impala, waiting. Berna could see him in there staring out, or she imagined he was staring out. She couldn't see his eyes.

"Whatever you say," Berna said, and turned to continue her walk home.

"Wait," Linda said. "We owe it to each other to be honest, and there are things that are heavy on my heart that I have to say to you." From there, Linda's honesty excoriated Berna, used the word *tramp* and claimed that Berna's behavior was damaging her, Linda's, reputation as well as her own.

"Like you're not doing it with Jimmy," Berna cut in.

Linda straightened her back. "I most certainly am not. You know me better than that."

"Well, bully for you."

"I thought I knew you. What's happened to you?"

"Are you done?" Berna stared hard at her.

"After all we've been through together . . ."

They hadn't been through anything hard together. Berna had been through plenty hard things—Gerald mostly, but her mom and brothers weren't easy either—had worn herself out hiding it from Linda. "I'm going home now," she said. She twisted on the ball of her foot and started walking.

Linda said her name twice and then called out, "Fine. Be that way."

Berna cried as she walked home. Linda. All up on her high horse. She didn't know the first goddamn thing about it. Berna wiped her tears with the heel of her hand, hugged her books to her chest, and quickened her pace.

Down at the A&P, Berna's mom caught wind of Berna's new popularity with the boys and grounded her. Now seventeen, Berna was banned from going anywhere except church on weekends and school during the week. "You're not going to be a whore and live in my house," her mom said. "Not while you live under my roof."

It wasn't her mom's roof she lived under anyway. They'd lived in Gerald's old clapboard house since she was nine years old, and he never let them forget that he was the one giving them a place to live and buying all their food. Her brothers, Bobby and Billy, never took to Gerald, and things between them were always tense. They'd grown tall but still skinny like Jimmy Creed and had that boy energy that was always just shy of an outburst of violence. Gerald didn't help by being an asshole. The house was small, and it felt like three wild bucks were couped up in a horse stall together, overheated from the glowing coal stove.

Bobby lied about his age and joined the Army right after he

turned seventeen. Last Berna knew, he was in Vietnam, or on the way there; it had been over a year since he'd enlisted. Billy was eighteen, freaking out on acid while he waited to get drafted. He lived in a crash pad he'd built out of scrap lumber and corrugated tin on the back of Gerald's property, down by Ice Creek.

Gerald kept hogs on his back property, and Berna's bedroom window looked out onto the pig yard. The stink of pig shit and creosote and coal smoke filled her waking and her sleep. Past the pig yard was a stand of trees, scraggly little cedars and big oaks and maples, and along the creek bank was a bunch of mangy locust trees with those light green clusters of leaves that always looked dry and rusty around the edges, even with all that creek water for them to drink. That's where Billy had his crash pad. Past the creek was a pasture with three cows and a bull that stayed way off by itself like it was always pissed off.

Billy's pad was in a stupid place because floodwater from the Ohio River overpowered Ice Creek's natural flow once or twice a year, pushed upstream, and filled in among the tree trunks. The ground near the creek was a stinking, mucky swamp. Once it had spilled all the way into the pig yard. Berna remembered looking out at those hogs, standing motionless in water to their knees, strands of snot and spit glistening all the way from their snouts to the stinking shit water. The creek *would* flood his crash pad, and she didn't care if he drowned when it happened.

Gerald's pig yard was fenced with doubled-up chicken wire nailed to fence posts. Inside was trampled and choppy mud. Berna's brothers used to hock loogies through the fence at the hogs as they walked by. Once she saw them pull out their dicks and piss all over the pigs. The hogs didn't bother to move, just lay there flapping their wide ears, as piss splashed all over them. Her brother's dicks looked weird to her at the time, before she'd seen other boys' dicks, like raw German army helmets—not at all like her stepdad Gerald's, which had a sloping hang to it like the length of water hose he used to swat the hogs but slid out of folded skin when it got hard in a way that made her think of this sea creature she'd seen in a *National Geographic* magazine at school.

Once, when she was eleven, Bobby and Billy had cornered her between the house and the pig yard, pulled down her pants and panties, and stood there pointing at her hairless peehole and laughing. Billy had reached and tried to hook his finger up into her, but she'd folded herself away from him. The two of them tripped her to the ground with her pants and panties around her knees, and Billy said to Bobby, "Let's corn hole her in the front." Bobbie reached down and pulled out his dick. Gerald saw from her bedroom window and hollered, "Hey, you boys!" and they jumped up and ran down along the pig yard fence toward the trees and the creek.

Gerald got them later. Made sure she was there to see it. He took off his belt and made them pull down their own pants and underwear, and then he told her to watch, and he put red welts across their bare asses, the two of them hairy teenagers almost as tall as he was, standing there using all the strength and anger they had to shut down their faces so they wouldn't bust out crying like baby girls. They didn't try anything on her again after that.

Where was her mom when all that was happening? So damn careful to keep her home from anywhere people might think she was being a slut, and nowhere in sight when Berna could have used her at home? She was on the front porch, spread out on that glider like a giant bullfrog, that's where.

When Berna came home from school or church, there was her mom, fat and mean as one of Gerald's hogs, always on the porch in her flower print house dress, even in cold weather, smoking cigarettes and watching cars and waiting for Berna, unless she had to go inside and slice baloney off the slab or make biscuits because Gerald was hungry. She always said something sarcastic or mean, and once even slapped Berna across the face and called her a whore just because she was late coming home from church, and she'd just stayed to help the janitor stack away all the basement classroom chairs for a wedding reception.

Berna didn't know why her mom hated her so much. She would have sneaked around and gone in the back door to avoid her, but that would have made it worse when her mom found out she was there. One day, out of the blue, as she climbed the steps to go into the house, her mom said, "If you come home knocked up, I will throw you out of this house." A fight is what her mom always seemed to want. With her. Not with her brothers or with Gerald.

Gerald had come into her room at night and made her do things with him for three years. Then he'd just stopped when she was six-teen, just before Linda abandoned her. Berna was sure her mom had known about it all along—how could she not in that little house—but she never said anything if she did. She just sat out on the front porch, in that metal glider.

Once Berna told her mom, "I wish you never married Gerald."

Her mom sat at the table slicing tomatoes to put on their break-fast plates with biscuits and squirrel gravy. She said, "He's a good provider." Then she said, "He's a good man. You don't know anything. You're too young to know."

"You better believe I know plenty," Berna said. "Looks like I know more than you."

Her mom took so long getting her fat body turned to take a swing that Berna easily slipped out of her reach and walked calmly to her bedroom. Her mom yelled, "Get back here, you little tramp. You piece of trash." Berna called back, "No." Her mom wouldn't come all the way down the hallway just to slap her. She hooked the door lock anyway.

She'd stolen the hook lock from the True Value and put it on the door herself, so Gerald couldn't get into her room at first, even though he hadn't come in for a long time, but now it was to keep all of them out. While she'd been installing the lock, Gerald had walked down the hallway in his green shirt and pants for second shift at the plant, the floorboards creaking with his steps. He stopped and looked puzzled at her as she worked the pliers, turning the latch loop screw into the door facing.

"What the hell you think you're doing?"

"Putting on a lock."

"I don't remember anybody asking if it was okay to drill holes in my goddam doors."

"Ask who?" She looked hard at him. "Ask you?"

He stepped toward her and said, "You best remember whose house you're living in." He smelled like soap. He'd shaved, but missed a spot, so there was a small triangle of gray and brown whiskers on his chin. It made her laugh at him.

"I'm keeping people out who I don't want in," she told him. From then on, she would decide who got to fuck her and who didn't, and it sure as hell wasn't going to be him ever again.

"This is my house," he said. "I'll go where I want when I want."

"Not in here, you won't. Not in here."

He stared at her hard while he decided what to do about her defiance of him, and she feared she'd gone too far and would pay for it.

"What's going on back there?" her mom hollered through the screen door from the porch, and they both realized they'd raised their voices. Berna didn't care. She was ready to have that conversation.

"Nothing," Gerald hollered out. "I'm fixing to go to work." He gave Berna a long hard look and walked off.

As usual, the fat bitch played dumb and let it drop.

Not long after that her mom heard two women at the A&P gossiping about Berna, and she came home screaming and cursing, and grounded Berna. None of them had ever gone to church, not even on Easter, but her mom must have thought getting religion might do her good. Berna decided church was better than staying home with her mother, so she started getting cleaned up and hiking it down the road to Bible Baptist. She didn't believe any of the religion stuff, but she loved it there because the people were so nice to her. The old women loved on her like she was their own grandchild. People showered her with attention, and she didn't have to let them use her to get it. An old man gave her a butterscotch candy or a piece of Juicy Fruit gum he dug out of his deep pants pockets. He was too old to be wanting her like that. Too good too, she could just tell.

The men in this place didn't behave like all the other male people Berna had ever known. It had to be church that made them that way. She felt safe, not safe like at Linda's, where nobody got yelled at, or beat, or worse, but safe like God himself was looking out for her. She never realized how much she craved that feeling until she experienced it there.

So, on that Sunday morning in 1968 when the singing group was coming, Berna walked with jittery anticipation toward a place she'd come to love. As she picked her way around the puddles, Billy jogged up beside her reeking of unwashed ass and armpits, and said, "You going to church? Think I'll join you."

He was just bored was all, and cold from sleeping in his crash pad out back—not cold enough to go sleep inside Gerald's house. He stepped his muddy boots right into the puddles as they walked, as if he didn't even know they were there. He kept scratching up inside his beard, like he had lice. It made Berna's head itch, being that close to him. His sour stink made her want to vomit.

She quickened her pace and said, "It's a free country." Up ahead, in front of the church, she could see the baby blue van with writing on the side and an orange trailer hitched to the back. She picked up her pace. Berna loved the music at the church, loved when they all stood and sang together. This was going to be extra special.

To rib him a little, she said, "Maybe you'll get saved."

"Nobody's going to lay that Jesus trip on me," he said. He tromped on beside her.

When they got there, people said hello to her, and greeted the stinking hippie beside her as if he were any good clean boy.

The singing group mesmerized Berna. The girls were so pretty and clean and all wearing matching new dresses. Their voices were sweet and high—they were like angels. The boys were pretty too, and she could tell they would treat a girl right.

Then the man got up and preached that you could be crucified with Christ, that Jesus would take away your old ugly life and give you a shiny new one. All you had to do was invite him into your heart.

Berna decided before Evangelist Minor gave the invitation that she was taking Jesus up on his offer, trading in her old ugly life for a shiny new one. She went forward before the organist had finished the intro to the invitational hymn. Billy followed her, but she didn't pay any attention to him. One of the beautiful singing angels took her to a downstairs classroom and showed her Bible verses in Romans and led her in a prayer asking Jesus to come into her heart and be her lord and savior. Then the girl hugged her and gave her a red New Testament that smelled like clean fresh leather.

"Start by reading the book of John," the girl said.

This was perfect. Berna leaned out to get another hug. The girl patted and rubbed her back and told her, "Now you're a child of the King."

On her way out, Berna picked up a Pinewood Bible Institute pamphlet off the tract table in the entryway. She looked it over as she walked home. The day had gotten bright and warm, and sun flashed up from the puddles. Billy loped along beside her, still tromping through mud and water. His boots went splash-suck-clomp-clomp-splash. One big puddle had slimy strings of frog eggs along the edge. Tiny black tadpoles were wriggling around in it too, stirring up little puffs of silt.

Billy said, "I feel all clean inside. Jesus is real." He said, "I'm so tripped out on Jesus that I'm not even craving a cigarette—he just took that addiction right from me—and I should be going crazy for a smoke right now." He swung his New Testament out in front of him as he walked and whipped his stringy hair from in front of his face with a head jerk that made Berna wonder how he wasn't damaging his neck.

The pamphlet had a charcoal drawing of a college building with one of those bell-tower things on top and a bunch of pine trees behind it, and it said, "Go Ye Into All The World." Inside was information about the institute, where you could train to be in full-time Christian service. There was a phone number.

"I'm going to go to this school," she said, not to Billy but to herself.

He snatched the brochure from her. Jesus might have taken away his urge to smoke, but he didn't teach him any manners. He looked at it front and back and handed it back to her. "That's good. If it's your scene." He squinted up at the sky and said, "I'm just going to roll with Jesus."

"I don't give two shits what you do."

At home, Berna dialed the number, even though it was long

distance, and let it ring seventeen times. They were closed. It was Sunday. She slipped back to her room, locked the door, and started taking inventory of what she would take with her. To be in a place where it was like church all the time? Where people always treated her the way people at church did? Jesus was giving her a brand-new life. This was her chance and she'd be a goddamned idiot not to take it.

Three days after her eighteenth birthday, Berna left Ironton with no intention of ever going back. Just as he promised he would, Jesus was busting her loose. She had to do her part too, though; step out in faith and brave a long car ride with Gerald as he drove her to PBI in Meadow Green, West Virginia. It was a grueling six hours, the last two a slow winding path into the Appalachians with Gerald cursing and twisting the radio dial trying to keep a signal for more than a song or two, to no avail in those mountains. Berna laughed to herself each time a song started crackling into static. At least the radio gave him something to focus on, so they didn't have to talk much.

At one point, he said, "Why you going to a *Bible* school?"

"Because I want to," she said.

"Girls can't be preachers," he told her. "I know. You're going look-ing for a man to marry."

"If I do, he won't be anything like you."

He chuckled and kept fiddling with the radio. "I tell you this: he'll be thankful when he takes you to the bed, thankful that you've learned a thing or two."

She fumed in shame and rage, refusing to let herself cry. She shut herself down and waited, and the car ride, like all things, eventually ended. There she was, standing in the middle of her new room—the newness of life that was promised to her in Jesus. In the brand-new gal's dorm, Evangel Hall. The window was barred with rebar welded into a grid and painted black, as were all the first-floor windows, to keep the fellows from temptation. The welds were raised and lumpy like scar tissue. Outside the window, a rise of mud and gravel ascended to the jagged edge of the pine forest where the hillside had been cleared for the building, and rainwater had eroded a whole series of little ditches that were striated like stretchmarks.

The door swung out and a high-pitched voice said, "Hiya." A gal with a strawberry blonde bouffant and a puffy face bounded into the room like a big, goofy puppy. "I was just down the hall," she said as she closed the door. She looked at Berna and stopped dead: "Heavens, look at you. You're no bigger than a minute. What's your secret? You're Berna?"

Berna nodded.

The gal was fat. She bulged from a white blouse and brown wool skirt. Her calves were like white hams. "Welcome to Pinewood," she said. "I'm Deborah. Deborah Vickers."

Berna didn't say anything. She nodded again.

"You have more stuff to bring up?"

Still, Berna just nodded.

"Right on," Deborah said. "I'll help." She turned and disappeared into the hallway. Her high voice called back, "Fat girls are as strong as oxen."

Berna followed. Deborah's thighs rubbed together, and her hose made zipper sounds.

The cement steps in front of Evangel Hall had been recently poured, and they were still dark and wet looking, with the broom strokes still crumbly on top. The late August day was warm and white without clouds, just a bright smear across the entire sky. The smell of the pine forest wafted across the parking lot. Two turkey buzzards circled high and silent over the mountain that rose behind Evangel Hall.

Gerald leaned against his VW Squareback Sedan, smoking

Winstons and surveying the campus. "You sure you don't want me to help?" he asked. He flipped his cigarette butt onto the gravel. A trembling string of smoke twisted from it.

"Yes, Gerald," Berna said. "I'm sure."

"Suit yourself." He sneered at two fellows walking across the parking lot toward the main building, Perkins Hall, in short-sleeved white shirts with skinny ties, dark slacks, and large, well-worn Bibles. He ground his cigarette butt into the gravel with his boot heel.

She could have stabbed him in the chest right there if she'd had a knife. Deborah flickered a nervous side glance at him as he pulled another Winston from the crumpled pack in his shirt pocket. He whipped open and lit his silver lighter with two smooth strokes of his grease-stained thumb and turned his head sideways as he lit the cigarette.

Deborah looked away, and then leaned into the open hatch of the Squareback. "This all that's left?"

"That's it." Berna wiped her hands on her new denim skirt. The religious girls in Ironton wore long denim skirts, so it's what she'd gotten. The skirt was too big for her, and she had to gather and pin it in back.

"We can handle this, sir." Deborah slid out Berna's box of blouses and under things.

"Okey-doke," he said, and took a long, satisfied draw on his cigarette. Deborah gave him another nervous, sideward glance.

As they entered the room with the boxes, Deborah asked, "How long have you known the Lord?"

"Four months." Berna leaned against the painted cinderblock and closed the door with her foot. The paint was still a little tacky.

"Far out." Deborah put the box on Berna's bare mattress, then took the box Berna had carried and put it on the bed too. She said she could tell Berna was a new believer. She told Berna that she and her parents were missionaries in Osaka, Japan, were on furlough, staying in the missionary apartment of their sending church in Charleston for the year. "They're already homesick for their babes in Christ there," Deborah said. "When they go back this time, I'm staying here in the States."

"You grew up in Japan?" That's why she was a weirdo.

"The Lord just told me to pray over you," Deborah said. She stepped up and stood in front of Berna and, like it was the most natural thing in the world, started praying: "Our heavenly father, Lord, we come before you now in Jesus's name and thank you for such great salvation . . ."

The air was acrid with fresh paint and bleach. The bed to the right was already claimed by Deborah with her pink and cherry patchwork quilt on top, and hard, green Samsonite suitcase underneath. The room had the beds, two plain wooden dressers, two recessed closets without doors, a full-length mirror on the door, and nothing else.

Deborah's voice grew louder: "Lord, for this babe in Christ. Berna." At this she reached out and took both Berna's hands in her own soft hands. She smelled like flowery lotion. "Thank you, Lord," she said, "for your promise that He who has begun a work in you will continue it until the day of completion . . ."

Berna was inches away from her new roommate's face: there were tiny blue veins on her eyelids that wrinkled as she squinted to pray and constellations of freckles spread across her cheeks and her pale nose, and she had downy fuzz above her plump upper lip. She puckered her mouth as she said *Lord*. Her breath smelled of caramel and vanilla.

Berna leaned her face closer, closer, until, in little earnest bursts like a message from the Holy Spirit, Deborah's warm breath puffed onto her face, into her nostrils and her open mouth. When Deborah finished, Berna leaned forward, and Deborah did too so they could hug.

As they pulled apart, in all the newness and excitement, Berna had the strongest urge to lunge forward and kiss Deborah's mouth. Instead, she said, "In a lot of countries people do little smooches on the cheek to say hello," Berna said. "I read that. It's a friend kiss."

"That's true," Deborah said.

"Me and my best friend back home used to do friend kisses. Do they do that in Japan?"

"Oh, no, but I know they do in other places. Like Europe. They don't think it's weird at all, over there."

"Isn't Jesus a loving God to us?" Berna said, and those words in her own voice rang in her ears like the awkward trying of an imposter who didn't know the lingo—she was sure Deborah heard it that way too. Her face flushed and she turned her head and looked at her closet and said, "Guess I'd better get settled in."

"There'll be time for that," Deborah said as she stood. "I want to give you the grand tour of campus, though that won't take long, it's so small." She reached for Berna's hand. Berna took it, and Deborah pulled her from the bed as she stood to her feet.

Berna let their hands unclasp naturally. As she followed Deborah down the steps, she looked at the spot where Gerald's car had been, and the reality of her new freedom swept over her. She was away from Ironton, in a brand-spanking-new place, and there was no way anything there could get to her here—she was safe. She could be a brand-new person too, in this brand-new place, and no one would know any different. "Deborah," she said as she followed her new best friend, "This is going to be the best year ever."

Pinewood Bible Institute Chapel
Sunday morning service, May 12, 1968

It has been a profitable year of exhortation, edification, and growth in spirit and mind. May you take what you have learned and put it to work, whether you are going into full-time Christian service, or serving as an essential layperson in your local church.

Student Sunday School Classes •••
9:45 a.m.
Fellas in Perkins Hall foyer
Gals in Moody Hall lounge

Morning Worship •••••• 11:00 a.m.

Opening hymn (all stand)
"Faith of Our Fathers" ••• chorale

Invocation •••••• Dr. Perkins

Hymn 380, "Standing on the Promises"
(all stand)
Hymn 231, "Stand Up, Stand Up for
Jesus" (all stand)

Scripture Reading •••••• Luke 9: 1-26

Expository Message from the Word
Worthy Conduct, Philippians 1:27

Benediction •••••• Hymn 386, "After
All He's Done for Me" (all stand)

_____

Evening Service •• 7:00 p.m.
(Please be seated before the opening hymn.)

This Week

Today
4:00 p.m. Chorale Practice
5:30 p.m. Men's quartet practice
8:15 p.m. Ladies' trio practice
(Please bring your sheet music. Those of you who have misplaced sheet music, see Professor Minor after morning worship.)

Monday
6:30 p.m. Jubilate Practice
7:30 p.m. Soul Winning teams meet

Wednesday
6:30 p.m. Chorale practice
7:00 p.m. Prayer Meeting

Thursday
5:30 p.m. intercessory prayer (Prayer
Warriors, Platoon B)
5:30 p.m. soul winners pair off for
prayer of preparation
6:30-9:00 p.m. door-to-door visitation

Don't forget to call your dear mothers and wish them a Happiest of Mother's Days.

Please continue to pray for our nation and for the brave men fighting to defend freedom and democracy overseas. The News reported yesterday that last week was the deadliest so far with over 500 of our brave men killed by the communists. These are perilous times and the need to win souls is more urgent than ever before.

Better to Marry than to Burn

(Professor Zechariah Minor, 1968)

IT WAS warming up from a wet, snowy winter; seams of snow cut along the gulches and gullies of the Appalachian Mountains that were in perpetual shade, and the trees still had no leaves, so the mountains looked like the bristly backs of giant porcupines, fallen trees here and there, flat like broken feather quills. Zechariah walked across Pinewood's campus to have dinner with a missionary couple on furlough from France. They were staying with their newborn baby in the missionary apartment in the basement of the Hopkins's house.

Zechariah had made good on his promise to God in the toilet at the pastor's conference. He had enrolled at PBI, he had sold his instruments, and he had put Izzy Manzano behind him because she was a stumbling block to his feet. She hadn't taken it well at all at first—a lot of crying and accusing, and in turns, saying she despised him, stating that he was not the boy she'd thought he was, and then declaring her undying love. Then she'd hardened her smooth, brown neck and shunned him right back. It had filled him with despair, but he stood firm in the Lord. He prayed and asked for strength and redoubled his efforts to stay strong in the Lord and the power of His might. He cried more than once at night, longing for Izzy, his love, his heart.

He longed for his banjo as well, and his mandolin and guitar. His dad taught him how to exposit the Word of God and basic homiletics and had him preach full sermons on two different Sunday evening services the summer before he left for PBI. When he graduated with a degree in 1958, Dr. Perkins asked him to come on staff to be the founding chair of the music ministry department.

This is when Khrushchev was threatening to bury the United States while he rubbed shoulders with communists in Hollywood, and Castro had just seized power in Cuba, bringing communism right to our doorstep. The Lord's return was obviously imminent, there was little time left to win the lost. Zechariah had taken the job, but only till he could find a church and get to the business of soul winning.

Ten years passed. Dr. Perkins died, and his son Harold Perkins Jr. took over. In addition to chairing the music department, Zechariah became the Resident Director of the men's dorm, and the Dean of Men, and lived in a small apartment on the bottom floor of the dorm. He taught Bible, theology, and music ministry. He directed the jubilate and the chorale, and he traveled with his student singers all over West Virginia, Kentucky, Ohio, Virginia, North Carolina. Occasionally to Maryland or Pennsylvania.

He'd stayed on the lookout for a helpmeet, the one thing he lacked, or he would have already been called to a church. He'd become a formidable preacher, souls were saved when he visited churches, and he was always invited back. But he was single.

Not only did his lack of a wife hamper his ministry, but it was also the source of his greatest struggle with sin. Gals passed through the school, and he considered each one who stirred lust in him as a potential helpmeet. For one reason or another it just never worked out for him. He still couldn't help, in weak moments, lying on his floor in the RD apartment, because the bedsprings squeaked, and abusing himself while he dreamed of one or another of them. He always prayed for forgiveness afterward and rededicated himself to moral purity. He consoled himself that they were all potential wives, so he could possibly be looking ahead to a pure marriage bed in his future life. That made it not feel so sinful.

World events grew bleaker—the war in Vietnam, the strengthening of the communist threat, the youth going wild and out of control; world leaders being gunned down in cold blood—and it was apparent that the Lord was at the door just waiting for the Father to say go. Here was Zechariah, sidelined, cloistered in a pine thicket on the side of a mountain, while his calling to win souls waited for him.

He wasn't in a particularly good mood as he walked across campus on that chilly March night to dine with Gene and Rhonda Niemeyer. He didn't know this couple well, and he had a strange feeling, from the over-friendly delivery of the invitation, that they wanted something from him. His first inclination was to say no politely, but lunch at the cafeteria had been stewed tomatoes with too much sugar, gloppy macaroni and cheese, burned apple crisp and sliced white bread. The husband, Gene, had popped his plastic coffee cup down on the table and said, "Come over tonight and let Rhonda turn you on to genuine French cuisine." Zechariah couldn't turn down a real woman-cooked meal. So that evening, he shaved, put on a clean shirt and his black tie, and walked over.

Gene and Rhonda were both originally from Aberdeen, Ohio. They had graduated two years after Zechariah. He had actually taught them both in jubilate for those years, but he'd been so new to teaching and so overwhelmed at the time that he couldn't remember much about them. They were already a couple then, so Rhonda wouldn't have caught his eye as a possible helpmeet in ministry.

Around the back of the house, down the hill, was the basement apartment. Gene opened the door and gave him a strong handshake. Gene was tall with blond hair that was still a little damp and was combed down over his forehead and ears. He had high cheekbones that seemed to crowd his eyes toward his bangs. His shoulders were wide, but his arms were thin. He had on a black turtleneck. Bell-bottom dungarees.

Dungarees were against dress code at Pinewood. While Zechariah personally didn't much care about dungarees in and of themselves—PBI's official stand was that they were part of the rebellious youth culture now, and therefore to be avoided as worldly—the fact that Gene wore them so boldly spoke directly to his heart attitude.

Right inside the door smelled of baby powder and baby spit up and baby poop all mixed together. As they crossed the living room to the brown and red horsehair couch, the smell of beef stew overtook the baby smell. Beside the couch was a wicker laundry basket converted with white sheets and a blue blanket into a kind of bassinette. The baby was not in it. Beside that was a battered beige guitar case.

The living room was dark, just had light from one shaded lamp beside the stereo. The stereo had a scattered stack of records on it as high as three Bibles—records were tossed around, in the white sleeves, in the jackets, bare vinyl on top of one another to get scratched and ruined. Zechariah would not be lending them any records. Through the open doorway, he could see that the kitchen, in contrast, was glaring and bright. White walls, a white Formica tabletop with specks of silver and blue. The ridged table edge was as wide as his hand; it and the legs were as bright and reflective as a chrome bumper.

"Rhonda," Gene called, "he's here."

Yep. Something was up.

Rhonda stepped from the bright kitchen holding a dirty white dishtowel. She was short with hair that was straight down the sides of her face and brown. She had a plain little face, her eyes close together with a perpetual half-squint of what looked like a mix between curiosity and confusion, like a beagle puppy trying to figure you out. She wore a brown apron over what looked like a safari shirt, but it was pink. Her breasts were too big for her small frame, and her shoulders hunched over like a bass drummer in a marching band.

She was wearing bell-bottom dungarees too. Right away Zechariah got the feeling they were backsliding, what with them openly flouting the dress code in front of a dean.

"How hungry are you?" she asked.

"I could eat."

"Music program going well?" Gene asked.

"Pretty good," Zechariah said. "I have a good group of students this year."

"Did I hear correctly that you used to be in a folk music outfit?"

"Hope you like *boeuf bourguignon*." Rhonda said through her nose, the way, Zechariah assumed, a French person would.

"It's made with red wine," Gene said.

"Anything sounds good," Zechariah said.

"Men will eat boiled boot leather." She waved the towel at him and disappeared into the bright kitchen.

Zechariah turned to Gene and asked, "How's the ministry in France going?"

This opened the gates. Gene said, "Fine," and motioned for him to sit. They both sat, and Gene launched into it: the established church has lost all contact with the real Jesus, the man who walked in Galilee, and they have utterly failed to make the gospel relevant to the young. They have become fat and lazy and concerned with nothing more than trying to imitate the anti-Christ modes of their secular establishment counterparts. He kept saying, "You dig it?" and waiting for Zechariah to nod before going on. The established churches were hooked on the ego-tripping system of the world and the devil.

Zechariah sat through an hour of this. The smell of the beef stew grew stronger, and his stomach groaned and growled. He could see through the door into the kitchen and prayed a silent prayer of thanks when he saw Rhonda setting it with plates.

Finally, she stepped into the living room and said, "It's time to *bon appétit.*"

Gene walked into the kitchen and Zechariah followed him. At the kitchen counter he turned in his black turtleneck and held out a bottle of booze. "In France," he said, "it's a sin to eat *boeuf bourguignon* without a glass of red wine."

He had just stepped from bad-heart-attitude to outright, willful sin. With his wide shoulders and thin arms, and his hair combed down over his forehead, he looked like a big silly puppet.

"You are drinking alcohol?"

"There's simply no other civilized way to do it," Gene said. "You're lucky. You are being introduced to good food and wine with a fine French red." He uncorked the bottle and poured wine into the long-stemmed glass in front of his plate. He poured into Rhonda's glass. It was darker than communion juice, looked more like blood. He leaned over and held the bottle over Zechariah's glass.

"Oh no," Zechariah said. He slid his palm over the mouth of the glass.

Gene shrugged. "It's here if you want to lose the legalism and do it right." He put the glass in front of Zechariah on the table.

"We have tea and water," Rhonda said. "Or milk, if you'd like."

"Tea," he said. "Is it sweet?"

"No, Gene likes it bitter. But I have sugar."

"That's okay." The sugar would just settle to the bottom of the glass.

Gene took a long drink of alcohol. His Adam's apple went up and down twice.

It was the best beef stew Zechariah had ever eaten. The long thin bread was fresh baked too, and they tore pieces off of it and handed it around. The kitchen was hot. Sweat tickled down inside his shirt from under his arm—all his undershirts were dirty—and he had to reach around and scratch it.

"France is a food culture," Gene said. "Wine making is an art, just like any other art."

Here he goes again, Zechariah thought. It was true, Gene set out on another monologue, this time about how Europe was so much better, and how they never had a temperance movement or a prohibition, and that they didn't have the problems with alcohol that the United States did as a result. Their children drink it. He'd never ever seen anyone drunk over there, not once, because they grow up with it and know how to handle it and don't consider it sinful at all, not even saved people. On and on he went.

He drank off his glass and poured himself more. His high cheeks were getting red under the hot kitchen lights. He again offered to pour Zechariah a glass. Zechariah refused. Rhonda had taken off her apron. Her heavy breasts hung down and swung a little under the safari shirt as she reached across the table for more bread.

After dinner, they ushered him into the living room, where Rhonda served bitter coffee in tiny cups that looked like they came from a play set. Zechariah was off his balance, not knowing what his responsibility was here. The dungarees were one thing, the diatribe about the evils of the church another; drinking alcohol was sin of a different level. He had to turn them in. What were they trying to prove anyway? Why prove it to him, of all people?

Then, when he thought it couldn't get any more perverse, Rhonda topped off the evening by brazenly flopping out her bare right breast and showing him the whole thing, nipple and all.

It happened as Gene leaned in for another monologue—how missions in France were so difficult because the folks there were

Catholic and so they thought they were already saved—working his way back to the evils of the establishment church. He had gotten out another bottle of booze that he called *digestif*, and he and Rhonda were each having a tiny glass of it. He was beside Rhonda, waving one hand as he spoke and holding the booze in front of him in the other hand, his fingers pinched tight on the stem of the tiny glass. He was turned, facing Rhonda, and Zechariah was in a kitchen chair beside the stereo so that Gene had to turn his head back and forth to speak to them both.

While Gene talked, Rhonda kept nodding at Zechariah, making eye contact with him, her half-confused little eyes seeming to say, *Isn't he brilliant,* and *Wasn't that the most profound thing you've ever heard?* Her hair hung limp and flat down the sides of her face, like she was peeking through curtains. Periodically she egged him on with a "tell him about" this or that thing, always priming Gene's pump, never just going on and telling it herself.

After a long instant, the baby in the dark back room yelped once, then twice. Gene was in the middle of a sentence about Street Christians, these saved hippies who are hip to something real and genuine. He stopped talking and rubbed down his bangs. They wouldn't stay flat on his forehead if he hadn't put Dippity-do in them. Rhonda and he sat motionless; their full attention turned to the back room.

The baby whimpered, and then burst into a full wail—in the cry Zechariah thought he could hear outrage at waking so hungry and in such strange and scary darkness. Why wouldn't a baby be outraged at being treated like that? Rhonda pushed herself up and hurried back there. She cooed at the baby and flirted with it, her voice high and soft. The baby stopped crying.

"So anyway—" Gene said, "and this is what I want to talk to you about—there's this whole new movement of the Spirit, and it's centered around music."

Rhonda returned with the baby. It was wrapped in a soft pink blanket that had yellow ducks with orange bills all over it. The baby had brown hair like Rhonda. She sat back at her place facing Zechariah.

Gene was talking about musical groups they'd encountered while they were out in California for several months: Harvest Flight, Dove Sounds, Children of the Day. "Fine musicians. You ever hear of Tom Howard?" Gene asked him, craning his neck around to look at Zechariah.

Zechariah shook his head; no, he hadn't.

"He does this jazz thing. You dig jazz?"

"Sure, I guess."

"They have these Jesus Festivals, and man you wouldn't believe the way the Spirit is moving. This is where it's at now. This is where the life is; the establishment church is dead." Gene turned back around and said to Rhonda, "You remember when we went to that coffee house and saw that group The Open Door?" He was animated, excited. Zechariah feared he was drunk.

"They were so good," Rhonda said. The baby started whimpering, and this is when she did it.

Rhonda reached up and deftly, with two fingers, undid a button on her pink safari shirt. She pulled down a flap and there was her white bra, exposed. Zechariah caught his breath. He didn't want to stare, but he couldn't look away. Thank goodness Gene was facing away from him. Rhonda didn't stop there. She undid a little clasp at the top of the bra and pulled down a flap on it. There was her bare breast in all its glory: blue veins just under the soft, almost translucent, white skin, a dark brown nipple that poked out like a missile tip, with tiny bumps all around the edge. The baby's neck stretched like a chicken's as it reached to latch onto the nipple. Rhonda said, "Hon, would you grab me a nappy?"

Gene sprang up and took five long steps into the kitchen. The bottle clinked as he poured himself more digestif. There are a lot of euphemisms for plain old sin, Zechariah thought. He stared at the baby's mouth sealed around the nipple. It's cheeks hollowed as it sucked. Zechariah had the hardest erection he could ever remember having. He'd never seen a woman's breast. These two were deep in sin, dangerously close to toppling into perdition. This evil influence could infect the whole campus.

Gene came back with a diaper and tossed it onto the baby as he sat back down with his little glass of booze. As Rhonda picked up the diaper, her nipple pulled loose from the baby's mouth. A string of milky spittle stretched from the tip of the glistening brown nipple to the baby's groping mouth, then it snapped and disappeared. As if that hurt, the baby cried out. Rhonda grabbed her breast from underneath and stuffed the nipple back into the baby's mouth with an energy that almost looked like she was trying to smother it to death. The cry was muffled, then it tapered off into a few satisfied grunts, and then the sound was rhythmic clicks, little slurping pops. Rhonda draped the diaper over the scene and pushed her hair behind her ear on one side and looked down at the baby with motherly gentleness. Zechariah was enthralled. He felt a wave of love for this woman, wanted to kiss her, to lie with her, to wrap his own lips around that nipple. Even with her close-set, confused eyes, and her hunched-over shoulders, right now she was the most beautiful thing he'd ever seen.

Gene talked his way around to the reason he'd invited Zechariah over. Gene wrote Christian songs, a mix of folk and rock and roll. He wanted to bring this new Jesus movement to Pinewood, give them a dose of that real energy; bring it to the whole East Coast. "So, I've got probably three records' worth of songs," he said, "but the problem is, I don't know anything about music theory—I can't read or write music." He turned and looked at Zechariah. "But I'm naturally musical."

Zechariah realized he was staring at Rhonda and the baby, so he turned to Gene. His heart rate was elevated, and his head all jumbled, and at the moment he wanted nothing more than to catch another glimpse of that beautiful breast, that glorious brown nipple.

"I thought we could collaborate," Gene said. "I'd give you full credit for your part in it, any money it made too. I'm not looking for riches or fame. I've seen where the Spirit is moving, and that's where I want to plug in. You dig it?"

Rhonda was this man's wife. Zechariah had crossed a line here; he was not just dreaming of a possible future marriage bed, but was lusting after another man's wife, committing adultery in his heart. He looked away in shame.

"I don't know," he told Gene, unable yet to look him in the eye. "I'm so busy with the chorale and the jubilate, and the quartet, if I can get it going again. Dr. Perkins Jr. wants me to put together another traveling team too. It's good for recruitment." Satan was mounting an attack and it was time for Zechariah to flee youthful lusts.

"Sure, sure," Gene said, "but this is an opportunity of a lifetime. We could be a part of a wave that's changing the world. It's a spiritual revolution, man."

"I have to go," Zechariah said.

"You don't want more coffee?" Gene said. "Rhonda can make more coffee."

"No." Zechariah stood. His erection was still hard in his slacks, and he turned his body toward the door lest they both see his sinful passion.

Gene stood and walked with him to the door. "Think about what I proposed." Gene gave him a hard and significant look. "This is where the Holy Spirit is moving in these last days, I'm telling you. You want to be left behind with all the other straights?"

"I'll think about it." Zechariah hurried around the house and up the hill. He walked in the cold brisk air back to his apartment in the men's dorm. He lay on the hard floor of his room and dreamed of Rhonda's shiny wet nipple and abused himself. His gasps bounced back at him from the bare block walls of the room.

Later, in his bed, he prayed, as he always did, for forgiveness. He came to terms with the fact that he was not, like Paul, given the gift of celibacy. He knew that now, since he had been blindsided by temptation, in the missionary apartment of all places, and had committed adultery, plain and simple. Though he couldn't say how exactly, it was also significant that this overwhelming sexual temptation had hit him right as the topic had changed to that of music. He had more and more given his time to music and not to soul winning. This was where it always ended, in gross moral failure. He had to get more serious about this thing. The welfare of his soul depended on it. First, he had to back away from the music ministry, devote his time to preaching the Word, which was the only biblical mandate, which was his sure calling. There was one other thing he had to do, and he saw now that there was no other option.

Zechariah could never be a true servant of God until he got his lust under control. He had to follow God's plan for his sexual relief. He had to get serious about this. It was time to find himself a helpmeet once and for all.

Pinewood Bible Institute Chapel
Sunday morning service, August 19, 1968

Welcome to another year in training for the Lord's service. May it be a time of preparation, exhortation, and edification.

Student Sunday School Classes •••
9:45 a.m.
Fellas in Perkins Hall foyer
Gals in Moody Hall lounge

Morning Worship •••••• 11:00 a.m.

Opening hymn (all stand)
"He Leadeth Me" ••• chorale

Invocation •••••• Dr. Perkins

Hymn 32, "'Tis So Sweet to Trust in Jesus" (all stand)
Hymn 60, "Leaning on the Everlasting Arms" (all stand)

Scripture Reading •••••• 2 Timothy 2:1-16

Expository Message from the Word
Disciple Makers   Matthew 28:19-20

Benediction •••••• Hymn 243, "Here Am I, Send Me" (all stand).

Evening Service •• 7:00 p.m.
(Please be seated before the opening hymn.)

This Week

Today
4:00 p.m. Chorale tryouts
5:30 p.m. Men's quartet tryouts
8:15 p.m. Ladies' trio tryouts

Monday
6:30 p.m. Jubilate Practice
7:30 p.m. Soul Winning teams formation

Wednesday
6:30 p.m. Chorale practice
7:00 p.m. Prayer Meeting

As we begin another year which the Lord has given us, let us be ever mindful of our high calling. These are not times for over-jocularity and "horsing around" but are times for soberness of mind and sureness of purpose. The faculty and staff take the job of training the next generation of soul winners, pastors, pastor's wives, and missionaries with the utmost seriousness. Please comport yourselves in a fitting manner also.

Old Things Have Passed Away

(Berna Cannaday, 1968–1969)

IN MISSIONS class, Berna sat directly across from the evangelist who had come to her church in Ironton, Evangelist Minor—except everyone called him Professor Minor here. Above the blackboard the great commission was painted in bright orange: "Go Ye into All the World and Preach the Gospel." Instead of desks, they sat in wooden chairs set in a circle. Guys and gals took this class together.

Professor Minor's suit coat hung from the back of his chair. His hands were on his knees like he was ready to spring up. His face beamed when he looked at Berna, and Deborah nudged her. He was in his late twenties, maybe even in his thirties, stocky, with dark-tanned skin, and looked kind of rough, like a roofer or a state road worker. She wondered what was wrong with him that he wasn't married yet.

He started prayer requests by asking them to remember Mr. Hopkins's family. Berna had heard students talking about that, Mr. Hopkins's grandson, Sgt. Geoffrey Bell, had been called home to be with the Lord three months earlier, in Danang, Vietnam. Mr. Hopkins was the name on Berna's schedule beside her Anthropology/Hamartiology/Soteriology class. (The older students called the class *an-ham-sot.*) Mrs. Hopkins was the name beside Berna's Marriage and Motherhood class.

Professor Minor opened the first day of class by asking for prayer requests. "The Lord tells us," he said, "in James 5:16 that the effectual fervent prayer of a righteous man availed much." He straightened his back and said, "Yes, Ida." He raised his arm and pointed. He was thick like a football player, no neck. Sweat soaked through the armpits of his dress shirt, even with an undershirt on.

Berna leaned out to look and scooted too far back in the slatted chair, which tried to fold closed on her from the back. Deborah grabbed her arm and waist and they giggled. Professor Minor looked at them, then back at Ida.

Ida Powers stood at her chair. "Pray for the work in my country," she said.

"Ida's parents are serving in Kenya," Professor Minor said directly to Berna, apparently the only one who didn't know.

"There is great unrest since the president was assassinated," Ida said. She had unbrushed blazing red hair, and her face and arms were covered in dark freckles. She wore a peasant dress with orange flowers on it and weird leather sandals. Her legs weren't shaved.

"John Purdue and I had the opportunity to minister there this past summer," Professor Minor said. "We were blessed to lead eighteen Kenyans to the Lord in a single night."

Guys said, "Praise the Lord," and "Hallelujah."

Deborah said, "Far out," and it made Berna laugh.

"Pray that God will continue to bless that work."

Deborah leaned close to Berna's ear and whispered, "Ida is leaving school after this semester. She's getting her M-R-S degree."

Berna turned to look at the girl with the wild red hair again. She whispered, "What?"

Deborah whispered, "M-R-S degree. She's getting married."

"Berna," Professor Minor said, "would you stand up please?" All the students in the circle looked at her. Two guys bounced their legs, and all the guys held worn black Bibles on one leg or the other.

She stood and stared at the great commission printed above Professor Minor's head.

"Berna is our newest chorale member," he said. She knew what it meant, the way he smiled at her.

She had no musical training, so Professor Minor tutored her two evenings a week, using notes shaped like triangles and squares and diamonds. She struggled and eventually told him she didn't want to learn notes. Still, he made her the alto in his traveling quartet. In chorale, Berna stood in line with the other singers beside the piano as Professor Minor played. He told them to put a finger in one ear so they could hear their own voices inside their heads. Berna put her finger in her ear and hummed the alto part for "Saved, Saved."

"Berna," Professor Minor said. The other students turned and looked at her. "Would you stay for a few minutes after class?"

She nodded. The other singers looked from Professor Minor to her and back. Ida Powers grinned wide. She had bad teeth. Probably bad breath too.

"Remember at the end," Professor Minor said. "Hold the first and second *saved* for three full beats, then for four on the final one." He flipped the sheet music over and positioned his hands over the keys. The part in his hair was like a map of a creek running into a pond, the bald spot on the back of his head no bigger than a silver dollar. He pressed down on the keys. "Take it from, *Life now is sweet*," he called over the reverberating chord. "Fingers," he said. Berna joined the other singers putting fingers in ears. He pounded the chord again and they started singing.

She sat and waited after class. Professor Minor waited until everyone else was gone. She was not surprised when he asked her if he could call on her in the dating lounge. She told him yes and he took her smile as excitement when it was really amusement at his being so nervous; she was sure he was a virgin.

82

———

Later that afternoon, Berna and Deborah were back in the room, taking off their blouses and skirts for their afternoon nap.

"I have something to tell you," Berna said.

"I'm getting so fat." Deborah pulled off her bra and had a sharp red mark where it had been digging into her flesh. Her breasts spilled out onto her stomach. She squirmed out of her girdle. Her legs were as lumpy as biscuit dough.

Berna said, "No you're not."

Girls were running up and down the hallway, laughing.

"It's a real bummer, man." Deborah picked up her Bible and prayer journal from her bed and set them on her dresser. "I don't get it. You eat as much as I do and you're still a skinny Minnie." She unwrapped an Ayds diet chew and popped it in her mouth. She offered one to Berna.

"To me you look perfect."

Deborah said, "What fella wants to marry a heifer?"

A gal out in the hallway let out a scream that tumbled into laughter. She went running by the door, thumping sock feet. Two or three gals followed. Squeals and laughter rang down the hallway.

Berna said, "I think you are the most beautiful person ever."

Deborah turned to face the closet. She sniffled and her jaw slowly worked the diet chew.

"I mean it," Berna said.

"You're sweet." Deborah pulled away. "But you know what I mean."

Berna said, "If I was a fella, I'd marry you in a heartbeat."

"That's sweet of you to say." Deborah crawled into bed and pulled her pink and cherry patchwork quilt up to her neck. She said wearily, "What did you want to tell me?"

"A fella wants to call on me in the dating lounge."

Deborah rolled toward the wall. "*A fella?* Really?" she said, mocking Berna's voice. "What on earth else would it be? A dog? A horse?" Deborah was so silent for so long after that Berna thought she might have gone to sleep.

Eventually, Berna said softly into the silence, "I would say no if you wanted me to."

"It's not up to me," Deborah said to the wall. "Take it up with the Lord."

Berna knew Deborah wasn't angry because she wanted her, but because she wanted a fella calling on her, wanted a husband. She said, "You'll never guess who it is."

"Professor Minor." Deborah's voice was a flat accusation. "Who else?"

"Are you mad at me? I swear I'll tell him no if you want me to."

"Swearing is a sin, and why should I be mad? Now please be quiet so I can get in my nap."

The dating lounge was a big room at the entrance of Evangel Hall with two couches, tables and chairs, and a Ping-Pong table with one broken net brace. The net stood on one side and lay flat on the other and guys came over and played with it like that. There were no bars on the dating lounge windows. It was dark out when Professor Minor came, and the night windows reflected the inside of the room.

One evening, after he preached at the campus prayer meeting, he brought a whole six pack of Squirt soda, green bottles in a yellow carrier, and a brown bag with oatmeal raisin cookies that Mrs. Hopkins had baked. There were two other couples in the lounge, sitting with their faces only inches apart, like they were trying to neck without breaking the no-physical-contact rule.

Berna sat in a chair with her Squirt soda and didn't eat any cookies while Professor Minor sat in another chair that he'd pulled to face hers, his big Bible on the floor between them. The *i* in the word *Squirt* on the green bottles was dotted with a tiny heart. He kept holding the bag out, offering her cookies.

Professor Minor talked, mostly about chorale, and then soul winning. He was nervous, looking around, scooting his behind up and back on the chair. He relaxed a little as he told her about his Road to Damascus experience right here at PBI, when he'd been living for Self and God had gotten a hold on him and impressed upon him the importance of soul winning.

"Nothing is more important than soul winning," Berna said because it seemed to be the thing to say.

"I can tell you are growing in the Lord," he said. He held the cookie bag out to her yet again, she said no thanks, and he got himself another one and pushed it into his open mouth. His chest and arms were like a bulldog. "I need to tell you something," he said. "I feel the Lord calling me into the pastorate. Three churches have asked me to be a candidate."

"You won't teach music anymore?" She took a sip of the soda. It was tart and bitter like grapefruit, fizzier than Coke or Pepsi or RC Cola. She liked RC with peanuts in it. If she told him that, he'd bring it to her.

"If I take a church—" He fidgeted and looked around, then leaned over his Bible and looked down at it.

He sat looking down for an uncomfortably long time, and then blurted out, "It is not good that man be alone." He sat up straight and said, as if preaching a sermon, "The Lord says in Ephesians 5:31 that for this cause shall a man leave his father and mother and cleave unto his wife and the two shall be one flesh." He leaned over and put his elbows on his knees, looking right into her eyes. His aftershave was strong. He was sweating, he was so nervous, which was kind of sweet, and sad.

She looked down, found the little heart dotting the *i* on the cold bottle. She stared at it. Nothing is free, not even freedom in Jesus. Here was the price God wanted her to pay: be a pastor's wife, be Zechariah Minor's wife, sing in his church. Let him fuck her.

"We need to seek the Lord in this," he said. "Are you actively praying for the Lord's will in your life?"

She nodded and said, "Deborah." She said, "Deborah and I, we pray together each night."

"Will you seek the Lord's will regarding joining me as my help-meet?"

She nodded that she would, but it felt to her like it was already a done deal and she might as well make peace with it.

Professor Minor—"Zechariah," he kept reminding her, "Call me Zechariah."—continued calling on her and she did nothing to discourage it. One Sunday, their gospel quartet was suddenly cut, without explanation, and Berna found herself in a duet with Zechariah. She traveled weekends with him. They got permission from the dean to ride alone together in a car. It was a new car, a Datsun, mustard yellow with a black vinyl roof. A few months earlier, Zechariah's dad had led a man to the Lord who owned a car lot in Ripley. He was so thankful that he gave Zechariah's dad a car, and his dad gave it to him. It still smelled new inside.

They went to churches all around; they'd sing several numbers, he'd preach, then she'd go back to the pulpit and sing an invitational hymn while he went down and implored people to come down front, give their hearts to the Lord, and have their sins forgiven.

Deborah became distant. Because she was jealous, Berna knew.

But then she got a guy to start calling on her, a guy named Jerry Epps, who Berna happened to know Deborah did not like at all—the first three weeks of school the two of them had secretly called him Booger Boy because he spent the whole breakfast the first day of classes talking to the two of them about world missions with a booger flapping in and out of his right nostril—how could he not have felt that? Booger Boy was graduating and looking for a church.

"Epps," Deborah said one night. "Deborah Epps—Debbie Epps has a nice ring to it."

"I don't want to change my name," Berna said.

Deborah sat on her bed and practiced signing her new name on a piece of notebook paper.

Jerry Epps came to be a fixture in the dating lounge. Deborah stopped praying with Berna at night. Berna did not mind being alone, but the Lord had other plans.

The last Sunday of Fall Break, Berna rode with Zechariah to his dad's church in Millwood. Snow flurried from a low and dark sky most of the way as they twisted through the mountains. Black and bare trees leaned in and seemed to be aware in a threatening way, like faceless watchers. Berna shivered and Zechariah turned on the heater.

Before the morning service, they sang "Softly and Tenderly," and then a new song Zechariah had come across, called "Pass It On." He played it on his guitar and taught it to the congregation while his dad frowned in the front row. Berna stood beside him and harmonized, staring at the words painted right on the wall above the exit: "You Are Now Entering the Mission Field."

After the service, they had dinner at Zechariah's mom and dad's. The house was bustling with people, like Christmas, and they were all there to meet Berna. Zechariah's mom and grandma and sisters made a feast: turnip roots boiled with neck bone, dumplings made with corn bread and the pot liquor, sausage sandwiches, home-baked peach cobbler, and pineapple upside-down cake. The dining room was so hot with a fire in the fireplace that Berna felt sick and dizzy. Zechariah's family grinned at her as they ribbed him and recalled embarrassing moments from his childhood.

On their way back, Zechariah said, "I've prayed a lot about the Lord's will for our lives." He adjusted the heater and pinched at his nostrils like he needed to sneeze. "I have peace that the Lord desires we get married over the Christmas Break. There's the missionary apartment in the Hopkins's downstairs that is unoccupied. The Institute has offered it to me. My dad will do the wedding, so there won't be any charge."

Berna crossed her ankles, did not respond.

"Have you prayed for the Lord's will?"

She nodded.

"Do you believe the Lord leads?"

She nodded again.

He reached out and put his hand on her hand. It was the first time he had ever touched her.

She froze.

He turned her hand over and interlocked their fingers. They rode this way for a number of miles. As they approached Hawk's Nest, he needed both hands to negotiate the hairpin turns over the mountain. When he put his hand back on the steering wheel, it was trembling.

"It's settled then?" he said. "Partners in ministry and in life?"

She nodded and looked out her window.

They drove past a Quonset hut with a sign that read, "Mystery Hole." It had a giant gorilla on top and a VW bug posed like it had run off the road and crashed into the side of the metal building. There was no real hood on the car, but a hood was painted on the wall of the place, all wavy on the corrugated outer wall. The road was a precarious ridge cut on the steep mountainside. In the ravine far below, the New River marked its low path through the mountains and made its patient way north.

One freezing cold afternoon, when the sky was gray and wet, sagging just above the mountaintops and ready to drop snow, Berna stepped out to the phone in the dark hallway. She called Perkin's Hall to the switchboard operator and asked for permission to make a long-distance call, which she was granted because she was Zechariah's bride now, part of the Pinewood family, and could have what she asked for. They probably would have let her anyway. Maybe.

She called her mom. Her hands trembled as she thought of how to say what she had to say about Gerald. When her mom answered, she said, "Mom, it's Berna. I just wanted to call and tell you I'm getting married. If you want to come, it's on the ninth. In Millwood, West Virginia."

Her mom didn't act surprised. She said Bobby wouldn't be coming, which Berna already knew. He was still in Vietnam. Her mom told her Billy wouldn't be coming either. "He's dropped off the face of the Earth."

"How do you mean?"

Turned out Billy had stopped tripping out on acid and grass. He'd moved back into the house, had talked about Jesus all the time. "Not the real Jesus," her mom said. "A pinko communist Jesus he made up in his own head." He'd refused to cut his hair or get a job, which made Gerald madder than his doing drugs. Then he'd got in with a bunch of Jesus freaks, took a brush, and painted in big, red, dripping letters on the side of his truck, *In Case of Rapture You Can Have This Truck! Not Much Is It?*

"One day he came home, loaded up his things in that truck, said he was going to a youth commune with the true believers—they called themselves The Family. He told me not to take the mark of the beast when the rapture comes."

"Where'd they go?"

"I asked him where this 'youth commune' was. All he told me was it was 'in the woods.'" Her mom said, "It was good he left. I used to could keep him and Gerald from killing each other. I swear by God, they would have done it soon if he hadn't left. A house gets too small for two grown-ass men is all."

Berna took a deep breath and just got it out: "Mom, Gerald is not welcome at my wedding." She could feel that same angry silence her mom used to use on her. Her heart was pounding. She took another deep breath, said, "I mean it. He can't come. It's my wedding and I will have his sorry ass thrown out."

"Who's paying for this *wedding*?"

"He can't come, mom. I'll call the police if I have to. I don't care if it's embarrassing." She felt faint. Her whole body was shaking.

"I ain't going anywhere my husband can't go."

"Fine," Berna said. She figured her mom would take his side, but it was still like a kick in her gut, which was her own fault for hoping her mom would ever change. "That's just fine," she said. "Goodbye." She hung up the phone and tensed her body to try and make it stop shaking.

Evangel Hall was so still and so dark with all the gals gone. No girls running or laughing. It was as still as a crypt. Zechariah Minor was a good man; he would be a good provider. She had gotten out of Ironton, and she was determined to be out for good. She sat down in the hallway with her back against the wall. The floor tiles were cold and hard on her butt bones. She stayed there in the dark and breathed in and out until her shakes went away.

Nobody gave Berna away in marriage. She walked her own self down the aisle in a dress Mrs. Hopkins hemmed up for her. Berna had stood in the thing on a chair in the middle of the Hopkins's den, and the old woman had worked away, pinning and tacking and measuring. She'd pulled the thing tight on Berna's waist and said, "My goodness, you're no bigger than a minute." The dress looked nice on her, except it was low and gaped in the front threatening to expose her tits to the whole world if she didn't keep her shoulders back, and maybe that's why they made them that way to make sure a bride stood straight on her special day.

Deborah was her maid of honor, and two other gals on the hall Berna didn't even know that well served as bridesmaids. Six months after she was wed to Zechariah, Berna served as matron of honor at Deborah's wedding, and she wept quietly through the entire ceremony.

Welcome to Clay Free Will Baptist Church
July 6, 1969

Sunday School   9:45

Morning Worship

PREDLUDE   Mrs. Joana Belcher

Pledge to the American Flag
Hymn #344, "My Country Tis of
Thee"

Pledge to the Christian Flag
Hymn #25, "Holy, Holy, Holy"

WORSHIP IN PRAISE

Invocation
Hymn of Praise #332, "To God Be
the Glory"

WELCOME TO GUESTS

WORSHIP IN MEDITATION

Scripture Reading
Psalm 33

Morning Prayer

WORSHIP IN GIVING

Offertory Hymn #335, "And Can
It Be"

WORSHIP IN PROCLAMATION

MESSAGE   "So Great Salvation"
             Pastoral Candidate
             Zechariah Minor

Hymn of Invitation #136, "Just as
I Am"

Benediction

The flowers were placed in the sanctuary today by Mrs. Glory Croston, in memory of her beloved husband, Roy.

Join us after morning worship at the picnic shelter for dinner on the grounds, where we will be celebrating our nation's birthday and welcoming pastoral candidate Zechariah Minor. Rumor has it, Pastor Minor is a guitar whiz and might be persuaded to lead us all in some patriotic songs at the picnic shelter. Pastor Minor will be ministering to us from the Word again tonight in evening worship.

Church Calendar

Sunday

9:15	Sunday School
11:00	Morning Worship
6:15	Church Training
7:30	Evening Worship

Monday, July 7, 1969

6:30	Handbell Practice
7:30	Choir Practice

Wednesday, July 9, 1969

6:30	AWANA
7:30	Prayer Meeting
	Sunday School
	Study Course

Thursday, July 10,

7:00	Deacon's meeting
	Pastoral search
	committee meeting

Extended Session:	Doris Goins Sandy Phelps
Counting Committee:	Archie Gwinn Colley Goins Henry Driggers
Deacon Visitation:	Colley Goins

And the Spirit against the Flesh

(Jordan Goins, 1968–1969)

THE EVENING of December 6, the day before deer season ended, Jordan got held up at work cutting and wrapping pork chops for Utahna Smith. She was running late for the pastoral search committee meeting, but she stopped by her house and changed into her gray and red AWANA shirt anyway, so the men, her dad included, would remember why she was part of the committee—she worked harder at the church than any of them, Pastor Jerry most of all, before he left. She wasn't a deacon, so she didn't get an official vote, but she was on the committee all the same, and they were going to get her two cents' worth.

She pulled on her red and black plaid hunting jacket as she walked to her Jeep and took it off a few minutes later as she walked down the dank hallway in the church basement. The voices from the meeting room weren't joking pre-meeting tones, but official, down-to-business ones—ten minutes late, and they had started without her. She slipped in and sat at the long fold-out table as quietly as she could. In front of her a peace sign was etched into the table. Freddie Sturgis, a rowdy boy in Pals who habitually raised his hand to flash the two-fingered peace sign, was the culprit, she was sure.

Her dad pushed a stack of papers held by a black binder clip toward her—the resumes, doctrinal statements, and sample sermons of eight pastoral candidates. She pressed her fingers down on the papers and slid them over the peace sign. Her father's hands were rough and hairy, his fingertips permanently stained brown from working on engines and changing tires; the fingernails outlined in black like they'd been drawn on with an ink pen. Henry and Archie had dark, working-man hands too; Archie had one knuckle scraped raw. Jordan's hands were pink and chapped. She worked as hard as any of them did, but if her hands weren't in rubber gloves, they were in Clorox.

"We're looking at Stephen Earnshaw," her dad said to her.

She shuffled his resume to the top, straightened the papers, and slid her white hands under the table. She said, "Where's Glenwood?"

"He had to work late," Henry said. "He said go on without him. We have a quorum."

The four of them poured over resumes, compared sermons, discussed slight differences in doctrinal statements, which began an argument between her dad and Henry over whether God knows who will get saved or blocks that information from Himself to make sure free will is actually free. The argument began to grow heated, so Jordan pulled out her legal pad and pen and said in a volume to match their own angry voices, "Back to business."

They stopped, and all three men turned and looked at her.

"I don't want to be here listening to you two bicker all night," she said. "What we need to do is make a list of one, what we have to have in a pastor, two, what we would like to have but don't absolutely have to have, and three, what we absolutely do not want to have."

Archie laughed and said, "We want a man who doesn't get our wives' hackles up all the time." They all laughed and the anger in the room dissipated.

Henry said, "A man who knows when to keep his goldarn mouth

shut." How they were all guffawing, Jordan more than the rest of them. It felt good to let the tension out like this.

"A man," her dad said, "who doesn't smirk at you so that you want to sock him one in the bill."

After Pastor Jerry had retired, they had hired a man named Darrell King, who'd gone to PBI but who had just left a church in Pennsylvania, and he hadn't been at Clay Free Will for two months before it was clear he was already on his way out. He jotted his life verse, 2 Timothy 4:2, when he signed his name, and he used Paul's charge to "reprove, rebuke, and exhort" as his excuse to be a flat-out rude and mean person. He'd personally offended an important segment of the congregation telling "the truth in love" and had lasted less than a year. Luckily, the Lord called him elsewhere before the whole thing blew up, but here they were, searching for a pastor again.

They made the list, and then went back to the resumes again. Another hour later, Henry looked at his own legal pad and said, "So, our candidates will be Jeremy Haig, John Sharpe, Randall Greene, Zechariah Minor, and Stephen Earnshaw. All agreed?"

"Agreed," Jordan said along with her dad and Archie.

Henry held up his papers in front of him and tapped them straight on the table. "I'll call them tomorrow and get this ball rolling." He said, "While I'm thinking about it, Jordan, there's something else I think you might want to do."

"Sure," she said. "What?"

"You've done such a bang-up job with the AWANA program these last two years. I mean, all our church growth is from families of AWANA clubbers that you got in here. It's your effort that's filling up that bus."

"Yeah," Archie said. "You're sure on the ball with that."

Jordan nodded because it was true. She had seen that a church up in Big Chimney was doing AWANA, which was like Boy Scouts and Girl Scouts together, and instead of keeping kids away from church, it brought them in where, along with tying knots and playing games, they learned Bible verses, and most of them ended up getting saved.

She started the AWANA program at Clay Free Will two years ago, when she was just nineteen. It was her baby. She ordered the materials. She recruited and trained leaders. She worked up budgets and got them approved by the trustees. She made the club calendar, came up with club theme nights, took care of rooms, inventory, setup, and cleanup. They'd bought a used school bus to pick the kids up for club on Wednesday evenings because they outgrew the church van. She'd used those kids to get their parents saved and into the church too: seven families so far—twenty-three souls—had been added to the fold directly because of her efforts. There'd been controversy over making her the Commander since she was a female and not to be in a position of leadership over men, but the deacons eventually decided since it was just boys and not grown men, it would be okay—her having authority over them.

"This came to the church." Henry slid a letter across the table. It was addressed to her with the church address. It had been opened already.

"What's this?" she asked as she pulled out the letter.

As she pulled out the letter to read it, Henry told her what it said: "It's an invitation to go to an AWANA Commanders conference come summer, at the church where it all started. In Chicago. The two men who started the whole thing are going to be keynote speakers."

"Both of them?" her dad said.

"I don't know. They're both speaking."

"Who goes last?" her dad said. "That's who's the keynote speaker. That's who's the big cheese."

"Been to a lot of conferences, have you Colley?" Henry said.

"Don't need to. The one who goes last is the big cheese. Who doesn't know that?"

Archie turned from their bickering to Jordan. "We've discussed it," he told her, "and we, the deacons, have agreed to pay for you to go out of the missions budget. That's what you are, a missionary to these kids up and down the Elk River. If you want to go, that is. If you can get the time off work."

"I have plenty of days banked at work," she said, looking at the AWANA letterhead.

"We'll fly you out of Kanawha Airport," Archie said.

"The way they're crashing planes, you might want to drive it."

"One plane out of hundreds," her dad said. "It was pilot error, and he won't be making that mistake again."

"He's dead."

"Exactly. Probably safer after a crash than any other time."

"Tell yourself that," Henry said. "I'd drive."

"Jordan?" her dad said. They all looked at her.

"I'd like to go," she said. "and I'd like to fly."

On their way out of the church, Jordan said to her dad, "I'm off work tomorrow. Want to hit the woods?"

He hesitated, and she knew the answer was no. He said, "Have to see. Doris's got me painting the living room."

"I'm going to my favorite ambush point," she said. "That buck is going to mosey down the path right into my sights. I won't even have to aim. I'll just pull the trigger and the bullet will be passing by when he accidentally walks into it."

Her dad laughed and shook his head. Doris was always the reason. From the start, she'd not only pushed all the relaxing air out of the house where they both lived back then with her overpowering essence of snooty judgmentalism, she had inserted herself right between Jordan and her dad. Their relationship before Doris had been so comfortable that Jordan had never even given it a thought—it was just the atmosphere in which they moved. She and her dad moved easily together like two people in synch, running along winning a three-legged sack race. Even now, as just the two of them spoke outside the church, she could feel Doris's leg shoved down in that sack with theirs.

Jordan had complained to her dad about it once, and he'd told her, "Honey, there comes a time in a girl's life when her relationship to her dad has to change. You know, like the Bible says, you have to leave your father and cleave to your husband."

That's not how the Bible verse went, but she didn't mention it to him. Instead, she said, "I don't want a husband."

"You don't want to give Doris and me grandbabies to spoil?"

The idea of growing a child inside her body repulsed her. "You want grandbabies? *Doris* wants grandbabies?" She snorted.

"My best memories are of when you were little."

"You could volunteer in the church nursery with the women."

He laughed as if that were obviously too ridiculous to even consider. He kept the van and the bus running. He mowed the church grass. He didn't sit around in a rocking chair with a diaper on his shoulder, holding babies. He said, "I do love babies, though."

"It's not going to happen."

"Sweetie," he said, "you're at the age where you need to find a man who takes your old dad's place, a man who will be a provider. A man who will take care of you."

A man to take care of her? After what had happened with Susan, Jordan had realized she would probably have to be alone for the rest of her life, and so she set out to take care of herself. When she was eighteen, she went down to the Kroger in Clendenin and got a job. She bought herself a new Jeep CJ-5. She rang up and bagged groceries until one of the meat cutters in back moved away, applied for his job, and got it—a union job, good money, good benefits. Six months later, she moved out of Doris's house, bought herself a small house in Maysel, on the riverbank beside Route 4, and started saving money to build a back deck on the house, steps down to where she'd put a dock on the river. Eventually she'd buy herself a fishing boat.

At twenty-one, Jordan made more money as a union meat cutter than any of the drunken derelicts she'd gone to high school with—except for maybe Harry Gillenwater who went to work over in the coal mine. Her dad's job as a truck mechanic wasn't union. She'd never dream of bringing it up because he was a proud man, but she was sure she also made more money than he did. She had her dad drive her into Charleston, where she bought herself a 1969 Honda CB750. It had a dark red tank with a golden stripe, and an electric starter—the kick starter was just there for backup.

"You need to stop spending money like it grows on trees," her dad had told her.

"I will now," she'd said. "I have what I need."

Now she told him, "I'm heading up the mountain tomorrow either way. If you want to come, I'll be turning up the path at five thirty sharp."

"I might just," he said. They both knew he wouldn't.

The next morning, she was awake when the alarm rang out at five. Last day of deer season and Jordan had been so busy with work and AWANA that she hadn't gotten out to bag one yet. The thermometer on her porch read 37 degrees. It would be in the low 40s once the sun came up, perfect temperature for field dressing a buck comfortably without having to rush. She drove her Jeep from her house over to Clay in the dark morning; no one else on the road, nothing stirring. She parked on the sloping, gravel road berm by her dad and Doris's house.

She'd called Harry, Timmy, Perry, and Ralph and was surprised to find all four waiting for her at the culvert where they would cut up the path by the creek.

"They're going to smell the booze coming out your all's pores for a mile," Jordan said. She offered them buck urine to mask their odor, but they all said no thanks and looked as if they would vomit.

"Get that shit away from me," Perry said.

"Piss," Harry said. "It's not shit, it's piss."

"Have too much booze last night?" Jordan shook her head.

"Nope," Perry said. "Just the right amount."

Just the right amount to make the hike up a quiet one; she was fine with that. As she made her way to her ambush point, they each peeled away to go climb their tree stands. Jordan didn't use stands; she couldn't stay still in a tiny stand, had to keep mobile, couldn't be treed like a coon. She found her spot and settled in against a tree to wait.

Just as the sun started flickering through the branches, two shots rang out from Perry's direction. About an hour after that, a shot rang out from where Timmy was. Jordan waited another hour among running and chattering squirrels and, not seeing her buck, packed it up and headed back down the path.

She found the three of them sitting against trees with their eyes closed. A four-point buck lay in the path.

"Who bagged him?" she asked.

None of them opened their eyes, but Timmy said, "Perry."

"I heard another shot."

"Missed," Timmy said, still not opening his eyes.

She looked down at the dead deer. "You aren't going to bother to field dress him?"

"You're the pro," Perry said. "We figured since you're so good at it."

"Yeah, yeah," she said. She always field dressed their deer for them, and she always processed it in her dad's meat shed too. For free. She suspected it was the reason they hunted with her—and because she was desperately lonely, she didn't bother to test her hypothesis by telling them to do it themselves. She dropped her pack and pulled out her knife set. She cut around the anus and pulled out the colon. She cut around the ball sack and penis, leaving them there as proof of sex in the highly unlikely event that a game warden showed up.

As she sliced the hide along the sternum, Perry stood and walked over to watch, it being his deer and him needing to feel like he was participating. She made a nick at the bottom of the sternum, slid her index and middle fingers into the hole, spread them, and slid her knife in between them. She pulled up so as not to nick the stomach as she slid down the carcass, knife and fingers slicing open the body to expose the full gut package.

"The way you stick your fingers in that hole," Perry said, "no offense, but it looks like sticking two fingers into a pussy."

Timmy started laughing. He said, "You got a dirty mind, Perry. There ain't nothing in the world that don't make you think about pussy."

"I'm a man. I like pussy," Perry said. "What's wrong with that?"

Ralph said, "Man, you two, that's uncool. You know Jordan's got church."

Jordan said nothing. She pulled out her bone saw, sawed through the sternum, and pulled the chest cavity open.

"There's no sin in a man liking pussy," Timmy said, still laughing. "Perry just talks about it all the time." He said, "I don't like hearing him talk about it all the time. Jordan, you like hearing him talk about it all the time?"

"No," Ralph said. "She doesn't. Hell, I love pussy too, and I don't like hearing him talk about it all the time. Matter of fact, I think he talks about it all the time because he doesn't get any."

Jordan reached into the chest cavity, severed the esophagus, and cut the diaphragm free.

"I get plenty," Perry said. "You know I do. I get it every night of the week."

Timmy and Ralph broke out into guffaws. Timmy said, "Now we know you're a lying sack of shit."

"Twice on Sunday. Ask Jenny."

"Hey Jordan," Timmy said. "We were talking the other day and Perry thinks you like to eat pussy."

Suddenly it was quiet, except for the slurp and squish of Jordan's hands inside the deer carcass. She pulled out the heart, then carefully cut away the liver and set them aside on a clean rock where they wouldn't pick up grit.

"One of these days the Lord's going to get y'all's hearts," she said. "Just wait. He's going to save you."

"Seriously, Jordan," Timmy said, "do you?"

Another long silence while she freed the kidney and set it beside the other organs. She straightened upright, one knee down one knee up, and said, "Well, if I did like that, if I did, Perry had better be scared because he might wake up hanging in my meat shed waiting for me to have him for dinner."

Timmy and Ralph hooted and laughed, and Perry nodded and smiled.

She stood, wiping her knife on the leg of her coveralls. "Gut package is laying loose in the body bowl, Perry. Get at it."

"Come on, Jordan. *Please.*"

She shook her head. "The least you can do is bag up the organ meat," she said. "Or are you that much of a good-for-nothing?" She knelt on one knee beside the buck, reached into the chest cavity and grabbed a fistful of esophagus, and pulled.

———

It was May of 1969 before Henry got around to lining up pastoral candidates to come in June and July. In his defense, the winter weather had made traveling rough, so it probably wouldn't have happened then anyway. Of the five, two had already accepted calls at other churches, and one had left the ministry entirely to coach high school wrestling. They had just two candidates to pick from. Jordan had grown the church by three more families since the meeting and was ready to stand proud of her work for the Lord when whichever one they called started rolling up his sleeves to get to work.

On the twelfth of June, she even dreamed vaguely that she would be publicly recognized—maybe not an award, but a mention—as she drove her Jeep to the Kanawha Airport and heaved her suitcase out of the back seat. She'd never flown before, but she was not afraid, even with the recent crash. She figured her dad was right: if those pilots were ever going to be extra careful, it was now. She had taken two hundred dollars out of the bank to carry in her wallet. It was way more than she would need but she hated to be anywhere without plenty of money in case of an emergency.

All the American Airlines employees were so nice to her, and the stewardesses on the 707 looked like dolls—all that makeup, yikes—in their red dresses with red-white-and-blue belts and scarves. She had the feeling it was going to be a dreamy trip until they were in the air, the no smoking lights went off, and the woman beside her—who looked lovely in a stylish, striped pantsuit, and who Jordan thought at first was going to be her travel friend for the flight—looked her up and down like she was a dead possum on the road and then pulled out a skinny pack of Virginia Slims and started smoking.

The woman smoked one after the other and snuffed them out in the armrest ashtray between the two of them. She purposefully—intensely—ignored Jordan, who felt the familiar sting of it and tried to shrink against the plane wall and stare out the window, but eventually they were above the clouds and there was nothing much to see but clouds beneath. Not only did the woman keep smoking, but she didn't stub her cigarette all the way out and it smoldered up in thin strands right into Jordan's face.

She grew nauseated and worked up the nerve to, as politely as she could, ask the woman, "I was wondering if maybe you could give those cigarettes a rest for a little while? I'm not feeling great in my stomach."

The woman raised her eyebrows at Jordan and said nothing.

"I'm sorry. I've never been couped up without fresh air like this before. My stomach feels weird, and I don't want to have to, you know . . ." She gestured toward the seat pocket in front of her, where the stewardess told them the airsick bags were stashed.

The woman said, "It's not my smoking that's making you weird."

"I'm not trying to be hard to get along with. I feel sick."

The woman stood and made her way up the aisle. She spoke to one of the stewardesses, who glanced back at Jordan twice. Jordan could hear the woman talking but couldn't make out the words. Except she thought she heard—she couldn't be sure; she could have heard wrong—the woman say *heshe*, and it made her look down at her blue jeans, her boots, her loose tee shirt. What was wrong with her? She was out in public, not up the Elk River in Clay, and she hadn't even thought to dress herself properly. Maybe that's not what the woman said. Keep calm, she told herself. The woman came back and, saying nothing to Jordan, not even looking at her, gathered up her purse, her book, and her newspaper, and moved to an open seat farther back in the plane.

Jordan spent the rest of the flight free of smoke, and alone, except for the huge lump in her throat that served as her companion after these things happened to her.

———

The conference kicked off on Thursday evening with a spaghetti dinner in a large gymnasium with the AWANA game circle underfoot. After dinner, they sang "Father Abraham," "Deep and Wide," and "Fishers of Men" with the words changed to "fishers of kids." They capped off the singing with the AWANA song, and Jordan belted it out right along with all the men around her. Then one of the two founders stood at the wooden lectern and preached. Jordan thought of what her dad had said, and decided since this one opened, the other would close, and therefore the other one was the big cheese.

After the preaching of the Word, they broke into teams for games around the AWANA circle—a black circle cut in four sections by a green, a red, a blue, and a yellow line—one team per line. They raced around the circle, hopping, leapfrogging, and on hands and knees blowing a ping pong ball. The end of each race was always a dive into the center of the circle for a bowling pin on top of a beanbag. Jordan took off her boots, competed for all she was worth, and dove for the center pin like Willie Mays stretching out for a pop fly. She was the reason her team won, and her teammates congratulated her and told her so. It felt good for a bit, but they weren't exactly athletic or fit. They began making plans to meet up in one another's hotel rooms for snacks and fellowship. No one invited her.

She rode a taxi back to her hotel. The driver was a Negro man, old, with frosty white hair. He made small talk with her, but she struggled to understand him. He must have had the same problem with her because he asked, "Where you from?"

"West Virginia."

"What brings you to my beautiful city?" he asked.

"A conference."

He nodded. "Well, I hope you get out and look around before you leave. This is my city. I love this city." He was quiet for a bit and then said, "I do. I love this city."

Her room was on the third floor, and she stood at the window for a while looking at all the lights of the city and felt utterly alone in the whole big universe. She prayed, "Why did You make me this way?" She told God, "I've tried so hard to please You, to do Your will. Why do I have to be so alone?" Out the window, she saw cars and people and lights all over, even this late at night. Seemed busier than it was during the day. She took a shower and climbed into the bed.

The next day was filled with workshops, and, since the previous night's game time was such a hit, they added another round of races around the circle. She claimed she had a headache and begged off this time. There was another dinner, another service with singing and preaching, and, as they had the night before, the men made plans for late snacking and fellowship and no one so much as looked her way. She caught a taxi back to her hotel. This time her driver was not Black, but he did not speak English well, and again they struggled to understand one another.

Then she was back at the window in her hotel room, looking down at the light and motion. The keynote address was scheduled for the next day, Saturday, and after that, she was off to the airport, and who knew if she'd ever come back to this city. Instead of her evening prayer, she decided to take the old man's advice. She walked back down and had the man at the desk call her a taxi. A different man showed up this time, another Negro, with an afro that smelled like coconuts, which made Jordan's mouth water.

"Where to?" he asked. Not turning around to look at her.

"I don't know," she said. "I'm from out of town."

"Yeah? Where you from?"

"West Virginia."

Now he turned and looked for a long instant. "What are you doing here?"

"A conference."

He cocked his head doubtfully, then shrugged and said, "Where you want to go?"

"I don't know."

He nodded. "Okay. What are you looking for?"

"A place to meet people?"

He lowered his eyebrows at her and said, "Any certain kind of people?"

She couldn't bring herself to name the sin she was flirting with.

His face brightened, and he said, "Ah, *people*. I dig." He turned around and pulled into the street. "I'm going to take you to this place down Hyde Park."

"What kind of place?"

"A little club," he said. "I'll have you there in two shakes."

"A bar?" Where did she think she was going to go? It was 11:30 at night.

"It's good people there," he said. "You'll like it, long as the fuzz don't show up."

"The police?"

He laughed. "Nah," he said. "I'm just playing. They don't go down there anymore."

She grew ever more nervous as he drove her to what began to look like a dangerous part of town. Closed storefronts, dilapidated buildings. Was he going to rob her? Did he have friends waiting somewhere to do it? She was the hick, the fish out of water, and what was she doing out now anyway? She said, "Where are we going?"

"Relax," he said. "I'm not dangerous. I'm cool." He laughed and said, "Just pay me right." He stopped in front of a bar that didn't have a sign out front.

"What is this?"

"Trust me, sister," he said.

She hesitated.

108 / VIC SIZEMORE

She opened the door and stepped one leg out. Music thumped inside the bar. The door opened, a woman dressed in a man's suit stepped out, and a choir of women's voices accompanied Joe Cocker's gravelly voice on the song "Feelin' Alright." She pulled out her wallet and handed a five-dollar bill over the seatback to him. He folded it in his fingers without looking at it. "I won't steer you wrong," he said. "I swear, I'm cool."

She stepped hesitantly out of the car.

He pulled forward, climbed out, and lit a cigarette. He wore bell-bottom hippie jeans and a blue tee shirt with a huge red *C* gaping around the letters *ubs* like a big round fish mouth. He took a long drag on his cigarette, waved, and nodded for her to go inside. Smoke rolled out of his mouth as he called out, "Trust me. Go on."

As she opened the door, her heart was pounding like she'd just shot a black bear with a bow, and it was turning to rush her with the arrow sunk in its thigh. She took a deep breath and stepped inside, into a loud and crowded underworld. She saw a man in a leather vest with no shirt underneath, another man in a ballgown with bright costume makeup on his face, towering tall in high heels. Other men dressed as women, some just wearing skirts and blouses like a secretary going to work. A short woman in a man's business suit. Other women dressed as men.

But also, she saw plenty dressed like regular people—what Jordan would call regular people, all mixed in, Red and Yellow, Black and White, like the song says—mostly Black and White—milling around and chatting with each other like they were at a church afterglow. Except there were hippies in jeans and tie-dye, and a few people dressed up all colorful like it was Halloween. At the tables, men sat arm-in-arm with men, and women with women, and Romans 1:26–27 popped into Jordan's head about how these were vile affections.

Her dad called the Smoke Hole in Clendenin a den of iniquity and it was just a little bar with one pool table; what would he say of this place? What would anyone back at Clay Free Will say? They'd paid for her trip.

A normal-looking man was standing beside her. She turned to him. He leaned in close so she could hear him through the pounding music and said, "Heidi?"

"What?"

"Heidi," he said. The accents sounded weird to her. "I have to see your Heidi," he said. She puzzled for a second before realizing he was asking for her driver's license.

She turned and walked back out and the taxi driver was leaning against his car, waiting just like he'd promised. She felt a surge of affection for the man. She didn't know him at all, but he was nice to her, felt like the closest thing she had to a friend in this town. She waved to get his attention and then gave him a thumbs up. He flicked his cigarette butt into the street and tossed a loose salute up to his afro.

Back inside, she pulled out her wallet and produced her license. The man squinted at it with a flashlight and handed it back, leaning in close and saying right at her ear, "If the music goes off and somebody yells *pigs*, find yourself a man to put your arm around, or at least don't have your arm around a woman."

While she was puzzling over what he'd just said, a stink burned her nostrils, like running up on a skunk in the woods. A common smell out in Clay County, but why would it be in a bar in the middle of a big city? "What's that smell?" she almost yelled to be heard over the music.

"I'll tell you what it's not," he yelled back. "It's not grass. Nobody is smoking grass in here. Big Brother wouldn't like that, and we are nothing if not a law-abiding establishment." He smiled at her. He said, "Go enjoy yourself, Jordan Goins."

When the bartender asked what her poison was, she wasn't sure what to say. Perry and them drank Jack Daniels. She called across the bar, "Jack and Coke." He nodded and flipped a glass up onto the bumpy rubber mat in front of him. A song ended and the conversations were loud and happy, then another song came on, just a piano, almost like chopsticks played fast, then the other instruments came in—Sly and the Family Stone singing "Hot Fun in the Summertime." The beat was nice, and bodies surrounding her just started moving to the rhythm of it, like it wasn't music but pulsing waves of water they were riding.

Jordan had never danced with another person in her life. She turned around and watched the moving bodies. Freaks, homosexuals, abominations, and not a one of them giving her a strange look like she didn't fit in, because she did fit in; for the first time in her life she felt like she was in a place where she could let down her guard and just be. She could not remember a time she felt this happy, this free. She felt like throwing her arms in the air and shouting for joy and crying at the same time. She took another deep breath to compose herself—she could still detect the distinct smell of grass—paid for her Jack and Coke and turned back around to scan the faces in the crowd for the person who would smile back at her.

Saturday afternoon, Jordan sat in her plane seat trying not to simultaneously have a nervous breakdown and dry heave a mouthful of bile. She'd closed down the bar the night before, danced with a lovely girl named Patti who told her that she, Jordan, was what they called a butch lesbian. "I'm a femme," Patti had told her, she'd pressed her body against Jordan's and said, "Look how we fit together, me and you." They danced. They drank. They kissed. Patti told her, "You are one sexy butch, you know that?" That's when Jordan fell in love with her. The booze had helped keep the Holy Spirit out of her head. At the end of the night, Jordan said she had to go back to her hotel room.

"Alone?" Patti had asked.

"I'd rather not."

Patti went with her. In her drunkenness, Jordan gave herself over to the lovemaking entirely, and then, while Patti was talking about her sister's son whom she adored, Jordan passed out. The next morning Jordan was too sick for pleasantries. They exchanged addresses and phone numbers, and Patti said, "I like you, Jordan. I like you a lot. Write me." She spelled her name Patti, with a big heart for the dot over her *i*.

"I will," Jordan said.

Patti laughed and said, "Liar," but then grew somber and said, "Please, Jordan. I mean it. Write me. Or call me. Collect if you need to. I'll accept charges. It'll be worth it to talk to you."

When Patti was gone, Jordan sat in front of the toilet and threw up until there was nothing left in her stomach, then dry heaved once after that. The joy—the glee—she'd felt the night before, the sense that anything was possible, had disappeared, and she plunged into a dark hatred and disgust for Patti and for herself. She wept and repented. She showered, packed, cleaned her room, made the bed. She'd already missed the morning sessions at the Commanders conference, so she skipped the keynote sermon and caught a taxi to the airport. Of the two hundred dollars she'd brought, she only had thirty left. She'd been generous the night before, had bought drinks for strangers all night, out of sheer happiness. How Satan disguises himself as an angel of light to lead believers astray. How weak Jordan was, how she had been blown over by the first little hint of temptation.

Back at home, the following morning, Sunday, she was supposed to stand before the congregation—they did pay for the trip after all—and give a testimony of the ways God had used the conference to educate and uplift her and give her new ideas to make Clay Free Will's AWANA program even better, great as it already was. At sunrise, she had recovered from her hangover, but her soul was still in the Slough of Despond and praying was not lifting her out. She ran her six-inch Victorinox across the steel a few times, slid it into a sheath she'd made herself out of deer hide, and hiked up to the creek where she'd lain her first time on the rag all those years before, hoping to bleed out and die. This time she planned to make it happen. She would sever her femoral artery, a short flash of pain, and then she'd be gone in just a few peaceful minutes. Mortify the flesh so her tormented spirit could finally find rest.

She sat on a rock beside the stream until the squirrels resumed their running and rustling in the leaves close by, unconcerned about her presence. She unzipped her jeans, slid them down. She unsheathed her knife with her right hand and with the fingers of her left found the spot in her groin where she would make the cut, vertical down the artery, not straight across, to make the outflow of blood fast and sure.

As she took deep breaths, her hands shaking as she tried to gin up the courage to make the slice, the guy in that play from her eleventh-grade English class came into her mind, how he wanted to do it too but was afraid God would put him in hell if he did, and her English teacher, Mrs. Bunch, assured the class that hell was exactly where a person who committed suicide would go. What misery, needing to escape unbearable present torment, but faced with worse—an eternity of worse—if you tried to get free. With eternal hellfire looming before her, Jordan wussed out. She sheathed her knife, pulled up and zipped her jeans, and hiked back down to the wide spot by her dad and Doris's house where she was parked. And she drove back to Clendenin.

She grabbed a quick shower, pulled on a skirt, donned her AWANA Commander shirt, and stepped into her penny loafers. She drove to church and spoke briefly about the conference before Henry delivered a sermon of sorts; she told the congregation that she helped her team win the races, but that she was a country girl at heart and didn't like the big city. That evening, she once again met with the men on the pastoral search committee. One candidate had visited already, and next was Zechariah Minor, from PBI.

"He's coming the beginning of July. It's our Independence Day Sunday, but we'll still do all the same things we did for the others, try to keep it fair."

Archie said, "He's bringing his bride." He shuffled through his papers. "Berna's her name. They're newlyweds."

Jordan's dad snorted and said, "Great. Get ready for a bunch of lovey-dovey nonsense."

"Be nice if we could find an unmarried man for Jordan," Henry said.

Archie agreed, said, "You'd make a perfect preacher's wife, the way you're going gangbusters with the AWANA clubs."

"Well," Jordan said, swallowing down the lump in her throat, trying not to break down crying there at the table. All she could think to say was "There are people the Lord calls to be single." As she said the word *single*, she thought the word *alone*. She blinked her eyes hard. She would not break down here, not as the only girl with a bunch of men.

"Not like the Catholics do it," Henry said.

"Well, no," Archie said, "not like that, but just look at old Paul."

They argued about Paul's admonition for a man not to be married so he could devote all of his time to the ministry. They had all agreed that they wanted a married man—Henry wasn't being serious with Jordan, just pointing out the elephant that was sitting on her lap as they spoke, that followed her everywhere she went like Mary's little lamb—because a married man was settled down, and an unmarried man was by nature an unsettled creature.

Book Two

Welcome to Clay Free Will Baptist Church
July 4, 1976

Sunday School   9:45

Morning Worship

PRELUDE   Mrs. Doris Goins

Hymn #346, "My Country Tis of Thee"

WORSHIP IN PRAISE

Pledge to the American Flag
Pledge to the Christian Flag
Pledge to the Bible
Hymn #231, "Stand Up Stand Up for Jesus"

INVOCATION

* Hymn of Praise #41, "Battle Hymn of the Republic"

WELCOME TO GUESTS

WORSHIP IN MEDITATION

Scripture Reading
Psalm 144

Morning Prayer

WORSHIP IN GIVING

Offertory Hymn #487, "Onward Christian Soldiers"

WORSHIP IN PROCLAMATION

MESSAGE   "Our Declaration of Dependence"

Pastor Zechariah Minor

Hymn of Invitation #136, "Jesus Is Tenderly Calling"

Benediction   "Crown Him with Many Crowns"

Please join us after morning worship at the picnic shelter to break bread together and celebrate the birth of the greatest nation to ever exist on Earth. Kroger fried chicken and drinks will be provided. Bring a side or a desert. There will be softball and horseshoes. Pastor Minor will bring out his guitar and lead us in patriotic songs. We will cap off the celebration with watermelon and sparklers for kiddoes of all ages.

Church Calendar

Sunday, July 4

9:15	Sunday School
11:00	Morning Worship
6:15	Church Training
7:30	Evening Worship

Monday, July 5

7:30	Choir Practice

Wednesday, July 7

6:30	AWANA Club
7:00	Deacon's meeting
7:30	Prayer Meeting

We continue to miss our dear brother, Henry. Brother Henry served this church faithfully for over forty years as a trustee, a deacon, and interim pastor. His death in the mining accident was tragic and from a human viewpoint too soon. But God's timing is always perfect even if we can't understand. Psalm 116:15 "Precious in the sight of the Lord is the death of his saints."

The beautiful flowers in the sanctuary are a gift from Sue and the kids in memory of their beloved husband and father Henry.

Extended Session:	Tessie Davis
	Jordan Goins
Counting Committee:	Archie Gwinn
	Colley Goins
Deacon Visitation:	Colley Goins

Behold All Things Have Become New

(Mrs. Zechariah Minor, 1970–1976)

BERNA HELD her new baby girl in her arms and watched Zechariah almost drown because of what she'd done. Sweet baby Miriam. Berna's heart burst with love and anguish when she looked at the perfect little face. She adored the child, was amazed that this kind of love, what she felt for her baby girl, was even possible. But there it was. She felt like she had found her purpose in life, had found her one true love.

What she'd done that almost killed Zechariah was supposed to just be a little joke—or not even that; she'd just done it without thinking anything about why. She had been fearful and upset about Zechariah making her sing with him in special meetings up and down the river, the fact that he was planning to put a set of songs together for them to do as concerts as The Singing Soul Minors, and that he hadn't ever asked her about it—she hated singing in front of people; it terrified her. She hadn't meant any harm, though, hadn't actually thought of the possible danger.

She had sliced open the crotch of his hip waders, the ones he wore to baptize people in the river—the waders made it easy for him to be right back out with the people after he finished baptizing, in his suit, having never taken off the pants, shirt, or tie, ready to shake hands and kiss babies. It was a warm afternoon, and the insects were buzzing loud as a constant heavy rainfall. She watched as he waded down into the water. He baptized two little girls who'd gotten saved in AWANA, and then a little boy who dove off to show how well he could swim, and he had to be sternly urged out of the water by Colley Goins's daughter who was the AWANA Commander, and who walked and talked like a man.

Berna focused on Zechariah's face each time he said, "Buried in the likeness of his death," and pinched their noses with his fingers. The people being baptized laid both of their hands on Zechariah's arm, one flat over the other like a corpse in a casket, and he plunged them backward into the river. Bringing them back up, he would yell out, "Raised in the likeness of his resurrection," and the people all clapped and hollered. She watched to see when he felt the water leaking in.

Once they had settled in at Clay Free Will, Zechariah had turned into this robot programmed to do four things. What he did most was church work, and he was gone all day, and most evenings too. The other three things he did were one, eat the food she cooked; two, wait for bedtime so he could fuck her; and three, fuck her. He was hornier than most, something that had become abundantly clear on their wedding night, but she had half-faked a panic attack when he climbed awkwardly on top of her—she just couldn't bring herself to let him at the time. He said he knew the first time was scary for a gal, like he was an old hand at it, and he backed off and left her alone. She wanted to obey 1 Corinthians 7:4–5, so eventually, after a few nights of cuddling in bed before going to sleep—his poor dick was so hard against her leg—she finally told him, "Go ahead and take me."

He was meek and mild as Jesus the first time. Tentative and clumsy, and eventually she had to reach down and help him guide it in. But his dick was thicker than any of the others—thicker even than Gerald's—and it hurt till she wanted to cry out. Mercifully, he always finished fast and didn't let his weight down on her and rolled right off after.

When he took her, his panting into the pillow beside her ear like a dog made her have flashes of specific memories, and she would lie still as if dead and smell his man sweat while he humped over her. Most of the time it was just a feeling, no specific memory at all, or more like her head didn't have any memories but her body did remember, and it would go stiff because it, her body, had no way of knowing it was her loving husband in her holy marriage bed. As far as her body knew, having marriage-bed sex with him felt just like getting fucked in the back seat of some boy's car, or by her stepdad Gerald in her childhood bed.

Poor ignorant Zechariah mistook her body's tensing up for pleasure. He moaned and groaned even more, and finished with hard thrusts, and rolled onto his back out of breath and laughing, thinking they'd just shared passion and that she was as satisfied as he was. He liked it most on Sundays after morning worship and dinner. Doing it in a room with the sun shining in made him even hornier.

Her getting pregnant with Miriam hadn't changed his desire any, but when her belly had grown big and round, she'd stopped letting him. Miriam was five months old now, sleeping through the night finally, and he'd started asking her when she'd be ready. It wouldn't be long till he'd be quoting 1 Corinthians 7:4 at her again.

Standing at the riverside for the baptism, holding their baby girl, she watched and waited. He'd been in there long enough. Surely the river was peeing freezing water right on his dick, making it shrink up like a turtle's head into its shell. What if a dick could get so cold that it shrank till it popped itself inside out? Then he'd have a pussy. A pussy and balls too. She laughed at the thought of it, and then asked the Lord to forgive her for having ungodly thoughts.

He was a stubborn one, which was why he almost drowned. His boots filled up with water as he stood there dipping those kids, and when he started to make his way back up the shoals, he lost his balance and got swept down the bank into deep water, and with a gasp, sunk down like an anchor by his water-filled waders. He first tried to swim, then started grabbing at the straps as his shoulders and his head went under. There was true panic on his face as he went under, and Berna liked seeing it there. She wasn't afraid he would drown. Not at first.

Glenwood Jarvis, Jim Miller, Colley Goins, and another man hurled off their shoes and suit coats and plunged in after him. Jim and Colley dragged him back to the shoals, all of them coughing and gasping, and pulled the wader straps off his shoulders. They dragged his body out of the waders, helped him stand, and walked him to Glenwood and the other man, who reached down and pulled him up the sand bar to the riverbank. Jim and Colley lifted the boots up and the waders hung like the shed skin of a huge green and yellow creature.

Colley poked his index finger like a little dick up through the hole in the crotch. "This has been cut with a knife," he said like a TV detective. "Somebody tried to kill Pastor Minor today."

"Looks like you got Satan running scared," a man said to Zechariah, "with all the souls being saved."

Zechariah stared at Colley's finger poking up through the hole in his waders like he was trying hard to recognize what he was looking at. His hair was swept to the side all wet. He'd lost his glasses and the two dents on his nose where they usually rested were blazing red.

"You got the old Devil worried, brother," Colley told him.

Another man said, "We have to put a hedge of protection around our pastor."

Others agreed, said yes, and bless God, that's just what they'd do. These men declared their willingness to fight and kill for God, and for God's man, if it came to that. They were hunters. They all had guns. It was just a little joke, and they were ready to grab the torches and pitchforks.

One of the women spoke up and said, "Don't you think it was probably just Freddie Sturgis or one of them other boys getting up to their mischief?"

Berna couldn't keep from laughing, but she was so nervous, people mistook it for crying and women came over and comforted her. Which did make her cry. The women were all over her personal space, telling her it was okay, the Lord wasn't finished with her husband yet, the Lord had protected him, God was good. Had she subconsciously wanted him to die? Was her deceitful heart that black and evil?

Then she heard Zechariah's voice, not big and preachy like usual, but small. "Let me tell you this," he said. He was shaken, must have thought he was kicking the bucket and now was putting a brave face on it. He said, "Nobody can touch God's man until he's completed the task to which God called him to do."

"Amen," Henry Driggers said.

Zechariah took a deep breath and said, now in his preacher voice, "The Lord still has work for me to do here yet," and the people clapped and said amen and hallelujah yes Lord, and praise God.

On May 13, 1972, Berna gave birth to her second child. A boy they named Andrew Philip. Berna was once again amazed at the love she felt. She'd loved her girl Miriam so much, she feared there wouldn't be any left for the baby boy, but her heart expanded, and she was amazed and thanked God daily, though two compounded her work and she was always tired.

The church was growing; AWANA was booming—up to sixty kids rode in on the busses on Wednesday nights. People were getting baptized regularly, and joining the church; new people were everywhere, and Berna couldn't possibly keep up with them all, preacher's wife or not. Women she hardly knew or didn't know at all dropped by with food they'd cooked. For a whole two weeks, women came lugging homecooked food up the sidewalk every evening, so much food she didn't know what to do with it all—lasagnas and casseroles, a ham with pineapples stuck on with toothpicks, scalloped potatoes, two broccoli casseroles, two big plastic bowls of green beans with bacon and white potatoes, packs of baloney, three loaves of Sunbeam bread, a fat glass jar of chili—she didn't have room in the fridge. She carried a lot of it across the parking lot and old train road to a family called Taylor, who was poor as anybody she'd ever known, and she'd known poor people growing up in Ironton.

All the sudden she was pregnant again. She went around in shock for a few weeks, knowing what her body was telling her. She'd been told it wasn't possible while nursing, but there it was, she was sure of it. She fell into a deep sadness. She could barely take care of Miriam and Andrew. She cried a lot. She didn't tell Zechariah for a while, because she was afraid she might just lose her mind and smash a lamp on his head.

When she did tell him, he laughed and hugged her and said, "Lo, children are a heritage from the Lord." He kept hugging her. He said over her shoulder, "As arrows are in the hand of a mighty man, so are children . . . blessed is the man who hath his quiver full of them." With that, he went happily off to the bathroom to have his evening shave before meeting the deacons for door-to-door visitation.

On June 28, 1973, she gave birth to another boy. Almost an Irish twin. Zechariah was making her pop them out like those missionaries who sent picture prayer cards back with single-family photos that looked like they could be pictures from an orphanage where the missionaries worked. They named the almost-Irish-twin James Allen.

That year, Zechariah bought two more busses and had them painted red and yellow and sent them straight up 119, halfway to Charleston, one for Elkview and one for Pinch across the river. He'd been visiting down there, had gotten almost all the way to Big Chimney; he was ready to expand downriver in a big way. It was time, he told Berna. The Spirit was moving on the face of the Elk River, and he had to strike while the iron was hot.

On July 7, 1975, Berna gave birth to Zechariah's third son and put her foot down, told him she was finished, she was not having another child, however she had to make sure it didn't happen. She loved them all. She did. She just wasn't up to caring for them. She couldn't do it. She wept as she begged him not to make her have more.

He told her to watch her heart attitude and that they should leave the issue of children where it belonged, in the Lord's hands. She didn't say anything to that. Zechariah named the boy Richard Michael—called him Ricky from day one—after a friend of his who was killed in Korea. Ladies brought food again, but not nearly as much. She figured they were getting tired of her popping out babies too and she was glad to not be buried in food.

However, Zechariah called from the church late one morning and told her Jordan Goins, the AWANA Commander, was coming by with a roast, and was now a convenient time? She told him it was as good a time as any other, and she could hear the anger in her own voice, and so she softened it and said, "Yes. Tell her now is fine."

Turned out Jordan Goins didn't have a roast, but apple dumplings that she balanced on one hand like a fancy waiter. She was tall with thick jaws like a man. She walked from her Jeep with the same kind of confidence as a man too, her arms out from her body, her stride long and forceful, like she wouldn't think twice about getting in a fight. She had beautiful blue eyes, and there she was, holding those dumplings, which were steaming up the plastic wrap and smelling of cinnamon.

Taking them, Berna said, "This smells so good." She said, "I never thought you were the cooking type."

"It's something new I'm trying," Jordan said. "These turned out real good."

"Will you stay and have a little with me?" They were still hot underneath. Berna switched hands.

Jordan looked behind her, as if nervous she would be caught in the act. What act? Why was she nervous?

"I'll perk coffee," Berna said.

Jordan turned back around and said, "Only if you'll have a cup with me."

"Deal."

Jordan kicked off her boots right on the porch, and they pulled her white tube socks half off her feet. She reached down and pulled them back up her calves one by one.

Berna percolated coffee and they split one apple dumpling, leaving five for Zechariah and the kids after supper. Jordan stayed until Ricky woke up, started crying, and woke up the others. At the door, while Jordan pulled on her boots and Ricky wailed away upstairs, Berna said, "Come by anytime."

"Okay," Jordan said.

"I mean it," Berna said. "I'm not just saying that."

Jordan grinned at her again and said, "I know." Then she jogged down the steps and strode off to her Jeep like a cowboy.

———

Berna fought the urge to cry as she stood in the church parking lot with six-year-old Miriam, watching for the school bus. The dirt road ran between the blacktop one above it and a row of houses stretched along the bank of the Elk River. The boys were in the parsonage, in bed, still sleeping she assumed.

At the church, the road, once the train tracks, blended with the dirt parking lot, emerged on the other side, and rounded a bend following the curve of the river. Railroad ties were discarded in the Queen Ann's Lace along its edges, with rusty spikes, chunks of coal, jagged rocks of coke. On hot days, the reek of creosote rose heavy and biting like the stink of a wild animal lurking among the black woodpiles.

The bus turned at the bridge and rocked slowly up the rutted road into the church lot where it turned around to head back toward the school. It churned up a cloud of dust that drifted high into the trees. The trees bordered the church and parsonage on the side and the back, blocking the view, but not the muddy stench, of the river.

The bus door squawked open. When Miriam grabbed the rail inside and climbed up, her knobby legs showed halfway to her hip. Her new culottes were already too short. Berna would have to let out the hems.

At the top of the bus steps, Miriam turned around and said, "Tell the boys goodbye for me." She was a frail-looking thing. Her black hair was stringy. It needed a wash.

Berna nodded.

"Tell Baby Ricky goodbye," Miriam said, as the bus door squawked closed on her.

Berna nodded. She loved that girl so much—she loved them all—but she was annoyed with her all the time. She couldn't stop the anger from welling up. As the bus lurched forward, Miriam's eyes turned and looked down on Berna. The girl's stringy hair lay flat against her head. The bus rocked back the way it had come, toward the bridge and the blacktop road.

The blacktop was Main Street, and then Route 4, and it ran between the river and the jagged hillsides right out of Clay County, hit 119 in Clendenin, and then followed the river all the way into Charleston where the river ended, maybe the road did too, she didn't know. Charleston felt like the big city to Berna. It had an airport. Berna walked the edge of the lot in front of the church and then took the bare and packed path that ran diagonally across the side yard between the church and the parsonage.

Inside the old Cape Cod with sloping floors, Berna walked past the bedroom where Zechariah climbed on top of her at least two nights most weeks. He refused to pull out and finish up on her stomach, though she begged so they wouldn't be like missionaries with fifteen kids, said it ruined it for him. In some ways this life felt harder and worse than the one she'd gotten saved to escape. The words of Romans 8:28 popped into her head: "We know that all things work together for good to them that love God, to them who are the called according to his purpose." She loved God, didn't she? She did. How could she know she was called according to His purpose? How could she know this would all be worth it?

She heaved herself up the steps. The upstairs room to the left, above the living room, was the boys. The one to the right, above her bedroom, was Miriam's. She turned into the boys' room and discovered that baby Ricky had pulled off his diaper and finger painted the wall beside his crib with his number two. The stink tripped her gag reflex, and she covered her mouth with her palm and dry heaved. Andrew and James were rolled up in their bunk beds against the far wall sniggering, and the sound of her gagging made them snort out little laughs.

"You two get out of here," she said to them.

Ricky was almost twelve months old. He wasn't talking or walking yet, but he crawled fast as running, pounding his knees across the floor, and he climbed like a monkey up whatever he could grab hold of. She believed he might be off mentally.

He sat straight-backed with his fat legs curved in deep wrinkles, proud grin on his number two–smeared face, and he had number two in his wispy baby hair too. He turned his smile to what he'd done on the wall. There was a bald strip across the back of his head from the way he lay on his back and turned it from side to side while he slept. The stink was overpowering Berna—she cupped her hand over her nose and mouth.

"But it's cold out," Andrew said from the top bunk.

Berna put her hands on her hips and thundered: "Obedience is?"

Andrew and James crawled out of bed and started getting on their Toughskins. They recited together: "Doing what you're told, when you're told, with the right heart attitude."

"Obey," Berna said, again masking her mouth and nose.

"Yes ma'am," they both said. They sat on the floor to put on their plastic-soled sneakers and bounded down the steps and through the house and out the back door.

She carried Ricky down the steps, spun on the ball of her foot and carried him through the living room into the kitchen. The heater grate in the doorway from the living room to the kitchen was a hot grill under her foot. To the left of the kitchen was the bathroom. She put him in the tub and ran it half-full. She stepped out and closed the bathroom door, an old paneled one like an outside door.

Zechariah's black plastic bowl of oatmeal was untouched on the kitchen table. As the oatmeal dried, it crusted around the edges. His coffee mug was gone.

She dragged the bleach jug and the bucket from under the kitchen sink, splashed a blue capful of bleach into the bucket and filled it with hot water. She stood and looked out the window above the sink. The two older boys were in the back yard under the apple tree, playing with Barnabas, the new puppy Zechariah had brought home. They were taking turns picking it up by the tail. The puppy writhed and snapped. Its mouth made silent yelps. When one or the other let it drop, it ran stumbling, too clumsy to make an escape. They threw apples at it. Andrew yanked it back up and held it upside down by its tail like a shot squirrel.

She stopped at the bathroom door and listened. Ricky was splashing and babbling. She went upstairs and smeared bleach water on the wall. She unhooked the sheet from the crib mattress and pulled the whole mess into a bundle and carried it down. Beside the bathroom off the kitchen was the utility room, the washer and dryer in it about one foot apart, on pieces of torn brown linoleum. The utility room floor was wood and piled with laundry so that the boys had to climb over it to get in and out the back door.

Berna heard a heavy thud from the bathroom. She stood still over the pile and waited.

No scream. No cry.

She dropped the soiled sheets onto a fat pile of laundry and went to the closet under the steps and tugged out fresh ones, heaved herself up to the boys' room and tossed them into the crib, then headed back down to check on Ricky.

When she opened the bathroom door, he was in the tub, but the mat was sopping wet, and water stood in pools beside it. The toilet seat was wet too. Ricky had Zechariah's toothbrush in his fat baby fist and was scrubbing his number-two caked hair with it.

Berna knelt on one knee and squeezed out a glob of No More Tears shampoo on his head and scrubbed hard. "No," she said. "No number two." She gagged as she scrubbed. Ricky winced and squinted, then slapped Zechariah's toothbrush on the water happily. She twisted to the potty and quickly vomited her oatmeal and flushed it down, then turned back to Ricky.

She held his head under the faucet and rinsed him. He screamed and squirmed, fought like he thought she wanted to drown him, but she held him firm. He writhed and jerked his head up and hit it on the faucet, inhaled for so long she thought he might not cry, but he did, and when it came, it was a banshee wail. She yanked him out of the tub and toweled him dry while he cried. Under the faucet, she thumbed the number two off Zechariah's toothbrush and placed it back in its plastic stand. Ricky stopped crying as she wrapped him in a fresh diaper and pulled on the plastic pants. She pulled blue footy pajamas on him and zipped them and half-carried, half-dragged him by one arm through the house, through the utility room and set him outside the back door and closed it.

Berna grabbed Zechariah's bowl and hefted herself onto the counter beside the sink and spooned the pasty cold oatmeal into her mouth as she looked for the boys in the back yard. Andrew and James were playing with Ricky. They dragged him around the yard by the footies in his pajamas. Ricky's face contorted into silent wailing. The tub water back in the bathroom gurgled down the drain and the heater grate between the kitchen and living room clicked and popped.

From the quiet of the house, Berna watched the boys outside. Andrew and James had made a game of it. They now ran back and forth from the apple tree to Ricky, dragging him over the grass by his pajama feet. His legs looked like they were made of rubber and stretched two feet long. The puppy jumped and ran circles and barked and stuck his wagging behind in the air. Ricky did not stop trying to crawl away, and he even stopped at times and rolled around to take swats at them. The blows were glancing and weak, and they played on.

Eventually the older boys tired of Ricky and went back to their yellow plastic Tonka trucks. He tried to join them, but they slapped him away, so he set out crawling back toward the house. The puppy stumbled after him, and when it caught up, it crouched and lunged repeatedly, nipping Ricky's face and ears. He tried to turn his head away and put up an arm. The dog was relentless. Andrew and James inadvertently rescued him when they scampered over and started playing with the puppy's tail again.

She walked into her bedroom and sat on the bed. The hamper was stuffed so full the lid would not close. The smell of sour clothes filled the room. The hamper was metal covered in white plastic with violets on it. There was a V-shaped rip on the side where the metal showed through. The bed's headboard was made up of three compartments with two sliding doors, so one compartment was always exposed. The two outer ones were filled with Bibles and commentaries. Zechariah's new alarm clock was in the center. It didn't have a normal clock face. It had real numbers that flipped in the middle on a roll like score card numbers. It was 8:33 in the morning. Berna lay down and stared at the rip in the hamper plastic. The house was silent. She was so tired. She couldn't keep her eyes open. She fell asleep.

The front door had slammed. It took Berna a few seconds to come to. She looked at the clock: 11:41. She jumped up, ran to the boys' room, and peered down. Zechariah and his associate, Pastor Jeff, were out at the edge of the church parking lot getting boxes out of the back of Jeff's car. The car was a black sports car with tiny back seats, not practical for a wife and kids.

Berna ran past a box just inside the front door, through the living room, to the kitchen, to the back window. The yard was empty, apples rotting under the tree. The boys were nowhere to be seen. Behind the yard was the swampy low field, a stand of trees, and a bank dropping to the sandbar and the river.

She panicked. She leapt through the utility room, stumbling across the laundry pile. The stink of number two from Ricky's sheets was as heavy as fog. She burst out the back door hollering for the boys. The air was cold against her arms and face. She ran to the fence and looked out on the side yard, between the parsonage and the church. One of the Tonka trucks was out there, and beside it, a piece of plywood with dirt and grass piled on top of it.

"Mommy," James called.

All three boys were against the house. They were digging in the cold dirt, pouring it in dump-truck loads over each other's head. Ricky was covered in filth. His mouth was muddy and wet. He was babbling to the tune of "Jesus Loves Me," leaning out and scooping dirt into his lap. Andrew poured a load of grassy dirt down his back.

Berna smacked dirt off James and Andrew and said, "Get to the utility room."

They bounded for the door.

She brushed Ricky and wiped his face as best she could. She picked him up and hurried inside.

The boys had not stayed in the utility room. They were in the kitchen, bent over shaking like dogs and laughing, and a shower of dirt and pebbles fell from their scalps. "We been playing funeral," Andrew said.

"Stop shaking your heads," Berna yelled. "Stand there and don't move."

She hugged herself in the cold and looked around the yard for the puppy. She ran around and out the gate and across the side yard to the Tonka truck and the plywood. She grabbed the wood and pulled, and the mound of grass and dirt tumbled off. The puppy was under it in a shallow hole–it wasn't moving.

She scooped under the dog's belly with her right hand and grabbed its snout like a bottle of pop with her left. She blew into the nose and squeezed the body between her body and her arm and blew into the nose again. She ran with the dog around to the back of the house. Grit and dirt from the dog's face crunched between her teeth. She spit as she ran. The dog moved. It wasn't dead. She carried it into the utility room and wrapped it in a towel.

The boys were playing with cardboard cowboy hats they'd gotten in Sunday school, and their shouting turned hostile.

"Mommy," James yelled. "Andy broke my hat. He has to give me his."

"Did not," Andrew yelled.

"Did too."

"You broke it." Andrew appeared at the door, and James jumped on him and grabbed the cowboy hat in his fist. Andrew balled his fist up and hit James in the ribs and James buckled and bit Andrew's ear, and Andrew grabbed a fist-full of hair and pulled, and both boys screamed in rage and pain.

Berna pulled them apart and dragged Andrew by the arm into her bedroom, whacking him a glancing blow on the behind. "Do not leave this room," she yelled. She whacked James on the leg, then dragged him to the stairs and pointed up. "March to your room, young man," she said, "and do not think about coming out till I tell you."

He started up the steps, stopped, turned around and cried, "It's not fair."

"March," she yelled.

"It's not fair."

"Life's not fair," Berna raised her voice. "Get used to it."

Glass shattered in the kitchen. Berna pointed again and repeated, "March." She ran in and found Ricky sitting in front of a broken tea glass, tea spreading on the linoleum like puppy piddle. She grabbed the back of Ricky's pajamas and lifted him.

"Bad," she said through her teeth. Palming the bald strip on the back of his head, she pushed his nose into the spill. "No."

He didn't make a sound.

She squeezed his leg and head and pushed his face harder into the floor.

He still didn't make a sound and he didn't struggle.

She squeezed and twisted his leg. She pushed her weight on his gritty head. "No," she said, mashing his face in the tea, "no, no, no."

Finally, he made a choking grunt. It frightened her. She let up the pressure.

He took a deep breath and let out a cry like a siren's wail. Little rippling rings moved away from his mouth in the spilled tea. She picked him up and held him to her breasts, smoothing his head with her palm. He buried his wet and filthy face into her neck and emptied his lungs with each bellowing cry.

Berna rocked back and forth on her shins. "It's okay, baby," she said. "Mommy's sorry, but you have to stop making messes."

For a while, she rocked Ricky as he cried. Tea soaked into the knee of her culottes. The puppy was free of the towel. He had his head inside Ricky's sheets, snuffling and licking Ricky's number two. Disgusting creature. His hind end was in the air, and his tail wagged happily.

Ricky settled into whimpering hiccups that convulsed his whole body. Berna's legs were getting numb, or she could have fallen off to sleep right there on her knees.

A door clicked shut.

Carrying Ricky, she hurried from the kitchen. The door to her bedroom was closed. Four boxes were stacked inside the front door. Jeff's car was still out front, but he and Zechariah weren't anywhere around.

She opened the bedroom door. "James? James, where are you, son?"

She heard giggling from the closet. She stepped softly across the room and listened at the door. Ricky hiccupped in her arm and trembled a long sniveling inhalation. Andrew and James were both inside the closet, shushing each other.

Berna cracked the door open. They had pulled down her blue dress. Andrew was covered and James only had his head stuck under it and the knee of his Toughskins was smooth with ground-in dirt. The two boys did not move.

She eased Ricky to the floor and pushed him gently in. She closed the door and twisted the lock.

"Mommy?" Andrew's voice said.

James echoed him. "Mommy?"

The knob on the door shook. "Mommy? We came in the closet."

Then the voices rose to a yell.

"Mommy we got stuck in the closet!"

"We came in the closet and got stuck!"

"Mommy!"

Berna closed the bedroom door, further muffling their yells. She put on her gray windbreaker that said AWANA in flaming red letters across the back and went upstairs to Miriam's bedroom.

She sat on the bed. It was unmade and sunlight through the window made the lumps of the covers look like a raised-up map of a mountain range. The tops of the ridges were bright, and shadows lay black in the creases that looked like they had been created by erosion and not a disobedient child. Berna had told the girl twice to make up her bed—direct disobedience. Berna pounded her fist on the bed. Dust motes and particles floated up and twisted in the sunlight.

She could leave. She didn't have to stay here. The tightness in her chest eased at the thought of escape. A bus ticket back to Ohio—no, she could go where Zechariah would never find her. A plane ticket. She could leave. She could go anywhere.

She leaned over on her elbow and stared at the plaque from VBS— white paper with a child's writing in black marker, shellacked to a piece of scrap wood. Zechariah had hung it on Miriam's wall beside the window. The black letters claimed *Only One Life Will Soon Be Past. Only What's Done for Christ Will Last.* Some of the letters were in cursive, some weren't.

Out the window, she could see the tops of the trees along the Elk River.

The boys had gone silent. It was their naptime, and they could nap safely in there.

Miriam would be home at three. Miriam, who always acted like the little mother, trying without shame to get Zechariah's praise and attention. The girl didn't know how good she had it—she didn't know that there were worse things in the world than being left alone by your father. That was for damn sure. Anyway, Miriam was already stepping in and trying to take over caring for the boys. As much as she loved these babies, she could see she was not made for this; she was broken, and she was going to break them too.

She knew the Bible said God wouldn't give her more than she could bear, but she was about to lose her ever-loving mind. In this moment, she thought of her own mom. She hadn't been made for it either. She had no education, no skill, no way to feed Berna and her brothers. Bad as he was, Gerald was all her mother had to grasp hold of. He was the only life raft she could find for them. Berna's exasperation briefly became a deep sadness for her mom. She'd been a girl once, hadn't she? With dreams of a happy life with a decent man? Maybe, maybe not. Maybe she always knew better than to dream such a thing. Maybe—probably—she'd had it worse than Berna when she was young. Berna almost decided to call her but, in the end, decided against it. The woman had stood by and let Gerald do what he did. Then blamed Berna. When she was just a little girl. She couldn't forgive that.

What she could do, though, right now, was pick up and leave. The prospect of freedom washed over her like the ministrations of the Holy Spirit, the Paraclete come alongside her to give succor, to wake her from this nightmare. God would forgive her—it was His mistake, putting her here. She tucked her freedom away as her secret treasure; what she would know, and Zechariah would find out when the time suited her. She already felt free—she had this hope, this evidence of things not seen.

The tops of the leaves were dark green, the bottoms lighter. They fluttered in a light breeze. She stared until the leaves blurred and it looked like the trees were covered in butterflies flapping their wings all together. The heater grate clicked and popped downstairs. The neighborhood below the treetops had fallen into bright and motionless afternoon silence—men off to work, kids all in school, wives inside watching *The Price Is Right*. The puppy's claws started clicking on the kitchen floor downstairs. It was fine. It was jumping around, playing. Probably already pooped on the floor, peed for sure. It was going to rile the boys back up.

She fell back on Miriam's unmade bed and pushed her feet under the covers and started to doze, but then she jumped up, sneaked downstairs, set the wriggling pup out the back door, and looked up the phone number. There it was: Jordan Goins. She stared at it for a bit and then slid the phonebook back on top of the fridge without making the call.

The next day, Berna began what became a routine several mornings a week of loading up the boys and driving down the river to the Kroger, where she would buy one thing or another so she could walk her cart by the butcher's window, looking to wave at Jordan back there working in her white coat, so strong and able, not caring who thought what of her. One day Jordan came out with her bloody white coat on, wiping her hands on a white rag.

"Hey there, pretty lady," she said.

Berna didn't know what to say. She was nervous. She said, "Hey there . . . butcher lady. I just wanted to say hi."

"Where are the little ones?"

"In the car," Berna said. "They have their toys."

"I could take my break now if you have time for a quick cup of coffee."

They sat in front of the store and talked until the boys got too restless in the car. People walked in and out. Most of them said hello to Jordan, asked her about cuts of meat, and she'd tell them she had it back there and it looked real good, or it was coming on tomorrow's truck, or they'd be out of it for a while. People recognized Berna too and said hello to her.

"I have to go now," Berna told her. "This is nice, talking to you."

Jordan leaned up and looked right at her, and an understanding passed between them. She held her empty Styrofoam cup on her knee. She said, "I think so too."

"Maybe you could come to the house for coffee when you don't have to work."

"That'd be nice," Jordan said. "I'd like that." She leaned back. "You know what? You should come be an AWANA leader tomorrow night.

We could do that ministry together. Nothing wrong with that, it'd be the Lord's work we were doing."

Berna nodded. Why not? She told Jordan she would do it.

"Maybe you could come have coffee at my house too. I have a back yard where they could play."

"Yes," Berna said. She couldn't stop smiling. "I'd love to."

Welcome to Clay Free Will Baptist Church
May 17, 1981

Sunday School   9:45

Morning Worship   11:00

PRELUDE   "Covered by the
                Blood"
                Miriam Minor

WORSHIP IN PRAISE

   Pledge to the American Flag
   Pledge to the Christian Flag
   Pledge to the Bible
   Hymn #23, "My Hope Is Built on
     Nothing Less"
   Hymn #29, "The Old Rugged Cross"

INVOCATION

   Hymn of Praise #30, "When I Survey
     the Wondrous Cross"

WELCOME TO GUESTS

WORSHIP IN MEDITATION

Scripture   1 Peter 1:18-25
Reading   Scott Driggers

Morning Prayer   Pastor Minor

WORSHIP IN GIVING

Offertory   "I Love to Tell the
              Story"
              Miriam Minor

WORSHIP IN PROCLAMATION

MESSAGE   "Power in the
              Blood"
              Pastor Minor

Hymn of Invitation #136, "Just as I
  Am"

Benediction   "Nothing but the
              Blood"
              Miriam Minor

Church Calendar

Sunday, May 17

9:15	Sunday School
11:00	Morning Worship
6:15	Church Training
7:30	Evening Worship

Monday, May 18

7:30	Choir Practice

Wednesday, May 20

6:30	AWANA Club
7:00	Deacon's meeting
7:30	Prayer Meeting

Extended Session:	Tessie Davis Doris Goins
Counting Committee:	Archie Gwinn Colley Goins Glenwood Jarvis
Door-to-Door Soul Winning:	Pastor Minor and Scott Driggers Colley Goins and Archie Gwinn

The Rod of Correction

(Richard Michael Minor, 1981)

SIX-YEAR-OLD RICKY followed his mom down the steps to the church basement, shrinking against the wall, bumping his shoulder along the cool painted bricks. The centers of the red carpeted steps were dirty brown. The rug on the bottom two steps had worn through to stringy holes. Ricky's face burned with shame and his heart raced as he thought of his willful disobedience and the punishment he'd earned for himself.

Just before they'd left for church, he'd stood in his mom's kitchen and watched in disbelief as his own hand had reached out and grabbed a cupcake off the counter, after she had just told him no—that same hand had refused to let go when she had grabbed it away, making it mash and crumble. Direct, willful disobedience. His mom had said, "I'll deal with you after church, young man."

More than just a switching was waiting for Ricky. She would tan his hide is what she'd do. And he'd be grounded to his room for the time between morning and night church. He longed to be upstairs listening to Miriam practice piano. He wanted to stay with her and not go to Sunday school.

The hallway in the church basement smelled like river mud—like dead fish and number two. The basement of the old church building flooded every year or so. Once he'd seen a fat river rat scurry along the wall and into the choir room when his mom turned on the hall lights. A round drain was in the middle of the cracked hall floor where Ricky—always there long before the other kids—squished crunchy black water bugs with the heels of his church shoes.

"Keep marching," his mom said. She quickly pulled away from him with long, angry strides and disappeared into the classroom. She was already straightening the flannel graph board onto the easel when he turned and stepped in.

The room smelled like river mud too. He sat down silently. He didn't scoot his behind back into the chair because he had on his brother James's old church pants, with the elastic waistband gathered and pinned in the back. When he forgot and slid back in a chair, the pin popped open and jabbed him in the back.

He watched his mom squat and pick up the flannel pieces out of a box under the easel. On the green board she smoothed up a blue flannel sky and brown flannel ground and a fence that peeled away at one end before she pressed it back on with her flat hand. The table was a piece of wall wood one of the men in the church cut to be like a half moon. It was painted bright blue even on the legs and bottom. When they did crafts, Ricky's mom sat at the flat side, and all the kids around the outside. The brick walls and the pipes running along the ceiling had so many layers of paint they looked lumpy, like they'd been shaped out of modeling clay.

His mom turned and glared at him. Her eyes were pretty and green. He liked her eyes when they weren't mad and looking at him. She said nothing, just turned back to the flannel graph. She pressed up fluffy white flannel sheep with black legs and faces, and brown-ish-gray goats inside the flannel pen. Her fingernails were cut to look like ovals on top. There were five sheep and six goats. Eleven animals.

When she finished, she turned around and put her hands on her hips and looked at Ricky. He dropped his stare to the blue table and slid the smooth soles of his church shoes back and forth on the slick tile floor.

His mom looked at him. She looked sad. She looked like she was getting ready to cry. It was his fault. He swallowed down the urge to cry himself.

There were twelve kids in Sunday school that morning, including Ricky. His mom taught on Matthew, on what it would be like when Jesus came back—how God was going to separate the sheep from the goats. Sheep are good, God loves them, and they go to heaven and are happy forever. Goats are bad, God hates them, and they go to hell and are sad forever. The choir practiced two rooms down, men and then women and then men and women together, singing the same short part of a song over and over, the muffled sound of voices and vowel sounds but no words.

Ricky stared at the table while other kids asked questions. For the craft, they pulled cotton balls apart and glued them onto the backs of smeary mimeographed sheep. Ricky liked the sharp scent of the purplish-blue mimeograph ink. He held the paper to his face.

"Ricky," his mom said. She stared at him with her eyes tight so that they wrinkled at the edges.

He put the paper down.

She got tissue paper and leaned over Rachel to dab excess glue off her sheep. His mom's blouse hung open and Ricky could see her bra. He could see the outline of bones on her white chest, and her collarbone was a ridge. She glanced up and glared at him—he thought of the switch on top of the refrigerator and quickly looked down at the blurry sheep.

"Time to separate the goats from the sheep," his mom said. "Get in line. Right here behind Rachel."

Rachel and her sister Leah both had their hair bobbed short like that ice-skater girl Miriam had on her wall, and it looked like shiny brown helmets on them. So did their mom, Miss Patty, but her hair was dry and frizzly. Rachel's face beamed from under the straight bangs at the other kids as they shuffled up to get in line behind her. The line curved around the table. Ricky scraped his chair back and got at the end of it.

"Some will be sheep, and some will be goats," his mom said. She sat low on a kid's chair beside the flannel graph board, and it made her knees point up. Her tights were shiny except over her knee knobs. She said that all of them would close their eyes and pick an animal. Sheep would go to the right, and goats would go to the left, to show how it would be if they didn't get saved and had to be a hated goat standing before the Great White Throne, where God would sit on Judgment Day. No peeking.

Rachel closed her eyes and Ricky's mom moved the flannel goats and sheep around on the board. Rachel picked a sheep and bounced on her toes when she saw it. She stepped to the right of Ricky's mom and grinned across the line. One by one the other kids went, until Ricky stood before his mother. All the flannel sheep and goats were gone. The pen was empty. Ricky was relieved. He turned to go sit back down.

"Wait," his mom said. She reached and said, "Rachel, let me use your sheep." Then she turned to a boy named Titus, who had a wide round face, and took his goat from him.

"Close your eyes, Ricky," she said.

Ricky squinted his eyes closed. Then, still squinting, he peeked as his mom put the sheep and the goat up on the flannel graph board. His heart pounded as he closed his eyes again: he wanted to be a sheep, to be at the right hand of God, to be happy and good. But, as his mom took his arm and guided it to the board, even though he didn't want to, he peeked again through his squinting eyelids. He saw that she had taken the sheep off the board and was directing his hand straight to the goat.

As he took the soft goat, he opened his eyes and looked at his mom.

"Go to the left," she said to him, not looking, already pulling down the pen and the sky and ground and smoothing them back into the box under the easel.

He stepped to the left. Titus said, "Give me my goat back." His wide freckly face seemed to float beside Ricky, and his breath smelled like old potato chips. He handed the floppy piece of flannel to the boy.

Ricky's mom sprang up and collected the goats and sheep, like she was in a hurry. She didn't look at Ricky. She didn't look at anyone. She told them to get back in their seats, and she passed out the mimeographed Bible verse for them to memorize with their moms. Her slip flashed white in back when she bent to lay a paper down. Now and then, as she stepped sideways, her anklebones wobbled in her shiny dress shoes.

Hot tears began to stream down Ricky's cheeks. She had done it on purpose—he saw her do it. She had picked him to be a goat that God hates. Ricky was a bad, disobedient boy. He clenched his eyes shut, and now he did cry.

That Wednesday, before Prayer Meeting, Andrew and James were bullying Ricky like they always did. They were throwing apples at him from on top of the picnic table under the tree in the back yard. The apples stayed green even when they were ripe and had rough brown spots on them. Ricky's dad would mow over them, and then more would fall on top of the sweet-stinking brown mush. A swarm of yellow jackets jerked all around the rotting apples in a silent frenzy. The heat made the church parking lot look wavy.

Ricky liked running through the cloud of wasps with great stomps of his bare feet into the apples. He'd burst into the sun on the other side and run far out into the safety of the back yard. If he got through, stomping apples and wasps alike, without getting stung, he'd take deep satisfied breaths and watch the wasps settle down so he could make another run.

He didn't mind his brothers aiming apples at him because neither one of them could throw. Ricky could run fast, and even hits were glancing and painless. This was how his play went with the two of them, and though his chest was tight with fear—play with his brothers always ended with him crying—at least they were playing with him.

He stopped and threw apples back at them. Andrew, who was nine, finally connected while Ricky was bending down. It was a hard apple and it hit Ricky's ear and made tears bloom in his eyes even though he was not crying. Before they could see the tears, he ran for the back door of the house with Andrew and James following, throwing too fast to take good aim. Apples bounced and skidded by him on the grass.

He yanked open the back door and ran into the utility room, where the washer and dryer were on the right, and the step up to the kitchen on the left. A wooden board full of hooks that held the church bus keys hung beside the back door. It fell with a jingling crash when he slammed the back door. Ricky backed himself into the narrow space between the washer and dryer, shimmying, twisting his hips and shoulders sideways. There he caught his breath and listened to the screen door hiss and click back into place. There was no sound after that but the fan in the kitchen window.

From his hiding spot, Ricky could see into the kitchen: the sink and stove, half of the kitchen table, two of the chairs that had fat round legs that stretched out what they reflected till it didn't look like anything but sliding, changing colors. The linoleum kitchen floor curled up at the edge of the utility room, with sticky dirt and dog hair and two dark, shriveled Cheerios underneath. The linoleum had different-sized brown and golden squares separated by thick gray lines—it was perfect buildings and city streets seen from above when Ricky played cars in there.

He smelled corn cooking. A tall pot on the stove gave off heavy steam, and the white trash can was in front of the sink with corn-husks poking out.

Ricky's mom strode into the kitchen, took the corn off the stove with two dishrags, dumped the steaming water into the sink and carried the pot back to the stove. He watched her skinny frame from behind. She had on her gray AWANA leader's shirt, denim culottes, and white sneakers. She stood with her feet together, and even in the culottes, Ricky could see how her legs bowed out from the top and didn't come back together till her ankles. She looked like Miriam from behind, only taller, whiter.

Ricky's mouth watered as he watched her work.

She plucked an ear of corn out of the huge pot. She took the stick of butter and ran it up and down the ear as she turned it, then shook salt all over, still turning it. Then she started gnawing the ear.

The corn appeared at the side of her head like the roller thing on a typewriter, with one whole row of bites taken off it. Then she did the same thing back the other way, and went back and forth, turning and munching, then bent and shoved the cob into the trash can. She wiped her mouth, buttered and salted another ear. She ate five ears of corn this way, shoving the cobs low into the trash can, pulling the husks over them.

As she crouched to push the last cob down, she turned her head sideways. Her eyes stared blankly at nothing as she pushed, but then slowly drew into focus on Ricky in his hiding spot. His heart leapt and pounded. Her arm was shoved past her elbow into the trash, her AWANA shirtsleeve crumpled against the top of the can. Her face was low beside the cornhusks. Butter smeared her mouth and cheek, and one kernel hung at the edge of her mouth. Another kernel was butter-pasted onto her chin.

Her face went all splotchy, and that's when he knew, by the color on her face, and the wide fear in her eyes, that he had caught her sinning. What the sin could possibly be was beyond him.

She stood, acting as if she hadn't seen him at all, brushed her hands together like getting dirt off, and walked so hard across the kitchen to the bathroom beside the utility room that he felt her heels shaking the floor.

Ricky worked himself out from between the washer and dryer. The skin of his arm squeaked painfully against the metal. He tippy toed to the kitchen trash and pulled at the cornhusks to look at the cobs hidden down inside. The smell of the corn began to mix with what was in the oven. He walked through the house and came back and stopped at the bathroom door. When the toilet flushed and the water came on, not knowing where he should be when she came out, and not ready to go back outside and face his brothers, he positioned himself beside the stove. His mom's switch lay on top of the refrigerator with the thick end curved over the side. He hadn't had a switching for two full days. It was time. He was being disobedient and he knew it. He felt like he did above the stairwell behind the old church building, almost within arm's reach of the wasp nest under the awning, arm cocked to jab the stick and run, wasps crouched on the nest staring back at him, ready to attack.

The bathroom door opened, and his mom stepped back into the kitchen. She didn't say anything to Ricky, or even look at him—it was like she didn't even know he was there. She walked straight over to the refrigerator, got her switch, and turned to him. He turned to run, but she was already on him. She grabbed his arm and switched him back and forth across his legs, so fast her hand blurred like when she scrambled eggs. He couldn't hop away from the stinging switch, so he ran, and cried, and she held onto his arm so that they went in circles as she switched, him running around her, her turning in place, still switching, until she stumbled and reached for a chair. She sat down and pulled his face close to hers. He could barely see her through the blur of his tears. She smelled like toothpaste.

"I told you to play outside until supper." She let go of him and sat back in the chair.

The sting in his legs turned to the familiar tingle and itch. He did not move from the spot in front of her because he didn't know if she had more to say to him about his disobedience. She rubbed the inside corner of her eyes with the finger and thumb of one hand, like she was trying to dig eye boogers out.

Ricky turned at his waist and looked at the stove. The pot was on top of it.

"Can I have a piece of corn?" he asked.

She said, "You committed direct disobedience." She stood and walked to the stove. "You will learn one way or another, young man." She pulled the oven door open and the smell of Shake-N-Bake drumsticks—his favorite—burst warm across his face and filled his mouth with spit. He wiped his tears with the palms of his hands and made an involuntary moan of pleasure and anticipation.

"Go tell your brothers to come and wash up. Your father will be home in a few minutes."

"Can I go get Miriam?"

"Yes," she said with a tired voice, as if he'd asked her to go do it. She pulled the pan of chicken from the oven with her dishrags and put it on top of the stove beside the corn pot.

"Can I have corn at supper?"

"Would I give corn to the rest of the family and leave you out?"
He didn't know the answer to that. "Can I have two?"
"Go get the others like I told you."
Ricky stood looking at her. Her eyes were not wrinkled in anger like usual. They were drooping, tired. "Go on." She turned around, scraped open the drawer and dug around for forks.

Ricky ran from the kitchen and pounded up the steps and down the hall to Miriam's room. He rolled onto her bed with her.

"Hey, Diggle," she said. She petted his head and didn't look away from her book. His legs were still tingling, but he was with his Miriam, and he was going to eat chicken drumsticks and buttered corn on the cob.

"Diggle, you smell like grass," Miriam said. Golden light slanted through her window onto her tan skin. The tiny hairs on her legs glowed in the sunlight like Lite-Brite pegs with the glow coming from a bulb that burned inside her.

He snuggled against her.

On Friday, Ricky was upstairs playing in the bedroom he shared with Andrew and James. He was waiting for their bus from school to see if Miriam would play UNO with him. He lay down in the doorway with his head in the hall.

His mom was in the room gathering laundry. She stepped over him to get out. "Go change into your play clothes," she said. She leaned with the basket against her bony hip and held the rail going down the steps.

Ricky rolled his head on the floor and looked at the hall light. It was round, but in bulging sections. It looked like a giant peeled orange, glowing low and soft. He turned his head so that his nose blocked his left eye's vision of the light. When he closed his right eye, his nose loomed in front of it like a white cliff, blocking not only the light, but also the entire hallway. He opened and closed his right eye, watching the light appear and disappear, and his nose become see-through and solid again, until his head started hurting.

He pushed with his heels to scoot on his back farther into the hallway. There was a runner rug tacked down from the back of the hall all the way to the bottom of the steps. It was brown and dull red and smelled like dust. Ricky pushed harder to get onto it and the pin in his waistband came undone and jabbed the bone right above his bottom. He caught his breath and rolled over, pulling the pin out of his pants. He cried quietly and looked at the pin and rubbed his back. He closed the pin.

His mom lumbered up the stairs with a basket of folded clothes. "Have you changed out of your school clothes?" She stopped and looked down. With the weak light coming from behind, her face was in shadow and looked like a monster's glowering down at him. Her voice boomed: "Get up and obey me." She disappeared into Miriam's room.

Ricky sat up and pinched open the safety pin. Then, just as he'd watched his hands grab the cupcake on Sunday, he watched his hands set to work, seemingly of their own willfulness.

He pulled with his fingers and the dark rug made a poof of dust as it popped off three tacks. He bent the pin and worked it under the rug and pushed it up through until it stood erect in the center of the hallway, making only a slight lump, nothing noticeable, especially if she was carrying a basket.

He ran into his bedroom to change. He wanted to be lying in the doorway again when she stepped on the pin. His heart thumped in his chest. He rushed and tripped himself pulling on his play shorts and banged his knee hard on the floor.

He thought of her falling down the steps. He didn't dream of her dying, only of how easy his life would be with her gone—maybe falling down the stair would make her be gone. All the women at the church who hugged him and rubbed his head, he would get sympathy from them. His dad could marry one of them—the associate pastor's wife, Ruth, was fat and nice, and gave him butterscotch candies—and he would have a new mom.

He was pulling his striped play shirt over his head when he heard the footfall—his mom was coming out of Miriam's room. She was saying that she'd better not find his school clothes on his floor.

Ricky froze. He stared at the lump in the rug. His mom appeared in the doorway and stepped down hard.

She had another load of laundry in the basket. Her head was cocked to the other side, so she didn't look in his room. Her foot rose as her other one fell.

She missed the pin.

Ricky watched her disappear from his doorway. She was still talking to him, telling him what he'd better and better not be doing.

Ricky sat cross-legged on the floor and let his face drop into his open palms. They smelled dusty like the runner rug and Ricky sneezed three times in a row and snot flung out of his nose. He wiped it with the heel of his hand and rubbed it into his play shorts.

His mom talked downstairs. It was a tone she used with his dad or with Miriam, not him or his brothers. He strained to hear, but the talking stopped, and he heard the bottom step creak—she was coming back up. He would have another chance.

The realization slowly dawned on him—the footsteps were wrong—that was not his mom. Then he heard humming. Miriam.

Ricky stared at the lump in the rug where the pin poked through and already knew what was going to happen.

Miriam appeared in the doorway, her skinny arms cradling schoolbooks and sheet music.

Ricky jumped for the door and shouted, "Miriam."

It was too late. The full force of Miriam's heel came down square and the pin slid in. A yowl came out of her that sounded like what a cat makes when you hit it with a piece of firewood. Books and music fell around her as she crumpled to the floor.

"Miriam," he shouted. "No." He rushed to her side, falling on his sore knee. He wrapped his arms around her.

"Why'd you do that to me?" she wailed.

He said, "It wasn't on purpose."

"It was too," she screamed.

Ricky buried his face into her shoulder and held on to her. She worked her arm between the two of them and pried him away. Her elbow bent backward like one of those long water bird legs.

His mom appeared up the steps. She got on one knee with her hand on Miriam's shoulder. She said, "What happened, Sis?"

"Ricky put a needle in the rug, so I would step on it." She wouldn't stop crying. She hung her foot out in front of her like it was broken. She rubbed her heel. It wasn't bleeding, not that Ricky could see. She said, "He's a demoniac." She put her forehead against her knee, cried and rubbed at her foot. "He's possessed by Legion."

"Not on purpose," Ricky said. "It came out of my school pants."

"Get away," Miriam shouted. She shoved him to his behind on the wood floor.

It didn't hurt but he let out a yell that tapered into crying.

Miriam jumped up, limped to her room, and slammed the door. The lock clicked.

Ricky's mom fingered around the lump and tapped the pin's tip with her finger. She looked hard at Ricky.

He stopped crying, met her eyes. Stared back at her. Did not look away.

"Why did you do this?" she said. She sat down to take the pin out. She pulled at the wrong side of the rug, where the tacks still held. She said, "What came over you?" She felt up and down the edge of the rug, her wrist bones poking out under her skin. She said, "How on Earth did you get this thing under here?"

Ricky stood up.

She hooked her arms around her knees. She said, "I just don't understand."

Ricky stared.

"I'm going to have to think this one over." She shook her head.

Miriam was silent in her room. The weak orange light glowed in the dark hallway. His mom worked her arm under the rug. She twisted and pulled at the safety pin until she got it out. She tried to clip it shut, but it popped open, and she fumbled to keep from dropping it. She sighed and held it up between them. She pursed her lips and raised her eyebrows at Ricky. The pin was bent out to an *L*. She looked back down at the rug, again shaking her head.

In nearly a whisper, Ricky said, "You're a goat."

Her head jerked up and she stared at him, her pretty, green eyes wide in astonishment and fear. He did not know why she was afraid, but he saw she was and that was enough.

"You're a goat too," he shouted. "You're going to the left side of God and you're going to hell to burn."

Her eyes stared like she was afraid, then she reached for him. "Come here," she said in her soft voice. "I love you so much." She wanted to hug him.

He pushed her arms away. He stepped past her, and she let him go. He walked down the steps—she did not yell at him, and she did not follow him—walked through the living room and kitchen to the utility room. He opened the back door and stepped out. He walked down the steps and across the parsonage yard. At the edge of the yard, he started running. He ran behind the old church building, and the new building, and the clearing for the new annex, and he plunged into the cool shade of the trees by the river.

Weeds sloped down the bank. A little way up-river were the shoals, where sand and smooth stones just inches below the surface stretched halfway across the river. Jar flies' grating calls rang out all around, grinding down like wind-up trucks, on the floor with their wheels up.

Not caring about snakes or bees, Ricky didn't go to the path, but plowed straight in with bare feet, ran through the weeds. Briars tore at his arms, and nettles stung his bare ankles. He didn't care. His vision was blurry and glistening through tears. He pulled up at the edge of the river and wiped his eyes. The river was green out in the middle, but close to shore and over the shoals it was brown. He caught his breath as he stared at the water.

He climbed out on the roots of what they called the claw tree because its roots grabbed at the riverbank like bird claws. Water spiders darted in the eddy the tree roots made. Bright green leaves and yellow pollen swirled gently there. The mud on the bank was drying into cracked and curling plates. It swarmed with gnats and smelled like number two and dead fish.

Ricky grabbed a stick and crouched on the root. He clutched a smaller root for balance. The root was covered with a thin coat of dried river mud, fine and soft as baby powder. Jar flies on the other side of the river called back to the ones above his head. Immediately he was lost in stirring the pollen and swatting at the water spiders. He played this way for a long time. Then he stood and heaved the stick out to where the water was dark and green.

Welcome to Clay Free Will Baptist Church
August 9, 1981

Sunday School   9:45

Morning   11:00
  Worship

PRELUDE   "God is in His Temple"
       Miriam Minor

WORSHIP IN PRAISE

Pledge to the American Flag
Pledge to the Christian Flag
Pledge to the Bible
Hymn #15, "High and Holy
  Sovereign God"
Hymn #19, "Immortal Invisible God
  Only Wise"

INVOCATION

Hymn of Praise #3, "I Sing the
  Almighty Power of God"

WELCOME TO GUESTS

WORSHIP IN MEDITATION

Scripture   1 Peter 1:18-25,
  Reading   Susan Driggers

Morning   Pastor Minor
  Prayer

WORSHIP IN GIVING

Offertory   "O, Worship the King
       All Glorious Above"
       Miriam Minor

WORSHIP IN PROCLAMATION

MESSAGE   "The Real
       Extra-Terrestrial"
       Pastor Minor

Hymn of Invitation #137, "I Surrender
  All"

Benediction   "Come Thou
       Almighty King"
       Miriam Minor

Church Calendar

Sunday, August 9

9:15	Sunday School
11:00	Morning Worship
6:15	Church Training
7:30	Evening Worship

Monday, August 10

7:30	Choir Practice

Wednesday, August 12

6:30	AWANA Clubs (in the gym)
	Cubbies Club (in the basement)
7:00	Deacon's meeting
7:30	Prayer Meeting

Counting Committee:	Archie Gwinn
	Colley Goins
	Glenwood Jarvis
Deacon Visitation::	Archie Gwinn
	Glenwood Jarvis
	Scott Driggers

Janice McMonagle would like to express her deep gratitude for the outpouring of love at the homegoing of her husband Roy. The food was delicious. She will return the casserole dishes to the tract table in the foyer. Her church family is so dear to her and Ruthie. She doesn't know where they would be without you.

Jordan River

(Berna Minor, 1981–1982)

ONE MONDAY when Miriam, Andrew, and James were in school and Ricky was home with an earache, Berna gave him two orange-flavored chewable Bayer aspirins, and walked him across the church parking lot with eardrops and cotton in his ear for Edna Taylor to watch. The smell of greasy food wafted halfway across the parking lot from Edna's house. Berna pushed the boy through the front door as Edna called out hello from the kitchen where she was frying scrapple and eggs, and Berna called hello back. She left Ricky with Edna and drove down the river to Jordan's house. She sat in Jordan's living room and said, "I've made up my mind. I'm going away."

Jordan's house was a two-bedroom place beside the river. The driveway that dropped down from the road was steep and washed out along one side so that Berna was afraid to turn the family van down it. She parked beside the blacktop road and lumbered down on foot. Jordan's front porch was streaked gray and black with train soot. It was clear no one ever sat in the porch swing—it was as black with soot as the rest of the porch.

The back yard was small and fenced in, and the woods went down the hillside to where there were telephone poles sticking up for a dock, but no dock on them. Those mangy old locust trees leaned out over the fence. Jordan stepped out onto the back porch and Berna followed. They sat together in the freestanding hammock Jordan had made that took up the entire porch. She had her own lawn mower, and hedge clippers, and a chain saw she could start up with one or two strong pulls right out in front of her, not holding it on the ground or even against her leg. She cut down trees along her fence, buzzed off overhanging limbs, beat back the weeds till her yard was a shady little sanctuary. Berna could not remember a time in her life when she felt as happy and safe as she did there, behind that little house with Jordan, staring at the peaceful river, green on clear days, brown when it rained.

Eventually, Berna had gotten comfortable enough to unload on Jordan; she spilled all she'd kept secret from Zechariah about her life—the molestation, the abuse, how Zechariah thought she was a virgin when they got married—and how she had always been the way she is, and she just couldn't be the preacher's wife anymore. She said, "I can't stay here. I have to go."

"You have to stay. You can't leave," Jordan told her. "It's your God-given duty to raise those kids, and you're doing better than you think you are."

Berna shook her head. "They'll be better off without me in the long run. He'll find a woman who'll be a better preacher's wife. A woman who can at least play the piano."

Jordan's eyes teared up. "Plus," she said. She shook her head and waited a few long seconds. She took a deep breath. "I don't know what I would do without you." She said, "You're the best friend I've ever had." She said, "I can't stand the thought of losing you." She'd kicked off her cowboy boots and her white tube socks were dingy, just plain dirty at the toes. She pushed her sock feet over next to Berna's bare feet, and then slid herself over and they hugged—hugged like lovers—for the first time.

Jordan talked her out of leaving her family. Where would she have gone anyway? She started going out to Jordan's on her own as often as she could, which was hard because Miriam whined that she should get paid for babysitting the boys all the time. Berna finally told her, "Stop being ungrateful. You get paid when I feed you," and she stopped asking.

Berna and Jordan were cuddling and talking like they did, and, just like that, Berna worked up the nerve, craned her neck and kissed Jordan on the corner of her mouth. Jordan was ready for it. She turned to meet Berna's mouth with her own. They kissed for a long time, softly and tenderly. Jordan gently took Berna's bottom lip in her teeth and pulled at it. She said, "I want to eat you up."

"I want to be eaten up."

They laughed and kissed more, playfully, like it was a big joke and nothing serious at all.

Jordan pulled back and said, "What are we doing? What is this?"

Berna leaned up and said into her mouth, "It is what it is. Don't think so much about it."

Things progressed quickly after they broke through that barrier and in no time they were petting. Berna cupped Jordan's breasts in her hands and kissed her way down to where her buttons were, and Jordan stopped her, pulled her head back up. Clothing was still a barrier Jordan would not cross.

They stopped kissing and talked. Jordan said, "This is bad. We have to stop this. No good will come of it."

"This is coming of it," Berna said. "This." She motioned between the two of them with both hands. "This right here is good."

"Lunchtime," Jordan said. She went into the kitchen and started making eggs. Berna watched through the doorway. Jordan had on a loose flannel shirt and no bra. Her dungarees were tight on her muscular legs.

Berna could not divorce her husband, and she could not give

Jordan up; she was in too deep to get free. She fought fleeting dreams of Zechariah's death freeing her to be with Jordan, and prayed, begging God to forgive her. Wishing for someone's death had to be about the darkest sin a person could harbor in her heart. Sure, sin was sin, but in God's eyes, that one had to be the worst. She didn't want him harmed—she *didn't*—she just wanted to be free.

In the kitchen, Jordan held the pan out and tossed the eggs up. Berna saw the flash of white and yellow as the eggs did a slow flip in the air. Jordan caught them in the pan, and none sloshed out. She set it back on the burner.

"You're good at everything you do," Berna called through the door. "It all comes so easy for you."

"You think?" Jordan turned off the burner, got two plates from the cabinet above the sink. She disappeared from sight as she carried the plates and the pan to her kitchen table. From behind the wall she said, "Soup's on. You want a piece of toast?"

Two days later, Berna woke up beside Zechariah and decided this was the day she was going to have sex with Jordan. Zechariah skipped breakfast, had a quick glass of Tang, and was off to the church. After the kids were on the school bus, she took a quick shower and washed herself especially well. Jordan had to work at 11:00, so they only had a couple of hours. Berna skipped their usual sitting and talking and went straight to kissing, and not long after that she tugged on Jordan's hand.

Jordan knew what it meant.

They held hands as they walked to the bedroom and, without saying anything at all, got on the bed and kissed and undressed and touched each other's bodies. Then Jordan slid down and used her mouth on Berna like she'd been doing it all her life. It was the first time in Berna's life that someone other than she herself had given her an orgasm. She writhed when it started because it startled her. Jordan grabbed her hips and held her so she couldn't squirm away and kept going.

Didn't she trust Jordan? She did. She relaxed into the bed, turned her head, and gave herself up to it.

Afterward, Jordan rested her cheek, wet with Berna's juice already gone cold, on the inside of Berna's thigh. Berna's other bare leg was hooked over her shoulder, her heel resting on Jordan's back. Berna stroked Jordan's hair and stared at the blue wall, where there were four nail holes that would make a square if they were connected; around the outside of them was a dirty oval, the shape of whatever had been screwed to the wall there. Next to it was Jordan's guitar, which she'd gotten for Christmas one year but never played. The top was covered with dust. On the other side of the nail holes was an old wooden icebox that Jordan's dad Colley had refinished, and Jordan kept her winter clothes in. It had brush strokes where he'd swiped on fake wood grain. The swipes were splotched at the bottom because he'd used too much and let it run. Beside that were two cardboard boxes. The one on top had written in magic marker *Xmas1973*, and it had a white label with the address all scribbled out.

This was a home. Berna loved that bedroom. It smelled like Jordan. It felt natural and right. Berna wasn't afraid. She rolled over and slid down, and used her mouth on Jordan, did it just as Jordan had done to her. It was not disgusting, as she thought it might be. It was beautiful, giving and getting pleasure. It felt right, and she liked it.

From that day, they were lovers. When they were together, Berna felt good and right, at home in her skin, in a way she could not remember feeling ever before. When they weren't together, guilt and shame crushed her. She wanted to please the Lord, she did, and she wanted to be a godly wife and mother. As natural and beautiful as it felt with Jordan, she knew it was the worst kind of perversion. She repented and prayed and made promises to God; if only He would free her of this wickedness. But she couldn't stay away from Jordan. She cursed Gerald, her perverted stepdad, blamed him for warping her this way.

"That man's not why we're in love," Jordan told her. "My own dad was as close to a perfect dad as anyone could be, and I won't let anybody say different. The only thing he did wrong was marry that bitch, Doris, excuse my French." She said, "If your stepdad made you like this, then what's wrong with me?"

"I don't think anything is wrong with you," Berna said. "I think you're perfect."

Jordan laughed. She said, "You know I've been in therapy on and off for years?"

"Therapy?" According to Zechariah, therapy was for people who couldn't learn to lean on the Lord, for people who sought worldly solutions instead of biblical ones.

"Psychotherapy first," Jordan said. "I started it at the same time you moved here. I drove down to Charleston when I got back from this AWANA conference where I fell—more like dove like a sailor off a ship—into sin, and I found a psychiatrist to try and get myself fixed. He told me my problem wasn't sin, it was mental illness—like having cancer, but it's in your mind and not your body. It was caused by my mom's death and being too attached to my dad, and that had blocked what he called my 'innate heterosexuality.' He told me that I had emotional needs my mom was supposed to meet, and they weren't met, and I sexualized those emotional needs.

"I believed him. All I knew was that I was miserable and had to do something. I said yes to each thing they said to try. I figured if it was like cancer in my mind; it was going to take whatever was the mental version of chemotherapy. I looked at pictures on the overhead projector and got shocked if I didn't click to immediately get rid of pictures of pretty women, but I didn't get shocked no matter how long

I left up pictures of men. Then I took this drug called apomorphine that makes you sick as a dog and then looked at pictures of women with women while I was trying to hold down the vomit. I mean, this whole time, all these years, I've been in love with you, since that first day with the apple dumplings, almost.

"None of it worked. He sent me to a woman therapist, and I was supposed to have a relationship with her like I should have had with my mom, replace my unhealthy attachment to my dad and make me bond with women the right way, not like I always tried to bond with them." They both burst into laughter. When it subsided, she said, "That didn't work either," and the laughter began all over again.

"After that, I went to this Christian counselor who told me I have what he called gender brokenness. He agreed with the psychotherapist about what caused it, but he said the only way to fix it was through relying more on Jesus, who can heal any kind of brokenness if you lean on him."

"Did you tell him about this?" Berna waved her hand between the two of them. "About us?"

"I did tell him, yeah." Jordan stared straight ahead. "Just that we were closer than we should be. Not *this* this." She grinned wide. "I stopped going to him when we started doing this. I'm guessing he has a pretty good idea why." She said, "He says for Jesus's healing to be effective, I have to do my part too. Stay away from secular music, secular movies, secular culture. Flee temptation at all costs, stay away from anything pro-homosexual. You basically have to stay away from anybody who isn't a Christian. And also, I need to do girl things instead of boy things, wear dresses and get dolled up, bake cookies, scream when I see a mouse. That kind of stuff. If I work hard at it like that, Jesus will reward my efforts with what he called a healed sexuality."

They sat in silence for a moment, and Berna said, "I like your sexuality."

"Me too."

"It's a sin. I know it's a sin."

"Yep."

"But still."

Jordan slid her arm behind Berna and pulled her close. She said, "Why is life so impossible?"

Berna cuddled into the flannel shirt, her head against Jordan's jawbone. She could not give the response that popped into her head: it was impossible because God was an asshole. She knew she should repent of the thought right then and there, but what was the point? She had no intention of stopping their perverse relationship. She rested her hand on Jordan's chest and twisted the pocket button between her finger and thumb. She said, "You're asking me?"

Welcome to Clay Free Will Baptist Church
February 7, 1982

Sunday School   9:45

Morning Worship   11:00

PRELUDE   "The Love of God"
           Miriam Minor

WORSHIP IN PRAISE

   Pledge to the American Flag
   Pledge to the Christian Flag
   Pledge to the Bible
   Hymn #401, "Oh the Deep, Deep
     Love of Jesus"
   Hymn #416, "I Stand Amazed in
     the Presence"

INVOCATION

   Hymn of Praise #14, "And Can It
     Be That I Should Gain"

WELCOME TO GUESTS

WORSHIP IN MEDITATION

   Scripture   Matthew 22: 34-40
     Reading   Leah Wright

   Morning   Pastor Minor
   Prayer

WORSHIP IN GIVING

   Offertory   "They'll Know We
           Are Christians by
           Our Love"
           Miriam Minor

WORSHIP IN PROCLAMATION

   MESSAGE   "Agape, the Greatest
           Love of All"
           Pastor Minor

Hymn of Invitation #137, "I Surrender
   All"

Benediction   "At Calvary"
           Miriam Minor

Church Calendar

Sunday, February 7

9:15	Sunday School
11:00	Morning Worship
6:15	Church Training
7:30	Evening Worship

Wednesday, February 10

6:30	AWANA Clubs (in gym)
	Cubbies Club (in
	basement)
7:00	Deacon's meeting
7:30	Prayer Meeting

Saturday, February 13

7:30	Sweetheart Banquet (in
	the gym)
	Spaghetti Dinner
	Fun games
	Special message on
	relationship building from
	Pastor Jeff
	$10.00 per couple (treat
	your sweetie)

Counting Committee:	Archie Gwinn
	Colley Goins
	Scott Driggers
Deacon Visitation::	Archie Gwinn
	Scott Driggers

ATTENTION TEENS!!!!!!!!
Don't miss the afterglow tonight at the home of Pastor Jeff and Miss Patty. There will be chips and Coke, pizza, and lots of fun Valentine's Day "games." A van will leave the church directly after evening service and return promptly at 10:30. Parents please be on time to pick up your teens.

The Prophet of the Highest

(James Allen Minor, 1982)

SUNDAY AFTER morning worship, James and Andrew were playing kick-and-get-through on Andrew's bunk, taking turns trying to crawl from the bottom of Andrew's bed to the headboard while the other tried to kick him off the bed onto the floor. In the middle of one of their battles, Andrew reared up and said, "Stop."

James didn't stop, not right away, but when he did he heard it. Their neighbor from across the church parking lot, Perry Taylor, was cussing at Timmy Jackson, saying he was going to kill him. Andrew's head was sweaty and even though it was winter, he smelled like outside in the summertime, like dirt and grass.

James didn't want to stop kicking. He felt strong; thought maybe he could win the game this time.

The past week James had finished all his AWANA books early, had done all the work to earn his Timothy Award even though he can't have it until after sixth grade, had even recited extra Scripture. He could recite 1 John all the way through, and the first three chapters of the Gospel of John, and the entire Sermon on the Mount— which he recited for the whole church from beside the pulpit, word-for-word without a single mistake—and a bunch of psalms and proverbs, and hundreds of other verses.

172 / VIC SIZEMORE

That morning at church, he'd heard an old woman, who smelled like Hall's cough drops and left her black rubber galoshes over her church shoes all through worship, tell his dad that he was *precocious*. She said he probably knew more of the New Testament than Jack Van Impe, and they called that man the walking New Testament. His dad had laughed and said, with his hand on James's head, "It's clear that the Lord's hand is on his life." James had come home and looked up the word *precocious*. Then he'd looked up *aptitude* which was in the definition of precocious. He'd also heard Archie Gwinn tell his wife on their way out, "That boy is a genius."

Because of that, James was feeling especially proud of himself this Sunday. He'd been holding his own against Andrew at kick-and-get-through, and usually Andrew kicked his butt hard. The game had gotten so rough they had torn the covers and sheets off the bed and the mattress was starting to slide off the box springs and slope down to the floor.

It was turning out to be a glorious quiet bedroom time. Some Sundays their mom would storm in with her switch and wallop them good, two or three raging times in a single afternoon, like she was waiting outside the door to catch them in willful disobedience. Those days she had prophetic fire in her green eyes—and watch out then, she would tan their hides, drive the disobedience far from them, Proverbs 22:15. Other days her eyes looked dead as peed-on fire pits, and the switchings and paddlings didn't have any oomph to them, didn't even hurt.

This was the other kind of Sunday: they could make as much noise as they wanted and she wouldn't come in once, like she was deaf or knocked out cold.

Andrew had kicked James flush in the ear last game, and it was buzzing, which was why he didn't hear the shouting outside at first. Plus, he was about to knock Andrew off the bed and win.

So now, when Andrew reared up on his knees and said to stop because he heard something, James didn't stop. James gave him a hard heel kick that grazed his ear and landed solid on his collarbone.

Andrew slapped his feet away and whispered hard, "I'm serious, *butt wipe*." His sweaty hair was sticking to his head in front of his ears. His face had three red marks from James's kicks and seeing that made James smile.

James still thought that Andrew was trying to trick him so he could lunge and touch the wall and be kicker again, so he put his foot on Andrew's chest and pushed.

Andrew punched a knot in his leg and hissed, "Stop." When Andrew whispered it was louder than regular talking, so he might as well have just talked.

James rubbed his leg and said, "I owe you one for that."

Andrew tried to punch his leg again, but he jerked it out of the way. Andrew said, "Shut up."

"Don't tell me shut up." James knew that Andrew was jealous of him, like Esau was of Jacob. Andrew was ten and wasn't anywhere near getting his Timothy Award. He didn't have a good memory. He had to go see a math tutor at school. Even Ricky could play guitar better than he could so all he did in the Singing Soul Minors was sing backup and recite Psalm 23.

Andrew's eyes widened and he cupped his hand behind his ear. He said, "Hear that?"

James jumped to the bunk ladder, thinking his mom was coming to switch them was what Andrew was talking about. Andrew's bed sheets were all on the floor. His hanging gray mattress had stains on it, both done by Andrew, yellow with dark brown edges. The big stain was from number one and the little one was spit up.

James closed his mouth and breathed hard through his nose and listened. Ricky was on his little mattress. He was asleep like always.

He could sleep through anything, and his mouth sagged open like a retard's. Drool strung out onto his pillow. Above his mattress was a plaque their dad had put up with a saying from that missionary, Jim Elliot, who got speared in the chest by Indians. Black letters on a white background: *He is no fool who gives what he can never keep to gain what he can never lose.*

Andrew tip-toed to the window and looked out. The window went straight up where the roof sloped down, so it was back from the wall inside a kind of box. It was low so that the windowsill was at their waists. When Andrew pulled the curtain aside, the bright white day flashed in and hurt James's eyes.

Andrew would get worn out good if their mom caught him out of his bed, and his bed all torn apart too. James felt a flutter of joy at the thought of watching it and turned to let his eyes adjust back to the dark room, so he could see if the doorknob moved, still perched on the bunk ladder, ready to climb to safety.

Nothing.

He looked back at Andrew.

Andrew's dark form in front of the bright window turned and put his finger to his lips and it looked like his arm fused into his body. James froze in place and listened. Men were shouting at the Taylors' house. The Taylors lived in a brown house with a rippled metal roof. It was across the church parking lot. It was two stories high, with a porch all the way across both levels, like a wooden hotel, except the upstairs porch sagged down so much in front, if you dropped a baseball, it would roll right off. The house was shoved back against the hillside below the blacktop road so that the only thing between the roof and the cars was a leaning guardrail and lots of weeds.

Men were shouting over there all right.

James tippy toed over and stood behind Andrew. He whispered, "What if mom comes?"

"Be *quiet*," Andrew said.

James stepped into the window box and shouldered himself a spot so he could see. The paint was all scratched off the windowsill where their dog Barnabas liked to stand with his paws and look out and bark at squirrels. James had to squint till his eyes stopped hurting. They could look straight across the parking lot to the Taylors' house.

Perry Taylor's black pickup truck was there, with its rusty bed piled with rusty junk. There was also a red and white race car with the numbers *442* painted on the side, jacked up with big wheels in back and little ones in front. The church parking lot was dirty tire-packed snow that you could dig up with a stick but not with the heel of your church shoe. It shone like water.

James couldn't see anybody, only the cars. "Where are they?" he whispered.

Andrew didn't say anything.

James looked down the dirt road. The yards were melted to patches of snow in the places that stayed shady all day. Through the bald and black trees on the bank, the river showed all the way to the bridge. Flat white ice chunks flowed along, all broken up; looked like if they were turned just right, they would fit together like puzzle pieces and cover the river again.

The previous summer, men had painted the old iron bridge down at the end of the dirt road light blue. Now it was easy to see it through the trees.

"Look," Andrew whispered.

James turned back to the Taylors' leaning house. Perry was striding down the front steps in his steel-toed boots and green work pants, a shotgun hanging loose from his fist like a stick of firewood. He only had on a tee shirt and no jacket. He was a trash man, and he was fat, so the cold didn't bother him any. That's what he'd told them one day when Ricky asked him where his coat was.

Another man came from around the racecar. It was Timmy Jackson from down the dirt road. His mom came to church. His dad wasn't saved, and neither was he. James's dad called them rough customers. Timmy was an ugly man; had shaggy red hair and always scowled like he was confused. He had on bell-bottom blue jeans and had his fingers shoved up high into his jean jacket pockets that were too small for his hands.

The two men met at the bottom of the Taylors' driveway and stood where the dirt road would be if it hadn't been covered in snow. Timmy took one hand out of a pocket and pointed at Perry and said something. Perry stopped, spread his legs, pulled the gun up and aimed it right at Timmy's head. His tee shirt was tight on his big belly.

Timmy pulled the fingers of his other hand out of their pocket and stood with his arms hanging down.

James could feel the cold from the window glass on his face. It fogged with his breathing. He wiped it. Andrew's nose made a tiny whistle when he breathed in. James said, "Breathe through your mouth," and Andrew was watching the men so hard, he just obeyed James without a word or a hit or anything.

"Think he'll shoot him?" Andrew said, not whispering anymore.

"I don't know. Maybe."

One time his mom had gotten Perry Taylor to drive them to the Kroger in Clendenin and had paid him twenty dollars for it—*twenty* dollars for a ten-mile ride, and he hadn't even asked to be paid. Perry had a big belly, but he was not soft, no, he was as hard as a train car. Once they'd bumped into each other by accident and it hurt so much James ran away so nobody saw him cry. On the trip Perry had thrown one of his Kool cigarette butts out his window and it blew into the truck bed on the cool river wind and got stuck between James's shoulder and the truck bed. It burned James's shoulder pretty good, made a black hole in his shirt. Perry didn't say sorry but chuckled and said, "That ain't the worst thing that'll ever happen to you, boy. I promise you that." Perry was the kind of man who hurt people on accident and laughed about it.

Another time Perry had left his truck window open, and James and Andrew snatched a crumpled pouch of Red Man from the front seat and ran with it to the riverbank. It was sweet and gooey in their mouths, and made James feel lightheaded and good. It made Andrew barf. But when they came back up, Perry was standing in the parking lot, and he walked over to them, and they were too scared to run. He had out his big pocketknife, held it in front of his fat gut. He said to the two of them, "If I ever catch a boy stealing my chaw, I'm going to cut his heart out and feed it to the dogs."

Thing was, James hadn't been able to tell if he was trying to scare them, which is what it sounded like, or if he was serious, because it was Perry Taylor saying it and not a man from the church.

Staring down at the two men on the bright, icy parking lot, James said, "Oh yeah." He nodded. "He'll shoot him all right."

"Here," Andrew said, reaching up to unlatch the window. James helped him push it up a crack. Icy cold air came in at their stomachs. They got on their knees and pushed their faces to the cold opening.

Perry Taylor and Timmy Jackson were arguing now, but so low that James couldn't make out what they were saying. Perry motioned with the gun as he talked. His big arms were stuffed into the tee shirt and were red and splotchy from the cold. His face was red too, glowing hot like a coal stove.

James understood enough to know that the fight had to do with sex. Ronnie Stewart brought pictures to school. Naked women with their boobies hanging, spreading their legs to show the hair and floppy skin down at their privates. "Look at that big old yummy pussy," Ronnie said once. Yummy? It made no sense. James didn't understand. Of another picture, Ronnie said, "Wouldn't you love to pork that?" as he folded open a page he'd ripped out of a magazine and held a centerfold spread in front of James and the other boys. James laughed with the others, but he did not understand.

The two men were just standing there talking now. If Perry didn't have a gun, it would look normal. It was starting to get boring.

Once Ronnie took James and Andrew to the riverbank and showed them a picture he'd gotten of a woman *and* a man naked, and the man had his dick stuck in the woman's pussy. She was squatted over him, and James could see her butthole right above where her pussy was stretched around the man's dick. It didn't look any different than Barnabas's butthole, or one of those stray cats sneaking around the riverbank. Except it didn't have fur all around it and a tail above, so the stirring it caused all down his body frightened him. He realized it was because this was a woman, and Proverbs 5 warned young men that *the lips of an immoral woman drip honey*, but her *feet go down to death, her steps take hold on hell*. The woman in this picture had the man down on his back. Her head was turned all the way around, so she was looking back right at James, and the look on her face brought down a fear and guilt that made him want to cry, to run away. He didn't understand any of it, but he did know this was an occasion to sin, a place for Satan to get a foothold.

James thought that Timmy Jackson probably took off his clothes with Perry Taylor's wife, and they probably kissed. He probably put his dick in her pussy. That was fornication. *The mouth of an immoral woman is a deep pit; He who is abhorred by the LORD will fall there*, Proverbs 22:14. *For out of the heart proceed evil thoughts, murders, adulteries, fornications* . . . Matthew 15:19.

If Timmy Jackson did put his dick in Perry Taylor's wife, they should both be stoned to death. They didn't stone people anymore,

James thought, at least not in America where people were turning away from God's laws. Shooting would do. Perry Taylor *should* shoot them if they were fornicators.

James wanted to see Timmy Jackson get what was coming to him: *Do not be deceived, God is not mocked; for whatever a man sows, that he will also reap*, Galatians 6:7.

"He'll shoot him dead, is what he'll do." James turned and looked at the side of Andrew's face. The red mark from his heel was still there. "He should shoot him too," he said. "And his wife."

"How come?" Andrew asked.

"Because Timmy Jackson fornicated with his wife."

"How do you know?"

"God told me."

"Shut up." Andrew leaned closer to the window and started chewing on the inside of his lip.

Timmy Jackson was the only one talking now. All calm looking, with his hands out, palms up, like he wanted to play firecracker. Perry Taylor was looking at the ground shaking his head slowly.

"We should get Mom," Andrew said.

Perry Taylor had lowered the gun barrel and it now pointed at Timmy Jackson's belly.

"Shit," Andrew said. "He's going to kill him." He shoved James. "Get mom. Hurry."

"You get her."

Behind them, Ricky's sleep-clotted voice said, "What're you looking at?"

"Shut up, retard," Andrew said. "This is important."

"What're you looking at?" Ricky repeated.

"Shut up," Andrew gave a half-hearted horse kick that Ricky easily sidestepped so that it only grazed his hip.

Ricky pushed himself between the two of them. "Let me see," he said. He had a sweaty head and sleep wrinkles all over the side of his face. His breath smelled like the roast beef gravy they had for lunch, only sour.

"You smell like number two, retard." Andrew said. "Get away." But he was watching the men and didn't shove Ricky out of the window box. "James, go get her."

Their mom made Ricky wear pajama bottoms and a special big kid diaper because he still did number one in his sleep. He was a big baby. Except he could play guitar better than James and Andrew, the little retard.

"Whoa," Andrew yelled, and James turned back.

Perry Taylor swiped down with his gun barrel like he was hoeing a garden and gouged Timmy Jackson's eye and cheek. Timmy Jackson put his hands over his face and bent over. Perry swiped up under Timmy's chin and made his head jerk back. Timmy tried to back away with his hands still over his face, but Perry smashed straight down on the back of his head with the gun butt like he was digging a post hole. Timmy fell to his knees from that one. He tipped and kept falling like in slow motion, without moving his hands to catch himself, and landed on the side of his head and his shoulder and was as still as a deer in a truck bed.

The blood pouring out of his face looked black against the bright snow. Perry's breath came in white bursts out of his mouth as he grunted and kicked Timmy, who just lay there. Perry stopped and rested for a second, looked around—Andrew and James both ducked down, then raised slowly and peeked back over the sill while Ricky just stood and stared. Perry aimed the gun straight down at Timmy Jackson's head. Timmy Jackson didn't move.

"He killed him," James said.

"Damn man," Ricky said. "He killed him dead."

"Get mom." Andrew shoved James toward the door. "*Go.*"

Switching or not, this was a bad thing. He ran across the room and pulled the door open. The hallway was dark. Miriam's door was cracked open, and though his eyes weren't yet adjusted, he saw her form peeking out.

"Perry Taylor killed Timmy Jackson in the parking lot," he said. "I'm getting mom." They crossed in the hall as she ran for the boys' room. He took the stairs three at a time and burst into his parent's room, yelling, "Mom, you have to come—"

She wasn't there.

He ran through the living room and jumped over the heater grate into the kitchen.

The plates from Sunday dinner were perched on the strainer where Miriam had stacked them. Beside them the glasses were upside down on a brown dish towel. In the light from the window, James could see the tiny ants that lived in the kitchen even in wintertime, crawling in and out from behind the creased metal strip that fit into the crack where the wall and the countertop came together. The countertop was cream colored with golden squiggly lines all over it so that if you squinted, it looked like fish guts all smashed together. The ants kept crawling in and out at the metal strip.

Their mom wasn't in there either.

The bathroom door was open. He ran and looked in there too. "Mom," he yelled. "Perry Taylor killed Timmy Jackson." He ran to the utility room. There were two piles of laundry as high as his waist. He got on his toes and looked out the back door, but couldn't see, so he opened it. He hollered out into the back yard, "Mom?"

He ran back through the house hollering for his mom, looked in her bedroom again, and then he ran upstairs and checked Miriam's room. He ran across the hall and looked in his room. Miriam and Andrew and Ricky were at the window.

"What's going on?" he said.

"Get *mom*," Andrew said.

"Hurry, Jamey," Miriam said. She was crying.

He ran back down the stairs and into the kitchen. He swiped the ants and hefted himself to his knees on the kitchen counter. He leaned over the dinner dishes and looked out the window. He smelled blue window cleaner and held the hand he'd swiped the ants with to his nose. It was the ants. They smelled like window cleaner when he smashed them.

Barnabas was at the back corner of the new church building, walking toward the river. James knocked on the window and the dog looked back for a second, then turned and disappeared around the building. James saw a flash of Jordan Goins's Jeep go around the corner from the back parking lot.

Jordan Goins was the AWANA Commander. She walked like a football player. Once James saw a pickup truck full of men going hunting. They were all in coveralls and orange hats. As they went by Jordan's voice came out of one of them. "Hey there, James," it said, and it scared him. Then he saw it was her, sitting there on the wheel well with her gun between her spread legs. She was evil. He saw it now. The filth of iniquity followed her like the dirt cloud around Pigpen in *Peanuts*, and he didn't know why no one else saw it, except that God was opening his eyes to special, spiritual truth.

Jordan and his mom had been best friends for years.

The back door opened, and his mom came in wearing her gray AWANA jacket, and he knew she'd been out in Jordan's Jeep. He could tell she was in sin by the scared look on her face when she saw him, like *she* was the one getting caught and not him. It only lasted a second, but that was enough. She fixed her face and said, "Young man, what are you doing out of your bed?"

He jumped off the counter and said, "Perry Taylor killed Timmy Jackson in the front parking lot."

"What are you talking about?" Her face was red from being out-side. Her nose was runny. She pulled a balled-up tissue out of her jacket pocket and dabbed at it.

"In the front parking lot," he repeated. "He killed him with a gun."

His mom shoved the tissue back into her pocket as she ran for the front door.

He followed her, his heart swelling with the importance of what he was a part of: matters of life and death, and him just nine years old.

His mom stopped on the front porch and hugged her AWANA jacket around her. James followed her out, saying, "He killed him, and I came looking for you. That's why I came out of my room."

"Hush," she said. She stared hard across the parking lot.

A police car was parked over at Perry Taylor's now, but the lights weren't flashing. It was Mike Humphrey, the policeman who lived in a trailer beside the high school. He was big as Perry Taylor, except his chest stuck out as far as his belly did. He leaned back when he walked, with his thumbs hooked into his wide black belt.

Perry Taylor was sitting in the back of the police car. He was crying and rocking back and forth, hitting his head on the back of the driver's seat. Not hard. The fornicator Timmy was still on the ground, but he was curled up now. Officer Humphrey was squatting down with his forearms on his legs, talking to Timmy.

"Go back in the house," his mom said.

James stared at the scene before him and knew the Holy Spirit was sending him a message: he was chosen by God because he was so smart. He was a special, precocious boy. If they called Jack Van Impe the walking New Testament, they were going to call James the walk-ing *Bible*. It wasn't called the *King James Bible* for nothing, he didn't think. God led his mom and dad to name him that.

He hadn't forgotten about his mom's sin either. Vile passions was what Paul called it. She'd better watch out, he thought. *For even their women exchanged the natural use for what is against nature . . . burned in their lust for one another*, Romans 1:26–27. James knew things. His heart leapt for joy at all the revelation he had received. He was a prophet of God, it had to be.

"Obedience, young man," she said.

Timmy's leg moved. Perry Taylor's wife came out of their house. She was flabby fat and only wore big loose dresses. James once heard his dad joke that she bought the material for them at a tent store. She didn't wear a coat either. All that fat. It was like having a coat on under her skin. Officer Humphrey stood and walked over with his chest stuck out and talked to her. She pointed and waved her arm, the bottom part of it swung back and forth.

Without looking away from what was going on, his mom said, "James, obedience is?"

"Doing what you're told, when you're told, with the right heart attitude," he mumbled as he turned and stepped back into the house. That wasn't even in the Bible, and she used it like it was. He skipped up the stairs and ran to his bedroom. Andrew and Miriam and Ricky were still at the window, watching Perry Taylor get arrested. An ambulance was there now. Its red lights flashed silently across the white and shiny parking lot.

They all three turned and looked at him.

Andrew said, "Did you find mom?"

"Did you find mom?" Ricky cut in and said at almost the same time but a split second behind.

Miriam's face was splotchy from crying.

What things the Lord had entrusted to him, to James Allen Minor. He put out his chest and said, "For he is a chosen vessel unto me, to bear my name before the Gentiles and kings . . ."

"Shut up, showoff," Miriam said. She turned back to the window.

James raised his voice and continued, "For I will show him how great things he must suffer for my name's sake. Acts nine—"

"Shut up," Ricky said.

"Remember what mom said about being a know-it-all?" Andrew said. He *still* had the red mark from James's heel on his cheek.

"Shut up," Ricky said again.

"You shut up," James told him. "You little retard. You can't even pass a Cubbies book."

"I don't want to."

"Because you're too stupid."

They all turned to look back out the window where the ambulance lights silently flashed.

A prophet has no honor in his own country, John: 4:44.

They would appreciate him in the fullness of time. God called Noah in Genesis 6:13. He called Abraham in Genesis 12. Jacob in Genesis 28, Moses in Exodus 3. Gideon in Judges 6, Samuel in 1 Samuel 3. Elijah, Elisha, Isaiah, Jeremiah, Ezekiel, Hosea. John the Baptist, Jesus, the disciples. Paul. Charles Spurgeon. Billy Sunday. D. L. Moody. John R. Rice, J. Frank Norris, Zechariah Minor.

And now James Allen Minor. He would surpass even the great things his dad was out doing. The Lord's hand was on him. He was going to speak the Holy Word of God without fear, not letting any man despise his youth. Righteous anger rose in him—be angry and sin not—at the Devil for the evil he poured on this old sin-sick world.

James would not neglect the gift that was given him by prophecy, 1 Timothy 4:12–14. He was sure—beyond the shadow of a doubt, he was sure—that God had already made him a better preacher than Spurgeon or Moody. He might be killed or crucified or scourged for the name of Christ, Matthew 23:43.

The others watched out the window. Whatever was going on out there was not important to him now. What a glorious day. He'd been called with a holy calling before the world began, 2 Timothy 1:9, and soon he would stand before the church and proclaim all things as the Lord revealed them to him.

Welcome to Clay Free Will Baptist Church
August 15, 1982

Sunday School   9:45

Morning Worship   11:00

PRELUDE   "For the Beauty of the Earth"
Miriam Minor

WORSHIP IN PRAISE

Pledge to the American Flag
Pledge to the Christian Flag
Pledge to the Bible
Hymn #314, "This Is My Father's World"
Hymn #17, "Shall We Gather at the River"

INVOCATION

Hymn of Praise #49, "Trust and Obey"

WELCOME TO GUESTS

WORSHIP IN MEDITATION

Scripture Reading   Romans 8:18-25   Rachel Wright

Morning Prayer   Pastor Minor
Special Scripture Recitation   James Minor

WORSHIP IN GIVING

Offertory   "We Walk by Faith and Not by Sight"
Miriam Minor

WORSHIP IN PROCLAMATION

MESSAGE   "Hope Is a Verb"
Pastor Minor

Hymn of Invitation #137, "I Surrender All"

Benediction   "Be Thou My Vision"
Miriam Minor

Church Calendar

Sunday, August 15

9:15	Sunday School
11:00	Morning Worship
6:15	Church Training
7:30	Evening Worship

Wednesday, August 18

6:30	AWANA Clubs
	Cubbies Club
7:00	Deacon's meeting
7:30	Prayer Meeting

Counting Committee: Archie Gwinn
Colley Goins
Scott Driggers

Deacon Visitation: Archie Gwinn
Scott Driggers

ATTENTION TEENS
Thursday Night at 7:00
Be there or be square
Be where?
Pastor Jeff's pad
Why?
Pizza, pizza, and more Pizza
Make your own banana split bar
Off the hook games (with prizes)
The BEST PART? No sermon!!! I Promise!

Whose Heart Is Snares and Nets

(Miriam Ruth Minor, 1982–1983)

MIRIAM WAS alone in the house with the boys so much she had basically become the house mother. She and the boys developed their own rules and most of the time they didn't fight much, especially while Andrew and James were outside playing with the neighborhood boys. Miriam and Ricky loved sitting beside the stereo listening to the secular music that was banned when their mom was around. They sang along. She would figure out the songs on piano, and Ricky would try to accompany her as best he could on his little guitar.

When their mom was home, she enforced her own house rules like a prison guard. When she entered a room, Miriam's shoulders and neck tensed up in anticipation of discipline for one infraction or another that she was still unaware she was committing. It seemed that whatever Miriam took pleasure in, her mom could find a way it was sinful and take it from her. For example, an old woman in the church made homemade root beer—root beer was Miriam's favorite and she seldom got it because it was too expensive—and left six fat brown bottles of it on the parsonage porch with a sweet note for them to enjoy it. But the lady had bottled it in old Stroh's beer bottles and so her mom poured them out. When Miriam protested, her mom told her it was sin to do anything that "causes your brother to stumble."

Once a couple of years earlier, Miriam had been riding to the

Kroger with her mom for the week's groceries, and she'd turned on the radio. The song "You Light Up My Life" was on. Miriam loved that song. It didn't occur to her that it would be sinful, since it was Pat Boone's daughter, and Pat Boone was a Christian, but her mom's hand shot out and snapped it off.

"Why'd you do that?" Miriam asked.

"Why would I willingly pump filth into my car?" Her mom gripped the steering wheel and pursed her lips.

"She's a Christian," Miriam said. "Her daddy is Pat Boone. He's a Christian."

"That's how the Devil tricks you, makes a thing look fun and right. 'It can't be wrong because it feels too right'? What's the message there?" Her mom didn't wait for her to answer. "It's a lie of the Enemy, that's what. Feelings will deceive you. You can't just *feel* like a thing is right. You have to *know* it's right, and the only way to *know* if it's right is if it is in line with God's instruction manual, *the Bible*."

Defeated, Miriam went silent and stared out the window.

"When we get home," her mom said, "I want you to dig through the trash can to get your lunch."

"Yuck. No."

"Yes," she said, "you will. I happen to know that there's perfectly good food in that trash can. You will find a nutritious lunch in there."

Her mom did not forget. After they got home and put the groceries away, she made Miriam go to her knees and dig through the kitchen trash for food. Miriam cried more as she put a half-eaten piece of Ricky's morning toast on the plate her mom held beside her. It had coffee grounds all in the grape jelly, and the smell of old coffee and jelly, mixed along with stinky eggs still in the trash can, made Miriam gag.

"There's a nice piece of bread you can have with your lunch," her mom said. She loomed over Miriam with the plate. "It won't hurt you at all. Keep digging." The egg smell was coming from the yolk of Miriam's own fried egg that morning—Miriam didn't eat the yolks. Her mom said, "Get that egg yellow," and Miriam did. She put it on the plate. The smells mixed with last night's Hamburger Helper, and sure enough, there was a glob of it, pasta and meat and gravy all pasty and cold. Her mom made her scoop it up with her bare hand, pluck the sodden napkin and a Columbia Gas envelope off it, and glop it onto the plate.

"Ah," her mom said happily, "now there's a healthy lunch for you."

Miriam sat at the table in front of the food trash and cried until she was gasping for breath, her mom insisting she eat it for lunch. In the end, her mom did not make her eat it, but Miriam decided Ricky's way—sneaking, and not bringing it up—was the best strategy.

Their mom was the same with TV. She banned *Happy Days* because it came on with a rock and roll song. Once Miriam was watching *Starsky & Hutch*, and her mom walked through just as Hutch used a curse word. Her mom turned off the TV and banned the show forever. Which meant, if she ever walked in and a banned show was on, even if Miriam wasn't the one watching it, she would face what she and the boys in their teenage years came to call "the wrath of mom." If they misbehaved, it was her fault. The boys were just boys, and God made boys without any sense or self-control.

In the fall of 1982, when Miriam's nipples started hurting, she had no clue it was puberty setting in. She could not stop reaching up and pressing against them, even though they were sore, and it made her wince. She asked her mom what was wrong, and her mom laughed at her. She said, "It means that now you're going to have to worry about men," and offered no further explanation. The next day her mom brought her two training bras that smelled like other people's detergent, one with pink trim and a little bow in the middle, the ribbons permanently curled into tight little balls, and the other with little purple hearts on it, faded and covered in hard little lint balls she obsessively pinched off.

"We have a house full of boys," her mom told her. "Don't leave your room without one of these on anymore, for their sake and for yours too. Don't want to embarrass yourself." Miriam was embarrassed of herself the next Sunday in Sunday school when Leah pointed and yelled, "Miriam's wearing a *bra*," and her classmates all laughed. Then, between Sunday school and big church, Jimmy Gillenwater snuck up behind her, pinched the bra strap, pulled it like a slingshot, and let it go. She arched her back against the sting while the other kids standing around laughed at her, and she thought this was what her mom was talking about when she'd told Miriam she would now have to worry about men.

Miriam wore the training bra and bore the torment from her classmates dutifully. Her mom told her, "You won't be a girl anymore soon. You'll be a woman, and it will all change for you. Nothing will be the same." Miriam had done much of the woman's work in the house for several years already: preparing food when her daddy popped in for lunch, cleaning her room and the boys' filthy room, doing the stinky laundry, folding it, sorting socks, doing dishes. She didn't believe her mom that it—whatever *it* was—would change; she already felt like the woman of her house. Since it was the only life she'd ever known, it didn't yet seem odd to her that her mom was gone all day; just gone and never told them *where*.

Her daddy had talked the trustees into buying the church a shiny black baby grand piano, and he, Pastor Jeff, and Mr. Goins had moved the old upright into the living room of their house. Miriam soothed her nerves by practicing on it whenever the boys weren't watching TV, or Ricky wasn't on his back on the floor with his ear against the stereo speaker, trying to listen to rock and roll music at a low enough volume to not get caught if their mom walked in. Only seven years old, and Ricky was already a sneaky little liar.

During the day, their dad never walked in. Their mom might or might not, so they had to stay alert when they were on their own. Being that Miriam was the oldest, she felt responsible, tried to keep peace and order in the house; being that she was the girl, her brothers ignored her instructions and laughed off her threats to tell on them. They were right to ignore her, she guessed, since she never could bring herself to tattle, even on James, who was a holier-than-thou know-it-all and, of all of them, was the one she wouldn't mind seeing their mom switch.

At the end of the school year, their dad withdrew them from public school and enrolled them in Elk River Christian School inside Bible Baptist Church in Clendenin. Pastor Jeff told her he would be their assistant principal, and they would have to start calling him Mr. Wright. He pulled Miriam aside though and assured her that she didn't have to call him Mr. Wright when no one else was around—as a matter of fact, he said, she could call him just Jeff now that she was not a little girl anymore.

The last Sunday in August, before school started, Pastor Jeff, Miss Patty, and Leah and Rachel came over for dinner and fellowship between morning worship and evening service. Things already felt strange to Miriam, knocked out of whack: not only were her mom and daddy both there at the same time, but a whole 'nother family was there too. That was the Sunday afternoon when Pastor Jeff got to her the first time.

She and the others changed into their play clothes while her dad and Pastor Jeff grilled hot dogs and hamburgers in the back yard, and Miss Patty helped their mom get the potato and macaroni salads ready and put the fixings on plates. After eating, Miriam and the other kids all changed into their swimsuits and their dad turned on the sprinkler for them to run through.

When they tired of that, Andrew unhooked the sprinkler and dragged the hose to the top of the grassless knoll in the back yard. The water ran down and created a flowing mudslide like the one Miriam remembered seeing on TV at that rain-soaked hippie festival. She joined the others in sliding down the muddy slope but hated the way the drying mud pulled at her skin. The others complained as she rinsed herself overlong with the water hose. "Shut up," she told them. Andrew grabbed the hose, and they did a short tug-of-war before he jerked it hard from her grasp. He called her a baby and drilled the center of her back with a beam of water as she ran for the house.

Inside, she asked her mom if she could take a shower before she got back into her church clothes.

Her mom was sitting at the kitchen table with Miss Patty, drinking iced tea. "Be fast about it," her mom said. "And put your play clothes back on. You'll get your church clothes filthy."

In the shower, she scrubbed her skin pink, and shampooed her hair twice. She left her soggy wet bathing suit on the floor, wrapped up in a towel, and scurried up to her bedroom. She dried off and let the towel drop to the floor. As she turned around to get her panties, she saw that the door, which she had closed and heard click, was open a crack.

From the narrow opening, one of Pastor Jeff's eyes stared at her. She could hear her mom and Miss Patty downstairs talking. She pretended not to notice him. She grabbed her clothes, stepped quickly over behind her dresser, and almost tripped stepping into her panties. She shrugged one shoulder then the other into her blouse and buttoned it. On top of her dresser, her ballerina jewelry box was open and empty, the spring where the ballerina once spun before Ricky broke it spiked up in front of the mirror.

Above her jewelry box, the space at the door slowly widened and Pastor Jeff's whole face pushed into it, creased smile lines at the edge of his mouth. They made eye contact.

"This is my room," she said. "I'm getting dressed."

"I was just looking for the bathroom," he said, and he stepped in and closed the door just shy of the clicking point.

"There's no bathroom up here." She froze, holding her skirt in front of her.

The floor creaked beneath his weight as he stepped over and stood above her. "It's okay," he said in a low almost whisper. "You don't need to be afraid of me. I'm good old Jeff." He led her to her bed and told her, "Sit down here with me and let's talk."

She sat still after that, as if in a dream, as if she were several inches above her body, hearing him talk, watching him touch her, the same as she would sit still and watch a TV show. He breathed heavily and told her she was such a beautiful young woman, not a little girl anymore, a young woman, so beautiful. His breathing was jerky and heavy, and eventually he just breathed and repositioned her legs, and groped with his fingers, and didn't say anything at all. After he finished, he told her not to tell or she would be in big trouble because she did it too.

She still felt detached from her own body as he eased his way down the steps and out the front door, but as she hurried through the kitchen to the back yard, shame swelled inside until she almost burst out crying. She had sinned against Miss Patty (she didn't care about Leah and Rachel; she didn't like them anyway). She had committed a horrible sin, an awful, shameful, horrible sin.

"Tell the others to hose themselves off real good and come inside to get changed," her mom told her as she rushed past. Miriam nodded from the utility room and pushed the screen door open.

Pastor Jeff had gone out the front door and walked back around to sit with her dad in the folding chairs. He picked up his iced tea and her dad started talking about the things of the Lord. Pastor Jeff stretched out his legs, crossed them at the ankles, and peered hard away from her. His black shoes were as huge as loaves of Italian bread.

She never forgot what her mom told her about how boys were not wired for self-control and it's the job of women to put on the brakes. She and Andrew rode out to Tastee-Freez with Jimmy Gillenwater when he got his driver's license. Andrew sat up front with Jimmy and Ronnie Stewart was in back with her. He kept putting his hand on her knee and she kept swatting it away and staring ahead trying to ignore him.

On the way out, they came up behind Jordan Goins on her motorcycle and at the straight stretch. She'd heard her mom and dad having an argument about Jordan. AWANA parents had asked that she not be the Commander anymore because she was confusing the children and not a good example to them of what a woman should be, and it might make them turn homosexual. Her daddy had fired Jordan. He tried to get her mom to take the job, but she refused. Arneda Sizemore was doing it, but she was old, and the kids didn't like her.

Jimmy pulled out like he was going to pass Jordan, but then he slowed down and started crowding her.

He rolled down his window and shouted, "Dyke."

She glanced at him, reached up and put two fingers on her handlebar brake. She slowed down, and he slowed down and crowded her more. He yelled out the window, "Rug muncher." Andrew yelled, "Get off the road, you freak."

Jimmy finally crowded her so much that she steered off the road and down across a narrow ditch and into a fence post; if she'd gone through the fence, she'd have tumbled, motorcycle and all, into the

Elk River. She was almost stopped by the time she hit the fence, it was just a bump, her head didn't even jerk forward.

Andrew rolled down his window, pulled himself out so he was sitting on the door looking over the roof at Jordan, and as Jimmy sped back up, he shouted, "Stay off the road, *freak*."

Miriam screamed at them to stop it, but it just made all of them laugh even harder. She cried the whole rest of the way to Tastee-Freez while they laughed, and she refused to get out of the car or have any ice cream. Jordan's motorcycle was gone. The only good thing was that Ronnie didn't try to touch her on the way back.

The boys' roving hands were because of her breasts and hips. In the hallways between classes, one of them would pinch her butt, or grab it with a whole hand. Not just her. Other girls yelled and smacked the boys, but Miriam ignored them, acted as if nothing had happened at all.

For her, Jeremy Cole was the worst offender. He sat behind her in West Virginia History class and would lean over and slide his fingers up against her butt in the desk seat. One day the electricity died, and, in the darkness, Jeremy forced his whole hand, palm up, between her butt and the desk seat. She reacted by sliding forward until she dropped out of the seat. Her head hit the seatback and she melted onto the floor away from his groping hand. The lights blew back on and there she was for the class to see, contorted so that her chest faced the bottom of her desktop, and her head was in the seat, staring up at the spitballs stuck to the drop ceiling tiles above.

She maneuvered herself out from under the desk in her dress, trying not to let anything show, while laughter rang out around her. She stood glaring at Jeremy. He had unpopped pimples around the base of his nose and on his forehead. He looked at her with innocent bemusement.

"Are you okay, Miriam?" Mrs. Ryan asked, half chuckling herself.

"I'm fine," Miriam said. She sat back down and scooted her desk as far forward as she could, until it touched the back of David Huffman's chair.

"Back off," David said, shoving her desk back.

"Simmer down now," Mrs. Ryan said. "Or you'll have two demerits each."

Miriam stared silently at her notebook and her cheeks burned with shame.

"We have to get through chapter eight today," Mrs. Ryan said, turning back to the pull-down map of West Virginia. "No more funny stuff."

Mr. Wright was in charge of discipline. He oversaw detention and suspended students for excessive demerits and for other things, like when Jinx Rupert stole all the faculty hub caps and threw them into the Elk River behind the school. Twice that year, Mr. Wright found Miriam alone at the school, in the band room, and he used his hands on her inside her clothes and guided her hand down inside his pants and told her how to use it on him. Each time she felt a strange detachment while it happened that she thought might even be pleasure, she couldn't tell, and crushing guilt as soon as it was over.

One day as he was driving them all back to Clay after school, she noticed how the sun shining through his ear made it translucent so she could see the veins inside. She leaned up and pulled his ear out and said, "Look, Jeff's ears are see-through." Jeff did not so much as flinch at her touch. Andrew leaned up and gazed at the pink ear in the slanting sunlight, and said, "Neat." Leah and Rachel both scowled. Miriam scooted back onto the seat, crossed her arms, and smiled at them.

———

A few days later, as Miriam walked home from piano lessons, a man started following her along the blacktop road in his car. She only vaguely noticed that the front left hubcap was missing the first time he passed. The second time, she took notice. He was slowing down and almost following her before speeding up and driving on. It was a blue Chevy Vega with the flipped-up tail thing. He kept turning onto the blacktop road and circling right back around to slow down and follow her again before gunning his engine and rolling past her. She walked faster. He pulled up behind her a fourth time and crept along. She glanced back. He was staring at her butt and his right shoulder was jerking up and down—he was playing with himself right there in the car. He gunned his engine, swerved around her so close she feared for an instant that his mirror would clip her arm, and drove on, turning onto the blacktop road, this time speeding away.

Miriam sprinted home, her shoulder bag swinging and banging against her hip until she grabbed it up into her armpit like a football, and ran harder. She did not stop until she reached the house even though her lungs burned as she panted in and out. She went upstairs and watched the road out the boys' window but did not see the blue car drive by again. She told her mom at dinner that she wanted to quit piano lessons, but her mom told her no, she couldn't quit.

A couple of weeks later, she walked over to the church where her daddy had given her permission to practice piano on the baby grand, instead of the cheap, out-of-tune upright in their living room, where the boys lay in front of the TV after school and watched reruns of *Hogan's Heroes*, *Little Rascals*, *Bewitched*, *I Dream of Genie*, and *Star Trek*, one after the other, before supper.

The sanctuary was dark and quiet. She turned on the piano lamp, set up her sheet music, and practiced for over an hour. When she was finished, she stepped down and looked around the dark sanctuary. The place seemed holier to her when no one was there. She sensed a person was there before she saw his shadow down the long center aisle in back.

"I thought that was you," Pastor Jeff said. "Playing a little piano?" He walked up the middle aisle toward her.

"I'm finished now," she said. "I have to get back home and help mom with supper."

When he reached her, he said, "It's been so good riding up and back to school with you."

Not knowing what to say to that, she responded, "It's fun."

And right there in front of the communion table with the words *This Do in Remembrance of Me* etched into the wood, Pastor Jeff started touching her, and again she froze like a rabbit. He started breathing heavily and he said, "You've grown into such a beautiful young woman." He said, "Come here," and led her into the choir room to the left of the pulpit. He locked the door and put his hands inside her clothes and guided her hand to touch him inside his pants. This time, though, this time he went further; he opened his pants and pulled it out. He told her to take off the culottes she was still wearing from cheerleading practice. She obeyed mechanically, and felt nothing, again outside her body and watching it happen like a TV show. There in the dark, locked choir room, in front of the alto chairs, beside a stack of blue hymnals with gold lettering, Pastor Jeff took her virginity. She cried because it hurt bad, but he didn't stop until he was finished, and then he was all jittery and apologetic, making her swear to secrecy.

She walked home in a daze, changed clothes in her room, changed her panties, balled up the bloody ones, and hid them inside a tee shirt in the hamper. She walked downstairs like a robot and dutifully helped her mom with supper. She did not cry until she was in bed that night and the boys were good and asleep. She refused to go back to the sanctuary alone to practice on the baby grand. Her dad's frustration boiled into anger. He told her he'd had to convince the deacons to spend the money on the piano, and he'd done it because she had real talent and needed a quality instrument. He told her she would be wasting the talent God gave her, which would be a sin. He called her ungrateful.

"It scares me going over there by myself," she told him.

He marched her across the parking lot and into the dark sanctuary. He walked her to the piano and told her to sit. He walked to the back and called out, "This church is the safest place all up and down this river. You need to grow up and stop acting like a silly little girl."

He wanted her to reach out her hands and play the piano—show gratitude to him for having the church buy it. She sat on the bench and waited until he left in a huff, the plastic heels of his black wing-tips click-clacking down the side hallway toward his office. When she heard his office door close, she made her escape out the side door and ran home in the orange evening light that slanted down through the trees up on the mountain.

Welcome to Clay Free Will Baptist Church
March 27, 1983

Sunday School   9:45

Morning Worship   11:00

PRELUDE   "Angels Your March Oppose"
Rachel Wright, clarinet
Leah Wright, flute
Miriam Minor, piano

Hymn #23, "The Fight Is On"

WORSHIP IN PRAISE

Pledge to the American Flag
Pledge to the Christian Flag
Pledge to the Bible
Hymn of Praise #64, "Victory in Jesus"

INVOCATION   Pastor Minor

Hymn of Rejoicing, (insert) "Greater Is He That Is in Me"

WELCOME TO GUESTS

WORSHIP IN MEDITATION

Scripture Reading   Psalm 121
Leah Wright

Morning Prayer   Pastor Jeff

WORSHIP IN GIVING

Offertory   "High and Holy Sovereign God"
Rachel Wright, clarinet
Leah Wright, flute
Miriam Minor, piano

WORSHIP IN PROCLAMATION

MESSAGE   "The Real Star Wars"
Pastor Minor

Hymn of Invitation #413, "Take My Life and Let It Be"

Benediction   Hymn #67, "This Is My Father's World"

Church Calendar

Sunday
9:15   Sunday School
11:00   Morning Worship
6:15   Church Training
7:30   Evening Worship

Monday, March 28
7:30   Choir Practice

Wednesday, March 30
6:30   AWANA
7:30   Prayer Meeting

Thursday, March 31
There will be no deacon visitation this week.

Sunday, April 3
9:15   Sunday School
11:00   Morning Worship

We will have a special treat next Sunday morning before Pastor Minor brings us a message from the Word. James Minor will recite the entire first chapter of The Gospel of John verbatim. Be sure to bring your Bible (KJV) and check his accuracy.

6:15   Church Training (cancelled this coming week)

7:30   Evening Workshop
Invite your unsaved loved ones for this gripping true story of faithfulness through tribulation. We will watch The Hiding Place, the moving story of Corrie ten Boom's family, how they followed the Lord's leading and hid Jews from the Nazis during WWII, and about the price paid for their faithfulness as they were imprisoned in the concentration camps themselves for their faithfulness to Christ. You will not want to miss this inspiring true story of courage and perseverance in the face of evil, and of God's goodness.

Counting Committee: Colley Goins
Scott Driggers

When You Pass through the Waters

(James, 1983)

IT SNOWED all the way into March that year, and in early April the rain and snowmelt flowed down the mountain gullies into the Elk. James saw his opportunity to go whitewater rafting. He'd always wanted to go whitewater rafting like the older kids got to do on the New River with Pinewood Bible Camp's Outdoor Adventures. The Elk rushed and crashed like the New River with all the snowmelt, except the Elk was mud brown, and milky froth gathered in the tree-root eddies like dirty soap bubbles. It might have been soap bubbles. James knew of pipes that poured straight into the river from people's washing machines and toilets. His dad said it was against the law, but the older kind of people still did it.

He slipped out the back door of the parsonage and walked the parking lot behind the church. Two red canoes leaned upside down against the back of the old building. They were too heavy for him to drag by himself. The youth group had a yellow two-man raft they used in the pond at Pinewood Bible Camp. It was in the basement of the new building, in the heater room, where his dad hung his green baptizing waders on a door peg so that they thumped softly against the door when you opened it.

He had a secret entrance to the church basement. He had un-locked the window to the primary room, and he could lie on the ground beside it and let himself down onto the teacher's table against the wall. Once his foot landed on a stack of workbooks and they slid, making him fall and almost break his neck.

Inside the teacher's closet were Hershey bars he liked to snack on, and he took quarters out of the white plastic church bank they used to collect offering. It was not stealing. *Thou shalt not muzzle the ox*, 1 Timothy 5:18. James was a servant of God if anyone was, so this was his to partake of as long as he wasn't greedy.

He eased himself down onto the teacher's table and slid the window closed. The room was dark and spooky. The smell of river mud came up strong from the drain out in the hallway. He skipped the Hershey bars and money this time, went straight to the door, and peered down the dark hallway toward the heater room. The window in the top of the back door was a small square with wire inside the glass that made little diamond shapes. Through the window, he could see the wet cement steps of the stairwell where, just a couple days ago, Ricky had killed a river rat with a brick.

His sneakers slapped the floor and echoed up and down the empty hall as he ran to the heater room. His dad's baptizing waders swung and kicked him gently. He grabbed the bright yellow two-man raft and pushed it out the door into the stairwell. He slid his body around it and dragged it up the steps by the shiny black rope that went around the top through black plastic loops. He ran back down and slammed the door—he felt like an evil presence was coming down the hallway after him and he'd just saved himself with the door slam. It was hard to believe he had just come from there himself.

Back up the steps, James looked at the parsonage yard: the apple tree with gnarled bare limbs, toy trucks against the house, bicycles thrown against the fence. The kitchen window reflected black tree branches and bright white clouds against the blue. That was his next source of fear. If his mom happened to be in there watching him right now, she would tan his hide. The wind gusted past his ears. He could hear the muffled hiss of a car passing up on the blacktop road in front of the church. He grabbed the black rope and ran as best he could with the raft bouncing behind him, knocking against his heels.

The river had poured into the clearing on the other side of the church, and it looked like a muddy swamp with trees growing out of it along the creek. The softball backstop was half under water. The river itself rushed and splashed; scrap lumber, branches, and trash churned downstream. A white plastic jug with a blue cap and no label bounced on top of the water like an invisible foot was kicking it along.

At a tree, James put the raft on the water and held the rope. The raft bounced and jerked and almost pulled him in, so he backed up, dragging it onto the grassy hillside to rethink things. The ground was saturated and squished under his feet. His Keds and his pant legs were already soaked. He stared at the river. It heaved and churned, roiled, and crashed like a living thing in pain. It sounded like hundreds—thousands—of voices whisper-shouting. Maybe he could hear the spirit world, maybe he was that special. They wouldn't be ghosts, there was no such thing as ghosts, but demons and angels waged warfare all around. He stood and listened hard, to see if any message came through those hard whispering voices.

From upstream, the river barreled down the chute of the valley. The motion seemed to push at his body. He took a step back to keep from losing his balance and toppling into the water. He made his way to the claw tree, whose grabbing roots were now under water; it leaned out over the river. With all the rain and runoff, one big branch was only a little bit above the water. He put his hand on the trunk and tested it with one of his Keds. His wet pant leg pasted itself to his calf and made him shiver. He realized that his feet were also freezing cold. His Ked slid a little and stripped off bark, but then held. He hooked the raft rope in the crook of his arm and started climbing out.

His shoe slipped and he thudded to his stomach and chest and held on like a koala bear. He started shimmying his way out over the water. Rough tree bark dug at his chest and stomach through his shirt—he should have buttoned his jean jacket. No, the metal buttons would drag sideways and hurt even worse.

The water splashing below blew cold gusts of mist, chilling his wrists and face. The raft batted and bounced in the eddy that was calmer than out in the middle—it still yanked at his arm like Barnabas on a leash going after a rabbit. When he got to the branch, he hooked his left arm around it and his right foot into the raft. He looked down and watched the raft bounce around until he saw a kind of pattern: it dropped away to the left, bounced once, twice, and then it swooped back up in a circle to the right, hovered for a brief second, then fell away left again.

He drummed up his courage as he watched the raft bounce, circle, bounce, four times in the same pattern. The fifth time, as the raft dropped away and looped back around, James let go of the tree and dove out over the water where the raft would circle under him. Free of his holding it at the tree by the rope, the raft shot forward with the river's rush. For an instant James felt weightless, hovered in the air above the raft, and then its bright yellow disappeared from under his sprawling body, replaced by the white splashing foam and water so close he could feel the freezing cold of it on his face.

Clay Free Will Baptist Church—"A Church on the Move"
Clay, West Virginia
The Lord's Day, April 24, 1983

Good morning and welcome to Clay Free Will Baptist. We trust you will experience Jesus in a new and meaningful way this morning.

WORSHIP THROUGH PREPARATION:

The prelude:	"It Is Well with My Soul" Rachel Wright, piano Leah Wright, flute
The Call to Worship:	"Great Is Thy Faithfulness" Adult Choir

Greetings and Announcements
Opening Prayer

WORSHIP THROUGH MUSIC:
"What a Friend We Have in Jesus," page 114

WORSHIP THROUGH GIVING:

Offertory	"Be Thou My Vision" Rachel Wright, piano

WORSHIP THROUGH MUSIC:

"He Hideth My Soul"	Leah Wright flute Rachel Wright piano

WORSHIP THROUGH THE WORD:

Message:	"The Only True Comfort" Pastor Jeff

WORSHIP THROUGH SURRENDER:
Invitational Hymn, "The Comforter Has Come," page 98

BENEDICTION:

"O, That Will Be Glory for Me"	Rachel Wright, piano

TEAM SCHEDULES FOR NEXT WEEK
NURSERY:
May 1, Cindy Phelps & Amanda Davis
May 8, Tessie Davis & Arneda Sizemore

CHILDREN'S CHURCH MUSIC
May 1, Leah Wright & Rachel Wright
May 8, Vivian & Linda Mosely

SOUND BOOTH:
May 1, Steve Burgess
May 8, Steve Burgess
Ushers for Next Week, May 1

Weldon Davis	Steven Jarvis
Colley Goins	Scott Driggers

Door Greeters:

Weldon Davis	Doris Goins

THIS WEEK:
Tuesday, April 26
Team Visitation, meet at the church at 5:30 p.m.

Wednesday, April 27
Prayer Meeting starts at 7:00 p.m.
AWANA starts at 6:30 p.m.
Choir practice starts promptly at 8:00 p.m.

Thursday, April 28
Ladies Bible Study (bring workbook) 10:00 a.m. at Patty Wright's house

Pastor Minor and his family would like to thank our church family for the outpouring of love during this time. His strength truly is sufficient. You can find your dishes on the tract table in the foyer. Please continue to keep Pastor Minor and his family in your prayers during this time of tragedy and testing. They ask that they be given time to grieve privately as a family. Thanks to Pastor Jeff for stepping up and taking care of the pastoral duties. You truly are in capable and caring hands.

You are hereby invited to the wedding of Amanda Davis to Steven Jarvis here at the church, Saturday, May 13, at 3:00 p.m. A reception will follow immediately in the gym.

Those Who Mourn

(Berna, 1983)

ZECHARIAH CALLED off church altogether on the Sunday after James disappeared at the river. Church members, at the church and in various houses, held round-the-clock prayer vigils, taking one-hour shifts right through the night so there was not a single second when prayers for James were not being lifted to the Lord. Berna paced around the house, unable to sit, or stand, or do anything for long. She let her other children lounge on pillows in front of the television set hour after hour—it didn't seem to matter anymore.

Colley Goins, Glenwood Jarvis, Jim Miller, other men from the church, and four volunteer firemen from the Methodist church went to work down at the river. Officer Humphrey was down there too. For four endless days Berna and Miriam and Andrew and Ricky waited around the house. Berna kept thinking hour after hour that James would traipse through the back door like usual—maybe muddy, hungry—and this warped reality would reemerge. After she scolded him and hugged him and wept, life would go back to the way it was. The slow passing of time was a pressure that filled the house. It pressed against her body until she opened windows to relieve it, but the breeze was chilly, so she slid them down again. At some point, the strange waking dream settled into a crushing certainty that nobody would say out loud, but the looks on their faces said it all: James was dead.

At first, the men tried to drag the river as best they could from the banks and up on the bridge. They had to wait four days to get out on boats because the water was too rough, and it rained steady for two days, which made it all worse. Then they spanned the river with ropes tied to trees on either side and used them to pull their boats back and forth. Zechariah took his waders down, but nobody needed them, and they lay unused on the bank beside the other gear. The men were concentrating on the bend, and the beaver nests at the bridge, the two places things always got hung up. Zechariah came back and told her all this. She did not go to the river. She did not leave the house. They were looking for a dead body. For the waterlogged body of her son. Her James.

Two more days she and the kids waited. Zechariah tried to stay there but paced like a tiger in a cage. Eventually he went back to the river. He stood around on the muddy riverbank with the men, though they wouldn't let him in a boat. He helped where he could— got coffee, ran down to Clendenin for greasy bags of Tastee-Freez burgers and dogs.

Women on the river did their thing: they cooked and they loaded up Berna's kitchen with food. Jordan brought her baked apples, and the cloying cinnamon smell made Berna need to vomit. Jordan sat at the kitchen table drinking coffee, not saying anything at all, except to settle the kids or get them fed or off to bed. Berna still kept waiting for James to come in the door. He was going to come in the door, and this was all going to be a story they told for years, maybe even laughed about. James, her special boy. Her baby boy. He wasn't coming in the door. He was gone.

The way she and Jordan didn't talk about it only emphasized that they both knew the reality of the situation. Other kids had drowned in the river, usually in summer. It wasn't a surprising thing, not even news if it wasn't your own child, or a child you knew.

On Friday, one of the firemen found him. He was jammed in the logs and trash caught against the bridge, just like they'd thought all along. Even though she knew, it was like a horse kicked her in her chest. She tumbled from the bright tension of waiting into black grief and guilt. She went to bed.

Jordan had called in her personal days at Kroger and stayed the whole week. When they found James, she called in and took another week off. She took care of the kids while Berna was in her bed. She drove them around in her Jeep with the top off and the heater on. She took them to Tastee-Freez twice and then all the way down to the Dairy Queen by the Smith's grocery store in Big Chimney.

While Jordan was out in the living room with the kids—Berna could hear her strange deep-voiced talking to them and their high responses, just the voices, no words—Berna was in her bedroom confessing her sin and getting right with God. The room filled with the smell of Berna's unwashed body and the full laundry hamper. Zechariah crawled in bed with her at night and held her, then crawled back out in the morning. Berna stayed there.

Here's what Berna knew, knew beyond the shadow of a doubt: she was not saved; the Lord had never truly gotten hold of her heart. She had not repented and truly been forgiven that day back in 1968 when she'd decided to use church to get out of Ironton. The Lord had taken her James because of her sin with Jordan. This is what He'd had to use to get her attention. Her boy was dead because of her.

Jordan opened the bedroom door and stepped in. The smell of burnt toast and grape jelly wafted in with her. She quietly emptied the dirty clothes from the hamper into a laundry basket. Berna shifted to get a look at her, and Jordan stopped.

Jordan leaned over, touched her face gently, and said, "Hey, pretty lady."

Berna rolled over, didn't say anything. At that moment, she did not love Jordan anymore. She hated her, loathed her presence in the house. She had ended it already, and Jordan just didn't know.

Jordan sat on the bed and started rubbing Berna's back. Berna tensed up. Jordan gently rubbed and scratched for a long time. Berna waited. Then the bed rose as the weight of her body lifted. Her knee popped when she squatted and picked up the laundry. She pulled the door closed and Berna was again alone in the dark, smelly room.

In the middle of that night, Berna woke up and prayed, "Dear Father God, I repent of my sin, and I ask you in Jesus's name to save me. Lord come into my heart, change my heart, and give me a new heart and pure desires. Make me a godly wife and mother. I am so sorry. You didn't have to take my James. Wasn't there another way? Why, God? Why that innocent baby boy?"

She realized she was sobbing when Zechariah rolled over and wrapped her up in a hug that was awkward and painful because he'd slid his arm under her ribs. And his breath smelled of gift lasagna. He wept too, though, wept with her, the first time she'd ever known him to cry, even when his dad had died with the heart attack, and he'd even preached the funeral service. He wasn't preaching this one. Jeff was.

She turned to Zechariah and wrapped him in a deep hug of her own, a thing she did not normally do. She resolved then and there to turn her back on Jordan and their sinful relationship, to devote the rest of her life to God, to her husband, and to her family. She had a lot to pay for. Then, almost audibly, she heard the Spirit's urging, the still small voice in her head saying, *It starts here, in the marriage bed with your husband, your covenant partner.*

She kissed his mouth. He responded immediately, before he'd even stopped crying, kissed her back as he tugged at her nightgown. She shut down her mind and threw herself into it, and they fucked. They fucked hard but not long because she hadn't given him any for a while. Then they lay beside one another silent and spent and both drifted into grieving sleep.

The funeral was a hazy dream, though the day was crisp and clear and bright. Zechariah had tried to talk them into singing "It Is Well with My Soul" as a family, but Berna refused. Jordan was there, and she came through and gave them all hugs, and was at the graveside service on the hillside graveyard overlooking Clay High School; behind that was the river where James had died. The sun flashed up off the water down there between the trees. Jordan kept looking at Berna, trying to get her attention, make eye contact. Berna did not let it happen. She was strong in her resolve. She had died to the flesh.

On her way to the car after the graveside service, she noticed that Jordan was maybe not doing as all right as she seemed, was not as strong as she'd made herself out to be. She wore her dark taupe gabardine pantsuit, the one she kept for such occasions, the one with the shoulders squared off by pads and the lapel that started on her right breastbone and crossed over her front to button at her left hip. That wasn't out of the ordinary.

The problem was her shoes. Jordan had put on one black and one brown shoe. They weren't even the same style. There she stood in her mismatched shoes. It was such a pathetic sight that Berna started crying again and wanted to run to her and hold her and tell her it would be okay. She did not however make the slightest gesture toward Jordan. She stayed strong in the Lord.

She let herself be led into the back of the funeral home car with the children, and Zechariah got in front. The children sat staring ahead. They were in shock. She supposed she was too; maybe Zechariah was, maybe not.

Zechariah said from the front seat, "Jeff's sermon was good."

Zechariah had been overly gentle and affectionate with her since the other night. She knew he sensed that things had changed

between them for the better and he was glad of it. She could tell he
knew it was because of what happened to James because he was tentative about it, wanting to be romantic with her, but not wanting to be
unseemly about it. How was it that a person could grieve the loss of a
child and at the same time take real pleasure in what had come about
as a result of it? Nothing made sense—nothing even seemed real.

The man from the funeral home agreed with Zechariah about
the sermon. He was a little man, had a big mustache, looked like he
colored it black. He was bald all the way to the base of his skull bone
but had this little strip of hair there that could have been another
mustache, except it had gray and brown mixed in with the black hairs.
Over the past three days she had seen him pop a cinnamon Certs into
his mouth from a red roll in his blazer pocket five different times. He
did have a nice smell about him though.

Nodding profusely, he said of Jeff, "I don't have to tell you, children's funerals are the hardest ones to do." Then he seemed to remember that he was with the family of the deceased, not just talking
shop with a preacher. He quickly added, "It's good that you all have
people who love you and support you. A lot of support. That sure is
a blessing to have."

In the church basement, the all-purpose room, the ladies had set
out on the long tables with what looked like more food than the
whole church could have eaten in a week. Berna heard the funeral
director telling Zechariah that he knew it would be hard, but he had
to get all James's stuff out of the bedroom he'd shared with the other
boys. "Bed and all," he said. "For those two boys' sake." He nodded
toward Ricky and Andrew, who were at the table helping themselves
to more than their share of deviled eggs, and no one was stopping
them this time. The man said, "Helps them move on faster, trust me."

All the core families were there, the deacons and trustees and their families. Others, too, people Berna recognized but didn't know. It was so crowded she got dizzy and had to sit for most of the time.

Zechariah stood and invited people to share memories of James. Most people spoke of how smart he was. Andrew stood and said he and James loved playing at the river, fishing, and floating on inner tubes. When it seemed clear no one else was going to say anything, Zechariah broke into "It Is Well with My Soul" on his own. He started in a soft voice, "When peace like a river attendeth my way," and wailed out the next words like he'd just been stabbed, "When sorrows like sea billows roll."

Berna hated him in that moment. Even the death of his son was just another chance for him to perform, to be the center of attention. Not that she ever wanted to be—Lord knows she didn't—but when he turned on the preacher, it went all through her, and she couldn't bear to be near him. His performance had its intended effect. People started crying. Berna did too, she couldn't help it. Her boy was gone. It was her fault. She longed more than anything to go to Jordan, to hold her love who did not—could not—belong to this moment. Jordan was off on her own, probably hiking up the ridge, and the thought of Jordan by herself out in those woods made Berna cry harder.

When Zechariah had sung through the entire song, he said, "The Lord giveth and the Lord taketh away. Blessed be the name of the Lord."

Clay Free Will Baptist Church—"A Church on the Move"
Clay, West Virginia
The Lord's Day, May 15, 1983

Good morning and welcome to Clay Free Will Baptist. We trust you will experience Jesus Christ in a new and meaningful way this morning.

WORSHIP THROUGH PREPARATION:

The prelude:	"How Great Thou Art" Rachel Wright
The Call to Worship:	"The Lord Is My Shepherd," Jessie Irvine, composer Adult Choir

"All Hail the Power of Jesus' Name" page 200

Greetings and Announcements
Opening Prayer

WORSHIP THROUGH MUSIC:

"Savior Like a Shepherd Lead Us," page 222

WORSHIP THROUGH GIVING:

Tithes and offerings

Offertory	"St. Matthew Passion" Leah Wright, flute Rachel Wright, piano

WORSHIP THROUGH MUSIC:

"Sing Your Praise to the Lord"	Amanda Davis, soloist Rachel Wright, piano

WORSHIP THROUGH THE WORD:

Scripture Reading:	John 24:20-29
Message:	Don't Make God "Prove It" Pastor Jeff

WORSHIP THROUGH SURRENDER:

Invitational Hymn, "I Surrender All," page 213

BENEDICTION:

Closing chorus:	"How Majestic Is Your Name" (see insert for words)

TEAM SCHEDULES FOR NEXT WEEK

NURSURY:
May 22, Sandy & Cindy Phelps
May 29, Tessie & Amanda Davis

CHILDREN'S CHURCH MUSIC
May 22, Vivian & Linda Mosely
May 29, Vivian & Linda Mosely

SOUND BOOTH:
May 22, Weldon Davis
May 29, Scott Driggers

Ushers for Next Week, May 22

Tom Friend	Weldon Davis
Colley Goins	Scott Driggers

Door Greeters:

Wolfe Counts	Larry Jackson
Kyle Mullens	Rachel Wright

THIS WEEK:

Tuesday, May 17
Team Visitation, meet at the church at 5:30 p.m.

Wednesday, May 18
Prayer Meeting starts at 7:00 p.m.
AWANA starts at 6:30 p.m.
Choir practice starts promptly at 8:00 p.m.

Thursday, May 19
Ladies Bible Study (bring workbook) 10:00 a.m. at Tessie Davis's house

Pastor Minor and his family would again like to thank our church family for the outpouring of love and support in this time of loss. We hold onto the promise that James is asleep in Jesus so we do not have to grieve as those who have no hope. Thanks be to God for his mercy endures forever.

Ask, and It Will Be Given to You

(Andrew Philip Minor, 1983)

TWO WEEKS after James's funeral, Andrew has his first day back in school. During Social Studies class, while Mrs. Combs talks about the different kinds of government—absolute monarchy, dictatorship, democracy, communism—Andrew daydreams. He can't stop thinking about the stupid girl shoes on his feet.

Fuzzy blue on the sides, shiny blue on top, he hates the shoes. He hates his mom for making him wear them to school. He thinks that if any boy calls him a queer like Mr. Cox—who Ronnie Stewart said lets other men put their dicks in his butt—Andrew will bust his head, and he'll get away with it too, this time, because of what happened to James.

Then the Lord impresses a verse of Scripture on his heart, one he'd memorized for AWANA last year while trying to get his Timothy Award: *Ask, and it will be given to you; seek, and you will find; knock, and it will be opened to you.* What he wants more than anything in the world is to have those blue shoes off his feet and baseball cleats on.

He remembers how Jesus said in Matthew 17:20 that if he has faith the size of a mustard seed he can say to a mountain, *"Move from here to there,"* and it will move; and nothing will be impossible for you.

Then the Lord puts a hymn they sing in church into his head—it is a miracle happening, he knows it—and he can see and hear in his mind his dad out beside the pulpit, waving his arms all weird like he's cursive writing on the air, his voice bellowing it out: *Nothing is impossible, when you put your trust in God . . . Listen to the voice of God to thee, is there anything too hard for me?*

Andrew has more than a mustard seed's worth of faith. He is all faith. Jesus will do it for a boy who believes like he does. Jesus rose Lazarus from the dead, Jesus rose himself from the dead. Andrew doesn't want a mountain moved. All he wants is his old blue girl shoes to turn into baseball cleats on his feet. Easy for Jesus to do.

Mrs. Combs is now talking about the Magna Carta, which took absolute power away from the king and gave it to regular people. All the kids are tired from just eating lunch. They're slouched and still, except for Georgie Porgie Shamblin who is against the back wall twirling his hair. There is a pipe behind his head with insulation on it wrapped and hard like a long cast, only yellow, not white. Georgie Porgie is digging at it with his pencil and flakes of stuff glisten like fairy dust in the air beside his ear.

"Forty-one of the men aboard signed the Mayflower Compact," Mrs. Combs says. She says, "A compact is an agreement, or a contract."

Tall windows go along the whole wall of the classrooms in the upstairs part of the gym where the middle and high schoolers have classes. The kindergartners are out on the playground beside the church building in the bright sunshine. The kindergarten teacher, Mrs. Dye, has on a tight skirt and wobbles silently among them on her high heels.

Andrew closes his eyes and starts praying his effectual fervent prayer: "Dear heavenly Father," he prays, "I come to you today in the name of Jesus, to claim your promise that if I have faith, and ask, You will do what I ask." He prays, "Father God, please turn these girl shoes into baseball cleats, and I will not forget to give You all the honor, all the glory, and all the praise. I ask these things in the name of our Lord and Savior, Jesus Christ. Amen."

The day before, after Sunday school and morning worship, Andrew had watched out the front window as Harry Taylor walked across the church parking lot after the rain stopped and knocked on his door.

Andrew opened it and Harry said, "I was thinking we could trade shoes for a while." He looked down as he talked. He smelled like dog crotch. There was a dirty sweat ring around his neck.

Andrew could see how Harry would be nice to him. Harry's dad had recently died, except he'd killed himself in jail, so he was in hell. Andrew's brother James had been saved and was in heaven with Jesus. Still, Andrew could see how Harry would be nice.

All the other boys in the neighborhood were being nice to him too since James drowned. Andrew hadn't been picked on or got in a single fight since that day. It was one more thing, like the sudden absence of James, that made Andrew believe the fundamental order of the universe had shifted.

The neighborhood boys, from Harry across the parking lot to the ones in the row of houses along the riverbank to the bridge—Jimmy Gillenwater, Ronnie Stewart, the Jacksons—were dirty, mean boys, on the welfare. They were stupid too, retards, impossible to talk sense to. They were like the Gillenwaters' pit bull that one time who had held Andrew at bay across the wide puddle in the dirt road. Andrew kept saying, "Go home, Harley. Go home," trying to sound mean, but the dog barked at him and stood there smiling with his tongue out, his eyes staring blank, like he didn't know one damn thing in the world but how to bite Andrew.

The Jackson boys always had their heads shaved bald, so kids said they had lice. They had Frankenstein foreheads and confused eyes, and if you tackled them or punched them in a fight, they didn't even feel it. Larry Jackson was in Andrew's class. His brother Robbie was in James's. Those two boys played outside in the cold without coats on and their arms would be all red and chapped looking, but they were like dogs; they didn't even know they were cold. Harry Taylor was like that too: Andrew once saw him wipe out on his bike. The whole side of his leg and his arm were scraped and bleeding, and he just stood there grinning, saying, "Shit," and "Goddamn," and "It don't hurt."

There stood Harry, ready to trade his baseball cleats for Andrew's Keds for a while. Andrew wanted those cleats. He'd been asking his mom for baseball cleats for months—he had begged, even cried one night at the dinner table—but she told him no. Harry's cleats were black plastic with a white stripe on them. The left one had a split on the toe that, when Harry stepped down, opened like a puppet mouth and showed his dirty sock.

"You want to trade for real?" Andrew asked. "You're not messing around?"

"Yeah," Harry said. He kicked them off and stood there in his mud-stained socks. He nodded hard. There was a scar above his left eyebrow. His eyes were pretty if you looked at them—handsome, not pretty; girls were pretty, boys were handsome.

"Okay," Andrew said. He sat on the front porch beside Harry and put on the cleats while Harry put on his Keds and pulled the laces so tight Andrew thought he might break them or cut off the circulation to his toes.

"We're going to play Indian ball," Harry said. "Or a real game if we get enough people."

"I'll play," Andrew said.

Andrew spent the entire afternoon in the clearing playing baseball in the cleats. His hits were solid, he stole bases and slid like Pete Rose, he ran down crazy-far pop flies. Once he heaved the ball from center field all the way over bald-headed Larry Jackson on second to Ronnie Stewart at home plate with only one bounce. He lost himself in baseball.

Then his mom called him in to get ready for evening church. He ran in and said, "Can I wear these cleats to night church?"

She frowned at them.

"Please, mom." His church shoes were shiny blue and had squared-off toes and fat heels. Kids at church teased him, called them girl shoes.

She sighed and shook her head and left the kitchen, but did not say no, which meant if he didn't mention it again, just did it, she wouldn't give him a switching. He chewed his peanut butter bread, swallowed it with milk, and tapped drumbeats on the linoleum kitchen floor with the cleats. If he rolled his feet heel-to-toe he could sound like a bunch of running horses.

The next morning was Andrew's first day back at school after James drowned. It had taken the men dragging the river four days to find him in a bunch of brush piled against the bridge piling because the snow melt had the water so high. The funeral had been on the next Saturday, and Andrew had stayed out for a week after that, eating food people brought and watching television. Now he had to go back. It felt like the first day of school all over again, like he'd been gone for a whole summer.

He climbed from the top bunk and stepped down onto James's bunk, then jumped to the floor. He put on his school clothes and then sat on the floor beside the baseball cleats. He pulled them on and carefully tied the frayed laces. Ricky was still asleep in his bed, his mouth open and flat on the mattress like a cat killed out on the blacktop road. Andrew could smell the number one. Ricky peed his bed again.

His mom and Miriam were in the kitchen and didn't even glance up as he strode in like Johnny Bench, his cleats clicking across the linoleum.

"You're up early, Drew," Miriam said. She had on her denim school culottes and her powder-blue Pinewood Bible Camp sweatshirt. She was at the counter packing their lunches. Three bags were lined in front of her, hers, Andrew's, and little Ricky's.

"You can sleep a little longer," his mom said. She was still in her nightgown that was thin as a slip. Usually she was up and dressed, with her hair all done and makeup on, even though she never had anywhere to go all day.

"Ricky did number one in his bed again."

His mom didn't say anything. She put two pieces of bread in the toaster and stood staring at it. Andrew sat at his place and waited. He swung his leg and clinked his cleat against the aluminum table leg.

The toast popped up. His mom buttered them by rubbing the butter stick right on the bread. She put them on a white plastic plate with flowers on it and set it in front of Andrew with a jar of grape jelly. She pulled open the drawer and got a spoon and set it by the jelly jar.

He jellied his toast—the jelly was purpler than usual and glistened like slime. His mom put a cup of milk, a sippy cup with the top off, in front of him and went into the bathroom and shut the door.

There was a hard knock at the front door.

"Get that," Miriam said.

"Why can't you?"

"I'm making your lunch."

He walked to the front door and opened it. It was just getting light outside. Harry Taylor stood at the door, a pink strip of sky above the mountain behind his head. He had on his *Keep On Trucking* tee shirt with the walking man's big foot coming forward like it was going to step right off the shirt. The neck was all stretched out already. He had on Andrew's Keds. They were muddy and wet.

"We have to trade shoes back," he said.

"It's just been one day," Andrew said. "How 'bout after school."

Harry shook his head. "My mom said." He still smelled like dog crotch.

"But you got mine all wet."

"Creek last night. Almost caught a duck with my bare hands." Harry held out his hands like he was holding a duck. He had a retard smile.

"I'm not trading back till mine are dry," Andrew said.

"My mom said," Harry nearly yelled.

"What's the problem here?" Andrew's mom said from behind him.

"My mom said we had to trade shoes back and Andrew won't do it."

His mom looked at the cleats on his feet, then at the muddy Keds. She said, "Andrew, trade Harry back his shoes."

With the heel of opposite feet Harry pushed his heels out of the Keds, one then the other. He stood flat-footed in his muddy socks. The smell of river mud rose from them and mixed with Harry's own stink.

"But mom," Andrew whined. "He got mine all wet and muddy."

"Obedience is?" she said.

He kicked off the cleats and flipped them out onto the porch. Harry picked them up and sat on the steps and put them on.

"You can wear your church shoes to school today."

"No." Andrew started crying. "I'll wear them wet."

"One day in church shoes won't kill you," she said. He could tell by her tone that the discussion was over. She said, "March up this minute and put them on."

———

As Andrew walked down the hallway of ERCS, the other students watched him pass like they were under a spell because it was his first day back and James wasn't with him like he always was. A couple of them glanced down at his blue shoes and his face filled with heat.

Leah Wright was against the wall. She had a fat round face with lots of freckles, and her hair cut short, which made her face look even fatter. Andrew hated her and she hated him too, he was pretty sure. She'd been around a lot the past two weeks and things with her had gotten back to normal pretty fast.

She smirked at him. He clenched his fists—he didn't hit girls, but she made him want to.

Cindy Rogers said, "Hi, Andrew." She reached out to touch his arm, and then pulled her hand back. She was tall and pretty and her mom curled her dark hair and made her walk funny to practice for beauty contests. Kids said she smeared dog poop on her face because she thought it made her skin pretty. That's why nobody would touch her, or they would catch Cindy germs and have to tag them off on another kid before they had a chance to yell out, "Shots."

When he saw her reach out, Andrew stepped back and put his hands on his shoulders and said, "Shots."

"You are so mature." She turned and walked her swaying walk into the classroom. She had to turn sideways to get by Jimmy Gillenwater and Larry Jackson, who were making fun of Georgie Porgie Shamblin. Georgie had a habit of twisting the hair above his left ear so much that he had a bald spot there. He got out of music class to talk to a man in the school counselor's office on Thursdays.

As Cindy passed by Larry, she said, "Move, Frankenstein."

He called her a bitch but moved and let her pass. Then he turned and looked at Andrew. Ronnie turned his head and looked at Andrew too.

Andrew felt his church shoes heavy on his feet, like those wooden shoes Dutch people wore. He ached to be out of them. He longed to have on baseball cleats.

Leah walked over to Larry and Ronnie—she didn't even like those retards—and she said, "Andrew is wearing his *girl* shoes."

"Shut up, pie head," Andrew said.

"Girl shoes," she said back.

Mr. Cox stepped out of the sixth graders' classroom holding a stapler and said, "What's the problem out here?" Mr. Cox was a youth pastor at a church in Charleston and drove up the river to teach. He had on parachute pants, all slick with zippers on them, and shoes he called turtles that had Velcro straps instead of laces. His dark hair was cut up over his ears but long in back and he had a big mustache. Ronnie Stewart called those shiny pants Mr. Cox's queer pants. Ronnie knew about sex. He had, folded up in his shoe, real pictures he'd stolen out of his dad's magazines. He showed them to the other boys in the bathroom.

"Get to your classrooms," Mr. Cox said. "Where's Mrs. Combs?"

"Not here," Larry said.

"Late," Leah said.

Mr. Cox shook his head. "Go on," he said. "Get in there and find your desks, or I'm going to start writing referrals." When his gaze fell on Andrew, his expression went blank for an instant, then he walked over—with all the kids watching, and Andrew in his girl shoes—and put his hand on Andrew's shoulder.

"I'm sorry about James, Andrew," he said. "I am so sorry."

"If anybody calls my shoes queer shoes, I'm going to bust his head open. I don't care if it is a girl."

"Violence is never the answer, Andrew." Mr. Cox patted his shoulder. "Go on, now. Get to class."

Andrew squirmed through the morning in his blue shoes. He watched Larry Jackson pick a slimy booger and take almost all of math class, concentrating like he was playing Operation, to wipe it into Cindy Rogers's curls without her or Mrs. Combs noticing. In Language Arts, Andrew doodled on his worksheet instead of doing his work. He went to lunch with his fists ready to punch anybody who so much as snickered at him. He pretended to play his trumpet in band. Scotty Driggers was the only other trumpet, so it was obvious he wasn't playing. Nobody bothered him. They had to sit in chairs in a circle back at the reading rug for English class. He pulled his feet under the chair so he couldn't see the damn shoes.

Now he is back in the classroom, the Lord has just put the Bible verses in his head, and he has just said his effectual fervent prayer for the miracle God has promised him. He feels a change around his feet and rises close enough to the surface of his daydream to be aware of the classroom around him, but he doesn't come out of it. He knows the transformation is happening, the miracle he's asked for. Ronnie Stewart looks at Andrew's shoes for a long time, and then looks up at Andrew. His face looks surprised. Andrew knows it is happening. He sneers at Ronnie. Ronnie slouches down more and puts his face in his open hand and yawns.

"So, it was the rule of law," Mrs. Combs says, "and not the whims—whatever he decided to do simply because he wanted to, and he was king—of an all-powerful King over in England." Mrs. Combs sits on the edge of her desk in front of the class. She has big fat boobs and presses the open blue Civics book against them while she talks. "The rule of law is what is important to remember," she says. On the front of the book there is a big star painted like an American flag.

Andrew dives back into his daydream, sees himself hitting home runs at the little league field beside the junior high. He jogs around the bases in his new cleats. Moms and dads stand in the bleachers and clap. He sees himself at shortstop, diving and snagging line drives because the cleats on his feet have been made by God and give him extra-special traction.

After the game people will gather around him to ask how he did it and he will say I give the glory to God. He does all good things for his children, gives them fish not snakes. Get saved, he will say, get saved, all of you.

His spirit soars. He believes with his whole heart, beyond the shadow of a doubt, that God has done what he, in all good faith according to God's promise, has asked. They are brand new, and leather, not like Harry's cheap old plastic ones.

Mrs. Combs snaps her book closed and stands. Kids sit up straight, close their books, and lean over to shove them back under their desks. Mrs. Combs says, "Line up at the door for recess."

It is time. Andrew closes his Civics book and leans over. He looks at his shoes.

Andrew's heart jumps up into his throat and he gasps. It feels like he's falling off a cliff.

Goddamned blue shoes. Motherfucking girl shoes.

The class lines up at the door. Desk legs scrape on the floor, paper rattles in desks. Sneakers squeak. Larry goes to the closet and gets the kickball. Mrs. Combs turns off the light. The wall of windows goes blinding bright, shines on Andrew like a mute accusing stare.

Andrew pushes himself up from the desk. He stands beside it with his arms hanging. He looks at the blue shoes. They look black in the dark room. Anger rises inside his chest. God has all the power in the world and could do this one little thing for Andrew and won't.

Andrew's eyes adjust as he pushes down the urge to cry. Damn them. Damn them all straight to hell. He'll show them queer girl

232 / VIC SIZEMORE

shoes. Square toes are perfect for kickball. He'll boot it over the fence into the street. Better yet, he'll knock the ball down the bank into the river and end the game for good.

He looks out the windows. The playground is empty in the bright sunlight. The swings hang still. A balled-up jean jacket is on the ground beside the monkey bars.

Book Three

Clay Free Will Baptist Church—"A Church on the Move"
Clay, West Virginia
Easter Sunday, April 22, 1984

Good morning and welcome to Clay Free Will Baptist. We trust you will experience the Holy Spirit in a new and meaningful way this morning.

WORSHIP THROUGH PREPARATION:

The prelude:	"Near the Cross" Patty Wright
The Call to Worship:	Praise Band will lead Words will be on the overhead
Opening Prayer	Pastor Jeff Wright

WORSHIP THROUGH MUSIC:

"Friends," Michael W. Smith	Leah Wright, soprano Rachel Wright, alto and piano
"Oh Lord You're Beautiful," Keith Green	(see insert) Rachel Wright, piano

WORSHIP THROUGH GIVING:

Offertory:	"Great Is the Lord," Michael W. Smith piano duet Patty and Rachel Wright

WORSHIP THROUGH MUSIC:

"When I Hear the Praises Start," Keith Green	Amanda Davis, soloist Rachel Wright, piano

WORSHIP THROUGH THE WORD:

Message:	"The Rest Is Up to You" Pastor Jeff

WORSHIP THROUGH SURRENDER:

Invitational Hymn, "I Will Arise and Go to Jesus," page 221

BENEDICTION:

Closing chorus:	"I Have Decided to Follow Jesus," page 112

TEAM SCHEDULES
NURSURY:
May 6, Sandy & Cindy Phelps
May 13, Tessie & Amanda Davis & Arneda Sizemore

CHILDREN'S CHURCH MUSIC
May 6, Leah Wright & Sally Friend
May 13, Vivian & Linda Mosely

Ushers for Next Week, May, 6
Tom Friend   Weldon Davis
Colley Goins   Scott Driggers

Door Greeters:
Wolfe Counts   Larry Collins
Kyle Mullens

THIS WEEK:
Tuesday, April 24
Team Visitation, meet at the church at 5:30 p.m.
Praise band practice, 7:00 p.m.

Wednesday, April 25
Prayer Meeting starts at 7:00 p.m.
AWANA starts at 6:30 p.m.
Choir practice starts promptly at 8:00 p.m.

Thursday, April 26

HIGH SCHOOLERS!
The place to be is at......the inaugural YoungLife party at Pastor Jeff's Pad. More fun than you can shake a stick at. If you miss it your friends will just have to tell you about all the fun we have planned.

Ladies Bible Study (bring workbook) 10:00 a.m. at Patty Wright's house

MARK YOUR CALENDAR:
The God Save America Rally with Harold G. Perkins and the Sounds of Freedom Chorale, Saturday, June 16. If you plan to ride on one of the church busses, please sign up at the tract table in the vestibule.

Work Out Your Own Salvation

(Berna, 1984–1990)

IN THE days following James's death, instead of spending his days in the church office and his nights out on visitation, Zechariah moped around the house, his sudden presence strange and off-putting to Berna, feeling sorry for himself because he'd lost his favorite child— even the other kids knew it was true, James was his favorite. Then he'd sat at the kitchen table and wept one night, telling Berna it'd all been his fault James died, because the Lord had to use something drastic to get his attention.

"The Lord tells us, that nobody who puts his hand to the plow and looks back is fit for the Kingdom of God," he said. "When I put my hand to the plow thirty years ago, and I laid my idol music on the altar of sacrifice, I looked back, I didn't turn my back on music. I made a promise to God I couldn't keep. I was so weak."

He sobbed with his head on his arms and it annoyed Berna, went all through her. Nothing he did ever felt like it was coming from a genuine, unselfconscious place—except when he wanted sex; he was as earnest as a child then—and no matter what he was saying, the sound of his voice rang false like a performance for other people.

She wanted to tell him it wasn't music he should have put on that altar way back then, but instead, she said, "'In my weakness I am strong.' Isn't His power made perfect in our weakness?" She could use Scripture too when she needed to.

"Paul's talking about physical infirmities there. This is different."

She preheated the oven and slid in a Stouffer's lasagna while he wallowed in self-pity. It wore her out just to be around him when he was like this. Anyway, blame for James's death fell squarely on her, not on him. She was the absent mother, the neglectful parent. She was the unfaithful wife. The perverted chaser after strange flesh—and the hole in her life where Jordan had once been gaped so much larger, so much more painfully, than the one where James had been. When she thought of it, she wanted to go to bed and never get up again. She managed simply to say, "Music ministry is ministry too."

"I made a promise to God," Zechariah repeated. "I broke that promise. 'Be not deceived; God is not mocked.'"

As always, she let it drop. She imagined that if one day she decided to keep a disagreement over doctrine going until Zechariah called it quits, they would both starve to death arguing, and he would spend his final breath hammering home an obscure point of theology. She didn't have the energy for it.

In the following days, Zechariah plunged headfirst into hyper-Calvinism. He drove all the way down to Charleston, to this Christian bookstore called Cokesbury, and bought himself a fat blue book called *Systematic Theology* by a man named Louis Berkhof. He studied that book like it was his second Bible. He underlined, filled up the margins with his own chicken scratch, kept a notebook that he scrawled in as he read and reread.

Before that book changed his mind, Zechariah's reading had focused on soul winning, books like *How to Lead Someone to Christ, Let's Go Soul Winning, The Art of Fishing for Men*, and *Seeking the Lost*. Those books disappeared in short order and were replaced by *The Case for Calvinism, Institutes of the Christian Religion*, and

The Bondage of the Will. Zechariah's obsession shifted from soul winning to winning arguments about theology. Whereas he once drove around Clay County trying to win souls and get them into the church, now he drove down the Elk River to that bookstore, spent money on theology books like normal men did on souped-up cars, porno, and booze. The upshot of it all was that Zechariah changed his mind about a lot of things, and that changed his preaching in ways the congregation could not countenance.

This caused all the hullabaloo at Clay Free Will Baptist, all the backstabbing and infighting—Jordan had stepped down as AWANA Commander during this time, had quit church altogether. The church almost split over Calvinism, families started leaving, and Scott Driggers and Colley Goins almost came to blows in the vestibule one morning before church. Then the deacons met with Zechariah and said they'd voted that it was time for him to move on to another church, one that believed the way he did now. He should have known how they would react; the warning was right there in the church's name: *Free Will.*

All the stink was about whether a person had the freedom to choose their own fate, or if God had predestined who He would save and who He would damn and it was already a done deal. Zechariah had come to believe that it was God who did the choosing and humans couldn't do a thing to change it. Best you could do was hope you were among the chosen; if you weren't, tough shit. The church men—it was only the men who were up in arms over this—found it offensive, un-American, smacking of communism, to even suggest God was the kind of God who would take away people's freedom.

As far as Berna could see, since it was God who formed you in your mother's womb and knew your secret thoughts, and God could do anything He wanted and nobody could stop Him, there wasn't a lot of difference. The argument was a silly one to her, not something to break off fellowship with a person over or fire a man who had a wife and kids to feed.

That's what Colley and the other deacons did, though, and there Berna was, driving their van out of Clay County in the rain, and she felt a despair that bordered on panic. She and Jordan had made furtive, longing eye contact through the butcher shop glass at the Kroger a few times, but they had not spoken. She had entertained dreams of their meeting up secretly. Things between them were left unfinished. They needed to talk. She wanted to hold Jordan again, and be held by her, and the possibility of that life fell behind her mile by mile, though she knew it had always been an impossible dream.

On the front bench seat Miriam slumped over on her purple pillow, her legs still hanging down. The non-frosted edges of her strawberry Pop Tart lay on the torn silver wrapper by her stringy brown hair. The boys were sleeping on the bench seats behind Miriam. Andrew was in his favorite tattered Cincinnati Reds tee shirt, Johnnie Bench number five, faded almost to pink, which he had become inseparable from like that cartoon kid, Linus, with his security blanket. For Ricky, it was his guitar, which Zechariah still hadn't bought him a case for, so he'd bundled it up in his blue sleeping bag and insisted on carrying it himself so it wouldn't be damaged in the move. Chiquita banana boxes full of linens and clothes blocked the back windows.

It would be that easy, she thought. They could all die right there, and Zechariah could drive on into his future, into his glorious calling, without them holding him back, and give a new, powerful testimony of how the Lord gives strength in times of suffering and all that. Over and over, she determined she was going to do it *now*, and then *now*, and for real this time, *now*. But her arms did not obey; they kept fighting with the loose steering wheel, so the van held its precarious course behind the U-Haul. At Mink Shoals, Zechariah slowed the

U-Haul and pulled into the turn lane as he passed under the inter-state bridge. The rain let up as she followed him up the ramp, out of that deep river valley, into a space where she could see more than just a sliver of sky. Big buildings came into view.

It was Charleston. They drove by the GoMart and a Rite Aid store with a police car in the parking lot. They drove by a brown dog standing soaked in the emergency lane watching traffic. Zechariah had convinced the kids that their dog Barnabas needed to stay in the country; he'd never be a city dog. He now lived on a farm out Big Otter. That old brown dog was watching traffic, looking for a chance to cross. City dog, adapted to city life. Zechariah was right about Barnabas.

They reached a place where Berna could see down where the muddy Elk flowed in a blooming brown cloud out into the gray water of the wider Kanawha. They passed a chemical plant over the hill by the river, pipes snaking all around metal buildings and storage tanks and smokestacks, like the back of the giant, ripped-open transistor radio. Exhaust pipes stuck up like middle fingers, smoked or steamed. One of them shot fire out the top. The river mud smell of the Elk was replaced by the biting stink of chemicals.

She followed on, followed as the U-Haul swung down a curv-ing off ramp in Dunbar, followed as it drove again, followed over a humped bridge, and finally, followed when it turned slowly into the parking lot of a huge church across a gritty four-lane from the Kanawha, a parking lot full of people waiting to welcome them. This was the first time Berna and the kids had seen the place. Zechariah had rushed his candidacy and taken the first offer he got.

This church was Reformed Baptist, what Zechariah called him-self now, and had lost their pastor over the same controversy that had gotten him kicked out of Clay Free Will, except here it was the church—or a man named Lowell Green, who Berna could see right away was the Colley Goins of this church; pastors would come and go but this was the man in control—that had changed to Calvinism and the preacher who had stayed free will and been thrown out on his ear. She knew now it was just what Baptist churches did, they fought, they kicked out preachers, they split, and suddenly there were two Baptist churches close together where there'd been one.

Lowell was tall and thin, but muscular, in an army green tee shirt tucked into blue jeans with a belt that matched his brown boat shoes. He had gray military-short hair, was a Major in the National Guard out at Coonskin. He flew one of those fat green cargo planes, which, as far as Berna was concerned, made him just a delivery driver in the sky. Owned his own construction contracting company in real life. Apparently, he had a lot of money.

"Okay," she said to the kids, "put on your smiles." She stepped down out of the van and closed the door behind her. A woman held a tray of treats wide and reached around Berna with her other arm.

"What a beautiful family," the woman said. Hugging Berna like they were old girlfriends, she said, "We think so much of Pastor Minor. He's made a real impression on us already."

The mist was cold on Berna's face. It felt good. The woman smelled like Breck hairspray—she'd given her hair a heavy spray that morning and the wet air was making a mess of it. She didn't seem to care. "He told us his wife was pretty as Miss America," she said. "He wasn't lying."

The kids walked around the van. Women converged on them, hugging them, stepping back to have a look, asking names and ages and interests. Ricky held his guitar in front of him so no one could hug him. Zechariah's voice blended with other men's voices over in front of the U-Haul. They were looking at the parsonage, pointing. One of them said, "We've been praying that the Lord would give us a break in the rain, and just before you pulled in, it stopped."

He said it like the Lord had stopped the rain just for them, right there in the parking lot of Tabernacle Baptist Church.

"Common grace," Lowell Green said, seemingly out of nowhere. Then he explained, "He sends his rain on the just and the unjust," which still didn't seem to fit anywhere into the conversation, so awkward and out of place, his trying to sound smart. Trying so hard to impress Zechariah. The man was insufferable. She disliked him intensely already.

Letting up on the hug, the woman leaned back and looked straight at Berna and said so earnestly, "You just don't know how happy we are to have you here."

Berna had to respond. She felt like she had a stone in her throat, that she couldn't possibly say a word without gagging. She prayed for strength; she took a deep breath and swallowed that stone down. She smiled and said, "We're happy to be here."

The woman hugged her again. She said, "I made baklava."

"Oh, wonderful," Berna said. She didn't know what baklava was, but it had to be food. She thought of Jordan again, and her dead son, and it felt she was using her last ounce of strength simply to keep from collapsing onto the wet asphalt. Lowell Green was now explaining to the man who had said God stopped the rain for them, "All creation enjoys common grace, the sun and the rain, and a glass of single malt Scotch. Only the elect enjoy special, *saving*, grace."

"Would you like some baklava?" The woman smiled at her hopefully.

Lowell said, "Atonement is limited, my friend. Not all are allowed in, and not all should be." He was talking not just to the man, but loud, to be heard far and wide. His voice boomed out, "Isn't that right, Pastor Minor?"

Berna could see right away that the man wasn't just unlikable, he wasn't a good person. Quite likely, eventually, she'd have to insist

Zechariah lock horns with him—or lock horns with him herself. What's more, his wife, Cindy, stood looking around like the queen bee, in her expensive clothes, under her perfect hair, like she breezed through life without a care. Staring at that woman and hearing that man's bluster, Berna had a vision of the future: this church unhappy with Zechariah, this church firing him over a personality conflict or another obscure theological squabble, this church forming a mob to run Zechariah out. It would happen, she could see it already. It would happen. Lowell and Cindy Green would lead the charge.

To Berna's surprise, Reformed Baptists drank and smoked as much as Catholics and Lutherans. The deacons and trustees welcomed Zechariah with cigars and brandy in the all-purpose building, which was the old sanctuary with the pews removed and a kitchen built where the pulpit obviously used to be. Lowell told Zechariah that a group of men met at his house one Saturday each month for "iron to sharpen iron." They drank good whiskey, smoked cigars, and did target practice with firearms. "We call ourselves the Coal River ATF," Lowell said. "Alcohol, Tobacco, and Firearms."

Berna wanted to say bully for him as he led Zechariah away, but she kept it to herself.

While the men did their man things, a gaggle of kids from the youth group welcomed Miriam, Andrew, and Ricky up in the youth loft. And, oh joy, Berna got to follow Cindy Green and a woman named Jennifer Cumby around on a tour of what they called the "church campus." Cindy wasted no time revealing that she was the chair of the decorating committee—and Berna soon learned that meant Cindy had to be consulted about all things related to decorating at the church, from the Passion Play and Christmas productions to the bulletin boards of the downstairs classrooms.

Berna would eventually discover why the woman's hair looked so perfect. She went to the most expensive hair stylist in Charleston, a gay man who was so popular he fired customers who aggravated him, and women waited six months and more for their appointments. The gay man also danced in drag at a gay bar called The Grand Palace, and Berna couldn't tell if it was because they were Calvinists—every person is totally depraved after all—or because they were from the city that they shrugged off what at Clay Free Will would have been considered more than reason enough to write the man off as a vile sinner to be shunned. There was no denying his talent though. Cindy's hair was smooth and shiny; the angles at her chin were so clean and sharp. Berna could see how women would find him worth the money if they had the money to spend. Berna would feel guilty spending money on that kind of vanity. Cindy chattered away in her expensive clothes, under her expensive hair, like she had not a care in the world, and Berna instantly hated her as much as her husband Lowell.

One wall in the dark gymnasium was lined with banners from tournaments the basketball team at Tabernacle Christian School had won. On another wall was a huge painting of a knight in armor holding a sword above his head with one hand, ready to bring it down on the enemy's head, and a purple shield in the other hand with a white cross on it. Above his head arced purple letters outlined in white, *TCS*, and under it, white outlined in purple, *CRUSADERS*.

They came across a gray metal door beside the locker rooms with a sign on the door reading *Benevolence Ministries*.

"Seems like an odd place for this," Berna said. Her voice echoed out into the cavernous, dark gym. "What do you do with it?"

"Well . . ." Jennifer said.

"Nothing right now," Cindy Green cut in.

"How come?"

Jennifer shrugged while Cindy Green said, "Nobody ever took charge of it."

"Can I see inside?"

Cindy unlocked the door with a universal key she called her magic key, and it was a broom closet, except the metal shelves were stacked full of canned food, peanut butter, boxes of cereal and pasta, and there were two clothes racks in back, like the kind in stores, with hanging shirts and coats. And pants, not on clip pants hangers but folded over the middle bar of shirt hangers.

"You need someone to take this over?" Berna asked.

"Do you want it?"

Berna could never make right the catastrophe her sin had caused the family, she could never bring back James, and she could not be with Jordan. Either she found a project to pour herself into or she killed herself. "Yes," she said. "I do."

Cindy waved her arm like the Good Witch Glinda and Berna wanted to slap her face. She said, "It's all yours. Knock yourself out."

Berna rose early now, determined not to wallow in grief. She packed the kids' lunches, sent them off with a belly full of breakfast across the parking lot to Tabernacle Christian School. She volunteered at the school when she had time, she checked homework, she oversaw devotions. She ordered a 365-day "Read through the Bible in a Year" devotional and pinned a copy to the wall in both Miriam's room and the boys' room. She set a goal to read through it with them, told them they could not go out to play on Saturday mornings until after their family Bible study. Zechariah joined them at times, but those turned into his giving a lecture, and she would join the children in zoning out until he wound it down so they could continue.

She found herself yet again horrified by the utter nastiness of God in the Old Testament and she had to stop reading it lest she lose her faith out of principle. She liked the God of Jesus in the New Testament, the one who loved and forgave, the one who championed the cause of the poor and downtrodden. St. Paul wasn't as bad as the Old Testament, but she didn't like him much either. She'd seen his type among traveling evangelists who passed through; he was a pompous, self-important ass, telling women to be silent, to submit to their husbands, to spread their legs for two things only: husband's dick in, baby out.

She discovered the novels of a writer named Eugenia Price in the church library at this time, romance novels, Christian romance novels. She started with *Beloved Invader*, and discovered halfway into it that it was the third in a trilogy, so she returned it and started from the beginning, with *Lighthouse*. For devotions, she decided she would read the gospels and leave the other parts for the men to shout at one another about. She released the kids from their reading routines. Berna gave up the hovering mother routine, to her relief and theirs too, and poured her energy into the benevolence ministries.

She put her head down and she worked. She set up a green dumpster in the side parking lot and painted *Clothes Donation Station* on the side in bright red letters. She got Zechariah to convince the trustees that it would be the best use of resources to open a resale store in a decrepit storefront building in Dunbar. She named it, Clothe the Naked, which a few church members balked at because of the word *naked*, but she reminded the hesitant women that those words were quoting Jesus straight out of Matthew 25, and not even Cindy could argue with that.

It didn't generate any income like she thought it might. As a matter of fact, it became clear that the ministry would always need donations of both clothes and money. She contacted community resource agencies and told them she was open for business; she called the Department of Health and Human Services offices in Kanawha and Putnam Counties. She went to welfare waiting rooms and handed out flyers to clients—and to the case workers, who were almost as poor as their clients. She was invited to give a talk to the gathered case workers one morning in North Charleston, and they liked her, so she got to speak to the Putnam County case workers the next month.

In her free time, she read Eugenia Price.

She stood boldly in front of the people of Tabernacle Baptist and called for donations, and for volunteers; she approached the stay-at-home moms whose kids were in school during the day, reasoned, cajoled, shamed. This is how she staffed the store with volunteers, so it was open weekdays from ten until seven, and on Saturday from nine until seven. She also made it policy that if someone came in and said they didn't have money, the item they were looking at was to be given to them, no questions asked. A few of the women caught her vision. They decorated the store, bought mannequins—two adult women, two girls, and one boy—and changed out the outfits like a regular store would. They donated their old clothes, called family and friends.

One day, when the Clothe the Naked store was up and running, Berna came home with a tub of extra crispy Kentucky Fried Chicken for family dinner, complete with mashed potatoes, slaw, and rolls, put it all on the table and said to Zechariah, "Now it's time to do something about the deplorable state of that food pantry."

The kids were still at their various practices, and he had just come over from a hard day of parsing Bible verses and theology texts and he was hungry. She told him, "I want to open a food pantry and call it Feed the Hungry and do the same thing with food we do with clothes. It can go in the empty space beside Naked."

He nodded as he pulled open the red and white tub of chicken. "Okay," he said. "I'll mention it to Lowell." He dug around and pulled out a drumstick.

"You do that," she said.

Working with the less fortunate of the Kanawha Valley brought Berna into contact with all sorts of religious and non-religious people. Zechariah voiced his concern one evening, not about the indigents— what they were was to be expected—but about the people she'd enlisted to help in the ministry, which was anyone ready to roll up their sleeves and help her alleviate people's suffering. "The Lord tells us to come out from among those people and be separate," Zechariah told her. "Welcoming unsaved people into the congregation like they don't need to be saved is like mixing rancid meat into a tasty stew."

"Lowell's been talking to you," she said. "He doesn't like Velinda, or Luci. Or any of the other Black people."

"This isn't about race. Like I've said, it's not a skin problem, it's a sin problem."

"About that," she said, "these people are doing God's work, and He's going to send them to hell anyway? They are better people than all the ones like Lowell and Cindy who do nothing but sit on their butts on Sunday and thank God they're not poor."

"Just because Carl Lewis can jump farther into the ocean than you, does that mean he can jump all the way to Hawaii?"

"What's that got to do with anything?"

"Pleasing God with your righteousness is like jumping from California to Hawaii. How much difference does it make that Carl Lewis can jump thirty feet out and you can only jump five? Neither of you get to Hawaii."

"That's a nifty metaphor, but there has to be a difference between being a good person and being a bad person," she told him. "It has to matter."

"Nobody gets close on their own. That's why our righteousness is described in Isaiah as filthy rags—which, by the way, if you look at the Hebrew word for *rags* means soiled menstrual rags."

His point with this, Berna knew, was that menstrual rags were the most disgusting thing imaginable, soaked as they were in a woman's menstrual discharge.

She shook her head. "Well, of course that's what it means." She'd lost her patience entirely with Old Testament God by this point, the old, woman-hating bastard who arbitrarily decided who he loved and who he hated. She was done with him, and all those woman-hating men who wrote the Old Testament. And that old crank, Paul, too. A verse that has stuck in her craw for a long time came to mind, I Timothy 4:7, where he tells Timothy to have nothing to do with "fables fit only for old women." Yeah, Timothy, stick to fables fit only for old men. Sexist old bastard. Berna would choose her own fables if she wanted, and she would choose love, not judgment. From here on, she was sticking with the God of Jesus, the God of forgiveness, tenderness, and love. Zechariah would just have to live with it.

She walked out of the kitchen while he was winding up to, yet again, expound on the doctrine of total depravity.

Tabernacle Baptist Church
1905 MacCorkle Avenue SW, St. Albans, WV 25177
The Lord's Day Services, January 7, 1990

Sunday School 9:30
Morning Worship 10:55
Evening Cell Groups 5:30
Wednesday Prayer Meeting 7:15

We extend a warm welcome to our visitors today. Please sign our Guest Register in the Foyer. We hope to greet you in a more personal way following the services.

Call to Worship   Congregation in unison
Psalm 100
Make a joyful shout to the Lord, all you lands!
Serve the Lord with gladness;
Come before His presence with singing.
Know that the Lord, He is God;
It is He who has made us, and not we ourselves;
We are His people and the sheep of His pasture.
Enter into His gates with thanksgiving,
And into His courts with praise.
Be thankful to Him, and bless His name.
For the Lord is good;
His mercy is everlasting,
And His truth endures to all generations.

Children's Lesson
"I'm in the Lord's Army"
Rev. Zechariah Minor

Children Leave for Children's Church

Hymns
"All That I Am I Owe to Thee," #117
"Grace, 'Tis a Charming Sound," #119

Scriptures
Romans 8: 28-30
And we know that all things work together for good to those who love God, to those who are the called according to His purpose. For whom He foreknew, He also predestined to be conformed to the image of His Son, that He might be the firstborn among many brethren. Moreover whom He predestined, these He also called; whom He called, these He also justified; and whom He justified, these He also glorified.

John 15:16a
You did not choose Me, but I chose you and appointed you that you should go and bear fruit, and that your fruit should remain, that whatever you ask the Father in My name He may give you.

John 6:44
No one can come to me, except the Father which hath sent me draw him: and I will raise him up at the last day.

Sermon
"God Is Still on the Throne"
Rev. Zechariah Minor

Benediction
"Hail Sovereign Love" #430

Announcements

Olivia June Ryder has an unspoken prayer request.

Harvey and Janet Stevens would like to thank their church family for the gifts and expressions of sympathy on the passing of Harvey's mother.

We are happy to welcome Susan West as a full member in our fellowship. Even though she's been worshipping with us for a long time, this is a big step. Please congratulate her when you see her.

The benevolence ministries need volunteers. This is an important ministry to those in need in the Kanawha Valley. If you wish to serve in this way, please contact Rev. Minor's wife, Berna.

The Spirit, and the Water, and the Blood

(Jordan, 1990)

IT WAS a relief when the classroom at WV Tech in Montgomery looked near enough like Jordan's biology classroom at Clay High School. Newer desks notwithstanding, it was just a classroom in an old building with tall windows on one wall. She didn't know what she thought she'd walk into, but the sameness made her feel she could do this. This was August 1990; she was forty-two years old, hadn't stepped foot inside a classroom for twenty-four years. She'd always been too distracted to do her schoolwork back then; she didn't know if she could do it now, but she was determined to try.

The Aquatic Biology professor, Dr. Butler, a bearded hippie in khaki cargo pants and tattered hiking boots, didn't go over the syllabus as her advisor said he would when she was fretting about the class, but walked them straight down the streets of Montgomery to the Kanawha where, at nine in the morning, fog still moved like disembodied spirits along the top of the water as the sun wasn't yet high enough to angle down into the valley. The insects created a roar in the surrounding hills, and inside of that general noise, the sound of traffic across the river rose and fell.

The water smelled good to Jordan, like a morning off work spent trying to land a muskie. The class dipped up water in little cups with screw-on lids, like the kind doctors had people pee in. Then they hiked it back to the lab, which was through a doorway at the side of the classroom, where they put drops on slides and stared at the water through microscopes.

"Now, the composition of a river changes a lot from headwater, through the middle, and on to the mouth, where it debouches into a larger body of water," Dr. Butler said, "but it also remains mostly, but not entirely, H_2O. Somewhere around 95, 96 percent. Oceans are around 96 percent actual water, and the rest is composed of a whole lot of things, including bacteria, plankton, archaea."

Jordan stared into the microscope as Dr. Butler continued to talk. "A busy world all its own in there," he said. "Life going about its business just as earnestly as we humans do. And why wouldn't it? The difference between that life and my life—your life—is one of size and complexity only. At the most basic level, we, like they, are using energy to try and keep ourselves from reaching equilibrium. And that, my dear students, is what the mystery of life is: using energy to avoid equilibrium. It began billions of years ago. These ciliates you see doing their thing and you are alike, part of that system."

She hadn't gotten through the first class without the professor spouting off about evolution. She still had vivid memories of Miss Arneda as her Sunday school teacher at Clay Free Will, and Mrs. Sizemore as her biology teacher at Clay High School, both telling the class that the theory of evolution was a lie of the devil, an attempt by atheists to remove God from science, just like they were trying to remove Him from politics and culture and even the schools. Jordan wondered if she'd made a mistake going back to school after so long. She was the oldest person in the class by at least twenty years.

"Let me see," Dr. Butler said into her left ear, his breath wafting the burnt tang of a serious smoker. She stood erect and stepped aside and he peered into her microscope. "That ciliate *Loxodes magnus* right there," he said, as if she were looking at it with him, "has eaten lunch. You can see the Trachelemonas inside him."

Jordan said, "Cool." What was she supposed to say?

"I hope I haven't put you off," Dr. Butler said. "I don't get social nuances like other people do and it makes people think I'm an asshole." His beard was unbrushed, twisted and tangled. It was brown shot through with strands of red and gray.

Jordan said what she thought he was fishing for. "I don't think that about you."

"Just wait," he said. "You will. When I was young, they said I had mild childhood schizophrenia. My childhood was not easy. Now they're calling it 'pervasive developmental disorder–not otherwise specified.'" He laughed. "PDD-NOS. You know what that means?"

"No."

"It's a euphemism for 'we don't know our asses from our elbows.'"

"Sounds like it," Jordan said.

"You're wondering why I'm telling you all this when you just want to learn about the squiggly things living in the river."

"No," she said. "It's fine."

"I guess it's because I'm a good scientist, but I've always been a social misfit. People don't like being around me. I can tell you feel like a misfit too."

"It's fine," Jordan said.

"Am I making you uncomfortable? You can just tell me to stop."

"This is interesting," she said, leaning back over her microscope.

"Yeah," he said. He stood beside her for a long, awkward moment, then turned to the class and called out, "What do you think about all the teeming life in that drop of water?"

"It's amazing," someone said.

"It's rad," another said.

"It's a whole world," he said. "It's a whole world you're looking at in there. All the world these little guys will ever know, just like this planet we're on is the only one we'll know, even though there are billions upon trillions of solar systems inside billions of galaxies out there in space. From space, Earth is nothing but a drop of water on a slide."

Jordan stared at the little creatures so busily going about their own business.

"That's the life we're going to spend this semester studying," Dr. Butler said. "I find it endlessly fascinating. Give it a chance and you will too." He said, "Now for the second most important lesson of the day: in this class you *will* clean up your equipment properly after *every single* use."

On the drive home, the Kanawha River below to the left of the road flashed in the late morning sunlight, each drop of it full of "teeming life." Jordan was overcome with emotion. It swept up from nowhere and surprised her, and she had a low-grade but sustained cry. Back at her house, she felt scoured out inside, and yet also light and at peace. There was no way she could describe it to Marisa. She decided not even to mention it.

Two weeks before that first biology class, Jordan had driven home on a Friday evening not only exhausted from a long week of overtime shifts, but sick to death of her job. She'd been a union meat cutter in various Kroger stores for twenty-two years. The job paid well, no complaints there. It'd allowed her to have a more comfortable life than her parents, and it'd allowed her to put Marisa through college, which she would never regret even if they didn't stay together. The job itself though: the endless cycle of assembling equipment, cutting, slicing, cubing, grinding, wrapping, slapping on prices and brand stickers, breaking down the equipment, washing, hosing, and sanitizing, all to begin again the next day. She felt like that guy who had to roll that rock up the hill, only to have it roll back down so he had to go down and start over again for all eternity. Also, the counting, tallying, inventory, paperwork. The constant smell of bleach that was so strong she left work feeling like her lungs were sunburned. And the customers. Once Berna told Jordan that Zechariah liked to say being a preacher would be a great job if it weren't for the people. Being a meat cutter would be a great job if it weren't for the people, and the cutting up meat, and the nonstop cleaning and sanitizing.

What else would she do at this point though? Quit a union job? Start over from scratch at the age of forty-two? What would she even do? But did she have it in her to stay a meat cutter for twenty more years? The thought made her sink deeper into her natural depression—Marisa and the rest of them already jokingly referred to her as either that depressed donkey Eeyore from *Winnie the Pooh*, or another cartoon character they told her was on *The Flintstones*, but she didn't remember ever seeing, called Schleprock, who trudged under a dark storm cloud saying, "wowzy wowzy woo-woo." Sadness was better than her other mode, anger, which she had, with age, learned to dive on like a grenade and take the brunt herself so no one else had to feel it. Not healthy, she knew, but it was her life, the best she could manage.

Since it was the weekend, it would undoubtedly be another night of late-night drinking at the Grand Palace, another night of skunky pot and Smirnoff screwdrivers, another night of drag queen performances, of lesbian dancing, of insistent, forced cheer. Jordan was so damn sick of that life she could barely muster the energy to shower and dress for the evening—yet she did, in her black jeans with wallet chain and rolled up cuffs, Doc Martens, one loose white tee shirt over two tight ones—one thing Jordan was thankful for was small tits; two tight tee shirts could bind them down so her chest looked almost like a regular dude's. Her youthful dream of losing them in a hunting accident returned to her even at this late age, and she still awoke from it with a bright happiness that her world had been set right. Over the tee shirts she wore a black leather motorcycle jacket. A bit much, she knew, but so what.

Marisa, per usual, got dolled up in a dress, eye shadow, red lipstick—the two of them were the dictionary pictures of femme and butch, with the interracial element added for extra spice—it amused Jordan that people out in town thought she was an edgy person, out on the forefront of a social revolution, when she was anything but. When Marisa looked hot like that, though, Jordan could muster up enough energy to get to the bar, and the screwdrivers took over from there.

Except they'd been fighting about the invasion of Iraq for several weeks. Marisa was rabidly against the war and ragged on America, calling it an evil empire, like it was just as bad as the Soviet Union had been. Jordan might have been a dyke, fine, but that didn't mean she wasn't a patriot. Saddam Hussein wanted to grab the bull, then the USA should give him the horns. Marisa went to marches at the Capitol building. Jordan couldn't help smiling when they watched the coverage of it on WCHS and the video showed a sparce little gaggle of protesters among a swarm of flag-waving patriots. Marisa saw Jordan's smirk, and their disagreement grew so heated that old grievances and personal insults slipped out and now festered as a dark resentment between the two of them, though they both pretended it wasn't so.

"You know what?" Jordan said. "I'm off work tomorrow, so I think I'll head to the woods and scout deer."

"Go into the woods tonight?" Marisa stepped out of the hall bathroom, where she was pulling her hair slowly through her flat iron, getting ready for a night of partying.

"No," Jordan said. "But I'll be getting up around four to drive out there, so I think I'll beg off tonight."

Marisa was still out when Jordan awoke the next morning at 4:00, not a rare-enough occurrence to cause concern. Jordan ate two boiled eggs from the refrigerator while the Mr. Coffee dripped her a thermos full of French roast. She loaded up her old Savage 99, a box of Remington 150-grain soft point Core-Lokt, and her Gerber Freeman gut hook knife. If she happened across a buck, she'd take him. She still had the keys to her dad's meat shed and he let her come and go as she pleased, even left meat labelled for her in his deep freezers—from him, that was as close to an apology for the hurtful things he'd said as she would ever get. She didn't visit them at the house.

She left a note for Marisa that she'd be home later that day, loaded up her truck and cruised down Quarrier Street—these early mornings were the only times Jordan had ever felt anything like affection for city life—past the courthouse on the right, the Town Center Mall on the left, Goldfarb Electric on the right, the streets still and empty, no cars, the lights straight green, not changing on her, radio off, only the rumble of her truck's engine—the aloneness of heading into the woods was a loneliness Jordan slipped into as comfortably as she did her old tree-bark camouflage jacket—across the Elk River, right at the light, and up the I-79 ramp.

She parked in the wide spot and hiked up before sunrise; had an invigorating day in the woods scouting; found tracks, rubs, and droppings where the oaks she'd always known were dropping plenty of acorns. Twice she sat against a tree, ate jerky and sipped the dark coffee from her thermos. The second time she leaned against a tree, her rifle across her lap, she dozed, woke, dozed again. Dipping in and out of consciousness, she felt she could almost blend into the tree and the leaves, melt into the forest and just *be*.

On her way back out, she went up and walked the mountain ridge before turning straight down toward where she knew she would come out along the blacktop just north of her dad's house. She smelled the carcasses before she saw them in the glade, and saw them well before she reached the glade, four deer, shot multiple times each, dragged and left there under the open sky where they lay rotting. No sign of any intention to field dress them. She'd seen shot deer before, who hadn't? But those were ones a hunter failed to track. These were just punks out for the rush of the kill and nothing else. No thought of herd management or harvesting, no intention to use the meat.

"Assholes," she shouted into the woods. "What is wrong with you, you goddamned assholes." It felt strange to her to be cursing this way in these woods where she spent so much time with her dad, who, though he was a stern and hard man, did not curse himself and did not approve of others doing it. He'd almost started a fistfight with a man at the Tastee-Freez who'd nonchalantly used *Jesus Christ* as an exclamation, and then *goddamn* as an adjective in the same sentence. "That's enough," her dad shouted as he jumped up and pumped out his chest, ice cream cone still in his hand. "I'm not going to sit here and let you take the name of my Lord in vain." The man had then stood himself, but Doris and the man's wife had both intervened before it came to blows.

Jordan gripped her rifle and might well have shot the bastards who did this if she'd seen them. These deer had been there for a couple of days already. The rest of the way down the mountain, Jordan fumed and cursed, and as she emerged from the woods onto the blacktop road, she decided she was finished with being a meat cutter, even though it was a union job and she had seniority. She was going to become a game warden.

Her dad's truck was gone when she got to her own truck, so she backed onto the blacktop and drove out of Clay County. On I-79 between Clendenin and Elkview, she got hungry and needed to piss.

Grabbing a burger was simple enough but bathrooms had remained a problem for her. She looked too masculine and freaked women out in the girl's room, and she didn't look quite right in the men's room. An urge to relieve herself away from home always gave rise to fears of being accosted or attacked.

Jordan was practiced at pissing standing up. She used the pointer and middle finger of her right hand to spread the inner lips of her vaj, and then pulled up to aim the stream, which was easy enough in the woods but still a problem, say, at a urinal in a men's room. She'd fashioned herself a piss funnel out of a 16 oz. Coke bottle and electrical tape to use if she couldn't get a stall, but she didn't like using it. One, it was messy. Two, if the men's room was crowded, her fiddling around with it made her worry that she was drawing the kind of attention to herself that would get her ass kicked. Or worse. At rest stops, if there was a stand of trees around, and there almost always was, she'd hike right into them to do her business in peace.

She wasn't so hungry. She could wait till she got home to eat. As for taking a piss, she decided to pull off a side road and piss in the woods rather than risk walking into the Hardee's or the GoMart, finding a crowd, and having to decide which bathroom would be the least risky to use.

Back at the apartment, she sat at her computer and began her search for college programs to become a game warden. The following Thursday, her first day off, she drove to Montgomery and enrolled to earn her BA in biology at WV Tech. She drove from there straight back to work and told her manager she needed to work all forty of her weekly hours on Tuesdays, Thursdays, and weekends because she was going to college.

Jordan had left Clay back in 1984 when James had drowned. She'd blamed herself, and it wasn't misplaced blame. Berna had hesitated to come to her a number of times, had felt guilty for not being home with her children, had said she needed to start being a better mother. Each time Jordan had begged and made her give in and come. They were together at her house when the boy drowned. She bore legitimate guilt for what happened and there was nothing she could do to make it right.

After that poor child's funeral, she sat in her truck for so long wondering whether to go over to the church and join the comfort gaggle that by the time she'd decided not to go, it didn't matter anymore; it would've been over anyway. She couldn't bear the thought of lurking around the edges of a crowd trying to make eye contact with her love. She decided to wait for Berna to contact her. At least they would have to reengage when Berna eventually came to the store, stopped back at the case for meat.

Berna didn't come though, at least not that Jordan saw. She could only assume Berna was avoiding her. Pastor Minor did the grocery shopping in the months after the drowning, a thing, as far as Jordan could remember, he'd never done, not even once, before. Now he always nodded cordially at her but never stopped to make small talk or even ask for a cut of meat she didn't have in the display case. She was always in back, the shop window between them, and she didn't feel it would be right to run out and ask how Berna was doing. As with Susan all those years before, Jordan knew she was on the edge of the abyss, and this time her perversion hadn't just gotten a girl in trouble and caused Susan's mom to uproot their life and move away—Jordan had caused the death of a child.

She shouldn't have been surprised about that either, though. Jordan had been causing death from the moment she was born. She'd learned over the years that her mother's death was due to chronic Hepatitis C, which had been a little unwanted gift slipped in with the blood transfusion after Jordan came out. Jordan had been too forceful, come too fast, and had given her mom what her dad called a fourth-degree tear. When she looked that up in a medical encyclopedia at the Clendenin library, she discovered what she'd done to her mom, she'd ripped her open all the way through the sphincter, leaving her not with a vagina and an anus, but with one big, bleeding hole.

Jordan remembered, at the end of her mom's life, the Hep C had damaged her brain so badly that she didn't recognize Jordan, was afraid of her when she entered the bedroom. Over the years Jordan had come to believe her mom had actually not lost her mind but had moved so close to death that she could see past physical, fleshly reality into the realm of the spirit.

Was it her evil spirit that insisted her flesh was wrong? According to the Bible, her flesh was the problem, its needs and desires evil, and her spirit was the thing she needed to nurture and protect. But what Jordan's mom saw when she was in between the two worlds was Jordan's spirit, and what she saw was evil. She recognized the real Jordan, who was her murderer, and she was rightly afraid. Jordan didn't believe this anymore, not in her head, but in her heart she still felt there was something fundamentally wrong about her existence in the world.

When Pastor Minor had packed up Berna and his living children and had driven right out of Clay County, Jordan had thought, there it is again. She'd made people die and she'd made people disappear. She decided it was time to disappear herself and save people the trouble she had a way of causing. She once again took her knife up to the creek, and once again did not go through with it. She couldn't live like this any longer, though, angry and sad and wanting to die. She stopped in the Smoke Hole one evening after work, drank two Jack and Cokes, and drove to her dad and Doris's. She sat at their kitchen table and told them she was a lesbian and the only way she was going to survive was if she stopped lying to herself.

Her dad did not take it well. Among the hurtful things he said to her was that her being a homosexual was worse to him than if she actually had died. "At least then I could grieve and get closure," he told her. "How it is now, it's just going to rip the scab off that wound each time I see you."

She moved out of Clay as she would have lived there: alone. She moved to an apartment in downtown Charleston, on Quarrier Street, two blocks over from the Kanawha River, one mile southeast of where the Elk emptied into it just past the Civic Center, emptied water that had flowed right past her dad on the riverbank with a fishing pole behind his house. His and Doris's house.

It was a lifesaving move. The meat cutter had recently retired from the Kroger on Ohio Avenue, so she transferred in, nice and smooth. She was running from God, she knew, but she had put space between them in order to get the lay of the land. How could she figure anything out with an angry God towering over her, staring down in fiery rage at her, no matter where she went? She had to get away from Him or be destroyed by Him.

The beginning of her second year in Charleston, she met Marisa, a Black woman who openly called herself a femme lesbian and who told Jordan there was not a thing in the world wrong with her, with Jordan; she was just the kind of handsome butch Marisa liked best. "My parents were religious too," she told Jordan. "I get where you're coming from. You've felt like you never belonged anywhere your whole life, right?" She said this over pizza and beers at the Anchor in Kanawha City. They were on their second date and Jordan surprised herself by tearing up—she was *not* a crier—as she nodded that, yes, except for when she was small, that was true.

Marisa nodded with her. "I'm telling you," she said, "I have a group of friends who will accept you just as you are—no, they will *celebrate* you just as you are."

"You can't say that," Jordan told her. "You don't know me as I am."

"I have a sense about these things," Marisa said. "Just ask my friends. You're a little rough around the edges is all. I can tell you have a good heart."

Six months later, Jordan and Marisa were living together and spending several evenings a week partying with Jordan's new friends, a core group of lesbians, and a couple gay men who came and went. All of them smoked pot, and a few did harder drugs, but Jordan stuck to bourbon whiskey, which she discovered she had a taste for. Marisa's friends didn't, as she had predicted, celebrate Jordan as she was. Jordan was conservative, rural. She killed animals with guns. She caught fish and cut them up, her hands covered in scales and blood. She sliced up mammal flesh for a living. She loved Ronald Reagan and thought it was unfair that she had to work so hard while welfare queens lived high on the hog from her taxes.

Maybe they didn't exactly celebrate her as she was, but they didn't reject her either. They spoke admiringly of what a strong, butch woman she was, and they let her be that, even if she had to keep her politics to herself. She'd never experienced anything like it, and so it seemed to be enough. A grand old house two blocks down from her apartment went on the market. With dreams of a home life with a woman she loved, Jordan took out a loan and bought the house.

One evening in 1988, when she'd finished her shift, she stopped into the ladies room for a quick piss before driving across town in the rush-hour traffic. The clearance rack beside the restrooms was full of overstock Nilla Wafer boxes. Jordan liked them in banana pudding, but they were too dry to just eat. Dipped in milk maybe, but she didn't like milk.

Inside the bathroom, there was a woman in a pink jumper washing her hands at the sink. A child stood beside her in a red tee shirt with that blue Smurf girl smiling on the front. The child stared wide-eyed. This happened enough for Jordan not to be surprised when it did. Except, when the mother turned around, she didn't just give Jordan a look. She yelped and jumped back, and yelled, "Get out of the women's room."

Jordan kept her cool. "I will. After I pee."

"Michael," the woman yelled. She backed around the edge of the wall trying to keep distance. Jordan moved to accommodate her, thinking this too would be over soon enough, most of the time it ended here. The woman yelled, "Michael," again, and then, "Michael, help."

A man burst into the bathroom, his face wide in fearful confusion.

"There's a man in here," the woman said to him.

The look on his face turned from fear to anger. "What the hell you think you're doing?" the man said. He didn't wait for Jordan to explain. He grabbed her shirt with one hand, and her neck with the other, spun her around, and pushed her out the door. He didn't stop there. He shoved her against the wall. "What the hell you think you're doing going into the women's restroom?" he said into her face. "My wife is in there. My little girl is in there."

Jordan grabbed the man's wrist. "You need to let go of me," she said, and his expression changed back to confusion. A crowd of shoppers had gathered to watch. He let go and stepped back. "What are you?"

"I'm Jordan Goins," she said. "I'm a meat cutter. I work here. What are you?" He had a crisp, short haircut, a white shirt, and a tie. A banker or a salesman. Or a preacher—that would just be her luck.

"What's wrong with you?" he said. "Look at you." He waved up and down her body.

"I could press charges against you for assault and battery," she said. "You can't just go putting your hands on random people."

"We thought you were a man," he said. "What were we supposed to think?" He looked to one of the spectators and said, "Does that look like a man or a woman to you?"

The store manager, Mike, appeared. "What's the problem here, sir?"

Jordan said, "I needed to use the bathroom . . ."

"This freak," the man spoke over her, "scared my wife and daughter half to death. They thought it was a man in the restroom."

"I just finished my shift," Jordan said. "I needed to pee."

By the time each of them, and the wife, had finished telling their side of it, a policeman had arrived. He got the story from the manager, looked at the husband, the wife, and then at Jordan. He said, "Anybody hurt?" Jordan said she was not, and they said they were not either. The officer called out for people to disperse and go about the rest of their day, and they did, glancing once or twice back over their shoulders.

"You okay?" Mike asked her.

"Fine," she said. "Not like it's the first time this has happened."

Her hands trembled as she yanked and slapped at the gear shift in her F150, making her way across town to her house on Quarrier Street. While the man had assaulted her, she pissed down her leg. (Urine is about 95 percent water, she would discover later in class, about the same as river water. The difference is in the other parts, which in urine are nitrogen, potassium, calcium.) Then she had to stand there, obviously wet with her own piss while customers watched the interrogation. She breathed in and out heavily to keep from lunging at the man as she opened her Buck knife, at that moment in her pocket, and slitting his jugular.

Marisa was cooking an Ohio Farmhouse chili recipe she'd found

268 / VIC SIZEMORE

in the library discard *Joy of Cooking* that slid from its cover and fell to the floor almost every time she pulled it from the pantry. She was using ground meat from the eight-point buck Jordan had shot last season. Marisa didn't like deer meat, she didn't like the idea of killing animals in the woods, and she didn't like Jordan's gun safe in the bedroom closet. She didn't like that Jordan had bouts of serious depression, bursts of anger, and also kept guns.

Jordan never told her it was at least partly due to experiences like the one she'd had at work. She didn't even mention them anymore—Marisa had seen enough to know. Most of the time it was just funny looks, occasionally a rude comment; it almost never got physical. Plus, her own gut reaction when she looked in the mirror confirmed their reactions to her; since puberty, when she stood naked and looked at her body, she didn't recognize it as her body, but there she was stuck inside it—that's why she kept guns too, though a knife would do.

Jordan's freshman composition class, her American history class, and her speech class were easy, but it was too much work along with her full-time job, so she dropped them. She stayed with aquatic bio. Over the course of the semester, she asked to meet with Butler in his office enough times that he was visibly exhausted with her. She didn't care.

One day toward the end of the semester, Dr. Butler rattled off again how river water and ocean water are around 95, 96 percent water. He told them that human lungs are 83 percent water. "Makes it seem odd that breathing water should kill a person," he said. "Before you are born," he said, "you're basically a fish inside your mother, breathing amniotic fluid, which is 98 percent water."

Jordan stopped by his office for a few minutes before getting back to Charleston for her shift, and they talked for almost an hour, and toward the end he shifted the conversation. They got on the subject of sex and gender, and Jordan told him how she had believed herself to be a boy when she was young, and how puberty had wreaked a devastation on her from which she had never recovered.

"Maybe you are a man," he told her. "Have you ever considered that you might be a man in a woman's body?"

"What do you mean?" she asked. She knew what he meant. She'd heard the drag queens at the Palace talk about "trannies," and she knew they got top surgery, breast implants, and, less often, bottom surgery to remove their penises. She also knew it went the other way, female to male, but for whatever reason, having a sex change—*her* having a sex change, taking T, getting top surgery, maybe even bottom surgery, living as a man—had never once occurred to her as a real, living option.

Dr. Butler told her that he had traveled to Thailand with a friend in 1988 to help with moral support while she had what he called "bottom surgery." He said, "People told her she was wrong, mutilating her body like that, but you know, we fix harelips and club feet and congenital heart conditions, and all sorts of other things we want fixed about our bodies. Girls get boob jobs. And why not?"

"I don't know."

"You ever think about doing it?" Dr. Butler asked, and immediately added, "You don't have to answer that. That's me being socially inappropriate again."

"No," she said. "It's okay." Jordan wondered why she'd never considered it for herself. The religion she'd been raised with mostly. God's judgment. Possible rejection from her dad. Marisa too, and all their friends; they despised men, were afraid of them—with good reason, Jordan had to admit—and might turn their backs on her. The absolute aloneness she feared might become her life. Except now it felt different: the prospect of living the rest of her days lying to herself felt worse than being alone.

"I'll go with you, if you want moral support," Dr. Butler said.

Once again, on the drive home, Jordan wept as Sinéad O'Connor sang "Nothing Compares 2 U" on her stereo. This time though, her skin itched and crawled as her mind swam—it did not swim disoriented and confused as most people meant when they said their heads spun; her mind swam strong and determined, like a muskie in the deep river, down where it was dark and cold. As it did, Jordan peered into the darkness looking for the thing her mind was down there swimming toward, and now she finally knew what it was.

All living things on Earth are mostly water. The river was water and so were the fish. Jordan was water and so was every person. Living flesh, living water, flowing, ebbing, flowing again. Where was the spirit in this? Where was God? Whatever god might be up there obviously didn't care enough to make Jordan's spirit and flesh match so she could live a normal life. Then she allowed herself to consciously admit what she'd secretly known for a long time: there never was a god up there to begin with. All these rules and laws were manmade. There was no Devil, there were no angels or demons. It all was water and mud, and when it died, it didn't fall into equilibrium, which was true death, but broke apart, changed its mode, and kept on living in other ways: water to water, mud to mud, as it was and is and ever shall be, world without end, amen.

Jordan turned down the music and drove on, her tires slapping on the endless strand of filled potholes lining both tire tracks of Route 60. Changing sex, living as the sex your spirit knew it was—people did it. Jordan could do it. It was this or suicide for real this time. She had to do it.

He had to do it.

"I am a man," he said into the car, and it felt like the first honest thing he had said to himself or anyone else since he was a child, and it felt beautiful for a split second before the fears assailed him: Would Marisa still love him? Would she stay with him? The person she thinks she loves has been a make-believe person, not the real Jordan—he had to stop pretending. He took a deep breath. "I am a man," he said. "I have always been a man." The fears: Where would he fit in? Belong? Who would love and accept him? If no one else would, could he at least finally love himself? He shifted in his seat, adjusted his grip on the steering wheel, and took another deep breath. Just to hear the words spoken aloud again, he said, "I am a man."

Tabernacle Baptist Church
1905 MacCorkle Avenue SW, St. Albans, WV 25177
The Lord's Day Services, November 10, 1991

Sunday School 9:30
Morning Worship 10:55
Evening Cell Groups 5:30
Wednesday Prayer Meeting 7:15

We extend a warm welcome to our visitors today. Please sign our Guest Register in the Foyer. We hope to greet you in a more personal way following the services.

Call to Worship   Congregation in unison

Psalm 24

The earth is the Lord's, and all its fullness, The world and those who dwell therein. For He has founded it upon the seas, and established it upon the waters. Who may ascend into the hill of the Lord? Or who may stand in His holy place? He who has clean hands and a pure heart, Who has not lifted up his soul to an idol, Nor sworn deceitfully. He shall receive blessing from the Lord, And righteousness from the God of his salvation. This is Jacob, the generation of those who seek Him, Who seek Your face. Selah Lift up your heads, O you gates! And be lifted up, you everlasting doors! And the King of glory shall come in. Who is this King of glory? The Lord strong and mighty, The Lord mighty in battle. Lift up your heads, O you gates! Lift up, you everlasting doors! And the King of glory shall come in. Who is this King of glory? The Lord of hosts, He is the King of glory. Selah.

Children's Lesson
"Father Abraham"
Rev. Zechariah Minor
Children Leave for Children's Church

Hymns
"All That I Am I Owe to Thee," #117
"Grace, 'Tis a Charming Sound," #119

Scriptures
Proverbs 21:31
The horse is prepared for the day of battle, But deliverance is of the LORD.

Ephesians 6:13
Therefore take up the whole armor of God, that you may be able to withstand in the evil day, and having done all, to stand.

Joshua 1:9
Have I not commanded you? Be strong and of good courage; do not be afraid, nor be dismayed, for the LORD your God is with you wherever you go.

Sermon
"What Is the Bondage of the Will?"
Rev. Zechariah Minor

Benediction
"A Debtor to Mercy Alone"   #434

Announcements

Linda Walker expresses her deepest gratitude for your expressions of sympathy upon the occasion of the death of her dear son, Richard. She would ask that in lieu of flowers you make donations to the addiction recovery program at the Union Mission. Even though our heart breaks until we think we might die, we cling to the promise that His grace is sufficient. Thank you.

As we celebrate the Marine Corps birthday today, and Veterans Day, let us not forget those who have been called up and are ready to make the ultimate sacrifice for us. The Ladies still need help with their letter writing campaign to our troops who are on their way to Kuwait to defend our freedom. Those of you who have served know how much a letter from home can lift the spirits of a soldier or airman who feels forgotten by folks back home. If you want to be a part of this important ministry, contact Cindy Green.

The benevolence ministries are always in need of volunteers. If you can spare even one hour each week, see Berna Minor and she will surely put you to work.

As a Good Soldier

(Andrew Minor, 1990–2002)

ANDREW GRADUATED from TCS in 1990 and enrolled at West Virginia State for fall classes. He tried out with the baseball team as a walk on, practiced with the team, and tried to impress the coach. He made good plays during practice but didn't think he'd make the team. Then Saddam Hussein invaded Kuwait, so he decided to enlist in the Army instead, go fight those raghead sons of bitches. The recruiters took him out for burgers and for fish and chips, bought him beer, took him to play paintball. While he was lying on the ground during a game watching for an enemy to shoot, one of the recruiters dropped beside him and said, "In these games, you're shot, you're dead. We have better war games in the Army. Your buddy gets shot and you get to fix him up right there on the battlefield. It's a lot more fun."

Andrew thought of the wounded turtle he and James had tried to fix up, one of the memories of James he cycled through occasionally. They had been setting up on the sandbar to fish, and they'd found a turtle half out of the water with a triangular shard of its shell broken out. Had to have been run over by a car and floated the creek down from the road. The edge was sharp like a broken dinner plate. It was up at the turtle's front left shoulder, and an open wound there crawled with white squirming maggots. The turtle went about its business as if they weren't there. The sandbar always had the stink of river mud, a smell Andrew loved. This turtle smelled different, like decomposing flesh, like it was already dead. He picked it up and carried it to the house, James skip-stepped alongside trying not to lose sight of it.

Their dad had stopped in for a quick lunch and surprised them all when he stayed to pick off all the maggots with tweezers and cleanse the wound with white fizzing peroxide. The turtle still just sat there, its dark eyes staring out from its broken shell into a prehistoric place known only to its reptile brain. After their dad cleaned and disinfected the wound, he let them keep the turtle in a cardboard box with wilted lettuce and shriveled tomato slices till it started to stink up the utility room porch so bad their mom set it out on the back porch, where it died in the box one night.

While their dad was picking off the maggots though, he did what he always did and tried to turn it into a teachable moment, told them how sin was like those maggots, eating away at the turtle, devouring its flesh, killing it little by little.

Object lessons and analogies were his dad's favorite preaching tools. No situation could be simply what it was—a blue robin's egg, a crawdad hiding under a rock, a bicycle wreck—but had to be a metaphor opening a window to the spiritual realm where what was of ultimate importance—the war between good and evil, where eternal souls were won or lost—was continually being waged, even as Andrew and James ran up and down the river to play.

"If you let Jesus, the Great Physician, tweeze away your sins," he told the two of them that day over the turtle, "He will cleanse your wounds and make you whole."

The recruiter said, "In training," bringing Andrew back from the memory. "In training you'll get to learn how to fix a sucking bullet wound on a chest using an ID card and tape."

"Cool," Andrew said, and he meant it.

He was set to sign the enlistment paperwork and head off to boot-camp when the coach at State called and told him he could be on the team, so he backed out on enlisting, even though the recruiters were pissed off and pressured him pretty hard. He practiced with the team but was nothing but a bench warmer when it counted. He was better than the starting left fielder, who he was convinced got the spot because he was Black. One day Andrew made one offhand remark about how, yes, WVSC was originally an all-Black college, but that was a long time ago, and if Black people were going to insist on affirmative action for themselves in White places, then they should have it for White people in Black places. Fair was fair. All the Black guys on the team hated him after that, went out of their way to make him feel uncomfortable, unwelcome. He complained about reverse racism to the coach, who was White, but the coach had bought into a bunch of liberal mumbo jumbo and didn't have Andrew's back.

Truth was, Andrew had never figured out how to fit in with his peers after leaving Clay County. When they moved, life went askew for him, and he couldn't figure out how to set it right. He hated St. Albans, the constant traffic, the chemical stink of the Union Carbide plant across the river. He despised Tabernacle Christian School. They didn't have a baseball team. They had soccer and basketball, and he wasn't great at either one of those. Ricky and Miriam seemed to slip right into friend groups. Ricky's guitar skills made him instantly "cool," even though he was a scrawny little runt who should have been picked on. Miriam was pretty so she didn't even have to try at all. Andrew slunk through the hallways between classes. He seethed when the other kids mocked his accent, called him a hick and a redneck. As a defense, he turned to antagonizing and insulting the popular kids. He had no friends.

When he'd been a junior in high school, TCS had hired a new Assistant Principal/PE teacher/soccer coach/boys' basketball coach named Jimmy Pederson. He'd almost had his arm ripped off by a farm machine when he was a teenager out in the Midwest. He shared his testimony about it in chapel one day. He'd been a wrestler, and he won a state championship. He was training to try out for the Olympic team when the accident happened, "but the Lord had other plans for me," he said from behind the pulpit, tears running down his face. "Praise God."

When he spoke in chapel after that, Coach Pederson held up his disfigured Grendel arm and cried about how good God was to save his life, how he could have been one of the best wrestlers the world had ever seen. He loved to grab boys and wrestle them to the floor, twist their bodies, pin them hard and fast, prove how the bad arm was not such a hindrance to him. He broke boards and cinder blocks with his Grendel elbow in chapel services, and then he cried again in front of the student body about the goodness of God who had cut short his wrestling career so he could minister to teenagers instead.

All forty-six students in the high school took gym class together with Grendel-arm Pederson. The girls had to wear culottes that did not rise above mid-calf, and tee shirts that were loose enough so no bra strap showed in back at all. This was the only class Andrew had with Miriam. One day, he whispered in her ear, "Grendel arm," miscalculating how well Pederson could hear. The man walked to him and lunged, grabbing him in a wrestling move. He slammed Andrew onto the basketball court so hard people gasped and the high school boys, who hated Andrew and he hated back, even hollered for Pederson to stop. Andrew struggled at first with grunts and sneaker squeaks, but Pederson clamped down on his headlock so hard Andrew thought he was going to pass out. The coach said, "How you like my Grendel arm?"

Pederson tried to pass it off as just horsing around afterward, act like he wasn't pissed off, which, they had all seen, he was. Humiliated, wiping tears from his eyes, Andrew didn't know what else to do so he walked over and stood beside his sister, the only person in there who he might call an ally. His humiliation was complete. Rage pumped into his chest and head like air into an already-tight basketball. Low, so only Miriam could hear, he said, "God damn you." She jerked her head and looked at him, then followed his hateful gaze to Pederson, who was still over animated, pretending he was just showing off like always. "God damn you," Andrew repeated. "God damn you straight to hell, you asshole."

The baseball coach cut Andrew after one season. The Gulf War was already over, so no use joining the Army. Not knowing what else to do, he followed his dad's exhortation to get serious about the things of the Lord and transferred to Pinewood University to prepare for the full-time ministry. He struggled, almost dropped out altogether over the Greek and Hebrew requirements.

Pam Williams was in his Greek class, and she was already fluent in Spanish and could also speak French. She had grown up in Chile, where her parents were still missionaries. She might have been good with languages, but she was ignorant about a lot of cultural stuff that most people took for granted in the United States, and it made her sort of an awkward outcast like Andrew. They got married in the summer of '92.

That fall semester, Andrew came across a magazine in the school library called *Chalcedon Report* and through it discovered R. J. Rushdoony, *The Institutes of Biblical Law*, and Christian Reconstructionism. It all tucked nicely into his own Reformed theology. It was clearly the only thing that could save America from her enemies: atheists, abortionists, socialists, liberals, and homosexual activists.

He earned his BS in Christian Leadership and Church Ministries in Spring of '94, and in the following months was a pastoral candidate at five separate churches, all of them small and struggling, old members dying off, no young blood joining to take their place. Not one church gave him a call back. He wept and prayed for God's guidance and provision, and God didn't answer, God left him to dangle.

He had signed up with Manpower and had to work various humiliating temp jobs for bosses who didn't even have college degrees and treated him like a peon. He quit that and made a go at selling supplemental insurance. His first two weeks he sat through training videos, studied for exams, and sat at a desk making a list of one hundred people he could call for an appointment—he used an old Tabernacle church directory to make the list, already knowing he could not bring himself to call most of them. As much as he saw the benefits of supplemental insurance, it wasn't his calling and he had trouble sounding passionate about it. He resented having to do it.

A female agent in the office chattered on all the time like the job was all sunshine and lollipops. She'd won a plaque the previous year for selling three million dollars' worth and got to go to Texas and speak at a huge convention. She had her own office, and on the wall was a poster with a picture of a regal male lion, and the adage was about the lion waking up in the morning knowing he had to outrun the slowest gazelle and the gazelle waking up knowing he had to outrun the fastest lion, so, no matter who you are, you have to wake up running or you will starve or be eaten. Andrew couldn't concentrate on learning the job for all her yammering around the office.

One day she told him, "Don't worry. Right now, it's like you're riding a bicycle uphill, but when you hit that crest, it's all coasting." She never came up with original analogies, only cliches, and that morning she had lipstick on her tooth. She was Miriam's age, she was rich, and she strutted around the office like the cock of the walk. "You'll see," she told him. "It gets easier." Then she clicked her high heels into the office kitchen and yelled out, "Okay, who's the asshole who brought in the Girl Scout cookies? You're trying to ruin my diet?

Oh my *god*, Thin Mints. I surrender, I surrender. You found my kryp-tonite." He listened to her rip into the Thin Mint box and fought the urge to cry.

Andrew lasted the four months of training while he got paid a salary. When they switched him to straight commission, he crashed and burned. He prayed in the morning, begging God to make life work out for him, asking God why it was so hard for him when good things seemed to drop into other people's laps.

Pam got a job as a teller at Fifth Third Bank in Hurricane to pay bills while he looked for work. She got pregnant, and July 14 of '96, she had their first child, a boy they named Chase. Andrew took the first job he could find so they wouldn't lose their house, working overnights at a plant that made PVC pipe fittings. He stood at a high-pressure injection machine as it squirted hot PVC compound into a mold, he took the pipe fitting out, cooled it in a water tub, then boxed it up. Almost six hundred times a night he did that same motion. His supervisor hadn't gone to college and couldn't get his subject-verb agreement right, and still he talked down to Andrew. On those long shifts, Andrew's fury at the unfairness of his life grew so bitter that he nursed dreams of going postal and shooting the place up. Then he would go home and try to stay awake with Chase while Pam worked her job at the bank.

He got laid off from the plant. He delivered pizzas, then he worked the grill at a Chili's restaurant, then he went back to Man-power. He called in each morning to see where they had work for him, did all sorts of construction and factory work, a few days here, a day or two there, days with no work at all. Pam gave birth to Hunter on January 20, 1998, in Women and Children's Hospital. After her ma-ternity leave, she told him he should stay home with the boys because the money he made doing temp work wouldn't even cover the cost of daycare. She was about to be promoted to loan officer at the bank.

She was climbing that ladder. She had little money signs in her eyes. "We were so poor all my life," she said. "I'm sick of being poor."

"Money is the root of all evil," he told her.

"The *love* of money is," she said. "Not money itself. Money is security. Money is quality of life. It's a future for my boys."

"You think I don't know that?" He felt enough like a failure. He didn't need her beating him down even more, telling him he wasn't worth any more than a babysitter or a housewife.

"Ecclesiastes 10:19 says 'money is the answer to everything,'" she told him.

He had no job, so he had no choice. He spent his afternoons while the boys napped listening to Rush Limbaugh. He watched Fox News and seethed with rage at how his country was being overtaken by illegal immigrants, welfare queens, socialists, gay activists, Democrats, and feminazis, while true American men like him were under siege and couldn't get a break.

During the days, the boys clung to him like baby baboons. Or they made messes. Or fought and refused to go down at naptime. They were parasites that jabbed him with giant straws and drank out all the strength in his soul until the only thing left in the dregs was despair. No matter how he spanked them, they wouldn't behave. A couple times he walked out of the house and stood in the yard, worried that if he didn't, he'd lose his shit and hurt one of them.

In 1999 Pam was careless with her birth control and got pregnant with what would become Baby Andy, whose due date was mid-April 2000. They were hand to mouth as it was, always behind on bills. His stress level was near the blowing point, so before he'd even thought about what he was saying, he surprised himself by suggesting they end the pregnancy.

Pam was outraged. "Did I just hear you say you want to murder this child?"

"It's not a child yet," he said. "It's just splitting cells right now." This was not what he believed—he was staunchly against killing unborn babies—but he was desperate not to have another mouth to feed when he couldn't take care of the ones he already had.

She told him, "I was too young and naïve when I married you. I never would have married a man who would murder our child."

"That's not what I'm saying."

"I didn't even know who I was when we met," Pam told him. "I'd grown up on the mission field and didn't know anything about living here in the States. I got married way too young." He cringed at her refrain, "I'm sick of being poor." Her telling him that he needed to man up and start being a provider. "The boys are growing up fast," she said. "We're way behind on their college funds." She said, "You haven't even thought about investing for retirement."

"How am I supposed to do that?"

"*No retirement*, Andrew. How can you not know anything at all about life?"

That was the first night he hit her. After, she told him if he ever so much as raised his hand at her again she would call the police and have him arrested. He cried and begged her to forgive him and promised he would never do it again.

After the Muslims flew planes into the twin towers and the Pentagon in 2001, Andrew decided he had to fight. He couldn't join the Army, not with Pam and the boys to take care of, so he carried the 30-30 Colley Goins had given his dad years ago out to Lowell's Coal River place and joined his militia. They required that he train with them one Saturday a month, like in the Army Guard. Here, Andrew finally found a group of men who accepted him. They fired their weapons, drank whiskey and beer, said what they thought openly, didn't have to worry about being politically correct.

His new friends admired the old 30-30. "These old Winchesters are one of the best rifles around for hunting elk out west," Lowell told him as he turned the rifle in his hands and admired it. Elk out west. Lowell's comment wasn't lost on him: they all had ARs that they'd bought legally and then retrofitted to be combat ready, Bill Clinton's assault weapon ban be damned. Lowell was telling him he needed a rifle designed not for killing deer but for killing men. That's where this thing was headed.

Lowell gave mini sermons when he mustered the troops. He held forth on the superiority of Western culture to any other in the history of the world, how European Christianity had created the civilized world and now enemies of God were trying to tear it down. "Not on our watch," Lowell would tell the gathered men who he called his troops. "Not while we are here to stand in the gap," and Andrew would join the other men calling out their agreement, proud to number himself among the patriots who would give their lives for this beloved nation.

During these days, he lost his temper and hit Pam a couple of times. He wasn't proud of it, but he never hit her as hard as he could have, just enough to make her shut up. Once she called the police and the deputy who came was Lowell Jr. The two of them chatted for a little bit and then Andrew explained how it was all a misunderstanding. Pam cried and refused to talk to Lowell Jr., and so he and his partner left. In a strange way, that scrape seemed to clear the air and make things better for a while. Their next fight got ugly, and he only raised his fist as a warning. He didn't hit her. He wasn't going to hit her.

"That's it," she said. "I'm done." She didn't even let him respond. She grabbed her keys and ran out the door. He followed her to her car, begging her to settle down, come back inside, and talk it out. She closed and locked her door, backed out, and drove away. She came back with a bunch of men from her work while he was out and packed up her clothes.

Now here Andrew is, brokenhearted and working the line at a startup called Jerry's Café inside Riverwalk Plaza in South Charleston. He fully expects it to go belly up within a year but he needs to work. He hasn't heard that old song "You Picked a Fine Time to Leave Me Lucille" since he was in middle school. Still, he can't get it out of his head, not the original Kenny Rogers version, but the one he and his friends sang on the baseball bus in middle school: you picked a fine time to leave me *loose wheel*. He's got these three boys and no one to mother them, except when they're with Pam, who's not much of a mother. She's still at Fifth Third and working on her MBA at Marshall. She's shacking up with her adultery partner, Sean Smith, a bank Vice President who runs the Hurricane branch. And here's that damn song, stupid as it is, filling Andrew with such despair he has to swallow hard to keep down the sobs. He watched *Because of Winn Dixie* with the boys the other night and had to slip out of the room twice, pretending to go to the bathroom, to keep from crying in front of them.

He has a free hour after the breakfast rush. He will have to bust ass on lunch prep to fit the break in, but Pam has finally agreed to meet him. She picked a coffee shop called The Daily Grind. When he walks in, he sees the two big tables in the middle are pulled together, full of stay-at-home mommies: muffin crumbs, toys scattered across the floor, strollers parked along the wall, diaper bags and shopping bags leaning together, babies on laps, babies sitting, crawling, ripping apart sugar packets on the floor. One woman is nursing without so much as a cloth diaper over her shoulder. She has on Gucci glasses and fingers her keys on the table, held together by a Mercedes Benz keyring.

The girl behind the counter reluctantly leaves her homework to help him. He orders a black coffee and drinks it, gets his free in-house refill. He is now sweating and needs to piss. He runs to the toilet. His lunch prep time is being gnawed away while he sits on his ass. He gets a third cup of coffee. Thirty-five minutes, forty minutes, no Pam. He stares at the cup, empty but still steaming, he sucked the coffee down so fast. The mommy club prattles on. People come and go.

"Excuse me," Andrew waves to the girl. "I was supposed to meet my wife here. Did anyone stop in while I was in the bathroom?"

"No," the girl says, "but we have another location across town. People get mixed up all the time." She closes her *Norton Anthology of World Literature* on her ink pen. "You want me to call over there?"

"Would you?" He turns and watches out the front doors. Each one has *espresso*, in fancy little black letters across it at eye height, backward from inside the shop.

"No problem." She pokes one button on the handset and waits.

Andrew needs to piss again already. Lunch will be hell. Jerry, the owner, will try to prep him and get it all dicked up and half-done and Andrew will be chopping peppers and onions in the middle of the rush with a bread knife because it'll be what's close at hand while waitresses stop for long instants to stare at him with their arms crossed.

"Katie?" The girl turns and smiles at Andrew. She has freckles across her nose. "Is there a woman over there waiting for someone?" She asks Andrew, "What's she look like?"

"Petite," he says. "Red hair. Obvious dye job—bad dye job."

She picks up another ink pen and twirls it in her fingers as she waits. "Hold on," she says, and reaches the handset across the counter to Andrew.

"Hello?"

"I specifically told you the *new* one." Pam says.

"I'm sorry. I'll come over there."

"I have to leave." He listens to her ask for a to-go cup to prove it to him.

"When are we going to talk?"

"I don't know."

"The boys cry for you."

"Please don't start this."

"Just come over tonight, we—"

"Not a good idea."

"Why not?" He hears a whine in his voice.

"It'll give the boys the wrong impression."

"That their mother abandoned them?"

"I love those boys—"

"You have a goddamned funny way of showing it."

"This conversation is over."

"I believe we can fix this," he says. "We owe it to the boys to try."

"It's far too late for that."

"How about we just meet for dinner," he says. "We can go out of town so your adultery partner doesn't see you with your husband and kids."

The call goes dead.

The barista is on her way from the back clutching sleeves of to-go cups like a farm girl carrying corn stalks. He puts a five-dollar bill in her jar. She says thanks and asks if he wants a free refill to go. He declines. His hands are already trembling. He drives to the gun store in South Charleston and puts $620 on the Visa card he and Pam still share for a used Colt AR-15. It is almost identical to a military M-16, and he's read online that all you have to do is file down one little piece of metal to make it totally automatic. It's so light compared to the hunting guns and rifles he's held it feels like a toy in his hands. They only let him buy one box of ammo but tell him he can buy more in a month.

Andrew cleans up after the lunch rush and preps the dinner shift. He drives home, where the smell in the house is a familiar one: his mom calls it *cowmoomush*, but it's just chili mac with potato cubes thrown in, topped in the bowl with tons of cheddar cheese and sour cream. It's one thing all three boys devour, so she makes a big pot of it each week. She swears she made it for Andrew and the others when they were kids, but he doesn't remember. And he would remember. On the housewife and mother front, she did the bare minimum. She's good with the boys now. It's like having grandkids finally activated her mothering instinct. And she's free.

"I have to run," she says, putting on her sweatshirt, "I'm working the Habitat build in Dunbar." At the door, she says, "I'd like to keep the boys for a few nights next week, if it's okay with you. We're having a *Veggie Tales*–themed, one-day VBS, all day Saturday, and it would be a lot easier if I didn't have to drive all the way out here to get them for it."

When she's gone, Andrew collapses on a kitchen chair. Baby Andy scrambles from the back of the house and climbs into his lap. There is a single orange dreadlock down the side of Andy's head that has the tomatoey tang of SpaghettiOs. Baby Andy squirms back out of Andrew's arms, takes a few wild, half-running steps, then dives to his hands and knees, which are already paddling before he hits the floor. He scurries like an alien down the hall to where Chase and Hunter are playing in their bedroom.

As his mom backs out of the driveway, one of the older boys starts howling. There is a heavy thud, a long pause, and the other one starts crying. Then Baby Andy joins in and they are all three crying. Baby Andy wails, "Mom!"

Andrew calls Pam.

"What do you need?" she asks.

"Please just come over and see the boys tonight."

"I could come and get them when I'm off work. Take them to McDonalds's play gym. Right now, I don't think it's the best idea for us—"

"To just talk?" Andrew takes a deep breath. "We need to talk this through."

"It's not getting us anywhere."

"Just tell me if there's a chance."

"Chance for what?"

"For us to be a family again."

"We haven't been a family for years, Andrew."

"That's not true." Andrew palms his forehead.

They are silent for a long instant, then she says, "Too much has happened. We're both different people."

"We're the same people who swore a vow before God. We are a core family unit. Don't destroy that."

"This is not a productive conversation."

The cowmoomush gurgles on the stovetop. The boys have gone silent, which means they're probably back there wrecking their room.

"You've lost your moral compass," he says.

"I'm so tired of this, Andrew. We're going to have to figure out how to coparent. Can't we find a way to—"

"You're nothing but a whore now." He raises his voice. "You're doing this for money and that makes you a prostitute. You are a prostitute. A *whore*."

The call goes dead.

Andrew prays as he scoops cowmoomush into three bowls to cool. He sprinkles shredded cheddar onto each and asks God to heal his marriage and bring reconciliation for the sake of the boys. He sets the bowls on the table, shoves in spoons, and pours three cups of blue raspberry Kool-Aid. He asks God again why his life is so hard and why nothing works out for him. He walks out to his truck and wrestles his new assault weapon from behind the seat, carries it to his and Pam's bedroom, and piles dirty clothes on it in the floor of his closet. In the hallway as he walks back to the kitchen, he hollers out to the boys, who are still quietly misbehaving, "Dinner's ready. Come and get your cowmoomush."

On his way home from work the following day, he stops into the Dollar Tree and grabs cheap toys for the boys—jack-o-lantern flashlights left over from Halloween for the older boys and a blinking, whistling ball for Baby Andy, because Andrew can just see him breaking a flashlight and trying to gnaw on the bulb.

His mom is pulling on her dirty flowerpot sweatshirt when he comes in the kitchen door. She struggles a little to get into it and he sees her osteoporosis has gotten worse: her shoulders roll over, collapse inside the loose bag of her skin.

"They're down the hallway playing," she says.

"Did they behave?"

"You know they did," she says. "They're good boys. Like you."

"Mom, do you remember that turtle me and James found?"

"Good lord, which one? You boys were always catching creatures and bringing them home. Snakes, frogs. That baby rabbit that died."

"The turtle was covered in maggots."

"I don't remember that no."

"I was watching TV the other night," he says, "just surfing channels, and I came across this show about how doctors are now using maggots and flies and bees to treat different illnesses."

She hoots a short laugh and shakes her head. "Well, isn't that something."

"They interviewed this one female doctor," he said. "She was British. She said a homeless man was brought in with maggots all over a big wound he had. She picked all the maggots off him, cleaned the wound, and the man died that night. She started looking into it, and because maggots only eat rotten flesh and leave the good healthy flesh alone, they were the ones fighting this man's infection. The maggots were keeping him alive."

"Makes sense," she says.

"You don't remember that turtle we found with maggots, and dad did the same thing to it, picked off the maggots and doused it with hydrogen peroxide and then it died?"

She shook her head. "Nope."

"It stank up the utility room, so you set it outside and it died."

She shook her head. "It wasn't me who set it outside. I wouldn't have allowed it to stay in the house in the first place."

"All I'm saying is Dad tried to save that turtle and he had no idea what he was doing, and he killed it."

"He didn't know."

"Remember how he said he was like Jesus tweezing away the maggots of sin from us?" His dad was wrong about Jesus. He wasn't there to tweeze away what was natural. He was there to affirm it. Lowell was right. Andrew was heir to the greatest civilization on earth. His birthright was to rule in power, not snivel and apologize. What was it Lowell had posted on the Coal River ATF blog: *Wolves don't lose sleep over the opinions of sheep.* Andrew said to his mom, "He was wrong. Dad was dead wrong."

"He did what he thought was best." She straightened her sweat-shirt. "There's chicken and rice in the oven. They're going to need baths tonight." On her way out the door she said, "You don't have to be so angry all the time. It makes the people who love you so tired." With that, she closed the door and was gone.

Andrew's weight fell into a chair at the cluttered kitchen table. He banged his head back into the wall so hard he knocked a dent in the sheetrock wall with a crack along the top. He leaned back and rested his head in the dent.

It's Friday night and Andrew's mom has the boys all weekend for the *Veggie Tales* thing they're doing at Tabernacle. After closing down the kitchen at work, he drives home to his own kitchen table, gulps down a six pack of Miller High Life and practices field stripping and reassembling his new AR-15. The next night, after breaking down the kitchen at work again, scrubbing, hosing, and squeegeeing the kitchen floor, he chugs another six pack of Miller High Life as he gears up. He drives to Sleepy Hollow Golf Club. The parking lot is empty, bright under streetlights, the clubhouse closed, the golf course dark. He pulls his Colt AR-15 assault weapon out of its hard case and moves tactically in the strip of trees between the course and the houses on Country Club Drive.

He is decked out in the camouflage gear he wears to the patriot militia musters at Lowell's Coal River place, including tactical knee and elbow pads, a MOLLE armor plated tactical vest, and a SWAT belt. His face and hands are covered in camo paint and his combat boots are laced tight, for hand-to-hand combat or running, should it come to that. His Glock 9 mm pistol is holstered at his side, locked and loaded. He carries his AR at the high ready, also locked and loaded, with a magazine of thirty 5.56 rounds. The enemies of America had infiltrated all levels of government and the time was coming when Andrew would have to join his fellow patriots and fight—this is what he was born to do, he can feel it in his bones; he has come into the kingdom for a time such as this.

Andrew finds the house where Pam and her adultery partner are shacking up. It's huge, has to be four thousand square feet. Andrew has stopped making payments on his and Pam's house—because he can't afford them, sure, but also because he hopes it will torpedo her career in banking. The garage door is open at the side of the house, the lights are on, and a red lawnmower with giant back wheels rests on the driveway, just inside the garage's light. Andrew sneaks into a copse of maple, oak, and beech trees between the golf course and the adulterer's yard. He spreads himself prone with his rifle, looks across his open sights, and waits. The dirt under the layer of dry leaves is not what he expected, not a wet layer of rotting leaves. It's gritty, sandy, like dirt at the edge of the river. All those good times he had on the Elk River. The good life, him and James playing at the sandbar behind the church.

After almost two hours, Pam's adultery partner emerges from the garage in baggy Bermuda shorts, grass-stained boat shoes, and no shirt. Andrew sights in and watches the man across his front sight post. The man has a fat, pale, banker's belly, and the thought that he is shoving his penis into Pam almost brings Andrew to pull the trigger, but he will wait. The man rolls the mower back inside but leaves the garage door open and the light on.

After two more hours, Pam's car pulls up and parks in front of the garage door. Andrew watches her over his front sight post as she gets out with her tote and walks into the garage. He can hear Pam and her adultery partner arguing. He can't hear what they're fighting about, but it's heated, and she has arrived late. Where was she?

He begins to wonder why he doesn't shoot them. They are sitting ducks. He realizes it's only because he is afraid of getting caught. He could pull it off if he overcomes his fear, if he makes a smart plan and takes bold action—bold action is the key. God helps those who help themselves. Always has. It's about time Andrew took out some mother-fuckers. Give them a little help on their way to hell where they're already headed. For now, it does his soul good to know things are shitty between Pam and her adultery partner—he dreams of her crawling back and him telling her to go straight to hell.

He strolls back across the golf course in the dark, his weapon slung over his shoulder. "Fuck with me and find out," he says aloud. "Just fuck with me and find out."

Coal River New Covenant Church
Sunday, April 1, 2002

SUNDAY BIBLE SCHOOL for the entire family .... 9:45 a.m.
Adult Class:"Ruling in the Midst of the Enemy" (Psalms 110)

Morning Worship Service: 11:00 a.m.

Prelude

Welcome & Announcements

Opening Hymn   "A Mighty Fortress" (page 55)

Pastoral Prayer   Scripture Reading (Psalm 110)

The Lord said to my Lord, "Sit at My right hand, Till I make Your enemies Your footstool." The Lord shall send the rod of Your strength out of Zion. Rule in the midst of Your enemies! Your people shall be volunteers In the day of Your power; In the beauties of holiness, from the womb of the morning, You have the dew of Your youth. The Lord has sworn And will not relent, "You are a priest forever According to the order of Melchizedek." The Lord is at Your right hand; He shall execute kings in the day of His wrath. He shall judge among the nations, He shall fill the places with dead bodies, He shall execute the heads of many countries. He shall drink of the brook by the wayside; Therefore He shall lift up the head.

Hymn   "Victory in Jesus" (page 448)

Offering

Hymn   "The King of Glory" (page 479)

*Special Music   Erin Griffin

* Children ages 4-3rd grade dismissed for Children's Church

Message   "Ready for the Day of Battle" Lt. Col. Lowell Green

Closing Hymn   "O To Be Like Thee" (page 31)

THIS WEEK:
Defending Freedom Committee
.... 4:30 p.m. today

Evening Cell Groups
.... 6:00 p.m. today

NEXT SUNDAY
Sound Room: Ronald Clendenin and Jack Stevens

Nursery: Hope Hill and Stephanie Shumaker

Budget:

General Weekly Funding Needs: $1.500.00

Last Sunday's Offering: $483.02

Unfulfilled Faith Promises:

$55.00 Ronald Klein

$135.00 Jeremy Smith

$40.00 Steven Shrives

$150.00 Andrew Minor

Upcoming:

Chalcedon Call Brass Band: Saturday, August 9, 1:00 p.m. at Joplin Park

Christian Soldiers and their wives Potluck Luncheon: Tuesday, April 10, 12:00 noon at Little Creek Park

"A lawless insurrectionist dares to call into question the justice of divine sovereignty. The distinguishing grace of God is seen in saving those people whom He has sovereignly singled out to be His high favorites. By "distinguishing" we mean that grace discriminates, makes differences, chooses some and passes by others. It was distinguishing grace which selected Abraham from the midst of his idolatrous neighbors and made him "the friend of God."

—Arthur W. Pink, *Attributes of God*

If One Devours You

(Miriam Minor-Knox, 2002)

MIRIAM SITS at the Applebee's bar and orders herself a house chardonnay. The restaurant is busy; two couples are dining at tall bar tables, and an elderly couple is on the other side of the U-shaped bar, facing her, sharing a plate of nachos and a pitcher of beer. Salt-N-Pepa's song "Push It" plays above her head and the television above the elderly couple silently plays CNN. A man talks while the chyron below him reads, "Blue chip average closes on another record high."

Miriam's day has been long and difficult. The judge recently appointed Court Appointed Special Advocates, CASA, to a case that has been open for a while. A man has five kids, two older ones with one woman, and three younger ones with another. This man, and the kids' bio moms, want unsupervised visits. The dad hasn't seen the teenagers in over a year. Miriam began the day visiting the younger three. The five-year-old was noticeably distraught; he thought Miriam was there to remove them from their paternal aunt's home. He started crying and it took a while to convince him Miriam was just there to make sure they were okay. The other two children played with toys and didn't pay much attention to her.

Then she visited the two older children. They were blunt about their feelings. They told Miriam they don't want to visit with their dad at all, ever. They were okay visiting their bio mom, but no overnights, and no guilting them when they didn't feel like visiting, or if they wanted a visit to end early.

Miriam orders a second chardonnay before finishing her first, drinks the second even faster. She watches as people come and go, waiting for a soul to sit beside her and strike up a conversation, but this evening no one is alone. The news plays silently, people come and go, and the '80s playlist circles back around to "Push It," goes to "Everybody Wants to Rule the World," and then "When the Going Gets Tough, the Tough Get Going," just like the first time. A picture of the Pope flashes up on the screen and the chyron announces, "More Priests' Names Added to Boston's Child Sex-Abuse Scandal." The unmistakable globby bass of "Sussudio," comes over the speakers, along with the thin '80s keyboards. Then the horns. A cramp stabs Miriam's abdomen and her heart starts pounding.

She excuses herself and makes her way through the restaurant to the restroom. She locks herself in the handicap stall and leans against the wall, grabbing the cold bar for support. She has broken out into a sweat and is trembling, and the pain has moved into her chest. She pushes herself away from the wall and stands in front of the toilet. She feels as if she's in an elevator that's just broken loose and is in a free fall. She grabs the bar again and eases to one knee. She tries to catch her breath. Fear sweeps over her, and she weeps as the sensation shifts and it's not her who is falling—she is planted solidly on the white tiles now and everything else has broken loose and is falling away, though nothing around her moves. She reels around, lands hard on her bottom, and hits her head on the bar. She waits out the attack with the massive, round toilet paper dispenser beside her head, stands slowly, still trembling a little, then pees before going back out to the bar. "Everybody Wants to Rule the World" plays over her head while she takes a shaky sip of wine.

When Miriam gathers her wits enough to drive, she heads, without thinking consciously about it, straight to Dorothy's house. Miriam and Dorothy are just getting to be best girlfriends again. They didn't speak for a while over a silly disagreement, but they worked things out. Then Miriam's husband Charlie got drunk and shot himself in the head—February 24, 2001, a date seared into her memory.

She was at Dorothy's house that night, when Charlie did it, and that's when Dorothy stepped up and proved herself a rock-solid friend to Miriam. Dorothy's husband Stephen is understanding. Miriam crashes in Dorothy's bed with her when they've been drinking, and he takes the guest bedroom. He did complain once that their clubbing was getting excessive, but he just mentioned it and let it drop. He looks like Tom Selleck—how Miriam had loved Magnum P.I. when she was a teenager—tall and fit with that dimpled smile. He works at Columbia Gas down by the river and is getting into business brokering. He's a hard worker, been with the gas company for fifteen years.

He is in the kitchen when Miriam lets herself in. The smell of Worcestershire sauce is sharp and Miriam's jaws clinch like she's bitten a dill pickle. A big blood-colored bottle of Lawry's Seasoned Salt with an orange lid is on Dorothy's new marble countertop beside Stephen's elbow.

"Smells good in here. What's for dinner?"

He doesn't answer. He's facing away and maybe didn't hear.

She raises her voice and asks, "When's Dorothy getting home?"

"You're her running buddy; you tell me." Stephen is beside the sink. He still has on his shirt and tie. His buns tighten in his thin dress slacks as he pounds on a piece of meat with a spiked pewter mallet.

"Haven't talked to her since this morning," she says.

"She won't be home till pretty late," he says. "You want to stick around?"

She drops her purse on the floor just inside the den. "Got wine?"

"How's alcohol mix with the new meds?" His voice is a rich baritone.

The Zoloft isn't working anymore so she's giving Effexor a try. "Doctor said don't," she says, laughing. "What's your point?" She pulls the chardonnay out of the fridge and brushes past him to the drawer for the corkscrew.

He wraps three potatoes in foil, tosses them into the oven and sets the timer.

While she uncorks the bottle and pours herself a glass, Stephen gets himself three fat fingers of Johnnie Walker Black over ice and splashes water from the faucet into it. He raises it to her. They toast and drink.

"Music?" he asks.

She nods while she is taking a drink.

He sets his glass clinking on the table and disappears into the den.

She steps outside and tries Dorothy's cell phone. A cloud front shifts as it moves in, purple and brown, deep as a car-crash bruise. They are calling for thunderstorms. Dorothy's cell goes straight to voicemail and Miriam flips her phone shut and goes back into the warm and spicy kitchen.

"Where are you?" she calls out.

Music blasts from the den as loud as a club. The song is "Brick House." It's Dorothy's *Pure Funk* CD. They have used that one a lot lately while they dolled up to go out. They danced around to the '70s disco music as they primed themselves with Chablis or chocolate martinis. Stephen drank Scotch and watched them, sometimes bemused, sometimes frustrated.

The volume softens, and she hollers, "Turn it back up."

He turns it up, then turns it up a little more. She can feel the bass through the floor, up the chair legs, into her body.

"Brick House" continues to pump in the den. She can't help but move to it.

"That okay?" he yells.

She yells back, "It's fabulous," and dances toward him as he comes back into the kitchen, holding her wine above her head, thrusting her pelvis out, right, right, left, left, shimmy. Stephen watches her, nods approvingly with the beat, even moves like he's about to dance, then goes down the hall to change clothes.

Miriam sits down at the table. It's a heavy wooden block she and Dorothy picked up at an estate sale. It had once been in a real French restaurant. The top is sloped and authentically hacked up. Above it hangs the pot rack Miriam bought Dorothy two weeks ago as a thank-you gift for being such a genuine friend.

Miriam is getting tipsy. She flips absentmindedly through their mail: bills, junk mail, a letter to Stephen from an attorney downtown, a *New Yorker* magazine. On the front of the magazine is a woman with her huge bag stuck in a revolving door. Miriam leafs through it. There is a cartoon of the Grim Reaper at a fine restaurant being forced to put on a dinner jacket before entering. Supposed to be funny. She takes a long drink of wine.

Charlie killed himself a couple weeks after Miriam left him for the third time—less than a month after she'd paid to have his vasectomy reversed so she could try to get pregnant. On her way out the door, she said to him, "You get help and I might come back."

"I'm not ready yet," he said. "I'm not strong enough." He laughed as he said it. He always laughed.

"You have to be ready," she told him. "I can't do this anymore."

The police officer told her that when Charlie pulled the trigger his blood alcohol level was 4.0, which is supposed to be comatose—5.0 is dead.

She closes the magazine and looks out the kitchen window. The

302 / VIC SIZEMORE

entire sky is dark and low now, and a few raindrops blow and spit against the glass. The Average White Band song goes off in the den, it's silent for a long instant, then the bass and blasting horns of "Shining Star" kick in. Stephen comes back into the kitchen wearing a wrinkled pair of khakis tattered at his heels and a faded blue Polo shirt tight on his chest. The blue of the shirt brings out his eyes.

He pours more Scotch into his glass. It's golden and swirls around the ice as if it has olive oil in it. Stephen dances a few steps. She can smell that he's reapplied his deodorant. She leans her head toward him and says, "You smell good."

Miriam snatches his glass and has a sip. It tastes like dirt.

He takes the glass back and drinks, keeping eye contact with her. She returns his stare. Dorothy has told Miriam that she and Stephen have grown in opposite directions, and she wants to leave him—they are such good friends, Dorothy might even give them her blessing and be glad to be free. They could all stay best friends. It could happen.

Miriam and Stephen drink and dance. They eat steak and baked potatoes with chives and heaping sour cream and real butter melting all over the plate for them to swipe their meat in. It is cooked perfectly—the man can cook too—pink but not bloody. They forget the salad but are too full to bother when they remember. Stephen molds aluminum foil over a plate of food for Dorothy, then pulls Miriam toward the den.

"One second," she says. She steps outside and tries Dorothy's cell again. It's raining now, mixed with hailstones the size of baby teeth that clatter off the hood of Stephen's car and bounce all over the black driveway. Again, it goes straight to voicemail. Dorothy always has her phone on in the car. They are still safe. Surely, he knows when she's coming home. Miriam goes back into the house and finishes off the bottle of wine.

Cameo's "Word Up" is playing. She dances into Stephen's body, and he presses back into hers. She straddles his leg and bumps. He grinds into her waist, her abdomen. They kiss. She rubs her hand on his hard-on.

"What about tomorrow?" he asks, breathing heavily into her ear.

She sings right into his ear, "The sun'll come up, tomorrow."

"Wow," he says. "You're an actual singer."

"No I'm not."

"You should be. You could make money with that voice." He slides his Scotch onto the stereo and wraps her in his arms. The rain becomes a steady drumming outside the window. Lightning flashes in clusters like paparazzi at the window. The thunder claps at times between songs, like stomping feet on bleachers. The room reels and things are finally turning her way. She dances. She spins around and grabs his glass and drinks down his Scotch.

They pull off each other's clothes and suck tongues all the way back past two empty bedrooms and Stephen's brokerage office to the master bedroom. At the door, he takes her hand and leads her to his and Dorothy's bed. Dorothy has put on the new denim and burgundy Ralph Lauren skirt and comforter Miriam picked up for her at T. J. Maxx. It is perfect for the room.

In bed Stephen is gentle and attentive. He goes down on her, takes his time. He is a beautiful man. Hairy as an ape down the front—she is fine with that since he doesn't have any hair on his back and he isn't going bald. He makes love to her, and she actually comes—before he does—and finds herself crying from happiness as she is waiting for him to finish. Listening to the rain. Listening to him grunt and moan into the pillow beside her ear.

She closes her eyes and sees Charlie as Stephen thrusts into her: her dead husband is sitting in his chair just like he always did, holding the remote and making pronouncements about TV shows with the authority of a Roman pope. Drinking his cheap vodka and lemonade out of a white plastic GoMart cup. Laughing.

"I love you, Stephen," she says. She wants to promise to cook and clean and earn money so he can quit the gas company and get his business brokerage up and going, and she can take care of the beautiful babies they will have. Dorothy will give her blessing. She wants out anyway—she's said as much more than once.

"I love you so much," Miriam says. She puts her hand on the back of his head.

He says into the pillow, "Oh God," he says. "Oh God, yes. Yes. Oh God."

His saying God over and over makes her think of her dad. The way he walked up to his pulpit, his stride as smooth as his voice. From the waist up he didn't move at all, like he was on an airport people mover. In her childhood it was like the holier he got the less he was made of flesh, the more he was just a spirit, so that any minute he might have risen and floated right over the pulpit and through the walls and off like Ezekiel to walk with God and be no more. It was the opposite in reality: he was a narcissist, her dad, put himself in the center of the crowd, soaked up attention like a black hole.

Miriam's certain her mom never had any kind of counseling or therapy—she escaped into those godawful Christian romance novels—but Miriam knows the woman is bipolar and probably borderline personality too. Miriam has only just started unpacking all the effects of that on her own life with her therapist, Jennifer. Her mom had cut off not only her own birth family—Miriam never met her maternal grandmother and her mom's childhood was a big blank space, dark and empty—but she had also cut off the extended family on Miriam's dad's side too, for no apparent reason, so that Miriam's dad drove alone to visit his family occasionally, but Miriam hadn't seen any of them since she was in middle school.

She's never mentioned Pastor Jeff to Jennifer, but Jen has intimated that she knows the general outline of what's there and occasionally asks leading questions to give Miriam a space to color in the specifics. Miriam has yet to step into that space. With all her training, all she knows about childhood trauma, she still hasn't gone there. And it has obviously messed her up bad. Here she is drunk and screwing her best friend's husband.

Stephen lets his full weight press her body into the bed for his final few thrusts, then he rolls onto his pillow and sighs, and says again, "God."

There are two chest hairs, curly like pubes, flattened in his sweat between her breasts.

Miriam almost crawled into bed with Stephen once before while he slept, with Dorothy right there in the house—they were so close, she and Dorothy, that once on a trip they shared a toothbrush. Miriam came down the hallway and said, "I almost snuggled into bed with your husband."

Dorothy laughed, waved her hand, and said, "Be my guest."

That was the night Charlie killed himself, she realizes now. Stephen had to work the next day, so he left her and Dorothy out in the den at one-thirty in the morning, starting their fourth bottle of wine and eating Chunky Monkey ice cream. Dorothy went to the hall bathroom, and Miriam had to pee too, so she sneaked through to the master bath. When she was finished, she stood and watched Stephen sleep, his broad shoulders, his thick jaw. She wished then that she could be married to him instead of her husband Charlie, who at that moment, though she didn't know it, was already dead.

A few minutes later her dad called and said, "You need to come home." "Daddy, I'm a grown woman," she told him. He asked her, "Are you okay to drive?" His pastoral coo shifted down to its sober, admonishing/exhorting end of the register. "I would admonish you," he'd tell the congregation, or "I would exhort you," before he'd explain to them how to stay in God's good graces.

She shrank inside at that tone of voice till she was a small child. "Daddy, what is it?" she asked. She knew. She said, "Is it Charlie?"

"You need to come home," he said.

Now Stephen stands hairy before her by the bed. She pulls Dorothy's comforter up over her breasts.

"Are you—have you . . ." He looks frightened. He blurts out, "Are you clean?"

"What?"

"You know." He shrugs his naked shoulders and gives a goofy grin, like he's trying to look like an awe-shucksing, innocent boy. "I'm clean as a whistle, by the way." He leans over, scratches his leg, tries to smile. "Are you clean? Do you have anything?"

She stares at him.

He glances at the master bathroom, then back at her.

"What do you think?"

He turns back to her. "Just tell me."

"You didn't just ask me that."

"I'm sorry. It's just . . . It's just that—"

"I honestly cannot believe you asked me that."

"Dorothy's told me." He shrugs. His shoulders are hunched over, and he has his hands in front of his penis as if he didn't just have it inside her body but was just caught naked in public.

"She told you I'm a slut."

He shakes his head. "No. It's just that you have self-esteem issues, and sex is how you deal."

That bitch.

"It's perfectly understandable," he says. "I mean, it's totally human."

She rolls away from him into the wet spot and squirms away from it. Bastard.

Her head slides down between Dorothy and Stephen's pillows. She shoves Stephen's off the bed so she can breathe. It makes a soft whump on the floor.

"Please just get dressed and be out in the den. *Please.*" He acts stone-cold sober now, suddenly thinking clearly. He goes into the master bath and turns on the shower.

She doesn't get out of the bed. She's beginning to feel sick.

The water stops. She turns and looks at the door. Steam rolls out when he pops his head out. He says, "I just . . . I just don't want any drama."

"Drama?" She clasps her fingers behind her head.

He steps out, still dripping wet, and says, "*Please*, Miriam."

As he starts naked for the hallway to grab their clothes, the front door opens and closes. Dorothy calls out, "Smells yummy in here."

Stephen looks at the bedside clock and whispers, "Shit." His white ass disappears into the master bath, the door closes and locks.

Dorothy's voice is a trusting singsong. "Where are you two kids?" The wet soles of her ugly, orthopedic work shoes squeak into the kitchen, and the sound of her pulling foil from her plate comes down the hall. From the kitchen she hollers, "You see the storm? A tree is across the road in Loudon Heights." She talks with a bite of food in her mouth. "You won't believe it, honey. I cut the hair of the lady whose husband owns the Mr. Donut in Kanawha City. She said he wants to sell. I gave her your card. I got his number. They're super nice people."

The fridge opens and bottles in the door clink together. It closes.

Miriam lies in silence. Her vision swims and her head throbs.

No sound from the kitchen.

Miriam swallows, and swallows.

Dorothy's shoes squeak and stop in the den where Miriam and Stephen's shirts lay strewn. The shoes squeak to the hallway, where the rest of their clothes—panties and bra included—lie where they were flung. The shoe-squeaking stops abruptly.

Rain on the roof makes a steady shush.

Miriam closes her eyes. Her head is suddenly clear, but the bed tilts and vomit surges into the bottom of her throat. Her mouth waters around her molars as she swallows and swallows and swallows. She breaks into a sweat and begins to tremble again. It isn't going to be all right. Nothing is all right. There's no going back and fixing damage that's been done. Nothing can ever be fixed.

Dorothy flips the hall switch and a slab of light invades the dark bedroom. Rain drums hollow on the roof. Stephen flushes the toilet in the master bath. Miriam's been running from the Lord for so long. It's time to do business with Him—rededicate her life to Christ. She can collapse into Jesus's welcoming arms, and he will fall on her neck with kisses wet from joyful weeping.

That alone won't be enough. She has to tell her therapist about Pastor Jeff. She has to open up those wounds and do the hard work of dealing with them. The thing she fears most is that she has known for a long time that she has to come out publicly and tell the world who he is. Just like all powerful men, he'll put the DARVO machine into action, and she's made plenty of mistakes in her life—his lawyers won't lack for ammunition. She will be publicly humiliated, vilified, pilloried; he will be praised and defended, not least of all by the women around him because he hasn't abused or raped any of *them*. Or maybe he has. Miriam hasn't made anything public yet. She doesn't have to. She still can decide not to go through with it. What good would it do? She'll tell Dorothy about it tonight though; it'll help her understand, and maybe not be quite so mad.

What she does know is, although she needs God back in her life, it can't be her dad's fundamentalism, where abusive men are coddled and protected. She needs a church that will take her side as a woman for once. She props up on her elbow and the comforter slides off her breasts. Nausea sloshes up in her throat. She swallows. She swallows again. She puts her hand over her mouth. Water rises in her eyes.

The high, piercing squeaks of Dorothy's rubber soles approach in the bright hall.

Tabernacle Baptist Church
1905 MacCorkle Avenue SW, St. Albans, WV 25177
The Lord's Day Services, August 4, 2002

Sunday School 9:30
Morning Worship 10:55
Evening Cell Groups 5:30
Wednesday Prayer Meeting 7:15

We extend a warm welcome to our visitors today. Please sign our Guest Register in the Foyer. We hope to greet you in a more personal way following the services.

Call to Worship   Rev. Minor

Hymn

"They Will Know We Are Christians by Our Love," #69

Scripture Reading

Ephesians 4: 1-16   Charise Jackson

Pastoral Prayer   Rev. Minor

Offertory Hymn

"Blest Be the Tie That Binds," #77

Hymn of Preparation

"The Church's One Foundation," #256

Piano Transition
(Sing 2 times)
Spirit of the Living God (see insert)

Sermon: "Called   Rev. Minor
to One Hope"

* * * * * * * * * * * * * * * * *

Evening Cell Groups: 5:30 p.m.

* * * * * * * * * * * * * * * * *

Please join us next week for a special service. We will be celebrating Pastor Rev. Minor's wife Berna, who was named the first ever Alumna of the Year at Pinewood University, a high and well-deserved honor. Dr. Jeffrey Wright, Dean of Pinewood University Theological Seminary, will be bringing a message from the Word to honor her. We will have a covered dish dinner after morning worship where the benevolence ministry ladies have put together a special program honoring Mrs. Minor's years of dedication to Feed the Hungry and Clothe the Naked. Meat and drinks will be provided. Please bring a side dish or desert.

The House of God

(Rick Minor, 2002)

RICK WAKES-AND-BAKES Sunday morning—smokes a bowl of kickass weed—to get himself into shape for morning worship. He is going to Tabernacle Baptist for his mom's big day. In begging him to go, Miriam said, "It'll be the first time the family's all been together in years."

"Not true." They were all there for Mother's Day at Tabernacle the previous year.

"Over a year," she said. "Come on, Diggle. It'll mean a lot to mom." Miriam was the typical firstborn: organized, self-sufficient, bossy, had her shit together. She'd found her calling early too; joined up with the first Court Appointed Special Advocates program in West Virginia in 1991 while she was in her senior year at Marshall getting her BS in criminal justice. She worked CASA in Cabell County and expanded from there to other counties, overseeing volunteers. She went on to get an MS in criminal justice, an MS in social work, became a licensed graduate social worker, and has managed the Western Regional CASA for, Rick isn't sure how long, their entire adult lives it feels like.

She was perpetually tired and stressed, but, when Rick would suggest she find other work, or just take vacations, she'd shake her head. It was her calling, just like preaching had been their dad's. Their dad offered salvation after death; Miriam tried to provide salvation in the here and now, to children, the most vulnerable. She labored tirelessly on their behalf, didn't tell anyone they needed to persevere through suffering by dangling postmortem bliss in front of them. Rick was absolutely sure his big sister had done more tangible good in the world than all the preachers and evangelists he'd ever known combined. Why hadn't he ever told her that? He should tell her.

Except, not surprisingly, her need to be the savior had made her personal life a disaster. She had savior-dated one worthless loser after another and married three of them. At least the last one spared her a shitload of lingering hassle by killing himself and being done with it for good—Rick feels like a bad person thinking that way, but it seems to him his sister is better off with the clean break from the soul-sucking narcissist.

After hitting the bowl, he takes an Alka-Seltzer and then drinks down a Gatorade at the open fridge to rehydrate. He's doing it for Miriam. He sometimes believes she's certifiably nuts, and he loves her more for her craziness. He'd rob a bank if she asked him to. Last time he talked to her she said she was walking with the Lord. She swings in and out of church the way people will diet and regain weight, so Rick never knows if she's in or out. She's been through a lot lately with her parasitic new boyfriend Tim.

A bright morning sun, along with a murderous hangover, sheared into his sleep this morning, and it felt like his brain was wrapped tight in a ripped aluminum can, so that if he remained motionless it was only pressure, but with slight movement the sharp edges dug in, slicing pain through his head into his eyeballs. The weed and Alka-Seltzer and Gatorade have knocked the edge off. He actually feels pretty damn good. He cracks open a Rolling Rock to drink as he showers: hair of the dog.

At a potluck after morning worship, his mom is being honored as the first Alumna of the Year by Pinewood University—it'd only been alumni for, what, almost sixty years? Rick's dad was never Alumnus of the Year, and he started their whole damn music program. They'd snubbed him over his Calvinism. Doesn't matter.

Yesterday, before his gig at The Empty Glass, Rick had gone to the Town Center Mall and bought a blue Oxford shirt and a pair of khaki pants for his mom's big day. He towels off and puts on the new clothes and realizes he doesn't have a belt, so he leaves the shirttails hanging, checks himself in the mirror, and decides the clothes look passable. Most of the tattoos are covered if he leaves the sleeves down.

He walks into the bedroom and grabs his hair band off the dresser. Grit sticks to the bottom of his still-damp feet. He scrapes them across the edge of his bed and slides his feet into his flip-flops. He pulls his wet hair into a ponytail with the red rubber band. He finishes off his beer with two long gulps, pops open another one for the road.

His front door opens, and his best friend Susan comes in and says, "Morning, Glory," and he remembers the previous night, inviting her to go with him. She has on a long navy coat over a dress. She has on high heels and is carrying a purse. It's small and compact like a book so that for a split-second he mistakes it for a Bible. She walks over and takes the beer out of his hand and carries it into the kitchen and sets it with a full clunk in the sink.

"I swung through Starbucks and got coffee," she says. "Let's go to church." Her hair is pulled back away from her face. Affection for him glows in her smile. He wants to kiss her but doesn't.

It is a warm summer morning. The sky is bright and cloudless blue and seems to have its own gravity when he stares up, gently pulling at him till he feels light, as if he's on a high mountain peak almost lifting into the sky. He throws out his arms to regain his balance. The winter-black trees are sprouting soft, light-green buds. He falls into the driver's seat. Susan stops at her own car and then appears at the passenger window with a cardboard tray with two coffees and a bagel on it. She hands them across to him but still struggles a little getting in. She's not used to the long coat or the heels. They work on her though because she is a natural beauty.

He cranks the ignition, and the car judders and stalls the first three times, sounds like it's laughing at him. A split down the center of his black plastic dash curls back at the edges; the hard, orange foam underneath is sun-faded to almost white. On the fourth crank, the Justy starts.

Cinder from the highway snow trucks still lines the interstate like grimy sand on beach roads—it blows against Rick's little hatchback in dark swirling sand devils as he passes semis. He calls the Justy his music cocoon. Right now, the CD he has in is Doves's *Lost Souls*. His guitar and amp are in the back seat from the previous night's gig. He isn't sure why he put them there instead of in his apartment with the rest of the band's equipment. He doesn't remember much of the previous night.

Rick hasn't been to Tabernacle—or any church for that matter—for the last seven years. When his dad was trying to get The Singing Soul Minors up and running, doing regular gigs, they were in one church or another several times a week, all week when they did revivals, their dad moving from one instrument to another, Miriam on piano, their mom quiet as a mouse but singing her parts when it was time. He and his brothers were just learning guitar then, learning chord progressions. He has to admit, those are fond memories.

He takes a careful sip from the tiny hole in the coffee lid and rubs his whiskered face. He forgot to shave. He starts the CD from the beginning; the song "Firesuite" is just the thing to get this drive started. He's delighted that his hangover is so thoroughly gone, and that he has a massive buzz on a bright Sunday morning. The coffee is dark and rich. It is just the trick. He's almost looking forward to church, and he is looking forward to spending the day with Susan. He's already jonesing for a big sloppy mound of potluck food.

As they pass the Montrose on ramp, Rick spies a state trooper in his blue and gray cruiser, nestled back in the emergency lane—dutifully watching for lawbreakers on their way to Sunday school, the bastard. Rick slows down till he's flowing with the sparse Sunday morning traffic, and uses his blinker when he changes from the left to the middle lane, and thinks about grabbing a piece of Trident out of the glove box but doesn't. He watches the cruiser in his rearview.

Susan turns around and watches it too. Her makeup is uneven, too rouged on the right cheek. She's doing this to meet his family. She's trying.

The cruiser doesn't pull out, the distance grows, it still doesn't move—a scowling old man passes Rick on the right with his hands on the wheel like bird claws—the trooper isn't pulling out. Rick's safe. He waits till the cruiser disappears around a bend and guns it past the old man. They'll make it to church in plenty of time for worship. They are missing Sunday school right now as they drive, which suddenly, all these years out, still feels naughty. The car is behaving, the girl he loves is beside him, and his stereo is kicking out the tunes.

Music is still his abiding love. Susan gets it, but his last girlfriend resented it. When he was playing music, she got pissed like he was blowing money on gambling or internet porn. Susan loves music too. They love this CD together. Doves aren't phenomenal musicians, but the production on this record is fantastic. Ricky's drummer Connor says the Doves play music, but they don't play any songs. Fine. Full and atmospheric, the music pours from the speakers and swirls into his car, music so thick and fluid he can feel it pressing on his skin, entering his body like a long flock of birds into a stand of trees.

An object is struck or plucked or strummed. Vibrations are

created that move air particles, which push more air particles, in waves of fluctuating pressure, across the room at varying frequencies. These waves are caught by the outer ear, directed down the ear canal where they cause the tympanic membrane to vibrate. Then those tiny bones, the hammer, anvil, and stirrup, amplify the vibrations, change their movement from air to the fluid of the inner ear. The fluid in turn moves tiny hairs which translate the vibrations once more into electrical impulses that shoot to the brain.

What happens from there is the mystery of mysteries to Rick. When the music hits him right, he feels like it gels him into a chrysalis, and he becomes one with the universe, and the music drives the car, and he just exists in the experience.

The moment he realizes it's happening, it's already over, but being transported like this is what he lives for, both playing and listening. The speedometer says he's going ninety. It feels like the Justy is sitting still, only rocking with wind off the river, even though he is soaring past all the cars motoring along in the right lane of I-64 as he crosses the river out of South Charleston into Dunbar, hurtling toward St. Albans and morning worship. He considers passing the exit and just driving on listening to music, but he's promised Miriam.

Tabernacle Baptist, that god-awful green aluminum building with a red brick façade across MacCorkle from the Kanawha. A prefab steeple bolted onto the flat metal roof with a white cross on top of the spire. He parks at the outer edge of the lot and clicks the key back only one notch, killing the engine but leaving the stereo on. The song, "The Man Who Told Everything" is coming on.

"We have a few minutes. You want to go in and meet a bunch of people I haven't seen for years?"

"Whatever," she says.

"After this song, we'll go in."

"Sounds good."

They listen to the song and finish their coffee. Susan says, "I'm going to need to pee before this thing starts."

Rick nods and kills the music. "Let's do it." He tightens his ponytail and squirts his neck with a shot of the Drakkar *noir* he keeps in his console. He pops in two pieces of Trident peppermint gum and chews slowly, gives the gum to Susan. She pops a piece into her mouth as he reaches across her to the glove box for his Bausch + Lomb All Clear eye drops. The bagel between them sits untouched.

He leans his head back and lets two cold eye drops fall into each eye and holds them closed. The drops run in cool streaks down his temples and into his sideburns. He sips in the mint-icy air and opens his eyes and rolls his head and looks out his window. People are dressed up, going inside. They glance at his filthy, beat up junker. He ignores them. He turns and stares through the eye-drop blur at the blue steepled sky.

"I'm not looking forward to this," he says. "Thank you for coming with me."

"It's not a big deal for me," she tells him. "I don't have all the baggage from religion that you do. But you're welcome. I'm happy we're here together."

"Welcome home, Rick," a loud whisper comes across the back of the church. Old Danny Jeffers. Rick hasn't seen Danny for at least seven years—he was old when Rick was a kid at this church. He's like George Burns, on a plateau and cruising toward death like it's a horizon line never seeming to get any closer.

They shake hands. Danny tells him, "We've got you a place saved up with your family."

The church is packed, and the congregation is seated, the teaching elder Larry Perdue sits in one of the two high wooden thrones behind the pulpit. He has on frameless glasses that reflect the over-head lights and hide his eyes. A man Rick doesn't know is giving announcements.

Rick picks out Miriam's straight black hair as he follows Danny up the side aisle. She's all the way up in the third row from the front. Their mom is beside her, her black hair streaked through with strands of white and more beautiful for it—but now lopsided with a wavy perm thing going on. Silver trays are stacked on the table below the pulpit—shit, communion Sunday to top it off—and on the purple cloth draped over the table, stitched in gold colored thread, *In Remembrance of Me.*

Rick sidles in at the end of the pew. Susan follows, holding his hand. They both nod to thank old Danny, who waves and strolls back down the aisle with a purposeful spring in his step. They sit down just as the man giving announcements says, "Standing together as we sing this morning," and the congregation stands, a few reaching down and pulling up the red hymnals out of the pew racks. The man repeats, "Standing together as we sing."

Miriam stands and hugs him and whispers, "Hey Digs." She leans in and says, "You smell good." She waves at Susan, who smiles and waves back. Rick has a one hitter disguised as a cigarette in his glove box, already loaded. He is already thinking about his plan to hit it between morning worship and the potluck dinner.

His mom leans forward and nods to him. He nods back at her and smiles, and she turns back to the front. Her face is thin and pale, but her makeup is smooth. Her large green eyes look all the more intense and beautiful. Looks like she's had her face and hair profes-sionally done. The powder-blue dress with wide white lapels and a white belt and fat white buttons looks brand new also. Her forearms are as skinny as a child's, she has constellations of small liver spots on the back of each hand, and as she flips hymnal pages her bones slide visibly under the skin.

His dad is on the other side of her at their mom's request, Miriam told Rick over the phone. He's not up front, behind the pulpit holding forth. This feels strange to Rick, like he's not in his dad's real church, but an alternate-reality version where the man sits quietly while others run the show.

"Turning with me please," the man says, "to page four hundred, 'Faith of Our Fathers.'" He has short hair, parted on the side and held perfectly in place, and a dark suit on. Not a single thing to distinguish him—he could be a mannequin come to life in a dumb comedy. He says, "Except today, in honor of Sister Berna . . ." He pauses and looks at Rick's mom with a sappy smile. He goes on, "In honor of sister Berna, we are going to sing 'Faith of Our *Mothers*.'"

The congregation sings the hymn that way, supplanting each *fathers* with *mothers*, skipping the third verse without being told; then Gloria Downy sings a song called "Prayer Warrior" clipping the ends off weak notes like she's working with just one lung. Old Danny and three other men go up, and Danny prays, and they collect the offering. The congregation stands and sings a particularly hopping rendition of "When the Roll Is Called Up Yonder," and then it's time for the sermon.

The guest speaker, here to present the award, is none other than Jeff Wright, their dad's old associate pastor in Clay. Pastor Jeff is now the Dean of the Seminary at Pinewood University—apparently the chancellor Dr. Harold Perkins Jr. was more interested in money and right-wing politics than the things of the Lord. As he begins his sermon, Miriam slips out to the restroom.

Pastor Jeff's sermon is on the inerrancy of Scripture, the tie-in being that this dear sister—Berna—would not be the example she is

322 / VIC SIZEMORE

if not for the inerrancy of Scripture. We could not trust a single thing Scripture tells us if it weren't inerrant, he says.

Rick goes into a daze in which Pastor Jeff's words come at him as if from a TV in another room. Susan digs her fingernails hard into Rick's hand. He glances over: her jaw tight as she chews her lip and stares daggers at Pastor Jeff. Rick knows generally that Pastor Jeff is talking about the liberal agenda so there are any number of things he could have said to piss her off. His dad is down the pew, sitting back in the congregation with the family for the first time that Rick can remember. Probably the strangest thing to Rick about this whole strange thing is this: Pastor Minor, the preacher, now just a congregant, another silent listener in the crowd. His eyes are half closed. He might be asleep.

Pastor Jeff wraps up his sermon, saying inerrant Scripture makes all knowledge possible. "Yes," he says, "that includes science and history." No one could know anything worthwhile without it. Thank God for his inerrant Word and thank God for faithful women like Berna Minor.

As Larry Perdue stands from the chair behind the pulpit and walks down to preside over communion, Miriam slips back into the pew. Rick turns her wrist to see her watch and her arm is limp. She stares out into nothing. "Hey," he whispers. "You okay?"

She nods and settles herself back in, pulling at the hem of her dress to cover more of her legs.

Larry Perdue recites the incantations, and the deacons serve the communion grape juice and stale cracker pieces, Rick becomes more and more amazed. It's a ritual he's observed hundreds of times in his life. He knows the words by heart: *This is my body broken for you, take and eat; this is my blood, spilled for the remission of sin, drink ye all of it.* He could easily lead communion himself if asked—it's all still there. The people in the congregation eat the cracker and toss back the thimble glasses of grape juice. Miriam partakes along with their mom. Rick declines. Susan shifts uncomfortably beside him. He glances over and she flashes him a weak smile.

The glasses clack and clatter into the circle holes in the flat board attached to the hymnal racks. His mom's skinny arm goes out with the thimble glass with her index finger and thumb. Her fingernails are painted the same sky blue as her dress. She places the glass into the rack and sits upright and smooths her dress on her legs.

Maybe it is because he is seeing it through the eyes of Susan beside him, but as he watches this time, he is struck by the incongruity: an ancient and violent ritual of blood sacrifice repeatedly memorialized in churches across the most advanced nation in the world, in 2002. What a brutal—evil—tribal god who has to see bloodshed in order to be appeased. A god who throws you into a burning hell for what you were born with and did not choose? A burning hell for *eternity*? It's too ridiculous to imagine people actually still believe it—and yet here they are.

It was his entire childhood and youth, this church and before it Clay Free Will. How has he moved so far from it? He might as well be in Bali, watching some elaborate religious rite he's never seen before and can't begin to understand. No. This is not his religion. He can't believe it any more than he could believe in Zeus or Odin— who can believe what they don't believe? This world is alien, these people are strangers.

How must Susan be experiencing it? He leans over and whispers, "You're a real sport."

She smiles without looking at him. Her smile is strained.

Susan walks with Miriam to the restroom after the service. Rick slips out to his car and gets his one-hitter. He steps to the alley behind the gymnasium and hits it. The back door of the gym is propped open with a folding chair and garbled voices rise and fall with laughter and children's shouts and clinking serving dishes and spoons. The heavy smell of blending home-cooked aromas emanates from the gym—to Rick it smells like collards boiled with a ham hock, a dish he hasn't encountered since his childhood in Clay County. Out in front of Tabernacle, trucks rumble by on MacCorkle Avenue, trailers rattling as they hit the uneven pavement. The fan at the top of the gym is on and through it Rick can see a glowing screen-covered halogen light and a basketball wedged in between the ceiling insulation and a green metal girder.

It's hot. Rick is sweating. He taps the ash out of his one hitter, slides it into his pocket, and walks up and enters the gym from the back. It's been decorated. The basketball backboards are wreathed in garlands of ivy and flowers. The volleyball poles and folded-back bleachers are draped in white sheets, and the long tables set around have white paper tablecloths rolled out on them. The centerpiece on each table is a real pineapple spray-painted gold.

A television and laptop computer are set up on a rolling metal stand in the middle arc of five curved green wall sections on casters that block off the other half of the gym. Kids are playing over there, shouting, and running. Now and then a ball rises above the wall sections and glides and disappears again like a flying fish.

The food tables are lined up beside the door to the breezeway that leads to the church kitchen. Women scurry to and from the kitchen, setting up trays and bowls and crock pots. Congregants stand around the gym in small groups chatting and laughing as they wait for the bustling women to finish setting out the food.

Rick's mom is already seated at the table of honor, the one round table in the gym, under the basketball hoop that is wreathed in fake ivy and flowers. She is staring at the golden pineapple, her face expressionless. Larry Perdue and his wife are beside her, Larry holding court.

Pastor Jeff and a group of deacons and their wives are sitting around listening and nodding.

Rick recognizes the older deacons from his youth. The man beside his mom is as young as Rick, or younger. He has no chin and he's going bald. He looks like a newt. His wife is pregnant and sits back with her hands over her round belly. She sees Rick looking at her and smiles. She has a blazing cold sore on her upper lip that almost reaches a nostril. She's just applied medicine to it because it glistens when she moves her mouth.

Rick smiles back and nods. Her husband turns and sees Rick. He gets up and walks over.

Rick scans the gym, looking for Susan and Miriam.

The newt man introduces himself and holds out his hand to shake.

"Rick Minor." Rick shakes his hand. Clammy, no grip.

"I'm the new associate. Just finished my DMin."

"Congratulations," Rick says. "Where'd you do it?"

"Bob Jones."

"Undergraduate at Pinewood?"

The newt man shakes his head. "Word of Life, in New York."

Rick raises his eyebrows and nods once, doesn't say anything.

"Your mother told me you like philosophy."

"Did she?" Rick chuckles and shakes his head. Where'd she come up with that? He hardly knows anything at all about philosophy. He spots Miriam as she comes in the door at the breezeway. Susan follows her and scans the crowd. She's looking for him.

The newt nods. "I like philosophy myself. You ever read Josh McDowell?"

"No," Rick says. He watches Susan and waves when her gaze reaches him. Her green eyes light up and she starts excusing herself through the groups to get to him. "Who is he?"

"Right now, I'm reading *Evidence That Demands a Verdict*. It proves beyond the shadow of a doubt that Christianity is not only . . ."

Rick watches his big sister and his best friend walk toward him. His mom and dad are over at their table, where there are no chairs left free. The newt wraps up his discourse, saying, "You should read it. He's like Paul on Mars Hill, using philosophy to win the lost."

"I'll have to do that," Rick says, still not looking at him. He knows the tactic: find a common point of interest, feign friendship, and rope him into the fold.

The newt says, "Nice that you could come," and reaches out again. As they shake hands, he says, "I'd love to get together with you and talk philosophy."

"Sure," Rick says. "Sounds cool."

As the newt turns to leave, Miriam reaches him. She hooks her hand into the crook of his elbow and says, "Where you want to sit?"

Susan steps up and stands beside them. She has her coat on her arm. The dress is green and blue and folds across itself on her chest so that when she moves, it gapes open and shows her blue bra.

"Doesn't matter," Rick says. Then he points to the table by the propped-open back door he just came in. "How about over there?"

The man in the dark suit who led the congregational singing goes to the TV stand and yells out, "Excuse me, can I have your attention please?" He waits. Asks again. After a lady goes around the rolling wall sections and hushes the playing children, he announces that the ladies are ready for lunch to begin, and that Berna gets to go first, along with the pastor and his wife and Pastor Jeff. Rick's mom walks to the front of the line. A gaggle of kids crowded at the front, already holding their plates—the front two boys already have three deviled eggs apiece sliding around—and plastic ware, grudgingly back into one another to make room.

Rick watches as the line slowly starts to move, his mom looking over all the dishes on the table, leaning over to study one or another. "Where's Andrew this morning?" Rick asks Miriam.

His mom takes a ham steak and then disappears behind a clump of people walking easily to the end of the line.

"He's joined Lowell's church," Miriam says. "They're doing their weekend warrior thing out there this weekend."

Rick snorts and says, "Big surprise."

Larry Perdue scoops a massive spoonful of what looks like tuna casserole. He's holding forth about something. Pastor Jeff glops on a spoonful of tuna casserole too. He is listening to Larry, nodding, almost stops nodding, then Larry makes a comment that gets it started again like a freshly tapped bobble head doll.

As they wait in line, Miriam says, "They asked Andrew to do a duet with mom, but he's so eaten up with this weekend warrior stuff out at Lowell's, he couldn't take a single Sunday away from it."

"Another big surprise."

"They asked him to do a medley of old songs with her, and I was supposed to play piano. Songs we used to sing as a family. You remember? You were young."

"I remember," Rick said. "Nobody mentioned it to me."

"You know better than that, Digs." Miriam palms his forearm. "You can't minister in music if your heart's not right with God."

The deviled eggs are gone by the time he gets to the table, and he doesn't see any collards and ham either, but he manages: seven-layer salad with iceberg lettuce and bacon bits and peas and shredded cheddar cheese, and broccoli casserole with Ritz crackers crumbled on top and more cheddar cheese, and string beans cooked with bacon and little round potatoes, and potatoes au gratin, and a slice of turkey, a slice of ham, a chicken wing out of a Kentucky Fried Chicken tub, a little spaghetti with sweet-smelling homemade sauce, and a fat buttered roll.

He puts the heaping plate of food between Susan's and Miriam's at the table by the propped-open door and goes to the dessert table. He gets a slice of cherry pie and a square of green Jell-O with fruit chunks and tiny marshmallows suspended in it. He starts to walk away from the table but turns and gets a small scoop of the pudding with banana slices and vanilla wafers layered in it. On his way back to the table, he picks up a plastic cup of sweet tea from a line of them already poured and waiting there.

Chatter echoes in the gym as they eat. Rick picks a bay leaf out of his mouthful of spaghetti sauce and puts it onto his napkin. Older church members come by and say hello, it's good to see the two of them. If he remembers the church member's name, he introduces Susan as his friend. She smiles and nods.

Rick takes his plate and gets more green beans and another piece of ham. He sees another plate of deviled eggs sprinkled with paprika has been put out, and the kids are too busy playing to snarf them all up. There are two left, and he gently pinches one up and pops it whole into his mouth. The mustard tang makes his mouth water as he chews. On his way by the drink table, he picks up a Styrofoam cup of coffee.

As he weaves between tables, he sees that the AWANA circle has been retaped onto the gym floor. Wednesday night throughout his childhood, he did these races, after reciting his memory verses. He'd earned his Timothy Award just like Miriam and James had. Rick sits back down beside Miriam and says, "You see they retaped the AWANA circle?"

She leans out and looks at the floor and raises her eyebrows. She doesn't care.

Larry Perdue stands and again introduces Dr. Jeffrey Wright, Dean of Pinewood University Theological Seminary. Pastor Jeff gives another sermon on the Proverbs 31 wife, after first reading it in its entirety. Miriam slips out to the restroom. Their dad sits and stares at his plate, where his crumpled napkin is slowly unfolding itself on top of a smear of spaghetti sauce and a chicken legbone.

Then the newt man gets up and talks for fifteen minutes about how for a quarter of a century now Berna Minor has worked tirelessly at the food pantry, has given aid and comfort to numberless needy and homeless people. She revamped the clothing store and started up the lunch program. All the workers at the Department of Health and Human Resources know her by name. The newt mentions that Matt Dodd from the Charleston paper did his column about her just two weeks ago. Rick hasn't seen it. No one bothered to call and tell him.

Susan leans over and says, "Your mom is a beautiful woman."

"She is," he says. That's impossible to miss. She looks like a porcelain doll in her powder-blue dress, skinny and frail as always—so breakable—but beautiful.

Pastor Jeff steps forward and presents her with a plaque, shaking her hand beneath the hand-off, like he must give out diplomas and Bible certificates at graduation. They sit back down. The halogens go off with loud clacks by section around the gym, and the mannequin man from the service announces that the ladies have prepared a special video to honor Sister Berna.

Chairs scrape all around on the new AWANA tape, as those with their back to the TV turn and those behind reposition to see. Miriam slips back into her chair and turns it toward the screen. The video begins with a recent Olan Mills photograph of Rick's mom and dad, accompanied by the two of them singing a duet of "Because He Lives."

Then it goes into a montage, all photos with Berna or Pastor Minor, or both of them, mostly recent. Pastor Minor's voice stops, and Berna's voice goes into the verse about the newborn baby. Occasionally an old picture pops up with the whole family in it. Pictures from prayer cards they sent out each year.

When they finish "Because He Lives," there is a gap in the sound due to poor editing, and then an old recording of their family comes on. They are singing "Just a Little Talk with Jesus." Rick remembers doing this one; when the family had performed, he was small, and he sang the solos on this one because he struggled to pronounce the words and would sing, *Jutht a wittle tok with Jethuth makth it wite,* and get the congregation laughing and disarmed for the gospel presentation.

The congregation is laughing at it now, just as congregations had laughed back then—little Ricky singing his heart out. More than the lisp, Rick notices how that Ricky had a pronounced Clay County drawl, like he'd just crawled out of a back hollow, dirty-faced and barefoot. A picture of their family flashes up on the screen, from when they all sang together, before James died. His mom in the photo looks eerily like Miriam, and when this photo was taken, she was indeed younger than Miriam is right now. Younger than Rick is right now too.

Pastor Minor's and Berna's voices come back on singing "Family of God." Rick had hated this song. He'd always hated "Because He Lives" too. Two jarringly unmelodic songs. Listening to them now, he sees he was right to hate them.

When they get to the part about everybody shedding a tear when one of them has a heartache, a photo of their brother James comes up and stays a beat longer than all the others. It's a school picture. James is grinning beneath crooked bangs. He's wearing his Pals uniform, the gray plastic Indian—Native American—chief's head is cinched tight up under his chin, the red scarf ends twirled into points the way he liked them. His body's twisted unnaturally, holding the pose the photographer maneuvered him into. A picture of the entire family together replaces it as his mom's voice sings that they also rejoice together whenever one of them has a victory. The pictures resume their regular rate of change.

When that song is over, a solo to the tune of "Oh Danny Boy" begins. Berna's voice again sings, not the words of the old Irish song, but about amazing grace and how that would be the song she sings forever because He looked past her faults and saw what she needed.

Rick glances at Miriam. She is staring at the video like it's a horror movie. A man walks behind their table and pulls the chair away from the door, and it bangs closed, clipping off the bright sunlight, submerging Miriam's horrified gaze in darkness.

The melodies he does love from his childhood—"Oh Danny Boy," Sibelius's *Finlandia*, "O So Lo Mio," "Ode to Joy"—he'd grown up thinking were church songs, and they are: they are forever ruined for him, he will never hear these melodies without those infernal lyrics running through his head.

His eyes adjust enough to see now that Miriam is crying, dabbing at her eyes with a beverage napkin. The video ends and the lights come on, a low, humming blue as they warm up. Larry Perdue stands and, in his booming preacher's voice, thanks those who stayed. He says that he's sure they all want to come by and congratulate Berna. Berna shakes her head and looks down, and he puts his hand on her shoulder and says, "Come on by and congratulate this dear sister in the Lord."

Rick opens the back door and pushes the chair in place. He looks out for just an instant, then turns and looks back into the gym. It is dark, the people move like shadows. His eyes adjust, and the overhead lights shift to a yellow glow, but are still not bright. Miriam stands and stretches. She says, "You work last night?"

Rick says, "Three sets."

In a loud confident voice, Susan says, "A benefit show. We were raising money to kick W. out for being the stupidest president to ever hold office."

A man turns and scowls at her.

"Behave," Rick says, laughing and shaking his head.

She gives him a wide-eyed *who me?* look.

"You know, it's funny," Miriam says. "I almost don't even remember James. I mean, he was there, but sort of not there too. Like Daddy and Mom, I guess. I don't know. It's weird." She asks Rick, "What do you remember?"

"I don't remember Mom and Dad being around either," he says. "James and Andrew ganged up on me for sport. The bullying was relentless. So, yeah, I remember James."

"We basically raised ourselves with no adult supervision," Miriam said. "Our house was *The Lord of the Flies*."

"I remember that when James died, Andrew stopped bullying me," Rick says. "I don't remember grieving. I was just a kid, and my life got a lot easier. I can't help it. That's how it sits in my memory."

The people are gathering around his mom's table. The family of God over there, her and Pastor Minor at the center of it. Rick has the overwhelming sensation that he doesn't know who any of these people are. His mom and dad no more than the others. His dad reaches out to him occasionally now that he's old and fat and has nothing to do all day; even told Rick once, "I want to be your friend. You know you can talk to me," which created a supremely awkward moment. The hinges on that door had rusted shut before they left Clay.

"You cruising home for a nap?" Miriam asks again.

"No," he says. "I feel good. What're you doing?"

"It's so beautiful out, I'm thinking about going over to that new Mexican place out Corridor G and having a couple margaritas on the deck."

"Get caught up in all that after-church traffic out Corridor G? No thanks."

"How about Joey's then? Come on, Diggle, we need to decompress after this." She said, "They play music on their deck. My nerves are wrecked. I'm shaking. I need a *drink*."

Rick has music—not cold comfort—and doesn't need to believe in anything else. What else is there? For him, nothing. These people. What does all of this mean, he wonders, these crazy things they believe and he grew up believing, and now coming back to it feels like stepping into the *Twilight Zone*? It's absurd, just like the guy he talked to last night said. There's no denying it.

"Joey's it is then?" Miriam asks. Always the bossy firstborn. Still getting away with it too. She asks, "Can I drop off my car and ride with you?"

The things these people believe are absurd, but no more absurd than believing we're all a product of blind chance—a bunch of wiggling organisms on a muddy glob of rock corkscrewing through space, following a burning glob of hydrogen that will one day burn out and all of human history will disappear and be gone forever, gone absolutely, as if it never was. Nothing at all makes sense.

"Yes," Susan answers for Rick. "Not a problem."

The crowd is thinning out at the round table. Rick sees his mom scan the room till she spots him and Miriam. She waves without a smile. Their dad sits slumped, his chest resting on his belly, smiling weakly as people file by and congratulate his wife, and then speak briefly to him.

"Come on," Rick says. "Let's get in the receiving line to greet the preacher's wife."

"Yeah," Miriam says. "If we don't at least say hello, I'll be the one to hear about it." She hooks her arm into the crook of his elbow as they walk across the gym. She starts to hum the tune of "Oh Danny Boy."

Susan sidles up and hooks her arm into the crook of his other elbow. They both press lightly down on his arms, but it feels like they're lifting him up—they're his comforters, his *paracletes*. It feels like he isn't walking at all but floating between them. He cannot feel the AWANA circle that moves there, beneath his feet.

Welcome To Kanawha Terrace United Church of Christ
An Open and Affirming Community

We Gather to Worship This Twentieth Sunday after Pentecost

Today we welcome Rev. Jennifer Brehm as our guest minister.

**all who are able are invited to stand

Order of Worship

Ringing the Church Bell

Meditation

"We have become not a melting pot but a beautiful mosaic. Different people, different beliefs, different yearnings, different hopes, different dreams."

—Jimmy Carter

Prelude

Welcome and Announcements

Collections

For those who are visiting, this is the time the children collect donations of clothing, food, and money for the Clothe the Poor and Feed the Hungry ministries of St. Albans and Charleston. You are welcome to donate if you feel so inclined, but it is by no means expected of you.

**Opening Hymn
"O for a World"—insert

**Call to Worship
Psalm 133:1–3

How wonderful and pleasant it is when humans live together in harmony! For harmony is as precious as the anointing oil that was poured over Aaron's head, that ran down his beard and onto the border of his robe. Harmony is as refreshing as the dew from Mount Hermon that falls on the mountains of Zion. And there the LORD has pronounced his blessing, even life everlasting.

Benediction

Adapted from an ancient Navajo ceremony

Today I will walk out, today everything negative will leave me

I walk with beauty before me. I walk with beauty behind me.

I walk with beauty below me. I walk with beauty above me.

I walk with beauty around me. My words will be beautiful.

In beauty all day long may I walk.

Through the returning seasons, may I walk.

In old age wandering on a trail of beauty, lively, may I walk.

In old age wandering on a trail of beauty, living again, may I walk.

My words will be beautiful.

I will walk in peace and beaty.

Amen.

Remember in Your Prayers This Week

Situational

Lynn Harrington, Elizabeth Dorsey, Ellie Eaton, Azari Mustafa, Jim Shipston

Long-Term

Sara Maca, Aubrey Piercy, Marcel Fusari, Daren Tucker, Jamey Mutembezi, Cynthia Shipston, Tricia Plucker, Willow Spotted Horse

Someone keeps destroying the pride flags we are flying in front of the church. Do not fear, we have purchased a box of them and will keep buying more. Remember, LOVE WINS.

Bereavement

Mindy Rauschenbach on the passing of her husband Steve, Rose Cordova Roca on the passing of her husband Jeorge, Ginger Stone on the passing of her son Dylan

New Members

We would like to welcome Miriam Minor-Knox into our fellowship. Miriam has jumped right into the thick of things here, working in support of our LGBT community, and we are grateful she is with us. Please extend a hand of fellowship to Miriam today after the service.

In Due Season

(Berna, 2003)

IT RAINED last night, and the McDonald's lot is damp. The boys' shoes will be gritty. Chase and Hunter dutifully follow her rule, hold hands, and look both ways as they cross the lot—they know she'll load them up and drive right back home if they give her trouble. She carries Baby Andy. The sky is clear this morning, no clouds at all. It's in the mid-sixties, a beautiful spring day. Corridor G is a jungle, all the traffic, and she's not sure why she keeps bringing them to this one. It's the nicest one in town but they're young and will play anywhere.

Inside the restaurant, she holds open the door to the play place. The din of rambunctious kids echoes off the high glass walls. Chase and Hunter scurry in and drop to their butts and yank off their Nikes and socks. Baby Andy trails behind and Berna has to hold the door open for him. The smell of greasy food mixes with the wet, oil-asphalt smell outside, and Berna has no appetite. These places are always too bright too. And too loud.

All the workers behind the counter are Black, too old for high school but too young not to be in college; they should be in college right now. Why aren't they in school? The injustice of it infuriates Berna. She doesn't see anyone in the button-down manager shirt, just all these poor Black kids, and they're having trouble keeping up. Four registers, all backed-up with lines of impatient White people. Here

338 / VIC SIZEMORE

she is one of them, and if she tries to be extra nice so they know she's on their side, it will ring false, and they'll roll their eyes. Better than treating them like Lowell and Cindy would. Cindy would never lower herself to eat at a McDonald's, but she's just a snooty bitch; Lowell is the real danger and Berna blames him a lot for how Andrew has turned out.

After the 9/11 attacks, Lowell and his ATF bunch had gone full-on white supremacist and had started training out at his Coal River place to fight. Berna and Zechariah always knew he was racist, but they didn't know the extent of it until last year, when he'd invited Zechariah out there to give the men an early morning message before they went to the rifle range on Lowell's back property. Zechariah had come home that day shaken as Berna had never seen him before. He sat at the kitchen table and wept into his hands. She scratched his back while he had his cry—the only other time she had ever seen him cry was when James died—and then sat at the table and listened to what had happened out there.

Lowell, and Lowell Jr., and that gang of men—retired military, active National Guard, two policemen, civilians playing soldier—had wanted to initiate Zechariah into their cause, which was a miscalculation on their part. "They believe there's a conspiracy to replace White people and White culture—that came from Europe—with Black and Brown people from inferior cultures."

"People are so fearful of those they don't know," she said.

"It's worse than that," he said. "Lowell told me to my face that he believes Jews and Black people are subspecies. He believes they don't even have souls. They die and are gone like animals. That's what he told me."

"He just came out and said that to you?"

"He did."

"He was messing with you. He can't really believe that."

"Sure sounded like he did."

"He can't. That's just crazy," she said. "What are you going to do about it?"

"He's the fighter," Zechariah said. "I'm not a fighter."

"You don't have to fight him. You've been preaching that God is the one in control for how long now? Do you not believe it?"

"Course I do."

"Then do what you've always done: stand in that pulpit and speak what you believe is the truth."

The next morning in worship, Zechariah did just that. His jumping-off point was Revelation 5:9b–10: "For thou wast slain, and hast redeemed us to God by thy blood out of every kindred, and tongue, and people, and nation; and hast made us unto our God kings and priests and we shall reign on the earth." He lambasted racists and bigots and singled out a history professor at Pinewood University for his public statements claiming all people who followed Islam were terrorists and should be run out of the country. "They are our fellow human beings," he said, "in need of Christ just like us. It is not up to us to decide where they stand with God—that is entirely within His sovereign prerogative. It is, however, our Christian duty to love them with the love of Christ."

Zechariah was on the right side of that issue. He called out Lowell and the other racists in the church even though he knew what would happen. It did happen too, the church split, Lowell took half the congregation with him and started a new church, the school had to close, and Tabernacle couldn't pay its bills anymore. Zechariah's health wasn't great already, and this sent him into a depression that broke his spirit and pushed him into his recent retirement. Even with all that, more than anything else Zechariah ever did in all the time she knew him, standing up to Lowell was the one that won her admiration and respect the most. He never said boo to Lowell about the sexism though, never spoke a word from the pulpit about the misogyny running warp-and-weft through Christianity.

What would he say? As far as Berna can see, the Bible does blame women for the suffering God unleashed on the world. From Eve in the book of Genesis to the Whore of Babylon in Revelation, women are bad, fit only for punishment with oppression and pain. Men throughout history have been more than happy to carry that out too—it seems men of God relish punishing women more than any other kind of man. Why not? God hates them.

God hates Berna too she's come to believe—even the God of Jesus and the New Testament. She thinks of the year following James's death, when Zechariah consoled himself with the doctrines of grace. Strangely enough, it was her husband's Calvinism that eventually set her free.

Sunday after Wednesday after Sunday, she sat listening to him preach, staring at the stained-glass window of that famous picture of Jesus knocking on the door. Before he'd come to believe in predestination, Zechariah had said from the pulpit that there was no knob on the door in that painting for a reason. Jesus was out there knocking on the door of your heart, but he couldn't open the door. He couldn't come in unless you opened it and invited him in. Berna thought, *Like a vampire*, but never said it aloud to anyone.

What she remembers is, over the years, banging on the other side of that door, asking God to open up and make her not who she was. It came as a huge relief when John Calvin convinced her that the picture was wrong and there was no knob on her side of the door. She felt as elated as Pilgrim at the cross when his burden rolled away. She was free to work at helping people not because she was afraid of God, but because it eased suffering, even if only in small ways. It's what she can do. If it's not enough for God, she's got nothing else. When she dies and stands before Him, she will say her piece and let the chips fall where they may.

She glances into the play place: Baby Andy is spinning the yellow tic-tac-toe wheels; Chase and Hunter are out of sight up in the tube maze. She turns back to get into a line and finds herself behind a thin man in a black motorcycle jacket. He has a gray mullet, that unfortunate hairstyle rednecks and lesbians share these days. He has on jeans and black boots and has a big black wallet attached to his beltloop by a swooping chain. He holds a black helmet against his hip, and it makes his jacket bunch up in his armpit. Looks like a rough customer.

Berna looks back and forth, watching the progress of her line and keeping an eye on the boys. Music plays under the general noise of people placing orders and the workers in back calling out things to one another, popular music that Berna doesn't recognize, but in the time she's been in line, she's heard two different songs use "like a diamond."

Berna watches the playing children, again spots the boys. She turns around as the man in front of her is looking out the side window at his motorcycle. Berna is transfixed, stares at the side of his face, with a thin, but well-trimmed beard, a light liver spot on the cheek, and tiny purple veins on the nose. As she stares, she feels the tiles beneath her have dropped away and she is floating in space. Who is this man, this man she knows, she knows well, but doesn't know at all?

She hears her own voice say, "Jordan?"

The man turns around and their eyes meet. Unmistakably Jordan Goins's deep, blue eyes looking at her from Jordan's face, weather worn, rough, textured, but Jordan's.

"Berna?" Jordan says in not-Jordan's voice. "Damn, look at you. You haven't aged a day."

"That's a lie." Berna knows the deep creases and sun damage on her own face, the liver spot starting to darken on her left temple. "You look different," she said. "You look good. Wow, I was not expecting this. Jordan Goins."

"Jay. I don't go by Jordan anymore. I go by Jay."

"Jay."

"I'm living as a man now. I'm a trans man."

Berna stammered, said, "What?"

"I've always been a man, Berna. I was a man back when you knew me. It was just . . . well, you know how it was."

"Wow," Berna says again, and again, "Wow." Jordan—Jay—must think she's a real airhead, standing there with nothing to say but *wow*. She says, "Well . . ." She just can't think of anything to say. She repeats, "Wow."

"Doesn't it make things fall into place back then?" Jay laughs. "When I realized it, my whole life fell into place like those Tetris blocks turning and dropping perfectly right where they fit. I've been in serious therapy too."

"You never got married?"

"No." Jay shook her—his—head and laughed. "I've had long-term relationships, but I've never been married. It's complicated."

Not knowing what to say, Berna simply nodded agreement.

"I've been living as a trans man for over ten years now," Jay chuckles, and it's the same laugh Berna remembers. The voice is changed; the laugh is the same, and the tilt of the head and smirk. Jay says, "I haven't gotten this reaction from anybody in a long time."

"Do you still live in Clay County?"

"Lord, no. I live right in downtown Charleston. I have a house on Quarrier Street."

"On Quarrier Street? All these years and we've never run into one another."

"I saw you a couple of times."

"Why didn't you . . ."

Jay waves off the question before she finishes it.

"Are you still a butcher?"

"Retired. Can you believe it? One day you turn around and you're old."

"Zechariah's retired too." He sits in his office looking at his computer now. When he feels okay, he golfs.

"Didn't think he'd ever retire," Jordan says. "I thought he'd keel over in the pulpit one day."

"He talks about filling pulpits, but he's not doing anything about it. I still work with the benevolence ministries some, but I have my grandbabies during the day now, so not much."

"Grandbabies?"

"Andrew's boys." She points to the play place.

Jordan—Jay—nods.

"How have you been?" she asks Jordan—Jay—and feels stupid, asking a question like that. They were lovers. They were *in love*. She can't help herself, she wonders if Jay has had her—his—breasts surgically removed, if he now has a penis. How do they even do that? Berna has questions, but she would never ask them, not now. The years have made them strangers now—but also *not*.

The people in front of Jordan—Jay—take their trays and move away. She steps up, places her order—*his, his, his*—and motions to Berna. "Put her order on my ticket too."

"No," Berna says. "I can't—"

"I haven't seen you in fifteen years?" Jay says.

"Longer."

"Let me get your lunch."

"Only if you'll come out and eat with me and the boys in the play place."

Jay grins. "Deal."

"Here." Berna hands him the buy-one-get-one coupon.

Jay lifts the tray with one hand—a small, but a strong, weathered, working hand. The helmet is under his other arm. He says, "Okay, pretty lady. Lead the way."

Berna holds the door and Jay steps through with the tray. They sit at a table where a *Mail-Gazette* is scattered. They fold up the sections and set them on the next table over. The play place stinks of sweaty kids and cold french fry grease. It's loud with squeals and laughter and the echoing thumps and squeaks of bare knees in plastic tubes. Berna sets out the chicken nuggets for the boys and pops the plastic top off her salad. She says, "I can't see you retired. Besides working on your house, how do you keep busy?"

"I do volunteer work. I build houses with Habitat for Humanity."

"That's good work. Jimmy Carter does that, you know."

"I like it because the people we help also have to work on the house too, have to invest sweat equity. I'm an activist on behalf of the LGBT community too."

Berna doesn't know what to say to this, so she nods and says nothing. They eat for a bit.

Berna wipes her mouth and asks, "How's your dad?" In her peripheral vision, she sees Chase and Hunter standing at the bottom of the blue tube slide looking at her and Jay. Baby Andy is inside the yellow plastic house with the red door and green roof.

Jay wedges his helmet between the window and his seat. "He passed four years ago."

"I'm sorry."

"It was a relief when it finally came. He had stomach cancer, lots of pain, couldn't go anywhere or do anything." Jay laughs and shakes his head. "He never lost his sense of humor though. A couple of days before he went, I was sitting with him, and a nurse opened the door and light came in. He rolled his head to look, then rolled it back so he was staring at the ceiling again and said, 'Wrong light.' The nurse and I just cracked up."

"How was he with . . ." Berna waves toward Jay, "with this?"

"It wasn't good, not good at all. I think he accepted me by the end, or not, I don't know, it doesn't matter now. Doris wasn't well herself—she's gone now too—and she was mighty desperate to reach out to me for help. Staring down death changes peoples' perspective on a lot of things."

"How is the church out there?" Berna looks over at Chase and Hunter and they turn and clamber the wrong way up the tube slide, all thumps and squeaks. Up in the maze, a girl's tiny voice yells, "Stop it. Jeffery, *stop.*" The girl yells," "I'm telling." Baby Andy is playing with another toddler in the plastic playhouse, acting like little adults, intense like they're on a deadline.

"Dad quit the church," Jay says.

"Wow. I didn't see that coming. What happened?"

Jay shrugged. "He quit religion altogether." He takes a big bite of his burger and chews. "You know, when my dad was done, he didn't pussyfoot around; he was done." He leans back, pulls the leather jacket off his shoulders—it is warm in the play place—and watches the kids play. With food still in his mouth, he says, "Which ones are yours?"

"I'll get them."

"Oh no—"

"They need to eat anyway." Berna stands and goes to the tube maze. She hollers for Chase until he answers and tells him to bring the other two and come eat, to which he says yes ma'am.

She sits back down. She's nervous, like she and Jay are on a first date. It's ridiculous at their age, she knows, but here it is, the feeling. Jordan is with her, in motorcycle clothes and a bad haircut, having a meal across the table. And Berna loves her still. Berna has always loved her—him. *Him.* What did any of that matter to Berna? Let the stodgy old men and their angry god worry about it. Berna still loves Jay, she can't deny it, and why would she now?

The boys come over. Chase and Hunter climb up into their seats. Jay jumps up and grabs a booster seat for Baby Andy, lifts him into it, saying, "There you go, Champ." The three of them snatch up chicken nuggets with dirty fingers, dip them in the honey mustard, gnaw on them. Hunter and Chase keep glancing curiously at Jay, while Baby Andy is engrossed in his chicken nuggets.

Jay asks, "How are your kids? What's Miriam doing these days?"

Berna says to Jay, "It's been hard for her. She's a sweet girl who's made bad choices."

Jay leans back and laughs. "Haven't we all."

"I wasn't the best mother."

"Do you know," Jay says, "the cells of your body are only 70 percent you; a full 30 percent of your body is not you at all, but interacting bacteria, viruses, various parasites? There are one hundred times more bacterial cells in a person's body than there are cells that they are made of—according to the National Institute for Health, there are more than ten thousand microbial species inside a person's body, and they actually contribute more to the body's survival than the actual body itself does. Think about it: What is each one of us but a small world of dirt and water, hosting a busy swarm of microbial life."

Berna stares at Jay. "Well, aren't you that guy from *Cheers* who has all the trivia."

Jay laughs. "Cliff Clayborn. Yeah, that's me. Did you know our brains are 75 percent water? So are our hearts. Hearts, by the way, that we share with other great apes. Chimpanzees. Genetically, we're more closely related to chimpanzees than chimps are to gorillas."

"I'm confused," Berna said.

"Basically, gorillas are our cousins and chimps are our brothers." Jay put his hand over his mouth and smooths down on his beard. It's a habit Berna has noticed.

"When I came to be with you back then," Berna says, "I'd leave them alone. I had people watch them, but mostly I left Miriam in charge. She was too young."

Jay says nothing in response to this, and Berna wants to cry. She tells the boys, "Eat up, and you can play a while longer." They cheer because usually she makes them leave right after eating to get back for morning naptime.

Chase looks at Jay. With his child's boldness, he says, "Who are you?" A small piece of nugget batter falls from his mouth and bounces from the table to the orange tile on the floor. He doesn't notice. He stares at Jay with his big brown eyes.

"Me?" Jay says. "I'm just an old friend of your grandma."

Hunter asks, "Are you a motorcycle man?"

Jay laughs and says, "You like motorcycles?" He picks up his helmet and holds it over the table. The boys stare at it in awe, nodding that yes, they do like motorcycles, they like them a lot.

"You want to sit on my motorcycle after you eat?"

They nod more vigorously. The little girl Baby Andy was playing with toddles up and stands staring at him. She needs her nose wiped. She has on a long-sleeved white tee shirt, the sleeve cuffs are brown with ground-in dirt. She has a small purple scar beside her nose, still a soft little baby nose. Behind her, kids are shouting and screaming and pounding around in the plastic tubes. Without saying a word, the girl turns and runs back to the plastic playhouse.

"You want to take a ride on my hog?" Jay says.

"Take a ride on a *hog*?" Hunter squeals. He starts giggling.

"Guess what," Jay says. "A hog is also what people call a kind of motorcycle. Because the motorcycle sits low and has a fat gas tank. Like a hog."

Chase says, "I never rode on a motorcycle before."

"I'll take them for a ride around the parking lot if you're okay with it," Jay says to Berna. "Nice and slow. Safe as sitting on a beanbag chair watching cartoons."

The boys both shout and cheer. Baby Andy cheers with them as he squirms to get out of his booster seat. Jay stands and helps him down. They run off to play. Jay sits back down, leans forward, and looks straight at Berna. "You ever let a man give you a ride on the back of his Harley?"

Berna puts her hand to her chest, looks away, and laughs.

"You're blushing," Jay says. She—he, he, he, Berna reminds herself—is grinning. Inside his neat beard, his teeth are straight and white—he's had work done on them. Berna laughs again and shakes her head. Jay laughs with her.

A few days later, Miriam calls and tells Berna she is back in fellowship with the Lord. "But I'm not in a church like Tabernacle," she says. "I've found my home in the United Church of Christ." Her church is hosting a social and economic justice conference in Charleston with other UCC churches, she tells Berna; other denominations will be there, even other religions. "I told them about you, and they wonder if you might come and be on a panel discussion, or even speak about your work with Clothe the Naked and Feed the Hungry."

"You know I don't do public speaking."

"You'll just sit at a table and answer questions about the practical aspects of running them."

Berna does know about running those places and it feels good to be asked, so she says she'll do it.

The conference is full of left-wing radicals, and a big group of them are nuns in trouble with their church—Berna can't get a straight answer on whether or not they've been excommunicated. Two of the nuns are an openly lesbian couple. Berna is fascinated, can't stop watching them all morning. Sister Bonnie Jo and Sister Jean. They are together, a *couple*. They look like two old grandmas. All the other women act like it's the most normal thing in the world.

The two of them tell Miriam they're ditching the boxed lunches and walking seven blocks to Leonoro's for Italian food. Sister Jean puts her hand in the air like she's being sworn in and says, "Their lasagna is to die for."

Berna is standing beside Miriam. She says, "I love eggplant parmesan. Wonder if they have that."

"Do they have that?" Sister Bonnie Jo said. "Put on your walking shoes, girl. You're about to eat the best eggplant parm you've ever tasted."

Over lasagna and eggplant parmesan, Berna and Bonnie Jo talk about the headaches of coordinating and managing volunteers in benevolence ministries. They compare their strategies for getting people to take ownership of the work. Miriam and Jean eat and listen.

Miriam waves at the waiter and points at her wine glass. He nods and smiles, and Berna can see Miriam and the waiter have done this a few times before. She realizes that though Miriam is kind to her now, she knows little about the girl's actual life.

In a pause, Miriam asks, "So how'd the two of you meet?"

Bonnie Jo does the talking now. Jean was an administrative assistant at the school where she did her graduate work. "She was a hottie," Bonnie Jo says. Jean smirks and takes a sip of her wine.

Berna wants to ask, how in heaven's name did they become nuns? Not just how, but why? They aren't real nuns though, she doesn't think. The church has rejected them. What does she know about it?

Not much. She picks up Miriam's wine and sniffs it. The tang makes her jaws clench, and her mouth waters in back around her molars. Miriam motions for her to have a sip. She scrunches her nose as if she's just caught a whiff of a dead mouse in the trap and sets down the glass.

Miriam says of their story, "I think that's fantastic."

At this moment, a sense of peace washes over Berna. God is not an angry old man. God is love. It's that simple. Zechariah is wrong about God. One thing she has to admit about his Calvinism is that it has, over the years, dulled his tendency to judge people harshly for their sins—seeing as all are equally depraved before God and he doesn't think it's his job to save people anymore. He wouldn't go as far as to approve of Bonnie Jo and Jean's lifestyle, but he wouldn't shame them either. He certainly wouldn't denounce them publicly, as their own superiors—men; all of them men—have done.

"You two make such a cute couple," Miriam tells them. They both smile and thank her.

Berna wants to cry. She takes two deep breaths and waits for the urge to pass. Then she asks, "Do you all know about Habitat for Humanity?" she asks.

"Oh, yes."

"Do we ever."

Miriam says, "Such a wonderful organization."

"I've been thinking," Berna says. "I might start working with them. Learn how to use a hammer and a saw."

"Why not?" Bonnie Jo says. "You're not so old. How old are you?"

"President Carter works on Habitat houses. So does his wife," Miriam says. "He's, like, eighty?"

"Still out there laboring away for God," the lesbian nun Bonnie Jo said.

"It's impressive," Berna says. She pinches the stem of Miriam's wine glass, lifts it, has a sip. She winces a little at the sharpness of it. Miriam smiles.

At the dinner table that evening, Berna says to Zechariah, "I ran into Jordan Goins a couple of weeks ago at the McDonald's on Corridor G."

Zechariah nods. With the edge of his spoon, he scoops out a bit of melon and cottage cheese from his cantaloupe half. He lifts the food slowly and winces as he closes his mouth around it. He chews and swallows. He says, "I've wondered what became of her. How is she?"

"She's fine." Berna decides not to tell him Jordan is now Jay. "She's retired. Never got married."

He nods. "No. I suppose not."

"What's that supposed to mean?"

He scoops out more cantaloupe and cottage cheese and eases it into his mouth. She has fixed him a plate of leftover ham steak and green beans too. He picks up his fork and tries to cut the ham steak with the edge of it, then puts his fork back down. He says, "My stomach is worse today. I don't think I can eat the meat."

"I need to tell you something. And I guess ask you something too."

He looks at her. It still surprises her, seeing once thick and solid Zechariah go bloated and red. Sixty-five is too young to look as bad as he does. He never kept fit, spent forty years at a desk with an ink pen in his mouth and his nose in a book, and then the thing with Lowell and his depression did a real number on his health. His gut troubles fill the house daily with intestinal stink so foul that she worries the doctors are missing cancer in there. He runs his tongue around his gums.

"I'd like to—I am going to—renew my friendship with . . ." She considers whether or not to use the male pronoun but decides one thing at a time with Zechariah and so finishes the sentence with *her*, "going to renew my friendship with her."

He sits for a long moment staring at his food. A hummingbird comes and hovers at the red feeder outside the kitchen window. It jerks and shifts, drinks, and darts away again. Berna needs more red food coloring for her sugar water. Finally, he says, "Your friendship with her back in Clay, it was more than just friendship, wasn't it?"

She eats a small bite of cantaloupe. Takes a drink of tea. "Yes," she says. "It was."

He nods, scoops more cottage cheese into his mouth. He chews slowly. Swallows. He burps into his closed mouth and swallows again.

"I think I'm going to start volunteering with Habitat for Humanity," she says. "Help build houses for people who need them."

"Jordan doing that?"

"Yes."

He nods.

They eat without speaking for a while. The old refrigerator suddenly starts humming as loud as an electric razor and a few seconds later just as abruptly stops. The automatic ice maker is on its last leg but it's still making ice.

Zechariah sets his spoon neatly on his napkin. "Do you think I wasted my life in those churches?"

"How could I possibly answer a question like that?" The grandfather clock in the living room clacks away. They stare out the back window at the faded hummingbird feeder.

"The neuropathy in my feet is getting worse," Zechariah says. "I need another appointment with Dr. Padilla."

Still staring at the feeder, she says, "I'll call tomorrow."

Tabernacle Baptist Church
1905 MacCorkle Avenue SW, St. Albans, WV 25177
The Lord's Day Services, May 4, 2003

Sunday School 9:30

Morning Worship 10:55

Evening Cell Groups 5:30

Wednesday Prayer Meeting 7:15

We extend a warm welcome to our visitors today. Please sign our Guest Register in the Foyer. We hope to greet you in a more personal way following the services.

Call to Worship   Rev. Perdue

Hymn

"The Law of the Spirit of Life," #415

Scripture Reading
Romans 8:1-11   Jennifer Kaufmann

Pastoral Prayer   Rev. Perdue

Preparation in Songs of Praise (lyrics on overhead)
  "Hosanna"
  "Where the Spirit of the Lord Is"
  *"Revelation Song"
  "Breathe"

*Tithes and Offerings will be taken during "Revelation Song"

Sermon
"Escaping the Realm of the Flesh"
Rev. Perdue

Benediction
"Awesome God" (lyrics on overhead)

Evening Cell Groups: 5:30 p.m.

Weekly Calendar

Tuesday at 6:00	P&W Band practice
Wednesday at 7:00	Service Projects
Thursday 5:00-9:00	Friendship Evangelism

Sarah Gardner would like to publicly thank her cell group for praying a hedge of protection around her during a difficult and grievous time in her life. She does not know what she would do without you.

The family of Susan Peters would like to thank the church for the beautiful flower arrangement at her funeral. This church was literally Susan's life. The peace lilies were beautiful.

Everette Jones would like to express his thanks to Clothe the Naked for providing so many needed items to the Baldwin family in their time of need.

This evening after church there will be a business meeting. All members in good standing are welcome to attend. We will discuss and vote on not renewing the leases for the benevolence ministries Clothe the Naked and Feed the Poor and redirecting those resources toward the children's ministry and the food pantry here at the church.

At the Sound of the Bird

(Zechariah, 2003)

HE GIVES up on sleep. The bird making all the racket outside his window is a bobwhite. It sings its own name tirelessly, *bob-bob-white*, pitching up on the *white*. Gray light is just starting to show through the closed blinds. He's been up most of the night, making trips to the toilet, sitting, sitting, squatting beside it, holding on to the sink counter, seeking relief from what felt like was a baseball trying to rip through his prostate. The pain had subsided and allowed him to doze only a while before the birds began their racket. Now his neuropathy is acting up making his feet itch and burn. He is no longer strong enough to do something as simple as untuck the blanket and top sheet without his soles cramping up, making his toes curl down while he grits his teeth and waits it out. His toenails look like yellow turtle shells. Not much to be done about any of it. He's old.

He can hear Berna down the hallway in the kitchen, clinking a spoon round and round inside her mug of coffee. Miriam had lived with them for a while after some of her man trouble. Now that she has moved back out again, their mornings have returned to the quiet routine of breakfast and devotions. Berna spends a lot of time these days with that Jordan Goins from out in Clay. Those two, what they did back then, and here they are at it again. But they're a couple of old women now and it doesn't seem to matter anymore. Down the hallway, Berna's spoon clatters into the sink.

He gets up and does a couple deep knee bends with his hand on the bed for balance, releases his morning gas in a long blubbering gust, and walks slowly in place to loosen up his joints and see if his feet will let him golf today. His legs are white as moons, long ago rubbed hairless and smooth by his slacks. He watches the muscles contract under skin as loose as an uncooked chicken's. He hasn't felt well lately, not just age, but he isn't sure what. He is determined to push through it, though he knows what's on the other side at his age, and it's not a return to health and vigor. A day at a time now. Each day a small lifetime, most days indistinguishable from the string before and after, broken only by trips to church. This morning however, he has eighteen holes to walk with his prodigal son, Ricky.

He opens the bedroom door, makes his way down the dark hall to the bright kitchen.

Berna is at the breakfast table, with her hair and makeup already done, in her peach terrycloth robe, *Our Daily Bread* open on top of her open Bible. She is drinking coffee she makes with a French press and grinder Andrew gave her for Christmas. She loves the thing, thinks it shows culture and breeding. She has unconsciously straightened her carriage as she sips her French pressed coffee in the mornings. He laughs to himself at her silliness this late in the game.

She is as beautiful as the day he first saw her, as small and frail as a little bird in the hand. She spends her days watching Andrew's boys now, and doing volunteer work with Jordan Goins. She keeps herself as busy as ever. Shows no sign of slowing down. She has his pink grapefruit half set in a cereal bowl at his place-setting, along with his granola-and-yogurt, and his pill organizer open to the pills he's to take this morning.

He doesn't speak to Berna so as not to disturb her morning

devotions. He pours himself a cup from the Mr. Coffee. She still brews his coffee. He doesn't like the French press stuff. Too strong and harsh. Cowboy coffee is what it was called when he was young—funny now, according to Andrew, it's apparently all the rage at the restaurant where he works. Along with eating locally grown turnips and collard greens, which in Zechariah's day just meant you weren't rich. Zechariah calls that French press stuff *le mud*.

As he pours his coffee, a charley horse knots up in his left calf. He has to abandon the mug at the counter and sit in his chair to stretch.

"Still golfing with Ricky today?" Berna asks, not looking up from her *Our Daily Bread*.

Zechariah broke down and called the boy yesterday, prevailed upon him to play a round. He says, "As far as I know." Ricky is supposed to swing by at seven so they can ride together. He might, he might not. He's about as dependable as the bums Zechariah occasionally hires from the mission to do work around the house. He's found that the same forbearance with which he deals with them is also the best way to handle Ricky.

"Where you going?" She sips her French pressed mud from a mug with a picture of pig students sitting at school desks looking at a pig teacher. It does smell better than his coffee.

"Shawnee, if he shows up." He stands and gets his coffee, then eases back down. In the light angling down the back hillside, he can see Berna's hummingbird feeder outside the kitchen window, a clear tube with red-faded-to-orange plastic flowers where the tiny birds hover and eat. It is empty. A shadowy white tail deer grazes at the back of the yard near the trees. Zechariah takes the steak knife from the table between them and works it around the edge of the grapefruit half, then between the wedges, loosening them for his spoon. He ignores her stare as he salts the fruit.

She shakes her head and looks back down at her *Our Daily Bread*.

"Eighteen holes," he says. "Going to walk it if I can get my feet to cooperate."

As he eats, gas gathers and shifts in his intestines, causing sharp cramps. He'll have to remember to take his Gas-X if Ricky comes along. He almost hopes Ricky doesn't show so he can get his relief the old-fashioned way.

"You should have invited Andrew to come."

"He can't get away from that place."

"True," she says. "Maybe you and Ricky can bond."

Zechariah digs at his grapefruit pulp, and as he does, he remembers when, coming from his study, he stepped into the carport where Ricky and a boy from his soccer team named Justin were horsing around. Ricky was around fifteen, a lanky man-child. As Zechariah entered the shade of the carport, he saw that both boys had their shirts off, and Ricky had Zechariah's mother's quilt in his fist, swinging it around like a lasso.

Zechariah remembers his mom making that quilt, needle-pointing the state flower for each state on baby-blue squares, then sewing them together in a checkerboard pattern and spreading them in the back room on a wooden rack to sew to a blue back with cotton under each panel. She'd spent months on it. She's gone now, along with his dad, his sister. His friends and colleagues in the ministry are going home to be with the Lord at an increasing rate.

"What are you boys doing today?" he had asked Ricky.

"Just messing around." Ricky was holding one end of the quilt in his fist and the rest was spread across the concrete carport. Justin stood about twenty feet from him with his hands in the pockets of his blue corduroy pants. They both had the fuzzy beginnings of mustaches and chin fuzz.

"My mom made that," Zechariah told him. "Don't let it touch the ground."

"It's just an old blanket."

"It's not just an old blanket. My mom worked hard on it. It's probably worth a lot. Take it inside right now."

Ricky stood and looked at him.

To avoid a power struggle in front of this other boy, Zechariah had said, "I want that quilt inside by the time I pour myself a glass of tea." He turned to go into the house, and as he reached for the screen door, something whacked him on the back of the head. It didn't hurt, but anger rose into his chest. He spun around and saw Ricky half crouched. The boy had just snapped the quilt at his head, the way boys did to each other's legs with towels in a locker room.

"Dude," Justin said, "that's your dad."

Ricky put his hand over his mouth and said, "I'm sorry. I'm sorry. I didn't mean for it to hit you."

Zechariah clinched his fists and took two steps toward Ricky, and Ricky stepped backwards ready to flee.

Zechariah said, "That was grossly inappropriate."

Ricky dropped his hand from his mouth and balled the quilt up in his skinny arms. "I'm taking it back inside. I'm sorry."

That was when Zechariah realized that if the two of them had any kind of relationship, he could have wrestled playfully with the boy, playfully reestablished the power dynamic, and they could have laughed it off. As it was, they stood staring at one another, each a mystery to the other, and what made it feel bizarre was not that they were strangers—that had always been the case—but that they were father and son.

Zechariah slurps a piece of grapefruit from his spoon, says to Berna, "Nothing that boy does makes any sense to me."

At six, Berna leaves to watch Andrew's three. Zechariah puts new strings in his golf cleats and cleans the cleats off with a rag, then walks around the house, stopping at the living room picture window now and again to gaze out as the day dawns on his yard and driveway. He sits at his computer searching for pictures of Izzy Manzano. He finds her address in Utica, New York, and searches through the city's records looking for pictures of her house. He discovers through his snooping that she has three adult children. It looks like she married a plastic surgeon. He can't find any pictures of her.

He has daydreamed about what his life would have been like had he married her. What their children would have turned out like. But the thought of his own children, disappointing as they have been to him, not existing in the world fills him with an existential grief so horrifying he immediately abandons his dreams of having married Izzy and returns to the more mundane sin of fantasizing about the two of them meeting up by chance and having a brief fling.

He's also looked up Rhonda Niemeyer. She and Gene went back to France and had six more children, for a total of seven. Zechariah had only seen them one more time, at an alumni event at Pinewood in 1996, and Rhonda still, almost thirty years later, stirred lust in his sinful heart. The one thing he remembered most vividly was Rhonda's milk-heavy breast, those blue veins, that brown bumpy nipple. Berna had stopped performing her wifely duty in bed right after they'd left Clay, and he'd resorted to sinful self-stimulation from then on, only when he was weak to temptation.

He would do it now—the desire is still in his heart—but at his age, his manhood rarely cooperates.

As he waits for Ricky, he sits on the commode twice more, once in the master bathroom and once in the hall bathroom, and releases gas, but the pressure builds back up quickly. He is headed to the hall bathroom once more when Ricky surprises him at the door.

The boy swings the door open and clatters in, already wearing a worn-out pair of golf cleats that look like he found them in a trashcan.

He has a new tattoo (a pagan tribal pattern) on his neck that matches the ones he wears like sleeves down both arms. The holes in his earlobes are big enough to wedge a dime into, never having healed from when he wore metal rings in them years earlier, and his receding hair is pulled into a ponytail. He wears baggy black cargo shorts and a black tee shirt. The smell of smoke follows him in.

"You had breakfast?" Zechariah asks. "There's cereal and granola. Grapefruit if you want. I'm going to make a quick bathroom run before we go. You should too."

"I'm good," Ricky says, smiling. He looks like a clown from a demon circus, like a devil-worshiping comedian dressed as a bum for a Three Stooges–style golf disaster. He clacks toward the kitchen. "I'll have sweet tea if you have any."

"We don't use sugar anymore, but help yourself," Zechariah says. "There's Splenda on the table. It's just as good as sugar." Gas pains almost double him over. "I'll be ready in a jiffy." He hurries down the hall and through his bedroom to the master bathroom.

After they park in front of the clubhouse, Zechariah drags his clubs out of the back seat while Ricky pulls from the hatch a motley array of beat-up clubs in a blue vinyl golf bag that is ripped down one side.

"Where are your clubs?" Zechariah asks. He'd bought the boy a nice set of starter clubs two Christmases ago.

"Right here," Ricky says, holding up the tattered bag.

On their way to the first tee from the clubhouse, they approach a well-dressed man at the ball washer, which makes Zechariah even more mindful—and now just downright embarrassed—of how ridiculous Ricky looks.

The man slams the washer up and down as if he is angry with it. When they get to him, he looms over them, six foot four at least. His striped shirt clings to the roll of flesh around his middle. He turns and looks at Zechariah, then at Ricky. He wears a gold necklace, a bracelet on his left wrist, and a fat gold ring with a square black stone on his right hand. On his left hand is his glove. His clubs are Pings. His watch is a Rolex.

"What's up, dude," Ricky says. He steps to the ball washer and gets on his toes, like he's trying to get his testicles into it. He says, "These ball washers aren't made for short dudes like me, are they?" He chuckles.

The big man straightens his back and looks out over the course.

"That was crude, Ricky," Zechariah says. "Crude and just plain silly."

"So what?" Ricky says. "It was supposed to be silly." He keeps chuckling. "You work with what you have, right?"

"Well, it wasn't funny," Zechariah says. He is pretty sure Ricky is high on drugs already, this early in the morning.

Ricky picks up the torn golf bag and says, "Probably a tired old joke if you golf all the time. I don't think I've ever seen one before." He starts laughing again, and says, "I have to take care of that in the shower."

Zechariah smooths his shirt with a gloved hand and says to the man, "Do you have a friend? We could make a foursome."

The man turns and peers at him as if Zechariah's just asked him if his wife was fat. "I am alone this morning," the big man says. His hair is parted on the side and looks like a politician's haircut—expensive but still ugly.

"Would you like to play this round with us?" Zechariah says.

The man looks at Ricky for an instant, then says, "Sure. Love to." He reaches out his hand to shake and says, "Patrick Pence."

Zechariah shakes his hand—the fella is wearing powerful cologne.

Ricky and the man shake hands. "Call me Pat," the man says.

"Nice to meet you, Pat." Ricky says.

"So, what do you gentlemen do?" Pat asks.

"I'm a pastor," Zechariah says.

Pat nods slowly and asks, "Where?"

"Tabernacle Baptist. Just across the bridge in St. Albans."

"Right there on MacCorkle," the man says. "I know of it."

"I'm retired actually."

Still nodding, Pat says, "I used to hear you on WJOY. You're the Calvinism guy."

"I hope it's been a blessing to you."

Pat looks back at Ricky.

Ricky grins at his ring and watch and says, "What do you do, Pat?"

"Right now, I'm in insurance." Pat slides his hand along the hair over his ear. Above his head is I-64, rushing with morning speeders. Over his left shoulder, on the hill, is the State Police Recruit Training Center.

"I was in the ministry myself," Pat says.

"Ah," Ricky almost yells. "I knew it. You're a *prosperity gospel* guy."

"I was a prophet."

"Is that right?" Zechariah says. Ricky is right. The way he flashes his money around, probably Assemblies of God. Health and Welfare gospel heresy. "When was that?" Zechariah asks. "In the area here?"

"A while back," Pat says, dismissively. He turns to Ricky and says, "So, what do you do?"

"I'm a rock and roll guy."

Pat nods.

"We're hot around town right now. We're the Striking Soul Minors. Heard of us?"

"No, but don't worry. I'm not up on things."

"Think a blend of ZZ Top, Wilco, and Pink Floyd: Americana, psychedelic alt-country, bluesy roots."

"I used to like ZZ Top before I was saved. Are you on Myspace?"

"Come to The Empty Glass this Saturday night and catch us live."

364 / VIC SIZEMORE

Ricky is the rhythm guitarist and lead singer in a thoroughly me-diocre secular rock band. He paints too and calls himself an artist. He also calls himself a writer and supposedly has a whole book written of some sort. Zechariah has yet to see a single page of printed proof, though he's asked several times.

Ricky reaches into the pocket on the ripped golf bag and pro-duces a glove, wadded and crinkled like a used tissue from a lady's purse. He works his hand into it and slams his ungloved fist into it several times, apparently getting satisfaction from the loud thwacking sound. "We have an LP," Ricky says. "We've gone as far as we can here. We're thinking of packing up our gear and going to Nashville."

"Nashville?" Zechariah says. He repeats, "Nashville?"

Ricky turns and gives him a proud grin and nods. "We're tight as we've ever been right now. We have a sheaf of solid originals. We're thinking hard about it."

"That's exciting," Pat says.

"If you don't know anybody in the business, it comes down to luck, or meeting someone with connections, which you can't do hanging around Charleston, West Virginia. Plenty worse bands than us have made it."

Zechariah couldn't disagree with that.

There is no one waiting at the first tee. The fog rises off the Kanawha River and hovers over the valley, blindingly white in sun-light slanting in almost horizontally from the east. Zechariah's first drive is straight but only about a hundred feet down the fairway. He stomps his burning feet a few times and moves aside for Pat to tee off.

Pat hooks his drive into the trees and takes a mulligan that lands in the rough near where the other ball went into the trees. "Still hook-ing it," he says to himself as he slides the club into his bag and tugs at the fingers of his glove.

Ricky steps to the tee. He has a driver, a three wood, but still holds it like a baseball bat. Ricky is thirty-two and still rides skateboards in the middle of the afternoon. His childhood pal Jeremy is a deacon at Tabernacle Baptist now, a chiropractor with a sweet Godly wife who is beautiful, and she's a stay-at-home mom. They have two girls just as beautiful as their mom, so beautiful they could win beauty pageants if they tried, and a boy who's so smart he's at the accelerated learning center. Ricky's never had a girlfriend or a job for long. He never grew up, never started an adult life with adult responsibilities. Zechariah felt personally humiliated when people asked about him.

Of all Zechariah's children, James was the special one. When Zechariah had tried to make a go of it with the family band, he'd started adding Scripture memory recitations for the kids as an added attraction—people liked hearing their child voices talking like squeaky little adults. Miriam had Psalm 23, Andrew had the Beatitudes, Ricky had John 3:16 and a couple other verses. James though. Berna's intense lack of enthusiasm sank the Soul Minors, but James was the real deal.

On Sundays when the sun was full in the church's back wall of windows, Zechariah would look out at the bright day as he preached, blinded to the dark congregation below him—he could hear coughs and sneezes, paper shuffling, an occasional elbow cracking against a pew—the people down there, a dark sea of souls. On those days he would preach with the awareness that eternity gaped beneath his flock. He had to use every means at his disposal to get their attention.

It was just such a Sunday morning when Zechariah had Berna put James in his best suit. He had a deacon go get the boy from Children's Church over in the old building while the congregation sang "Blessed Assurance." He waved the boy up beside the pulpit.

"You may be seated," he told the congregation. "Turn with me if you would to Matthew 5, please." Thin Bible pages rustled all over the sanctuary. "Matthey 5," he repeated.

James stood and stared confidently out at the dark congregation of over four hundred people. After the paper shuffling subsided, Zechariah pulled the microphone from its stand, handed it to James, and whispered into his ear, "Give it to them good, son."

In a strong and sure voice, James began, "And seeing the multitudes, he went up into a mountain: and when he was set, his disciples came unto him. And he opened his mouth, and taught them, saying, 'Blessed are the poor in spirit; for theirs is the kingdom of heaven. Blessed are they that mourn; for they shall be comforted. Blessed are the meek . . .'"

Zechariah stood as if in a dream and watched his middle son. The only way he knew the boy was under any stress at all was by the blazing red of his ears. Otherwise, he comported himself like a pro, stood erect, and projected his voice out over the crowd; he enunciated clearly, did not rush his words, did not move the microphone to cause distracting changes in volume or clarity.

When he finished his recitation, the people rose clapping, their shadows moving here and there in the blinding sunlight. Zechariah stood behind James with his hands on the boy's shoulders, and just as he'd been taught, Zechariah's little man pointed upward to give God the glory. Zechariah tousled his hair and set loose the crisp smell of Ivory soap, which Berna, always pinching pennies, bought for all the family's washing needs, including hair.

There would be no limit to what they could accomplish. A new building, yes. But not there in Clay County. Not up this river where the potential had all but been tapped out. They would move closer to Charleston to build the new church. He would start looking for properties the next day. Charleston had virtually unlimited potential.

All this had occurred to Zechariah as he stood and basked in his son's applause. When it subsided, he was choked up as he said, "How about that boy?" He leaned down and James's clean hair tickled his bottom lip as he whispered, "You can head on back to Children's Church now." He hugged the boy to his legs, patted his chest, and then pushed him gently toward the steps.

As James descended from the platform, Miriam started the intro to the offertory hymn, the next thing on the order of service he'd given her. It was a nice arrangement of "Jesus Is a Friend of Sinners," and Zechariah sat in his wooden chair behind the pulpit and hummed as the men took up the offering. His vision had been refreshed; his soul reenergized. His calling was sure.

Ricky's drive is long and straight. The ball lies just off the green on the left edge of the fairway. He laughs and says, "Dang. Check that out."

"You golf a lot?" Pat asks, looking with his hand cupped over his eyes.

"Never." Ricky slides the three wood back into the bag and says, "Beginner's luck." He slings the ripped bag over his shoulder and saunters off down the middle of the fairway.

Zechariah and Pat wheel their bags down the cart path. Zechariah stops at his short drive and pulls out a wood for another drive. Pat veers to the trees and whacks around with an iron, looking for his lost ball.

Because his feet are giving him trouble, Zechariah limps the front nine with a modified stride, which pulls a kink in his back. He is still suffering from cramps. He's been walking wide off the path so he can pass gas without offense, but his back is getting worse, making that less of an option. He's afraid they're going to notice he's in pain, so after the front nine he asks if they can grab a Coke or a cup of coffee in the clubhouse. He'll see if he can recover enough to play the back nine. Pat says okay. Ricky doesn't care—he doesn't care about anything.

Zechariah buys. He and Pat order coffee. Ricky gets a big bottle of pink energy drink with a picture of a lizard on the label and chugs it down like he's at a frat party before Zechariah and Pat have finished adding sugar and cream to their coffee.

Pat asks, "How long were you in the ministry?"

"Fifty-four years, all told," Zechariah says. He still has his first preaching Bible, the old Scofield Reference Bible his dad gave him. Zechariah keeps it displayed on his office shelf at home, the way an old soldier would his first service revolver.

"That's amazing," Pat says.

A college-aged girl is working the snack bar. Ricky is engrossed in watching her. He slouches in his chair and flips the empty drink bottle from hand to hand on his lap, his baggy cargo shorts sagging beneath his legs. Strands of hair have come loose from his ponytail and are pasted to the sweaty skin of his tattooed neck.

"Quite an achievement," Pat says. "You want to hear a story I have?"

"Sure," Ricky says.

Sitting in the clubhouse, Pat tells them this story:

"There was a man who had his own investing business. He made a lot of money—over four hundred thousand dollars a year—in the early eighties when that kind of money was a lot; loved his work in finance and was happy doing it. He married his high school sweetheart, they built a 3,200 square foot house, she had three beautiful children, and he drove a Mercedes Benz and rode a BMW touring bike; his wife had a Jaguar and a minivan. They had a boat for deep sea fishing they docked at Murrells Inlet, just south of Myrtle Beach. They had all this old world had to offer.

"But the man grew unhappy. You see, when this man was a child, a prophet had spoken a word over him in church, had prophesied that he would grow up to be a mighty man of God. It weighed on the man's conscience that he was not in God's will. He labored under the weight of the Holy Ghost's conviction. He started doing cocaine and drinking to keep the guilt away; started living life in the fast lane. He cheated on his wife with various party girls. She threatened to leave him if he didn't straighten up.

"Then one night, drunk and high, the man was driving with one of his party girls, and he started praying. He shouted at God and asked what he should do and said, 'Give me a sign.'

"What he remembers after saying that prayer is waking up in a hospital bed. He had crashed his car over an embankment and had almost died. (The girl, who he had picked up at a bar and turned out to only be twenty-two, had been killed.) They hadn't been found for nine hours.

"Well," Pat said. "That was this man's unmistakable sign from God. He sold his business and the house and the expensive cars. He bought a Fleetwood Bounder RV and hit the road as a traveling evangelist. It soon became apparent that he had the gift of evangelism and prophecy. His wife homeschooled the children as they canvassed the United States preaching and prophesying."

"That's quite a story," Zechariah says. He accidentally passes gas, and it makes a short honk on the wooden chair. Ricky glances at him and suppresses a smile, and he feels his face flush with embarrassment, but Ricky turns right back to watching the girl behind the counter.

She is dropping frozen hot dogs out of a big white box into a rectangular pot of steaming water.

Pat waves his hand with the fat ring on it, with the Rolex on the wrist. The hand is as wide as a porterhouse steak. He says, "Oh, there's more."

Ten years the man devoted his life to serving God. He preached and prophesied from coast to coast. Souls were saved, people broke through, lives were changed. Then one night, as he was traveling through to reach his next evangelistic crusade, he fell asleep, and the RV ran itself off the road. "Fancy Gap, North Carolina," Pat said, that's where the RV rolled seven times over an embankment, killing his wife and three children, who had all been sleeping on the bed in back. He was the only one buckled in and he was the only survivor.

"That's how God repaid him for sacrificing his life to the Lord. It turned out his own life wasn't enough. God took his family from him."

"*Damn*," Ricky says. "That's heavy . . . stuff."

Pat turns to Ricky, his face showing no emotion. "You guessed it." Ricky hadn't guessed anything, not aloud. Pat says, "That's my story. All of that happened to me."

"*Damn*," Ricky repeats. "I'm sorry for your loss."

Pat looks at Zechariah. He says, "What kind of God would do that to a man?"

Zechariah prepares to answer that it's not up to us to question the ways of a sovereign God, and not ours to know why things happen the way they do, only to obey, live faithfully, and persevere. He doesn't get the chance.

"I'll tell you what kind of God. A bully. An asshole." Pat takes another drink of coffee and says, "What I say now is God can burn in hell."

Ricky sits up in his chair and snorts a laugh, looking first at Zechariah, then at Pat, then back at Zechariah, a huge, bemused grin on his face. The first time all morning he looks like he's enjoying himself. He's waiting for Zechariah's comeback, might as well be rubbing his hands together in anticipation. He expects this to become a theological debate, in which Zechariah enumerates the fallacies of this man's theology and logic.

Zechariah doesn't have the energy for it anymore, so he parrots Ricky's, "I'm sorry for your loss."

Two old men walk into the clubhouse in their sock feet, shuffling comfortably, like they're puttering around their own homes. One calls out to the girl behind the counter and calls her beautiful. Old lechers—such as is common to man. Pat leans back and the chair creaks under his bulk. He sighs. Zechariah starts to lean over and rub his calf, but his back catches and makes him take a sharp breath.

"I don't think I'm up to the back nine," he says. He stands slowly, holding the table.

On the way home, Ricky's driving recklessly again without even realizing it. He says, "That dude was so full of shit his eyes were brown." He says, "Sorry I said *shit*," and laughs that he's said it again. He puts his hand up as if in surrender. "Sorry, but you aren't buying that crock of . . . dookie are you?"

"No idea. I've heard stranger ones that were true."

"He's a charlatan," Ricky says. "You know, on the back nine he'd have been trying to sign us up to sell Amway."

Zechariah changes the subject, asks about Ricky's Nashville plans, and it is clear the boy has no idea what he's talking about. "I'll tell you what my dad told me," he says. He prepares to say, "Just because you're a pretty good baseball player on the sandlot doesn't mean you can just decide to play for the Yankees," but he surprises himself when, "I've been thinking about breaking out my banjo. Maybe I could sit in with you," comes out of his mouth instead.

"Maybe," Ricky says. "Yeah, sure. We're rehearsing right now for a festival in Virginia we might get a gig at, but when that's over . . ."

"You could bring your guitar over and the two of us could jam. My fingers aren't as nimble as they were, but when I was young I was the best there was."

"Sure," Ricky says. "Yeah. I'm focusing on this festival right now, but when that's over, sure, maybe we'll jam."

When Ricky pulls up the driveway to drop him off, he says, "Come in and have lunch. We have leftover spaghetti I can nuke."

Ricky says it sounds great, thanks, but he's got to run.

Zechariah turns on Fox News and falls asleep in his La-Z-Boy. Later Berna calls the landline. "I didn't think you'd answer," she says. "I was going to leave a message."

"I knocked off early," he tells her. "My back is bothering me. And my feet are burning, as usual."

"Anything new with Ricky?"

"I threw it out walking the front nine."

"I'm dropping the boys off at Pam's and running a couple errands," Berna tells him. "There's a rotisserie chicken from Sam's Club in the fridge, and mandarin oranges and cottage cheese. There's that leftover spaghetti too."

"I ate that for lunch."

"We're unloading a truck and stocking shelves. Don't know when I'll be home. There's that chicken in the fridge if I'm late."

He tells her he'll manage and ends the call. He drags his old bones back into the living room where sunlight blares through the picture window onto the blue carpet. The pain in his back radiates up his spine, giving him a throbbing headache at the base of his skull. He sits back down in his La-Z-Boy. The grandfather clock's pendulum clicks and clacks beside the fireplace. The face reads 4:30. The entire evening spreads before him.

He pushes the lever, raising the footrest to recline. He carefully, slowly, pushes off each shoe with the other foot. He can feel the pain in his back, as if a sharp little stone has been lodged between two vertebrae in his lumbar, waiting there for him to make a wrong move so it can grind at his nerve endings. He presses a throw pillow behind his throbbing head, rubs his burning feet together, and closes his eyes.

Charleston Daily Mail

JULY 14, 2004

ZECHARIAH WYCLIFFE MINOR

(1938–2004)

Pastor Zechariah Minor went home to be with his Lord and Savior at 3:57 a.m. on Monday, July 12. Reverend Minor was born in Mill Wood, West Virginia, in 1938. In 1954 he received the call to full-time Christian ministry. He graduated from Pinewood Bible Institute (now Pinewood University) in Meadow Green, West Virginia, in 1959, and served as professor there from 1960 to 1969. While there, Reverend Minor founded the school of music ministry, which has grown into one of the most successful programs at the school, with many ministry teams that travel all over the world today and which has produced several Dove Award–winning artists. In 1969, Pastor Minor received the call to the senior pastorate at Clay Free Will Baptist Church, where he served until 1984. During his time there, Clay Free Will Baptist grew from one hundred and thirty members to almost six hundred. In 1984 Pastor Minor followed the Lord's call to Tabernacle Baptist Church in St. Albans, West Virginia, where he served faithfully until his retirement in 2003, and remained on as Pastor Emeritus until his death.

Pastor Minor is survived by his wife Berna Cannaday Minor, of Dunbar; one daughter, Miriam Minor-Jeffreys of Scott Depot; two sons, Andrew Minor of St. Albans; and Rick Minor of Charleston; three grandsons, Chase, Hunter, and Andrew (Jr.) Minor; and a brother, Pastor Stephen Minor, 69, of West Union, Ohio. He is preceded into the Lord's presence by a son, James Allen Minor; and a sister, Naomi Hammond.

A viewing will be held from 6:00 p.m. until 8:00 p.m. on Friday, July 16, in the Hoyt Chapel of Tabernacle Baptist Church in St. Albans. A celebration of Reverend Minor's life and ministry will be held at 2:00 p.m. on Saturday, July 16, also in the Hoyt Chapel. The family asks that in lieu of flowers, you make donations to Habitat for Humanity.

"He is no fool who gives what he cannot keep to gain that which he cannot lose" (Jim Elliot).

We love you Daddy.

Yet the Sea Is Not Full

(Jason Robert Goins, 2004)

JAY STOOD in Berna's front doorway with the outdoor smell of summer wind on him. He had just handed the bowl of muffins to Miriam. He reached up and rubbed his hair to smooth out the helmet head. Behind him, the day was bright and hot; inside, the hallway was dark and cool. On the other side of the entryway was the open passage into the kitchen, which was bright again with white, electric light. The white plastic waste basket stood against the side kitchen wall beside a doorway to the basement, and almost lined up with the front door was a doorway to the back yard. The window in the door framed Berna's red hummingbird feeder on a tall, black, shepherd's hook pole. The smell of cold bacon grease lingered in the interior air.

Miriam had just told Jay she loved pumpkin chocolate chip muffins as she reached out and took the bowl he offered. He said, "A lady I volunteer with calls them better-than-sex muffins."

That's when the panic swept in and took control, flipped a switch inside Jay's head, and he didn't realize it was even happening until he was back on his bike, leaning into his U-turn around the cul-de-sac, and speeding out of Berna's neighborhood.

Berna had called with the news of Zechariah's death at 4:20 a.m. "It's over. He's gone," was how she had opened the conversation.

"I'm so sorry," Jay had said. It had been a long, miserable death watch after his stroke.

"He took a big, deep breath, opened his eyes wide, and that was it. I almost felt like I saw his spirit leave his body."

"I'm so sorry," Jay said again. "It's a mercy though. He's not suffering anymore."

"No," Berna said. "He's not."

"Is Miriam there with you?"

"Miriam's here. Andrew is on his way. Ricky never answers his phone even in the daytime. I left a message."

"Is there anything I can do?" Jay would have done anything for her, anything at all; he wasn't just saying the standard thing. "Whatever you need—a bank robbed? a hit on somebody?—just say the word and I'm Johnny on the spot." What he wanted to ask was please can I come and be with you? Come sit with you? Help with the details? Run errands? Anything. Whatever. He didn't even know if it would be appropriate for him to go to the funeral.

Berna let out an exhausted laugh. "My head's all messed up. I didn't think it would be like this since it's been coming for so long, but it is."

"Are you doing okay?" Jay asked. "What do you need?"

"I don't know," Berna said. "I'm okay. I'll call you when my head is straight."

A police siren over on Washington Street had set two of his neighbors' dogs barking a couple of hours earlier, and when the siren died away, the dogs barked at each other for another two or three minutes. Then he'd had to piss and have a glass of milk. He still hadn't managed to get fully back to sleep when Berna called. After the call, he was wide awake for the day—there was nothing to do but go for his run a little early, work off the nervous energy.

———

Jay ran four miles on the Kanawha River Trail. The fog hung heavy on the early morning river, and he didn't see another human so early, only the occasional car passing above. Back at his house on Quarrier Street, he trimmed his beard with his electric razor, and stepped into the tub for a shower. When his skin was pink and tender from the hot water, he toweled his short hair dry and brushed his teeth. He slipped into his one clean pair of cargo shorts—the ones with the left pocket torn off, exposing a wide square of unfaded green—and his black Alley Cats tee shirt. The sun had crested the horizon by this time and the temperature was started its rise to a forecasted 97 degrees.

The boom box on his kitchen counter was twenty years old, paint spattered; the cassette door sheared off entirely. He switched on the radio and NPR filled the kitchen with a story about President Bush inviting a bunch of people to the South Lawn of the White House to play tee ball, a welcome distraction from the wars in Iraq and Afghanistan. Jay set out two sticks of real, unsalted butter to soften, turned the oven under his Viking range to 350°F, and put on his reading glasses to snatch down the spices. He tried to remember them all without looking at the recipe: cinnamon, clove, allspice, nutmeg, baking soda, baking powder, salt. What else? Ginger.

He dragged the eight-quart square Rubbermaid tubs, one sugar, one flour, from the pantry, and scooped out five cups of flour, sifted it into his seven-quart mixing bowl, then dumped three cups of sugar into it. He tossed in five teaspoons of cinnamon, one and a half of allspice, one of clove, one of nutmeg, a pinch of salt—another pinch of salt—and quarter teaspoon of baking soda. He threw in a heaping tablespoon of baking powder because the pumpkin was so heavy. He blinked hard trying to suppress a sneeze as the spice powders went airborne, the warm smells of winter holidays.

When the butter was soft, he mixed all the wet ingredients in the

380 / VIC SIZEMORE

countertop mixer, then slowly incorporated the dry. He folded two cups of chocolate chips into the batter, then turned to get out the pans and spray them down good with oil. NPR looped back around to tee ball on the White House lawn. Cal Ripken Jr. would be there because he was the Tee Ball Commissioner. Jay chuckled and shook his head. A Commissioner of Tee Ball.

As he slid the muffins into the oven, NPR switched from morning news to classical music, and thirty minutes later, the aroma of sweet cinnamon spice filled the house. Of all the items in his limited baking repertoire, his pumpkin chocolate chip muffins were by far the most popular at Habitat. He'd gotten into cooking for a while, bought the Viking Range and a set of Henckels knives that now sat dusty in their wooden block, staring at him like well-behaved but neglected pets while he used the old twelve-inch Victorinox chef's knife he's had longer than the boom box. He'd gotten good at cooking but hadn't had the patience or concentration for baking—and after a while, it had shifted from enjoyment to sadness because when he said, "Man, I outdid myself this time," or "This is delicious," he said it into an empty house over what he knew would be leftovers until the dish disgusted him.

When the muffins cooled, Jay pulled out the green-and-blue box of Reynolds Foodservice Film he'd bought at Sam's Club—2,000 feet of it—and wrapped each muffin individually, as if he planned to set them on a bake sale table. He pulled down his huge wooden salad bowl, which he'd only ever used for popcorn, piled the muffins into it, and slid it into the fridge. He switched off the boom box and the house fell silent except for the whir of the air handler in the basement.

He jumped into the tub for another quick shower, not getting his hair wet, threw on a pair of khaki pants and a polo shirt, and stepped without socks into his Timberland boat shoes. He strapped the bowl onto the back of his Harley Low Rider and rode to Berna's house, where her car was in the driveway, behind Zechariah's. Three cars—Jay assumed they belonged to the kids—were parked along the street. He hadn't seen any of them since he and Berna reconnected. He didn't know if Berna had told them anything at all, if they knew about his transition.

He pulled up behind the last car, a red Subaru Justy, and flipped down his kickstand. The Justy was obviously Ricky's car. It had a dented left rear quarter panel and rust lining the wheel wells like chocolate milk around a child's mouth, and it had two bumper stickers on the bottom of the hatch—one a simple black rectangle with *got music?* written in plain white letters, and the other round and red with what looked like a teddy bear with devil horns and triangular jack-o-lantern eyes that poured tears out on either side. The devil bear looked like it had one Captain-Hook pirate hand too. Some band. Or skateboard brand.

Jay cradled the wooden bowl of wrapped muffins in one arm like a baby and walked past the car. The back seat was full of rock band equipment, confirming for him it was Ricky's car: a fat amplifier that said Marshall on the front, two speakers the size of a laundry basket, black poles and microphone stands, two transparent plastic tubs full of cords, power strips, and microphones. On the front quarter panel, the little car announced in white that it was 4WD, and this broke Jay's nervousness into laughter, thinking about that Fisher-Price car trying to muscle its way up a logging road.

Still chuckling, he stopped at the Ford Aerostar minivan in front of it with its own stickers. An NRA window sticker with the eagle on it clutching two rifles instead of arrows and no olive branch in sight. This was Andrew's car just as clearly as the Justy was Ricky's. The bumper sticker directly beneath that had a waving American flag on it that said, "Support Our Troops." On the other side, for balance, there was a sticker with a picture of a black 9 mm pistol and the words, "There wouldn't be a First Amendment without a Second." Beside that was his "W" sticker.

Jay had voted for George W. He knew it was a cliché, but he did consider himself a social liberal and a fiscal conservative. He'd been a supersaver all his life, and he'd had good investing advice. His net worth was closing in on two million dollars—it took a dive after 9/11, but was moving in the right direction again. He had a real problem with the government deciding they knew better than he did how to spend it. He donated his money and time to Habitat, and still those people treated him like a pariah for his political beliefs; it was like because he's transexual, he was supposed to be a freaking socialist too.

One thing about his money: he didn't know where the switch was inside his head, the one that flipped him from scrimper-saver mode to spender mode. He wasn't interested in buying a bunch of crap, but there were things he wanted to do, places he wanted to see. Problem was, doing fun things got old mighty fast when he was always doing them alone while all around him people shared their experiences with loved ones and friends. He'd wondered at times if he'd have been so into solitary hobbies, like hunting and fishing and riding his motorcycle, if he'd been allowed to have friends like a normal person. He liked tennis. He liked board games.

As he walked past the minivan, he saw it wasn't in any better shape than Ricky's Justy. The back seat had a car seat in the center, flanked by booster seats. Filthy, all of it, crumbs and French fries, and shiny spots gummy with ground-in food. The stink of burnt oil emanated from under the hood.

When he got to Miriam's VW New Beetle, he had to laugh aloud. Sunflower yellow and as spotless as if she'd run it through the car wash on her way over, it had a bud vase with a white daisy in the dash beside the steering wheel and two bumper stickers of its own on the rear bumper, spaced perfectly between the license plate and the reflectors on each side. The one on the left was "namaste," and the one on the right was "Commit Random Kindness & Senseless Acts of Beauty."

He backed into the middle of the street, rubbing his face and laughing. He stood holding the bowl of muffins, the aroma of holiday spices rising just as insistently as the stink of burnt oil from Andrew's car. It would have been easy enough to know which car belonged to which kid without the bumper stickers, but the stickers—those poor kids, raised the way they were; how it was drilled into them that they couldn't just live a good life and try not to hurt anybody else, they had to be about a cause, and they couldn't be about it quietly either, they had to shout it from the rooftops. How Zechariah beat into their heads that God had enlisted them at birth, like it or not, into a universal war between evil and good.

At the door, Jay took a deep breath, rang the bell, and held the muffin bowl between his body and the door as it opened, and there stood Miriam. Jay had seen pictures of them all, of course, but Miriam in person—a petite porcelain doll, with black hair, blue eyes, and clear pale skin—was the spitting image of young Berna.

So, Jay said it, told Miriam, "Aren't you just the spitting image of Berna."

"That's what people tell me." Miriam smiled. It was a kind smile.

"You could have done worse," he said. "I'm Jay. You don't recognize me."

"I remember you," Miriam said. "Mom told me about you. It's good to see you again."

"It's been a long time," Jay said. "Those Clay County days seem like ancient history, don't they?"

Miriam looked down at the bowl of muffins. "Ooh, those look delicious. Did you bake them?"

"I did."

"They smell delicious."

"Pumpkin chocolate chip."

"I absolutely *love* pumpkin chocolate chip." Miriam reached for the bowl and said, "My mouth is watering already." She stepped aside holding the bowl in both hands and said, "Come in, come in."

Jay stepped up into the doorway, saying, "Funny thing is, I don't like them myself, but other people go crazy for them. A lady I volunteer with calls them better-than-sex muffins."

As he said it, Berna's oldest son Andrew emerged from the basement into the kitchen, and he was laughing about something Ricky had said from on the steps behind him. He turned as he laughed and caught sight of Miriam and Jay. He was still laughing—that same strange laugh of his that glugged up from his throat and sloshed out of his mouth like water from a jug—as he and Jay made eye contact.

Jay didn't regain awareness of himself moving through space until he was circling the cul-de-sac on his Harley and roaring out of the neighborhood. He didn't even remember strapping on his helmet, kicking up the stand, or starting the bike.

Out of Berna's neighborhood, he got on I-64 east and rode back into Charleston, where he didn't get off at his usual exit, but rode on out I-79. He let his mind drift off to where it liked to go when he rode, out where thoughts and images floated blurry all around, came and went, one or another pulling into focus occasionally but not for long—it was as if the wind battering his body and the road whipping past just beneath him continually swept it all away and kept his mind clear. He'd passed the Elkview exit before he consciously thought about where he was going. At Clendenin, he got off the interstate and headed out Route 4 toward Clay.

When he nears his first house, over the hill from the road by the river, he slows and pulls carefully off onto the gravelly wide spot, where there's a new steel guardrail. Fresh, powdery gravel covers the driveway. The house has a new roof. That house: where he and Berna first declared their love for one another; where they made love in his bed, and on the sofa, and once on a blanket spread in front of the TV.

He turns around and heads back toward Clendenin, and when he passes the spot in the straight stretch where it happened, he realizes why the muscles of his body steered him out this way even before his mind was aware, the memory was there in his body all along, down deep, and now it floods up into his mind as clear as the day it happened.

He was riding his Honda CB750 home after a day of riding, and Harry's boy sped up behind him in Harry's 77 Cutlass 442, pulled out as if to pass, but then slowed down and started crowding Jay off the road. Instead of gunning it and leaving the Cutlass in the dust, which he could have done, though the boy, teenager that he was, would no doubt have made mindless chase like an untrained dog after a squirrel, Jay instead slowed down hoping he would lose interest and drive on.

When it became clear that Harry's boy wasn't going to stop until Jay was in the ditch, he decided to go ahead and get it over with. He steered down into the grassy mud and the wheel caught a rock and jerked the handlebar over into a fencepost—where the fence used to be, there is now a guardrail. Slow as he was going by then, it still messed up his left wrist—he thought it was just a sprain, but it turned out to be a fractured scaphoid bone. The bike was muddy, and the brake lever a little bent, but it was rideable. It had become clear to him that he wouldn't be able to muscle the bike out of the ditch with his bum wrist when a man he didn't know well named Randy Jenkins pulled his pickup truck over and helped.

Jay silently listened to the man's commentary on why "girls" shouldn't be out riding motorcycles by themselves in the first place, and was relieved to think that, since Jenkins was a heathen and didn't go to church, it was unlikely he'd have an opportunity to bring it up to Colley in casual conversation. Jay thanked him and rode his bike the rest of the way home, slowly, twice catching a sharp breath and crying out when he squeezed his fingers around the brake lever. He told the guys at work he'd hurt his wrist in a fall while hunting.

When he was young he had no friends—no real friends—and he couldn't be in the woods all the time. He spent a lot of time out riding under the bright sky, whipping through waves of sunlight and shade on backroads, in and out of overhanging leaves, leaning into curves, gunning it into straight stretches, nothing between his body and the road, the buffeting wind, the trees whipping past.

Riding his bike was what made him feel free of a mostly miserable life. Fayetteville, Summersville, Sutton Lake. Snowshoe, on over to the backroads of Virginia. He'd ride with no set destination, carrying nothing but a little cash for food and gas. In 1974 they passed a law so women could get credit cards without needing a man to cosign, and Jay did just that, got himself an American Express card. He still carried a little cash because smaller gas stations didn't take credit cards, but mostly he used it.

As Jay remembers it, that bike saved his life more than once. At times, when he was thinking of ending it all, he'd go out and ride, and the exhilaration of the wind and the speed would be pleasure enough to make him decide to keep living for a while longer.

He rides back to Clendenin and gets back on I-79 toward Charleston, still trying to figure out what had happened at Berna's doorway; he realizes the two things—his running from her doorway and Harry's boy running him off the road twenty years ago—are related.

At the time, Jay filed his being run off the road as just one of the countless times someone—young men; almost always young men—harassed him, or worse. At the time, it had seemed mild compared to the times when he'd been younger and boys had cornered him when no one was around to stop them. They had threatened to kick his ass or rip off his clothes to see if he was a boy or a girl, or rape him. The assaults had grown less frequent, but not the countless insults and indignities large and small. It was just another experience in the life of Jordan Goins. What's more, back then he believed he was deserving of the abuse—as Zechariah Minor preached of homosexuals, an abomination—he had it coming just by being what he was.

Not long after that, James drowned. There was talk around town, and Jay's dad had a sit down with him and told him the deacons had all agreed that he should not be the AWANA Commander anymore. "You agree with them?" he asked his dad. His dad didn't say anything, just nodded his head and looked right at Jay. Jay sold his house and moved away from Clay. He drove away and left the Honda under its blue tarp outside the house; never went back for it. It wasn't until 2000 that he decided to start riding again.

Now he realizes what dredged up the memory of Harry's boy running him off the road. The same thing that caused him to flee Berna's house: Andrew's laugh. That dumb, glugging laugh. Of all the things Jay remembers clearly about his being run off the road, that laugh is the clearest. What he can't remember is what specifically they were yelling at him as it all happened, or who else was in the car, but Andrew's laugh rings crisp and sharp in his memory. His body reacted to it before he even knew what was happening, and it reacted the way it always did. For his entire life, in times of fight or flight, Jay's default has been flight. It angers him to realize it was that stupid laugh that had sent him bolting like a rabbit for its hole, but there it is.

Back at his house, Jay sees that Berna has called his phone twice and left one message, and a text message saying she wished he would have been able to stay, and would he call her when he got her message. They spent time together when they reconnected—Berna working on Habitat houses with him—but then Zechariah had his stroke and Berna became his primary caregiver, and that had consumed her life. Jay wanted to help, but it didn't feel right. He didn't belong there. They both tried to call occasionally, but once again, they went on with their separate lives.

Jay steps out of the heat into the air-conditioned house and sits on the steps to the upstairs bedrooms and calls.

"Jay," Berna says. "The muffins were divine. I wish you could have stayed."

"Yeah, me too," Jay tells her. "I had errands to run."

"For Habitat?"

"It didn't feel right. It was just your family there and I felt like I'd be a fifth wheel."

"That's not true."

"But if felt that way."

They talk for an hour. Berna details the funeral arrangements, talks about how helpful Miriam has been, how she's taken care of arrangements while Andrew and Ricky have been more-or-less useless.

"That's a lot of stress," Jay says. He tells Berna, "I saw on TV the other night about this company that puts people's bodies into pods around the root ball of sapling trees, so their body feeds the trees. The molecules of their body move up into the tree. They actually *become* part of the tree."

"Wow," Berna says. "The things people think of."

"That's what I want," Jay says. "I don't want my body locked away in a crypt. I want all my molecules to spread out and rejoin the living, breathing world."

"It won't be you though," Berna says. "You'll be in heaven."

"It wouldn't be me in heaven either. Not without my body, and the earth under my feet, and real things to do other than praising God all day long, except it wouldn't be all day because there'd be no time, and things would be perfect, so there'd be nothing to do because it wouldn't change anything because everything's already perfect. That doesn't sound like heaven to me; it sounds like the other place. No thanks." Jay waits to see what Berna says to that. She doesn't say anything. Jay says, "I don't know. What do I know?"

"You're coming to the funeral, aren't you?"

"I wasn't planning on it."

"I wish you would."

"It feels like maybe I shouldn't."

"If you're not comfortable coming, I understand."

"I'd be sitting in back by myself getting funny looks from people."

"Sit with me."

"That would be too weird. I'm not family."

"I'm the widow. I get to say who sits with me."

"I don't know."

"If they don't like it, they can go get fucked."

Jay breaks into laughter. "I'm going to tell. The preacher's wife just said a dirty word."

"I mean it," Berna says, laughing now herself. "Fuck them."

Jay wants to tell her he's had a lot of practice ignoring what others think about him, except he has to watch out for his safety. Beyond that, he doesn't care. Except there was Andrew. As much as it angers him to know it, he can't deny that he's afraid of Andrew. He's afraid of Berna's son. He doesn't say any of this to her. He says, "I don't know."

"Do what's right for you," Berna says. "But if you want to come, come. I want you to come. I mean it: if they don't like it, fuck them."

Jay goes back and forth on whether he should attend the funeral. His presence is quite likely to cause more than a slight distraction, if not outright trouble. He finally decides it can't hurt to have a clean new suit just in case. At noon the next day, Jay locks up his house, cuts over to Lee Street, and it's a straight shot of about a mile to JCPenney in the Town Center Mall. It's hot out. He'll be sweaty as a pig when he's trying on suits. He'll be drenched walking back home with a plastic garment bag slung over his back. He's been crawling out of his skin since he and Berna talked yesterday. He's paced, tried to read, done curls with his dumbbells. More than once he's almost decided to jump on his bike and ride out to her house. Andrew is there though.

JCPenney doesn't have charcoal gray suits in Jay's size and there's nobody on the floor to help him, so he settles for black. Since he's already on this side of town, he walks across the river to the tailor's, D'Alessio and Son on West Washington. He's never had a reason to have a suit altered before. The old man is friendly and chatty, though his accent is so thick that Jay has to concentrate to understand him. He hems Jay's pants for him lickety-split while Jay sits right there talking to him, and the gratefulness Jay has for the friendly exchange, the absence of strange looks and questions, feels like love for this old guy.

When the old man finishes the hemming, he smooths Jay's suit into the garment bag and presents it to him. "There you go," the man says. "Now you will be sharp. All the ladies will want to be on your arm."

Jay is so thankful for that short, uncomplicated exchange, he cries just a little for happiness on the sweltering walk home.

The funeral is at Tabernacle Baptist. Jay arrives ten minutes before start time. Andrew stands staring out the double glass doors from the back wall of the church foyer. Jay tenses his stomach, shoulders, arms. As he walks forward, he sees that Andrew has on the same, brand-new black suit that Jay does. From JCPenney's.

"Hey," he says, fingering the lapel of his suitcoat, "I like your taste in formalwear." It sounds awkward, smacks of insecurity and trying too hard. His hands are shaking. It takes effort and concentration to stand there, not to turn and flee the building at once.

Andrew glances at Jay's suit—not his face; never his face directly—nods and looks back out the doors. Outside it's bright and hot.

"I'm Jay." Jay reaches out for a handshake. Andrew obliges. "Back when you knew me, you knew me as Jordan."

That gets Andrew's attention. He tilts his head a fraction and looks at Jay with that empty confusion he's so used to from people who haven't seen him since before his transition. He braces himself and runs through scenarios again in his mind, trying to be ready for any reaction he might get. Andrews brows unfurrow as the realization dawns on him. "Jordan Goins," he says. "You're Jordan Goins?"

"I was," Jay says. "Now I'm Jay."

"You sure have changed," and turns back to the door. "Not that much, now that I think about it. It's been a lot of years."

"It has been a lot of years," Jay says. "You waiting for your boys?"

"Yeah," Andrew says. "Their mother is supposed to bring them, but I don't trust her."

"I'm sorry you have to worry about that," Jay says. "Today of all days."

"They had a tee ball tournament in Milton this morning. She said she'd get them back."

"Doesn't seem like a reason to miss their grandad's funeral." Jay missed his own dad's funeral, didn't even know Colley had died until Doris called and told him six months after the fact.

"You don't know my ex-wife. She's a vindictive little . . ."

"Did you know that Cal Ripken Jr. is the Tee Ball Commissioner?"

"No," Andrew says, still watching out the doors. "I didn't even know that was a thing."

Jay laughs and tenses up his arms to still the shaking. "I didn't either until I heard it on the radio. He was at the White House playing tee ball with a bunch of kids."

Andrew nods. He's not interested. He stares out the front doors.

"Your mom in there?" Jay gestures toward the sanctuary doors.

"Yeah," Andrew nods. He crosses his arms and stares out the glass doors at the parking lot.

"I'm going to go find her," Jay says.

"Okay." Andrew nods and stares out the door.

At the back of the sanctuary, Jay scans the crowd, sitting all prim and proper, ready for the service to start. The organist plays "Abide with Me." These people don't know him. He spots Berna up in the second pew, middle left. Miriam is to her right, and Ricky is to Miriam's right, with an open spot on Ricky's right, which is the aisle seat—Andrew's spot; probably so he and Ricky, maybe Miriam too, can slip out at the end and be pallbearers. To Berna's left is another empty spot. From there is a string of family members Jay doesn't know.

The organist stops playing, flips pages of sheet music, and starts playing "It Is Well with My Soul." Berna cranes her neck around and spots him. He tenses his body again and relaxes, tenses, and relaxes. His heart pounds like mad. Berna waves for him to come up. She motions to the empty spot where she wants him to sit beside her. She has saved him a spot. It's crazy. He doesn't belong there, especially not at a time like this. Berna scowls a little as she motions more insistently for him to come sit beside her. He steps, and steps again, and then he is walking down the aisle toward the front of the church.

.

Charleston Daily Mail

SUNDAY, MAY 21, 2006

GOINS-MINOR

May 20, 2006

It is with great pride and happiness that Miriam Minor of Scott Depot and Rick Minor of Charleston announce the commitment of their mother Berna Mae and Mr. Jay Goins.

Jay was born and raised in Clay, West Virginia. He attended Clay County High School. Jay is a retired union meat cutter with The Kroger Co. and currently works as a volunteer builder and general handyman with Habitat for Humanity of Kanawha and Putnam County.

Berna was raised in Ironton, Ohio. She attended Pinewood Bible Institute (now Pinewood University) where she earned her one-year Bible Certificate. Berna is the founder and former director of the charities Clothe the Naked and Feed the Hungry that cared for the needs of the less fortunate for many years in St. Albans. She now volunteers with Habitat for Humanity of Kanawha and Putnam County, mostly as a gofer for Jay.

Jay and Berna were joined in committed union at 2:00 p.m. on Saturday, May 20, before a small group of family and friends at Daniel Boone State Park in Charleston. After the ceremony, the happy couple plan to travel by motorcycle, to the chagrin of Berna's daughter, to St. Simons Island, Georgia, for their honeymoon.

Acknowledgments

Thanks first to my mentor Sandra Scofield who worked with me through early drafts of this novel. Thanks to the editorial staff at WVU Press, especially to Sarah Munroe—without your keen insight and guidance, this book would not be. Thanks to Sandra Scofield, Joe Alderson, Marcelo Asher Quarantotto, and Heidi Stauff for critical feedback on the work that grew into this novel. Thanks to Kim Runyon Wilds for explaining the important work CASA does.

Jay's stories are informed by the following books and documentaries: *Stone Butch Blues, Becoming a Visible Man, You Don't Know Dick, A Boy Named Sue, Real Boy, Boy I Am, Finding Kim, My Transgender Life, For the Bible Tells Me So, Love Free or Die, Born to Be, Proper Pronouns, One Nation Under God, Gendernauts, Last Call at Maud's, No Secrets Anymore, Love the Sinner, An Act of Love, Born Again: A Personal Struggle with Faith and Sexuality, Fish Out of Water,* and "Transgender," episode 3 of the series *You Can't Ask That.*

Earlier versions of stories adapted and/or cannibalized for this book appeared in the following publications: *Portland Review, Blue Mesa Review, Relief: A Journal of Art and Faith, Connecticut Review, Atticus Review, Rock & Sling, Burrow Press Review, Pithead Chapel, Letters Journal, The Stockholm Review of Literature, Drunken Boat, St. Katherine Review,* and *Connotation Press.* Chapter titles and passages of scripture are from *The Holy Bible, New King James Version.*